Karina Natalia Vasquez is a fantasy romance author based in England. She is of Peruvian and Spanish descent and adores anything that has dulce de leche in it. When she isn't writing, she is reading fantasy, romance and fangirling over Star Wars. You can usually find her holed up in her room, cuddling her two dogs, collecting crystals for her superstitious mind or daydreaming in the hopes that she will magically end up in a Fae kingdom one day.

By Rina Vasquez in the Solaris and Crello *trilogy*

A CITY OF FLAMES

And coming soon:

A KINGDOM OF SHADOWS
A WORLD OF RUIN

A CITY OF FLAMES

RINA VASQUEZ

First published in paperback in 2023 by
WILDFIRE
an imprint of HEADLINE PUBLISHING GROUP

3

Cataloguing in Publication Data is available from the British Library

ISBN 978 1 0354 1435 2

Offset in 10.18/14.8pt Adobe Caslon Pro by Jouve (UK), Milton Keynes

Printed and bound in Great Britain by Clays Ltd, Elcograf S.p.A.

Headline's policy is to use papers that are natural, renewable and recyclable
products and made from wood grown in well-managed forests and other
controlled sources. The logging and manufacturing processes are expected
to conform to the environmental regulations of the country of origin.

HEADLINE PUBLISHING GROUP
an Hachette UK Company
Carmelite House
50 Victoria Embankment
London
EC4Y 0DZ

www.headline.co.uk
www.hachette.co.uk

For my grandma, you are the sun to my day
and the moon to my night.

Zerathion
Emberw
Aurum Castle
City of Flames
Aeris
Isle of El
Undarion
Sea of Serenity

Ocean of Storms

Naralía's Village

Screaming Forests

Olcar

Terranos

Thalore

Melwraith

CHAPTER ONE

'What a great day to shit oneself to death, don't you think?' My second oldest brother whispers beside me.

I roll my eyes and turn to face him. 'Careful Illias, your sarcasm could get you killed, and then you'll be shitting yourself *postmortem*.'

His thick dark brows bunch together as he huffs, cutting a gaze towards the woods in front of us. A broken tree has blocked our pathway, making it merely impossible to jump over the height of it, yet excellent when it comes to hiding from whatever creatures lie ahead of us.

'Why is it that you drag me out on every hunting escapade of yours?' He groans quietly as the spring morning sunlight streams through branches and high trees. 'Why can't you ask Iker to do this instead?'

'Iker . . .' Being two years older than me and cannot tell whether it is night or day most of the time. 'Iker is dreadful when it comes to moral support, unlike you. Besides, you're my favorite out of the three.' I smile. Illias is known as the lenient one out of the four of us.

He can never say no to my offers to purchase him cans of paint for his canvases if he tags along.

He scoffs, brown doe eyes locking with my light blue ones. 'Now you are outright lying—'

I lift a hand to silence him and listen carefully as the bushes to my right rustle in the distance.

'What? What is it? Should I start running?' Illias asks. The lining of his dusted tunic frays at the edges.

My eyes search every thicket surrounding us. 'Where did you set the trap?'

'Trap? I was supposed to set a trap?'

I turn my head slowly and grit my teeth. 'I *asked* you yesterday!'

He gulps, short chestnut curls fall across his forehead, just about touching his brows. 'Oh, we really are going to die, aren't we?'

It's a possibility, yes, but am I telling him that? No, I am not. 'I'll just have to catch it a different way,' I say and rise to my feet. Birds scatter towards the skies, and the wind blows wisps of my hair across in a dark and eerie ambience.

I pull the cloak down from my head and draw two daggers out of the leather sheath strapped around my corset. I wait five short seconds before a crack of a branch comes from my side, and I whisper, '*Now* . . . you can run.'

On cue, Illias takes off in the opposite direction as a rümen catapults out of the bushes, heading to the main forest. I waste no time leaping over the tree. One of the blades warms against my non-gloved hand as my boots sink into the crusted grass. I pass darker branches, lichens, and shrubs as the rümen screeches in the distance.

Rümens rely on scent and hearing for everything. Where eyes should be, slits can be observed on either side of their head, rendering them blind. With the grimy slim body of a long snake and the wings of a bat, they look intimidating enough, but their screech? That is a deathly sound no one should experience at proximity.

I don't intend to kill one. My primary purpose is trapping, even if rümens are one of the hardest species to catch due to their speed and agility. Yet, a simple nick to the scales on their back renders them weak.

Pausing in the middle of a clearing when it's no longer in sight, I keep my grip steady and bring the dagger to the side of my head.

More birds flee from their nests, and I wait . . . I wait for any movement, any noise to show the rümen is still lurking within the depths of the woods.

Turning in a slow circle, my breath wavers. And just as I spot a glimmer of sun bounce off the scales of the rümen hidden between bushes, a snap of a twig behind triggers the creature, causing it to fly out, fangs at the ready as it sends me to lie flat onto the ground. Both knives fall from my hands, and I bring my forearm out to its neck, stopping the horrid creature from biting me.

Everyone knows the bite of one is lethal – a death unimaginable.

I wince, trying to reach for the blade that has fallen on the far left of my body while the rümen's head comes down, snapping its razor teeth and bellowing out its cries which only remind me of something far more feared in our land.

Dragons.

Suddenly, flashes of that day when I was twelve years old echo in my mind. How my mother's screams resonated in our cottage as I stood there paralyzed with fear, helplessly watching a dragon kill my father in broad daylight.

I grunt out a cry as the rümen's talons sink into the side of my leg, the same way the dragon had sunk his in my flesh, slicing down from my palm to my forearm. I had raised it as a shield at the same moment my oldest brother Idris shot an arrow to its back, projecting the dragon forward.

The memory comes back to me so vividly it all but blends with the present, the blurred images fogging over the reality of the moment. I had raised my arm as a shield back then, yet the blunt force of the arrow made the dragon's claw slice down into my palm.

As my mind finally allows me to focus on the present, the rümen stops, looking into my eyes as if it can see me—as if it's analyzing me, just the way the dragon had done, right before taking Idris's arrow. I take that as my chance, and once my hand latches onto the handle of the blade, I bare my strength and ram it into the side of the creature's neck, deepening it until blood, warm and thick like lava, erupts down my hand.

The rümen screams out its agony one last time before slumping. Membranous wings fall limp, and I push its body off of mine, scrambling to my feet while catching my breath.

So much for not wanting to kill.

Picking up the other blade, I half turn to try and find Illias when a sense of darkness up ahead draws my attention. I stare at the thorns encasing the path leading to the Screaming Forests, a territory that separates the land of Emberwell from Terranos and a place where rulers of earthly immortals reside. No human on our side ever dares pass it. Not after the settlement was forged for all of Zerathion and its four lands, three hundred years ago. Each to their own land except for rulers.

'What did you do?' Illias comes over, panting, and pulls me out of my thoughts. 'Ivarron always wants them alive!'

I tear my gaze away from the thorns that almost block the forest and instinctively wrap calloused hands around my other wrist. Glancing down at the fingerless leather glove ending just below the elbow—at the scar that hides beneath, I say, 'It had the upper hand . . . I had no choice.' And look at Illias.

He stares and his brows furrow like he knows that's not the case. I might be good at hunting and trapping creatures, but Illias has always possessed the talent of detecting when something bothers me, much like Idris, and that something usually tends to be what had happened all those years ago.

'Come on.' I motion my head before he can say anything and start walking out of the woods towards the main village.

The fresh scent of baked goods fills the clammy air of the market square as we make our way past horses and carts. People smile to greet Illias, and I watch as he does the same, but the minute they see me next to him, they duck their heads and scurry off. Something I'm used to, since it started the moment everyone found out I work for Ivarron as a trapper. It's not a safe job, and Ivarron is known as a scheming pig.

'Shit, kill me right now,' Illias mutters. I glance at him with a wary frown, stepping on chunks of stray hay across the cobbled ground.

I stumble to a pause from the pain that the rümen's talons had caused when it sliced my thigh. 'What is it?'

'Kye is over there.' He nudges his chin forward. I look in the direction he indicated seeing his former lover Kye – someone that happens to work as a woodcutter alongside Idris – casually leaning against a murky stone wall and talking to a friend of his. An immediate glare forms on my features as I remember how broken Illias was over Kye's infidelity.

'He's been spreading a rumor about my hand,' Illias continues with a murmur. My glare deepens as I lower my eyes to Illias's left hand, a birth defect, designing it only with an index and a thumb. Still, it never stops him from creating artwork beyond imagination. 'That I was born a beast worse than the rümens and that no one should approach me or the venom I'd spew would kill them in an instant.'

'How come I have not heard of this rumor?' I seethe. If anyone in the village dares to believe such an absurd rumor as this when so many know and adore Illias, they must be the stupidest people on earth.

'Because half the village is afraid of you,' he retorts, making a solid point. Not only do people fear me as Ivarron's trapper, but they also expect me to have a drastic reaction when it comes to protecting Illias. One of the reasons why no one ever befriends or finds interest in me, not that I want someone. Either I end up chasing them away, or Idris does it for me.

Focusing my deadly gaze on Kye, I see his long blond hair looks dry and brittle even from afar. 'Stay here,' I say and ignore Illias's pleas not to get involved as I start heading Kye's way with a slight limp.

'Kye.' I greet him with a mocking smile on my lips when I near him. His golden complexion turns white as he spots me and stiffens. His friend mimics his moves, and I swear I can see a slight tremble come from him. 'You remember me, right?'

He nods, swallowing and unable to look away as if he fears I will snap at any moment. I mean I *could*, obviously, but that requires effort, and it has been an awful long morning already.

'Well, I couldn't help but overhear this rumor—' I place a dry, bloodied finger against my chin. 'That has something to do with Illias . . .'

He opens his mouth, but I don't let him even get the first word out. 'Now, it's strange because I'm not sure how you found out.' I sigh dramatically. 'But even though you were right, we can't have you telling everyone around now, can we? So—' I move my cloak and show the knives strapped to me. 'Perhaps I should kill you before you inform anyone else.'

His face blanches. 'I didn't mean to say anything, I swear it. It was just a stupid joke—'

'Listen, Kye,' I say and lean in, making sure he and his friend can hear me as I whisper a menacing threat, 'If you ever make up a rumor or break my brother's heart again, I assure you; no amount of healing will manage to fix you once I'm done with you.'

I step back, satisfied, and a smile shapes my lips as I watch Kye's throat bob. His wide green eyes slide from me to his friend before both nod frantically and rush away.

I inhale with pride and spin on my feet, heading back to Illias as I take out my wood carving of a crescent moon from my pocket, weaving it through each finger. A lucky carving, I call it. Something I've carried around with me since the age of ten.

Illias grimaces, rubbing his face. 'Do I want to know what you said?'

'No,' I say. 'No, you do not.' As I'm about to grab his arm, he stops me from doing so and peers over my head.

'Shit, Venators.'

Upon hearing that word, my head whirls around, scanning through the villagers passing by in their tattered dresses and tunics, until my eyes set upon what they are all looking at . . . Venators. The Queen's noble warriors, who reside in the infamous City of Flames, and whose job is to protect the population from threats such as dragons, rümens and others of their ilk. They are the official dragon hunters of the kingdom. What my father once served as, and my one dream profession – what I've always dreamt to become.

I inhale softly at the dark leather-plated armor shaping each strong Venator. My eyes travel from a few of them standing guard in every corner of the village to one of the female Venators in particular. She holds her firm posture as the sun shines down on the flame designs of the leather cuffs wrapping around her forearms.

Surveying them all, my sight soon catches the color of red across from me – a band on the arm of another hunter. From this distance, a normal person wouldn't be able to make out the engravings, but I can. A golden scaled dragon roaring, surrounded by a swirl of fire . . . Only the leaders of the Venators have one of those armbands. I know, because my father had one.

Bringing my gaze up, curious to see the face of the person who has taken on my father's responsibilities, I freeze in shock when I do. He's young. Barely a few years older than me.

His hair is short, shag at the neck. The copper color resembles that of the flames on his leather cuffs. His defined muscular arms, as he crosses them over his chest, draw my attention. And from how sharply cut his face is, you can see even from here he is without a doubt a handsome man – a warrior of elegance.

His eyes, whatever color they may be, cut straight to me, and for a minute, neither of us makes an effort to look away.

'What are they doing here?' I ask Illias, placing the carving back in my pocket, as the Venator and I continue our staring contest.

'They look to be patrolling,' he states the obvious. I give him a severe look, and he sighs. 'Maybe a dragon was spotted nearby. It'd make sense since many houses have boarded up their windows.'

A dragon . . . we haven't seen one in our village since that day, nine years ago.

Whipping my head back around to look at the Venators again, the one with the red armband doesn't step down from his stare. I glower in his direction, hoping he's the first to look away, and to my contentment, he does but a tug at the corner of his lips has me questioning what he finds so amusing.

I'm ready to go there and ask myself when Illias links his arm with mine and pulls me out of the way of an oncoming traveller and his cart. 'Let's head to Ivarron's and get this shit over and done with.'

Right . . . Ivarron.

Chapter Two

Everyone in the village knows where Ivarron lives, in the little district past the market square. But no soul will be found wandering about his street if they can help it. Though some poor unfortunate ones have no choice, living in the few thatch-roof houses flanking Ivarron's. What a dull sight our village makes.

I sigh, gazing at the busted door, its wooden exterior – much like every place here – starting to get moldy at the sides. The smell of rotting flesh rises to my nose when I enter alongside Illias. He shivers next to me as we glance around at slanted shelves filled with jars containing fangs, hairs, talons and then maps spilling across other areas of his home.

Ivarron used to be a trapper, selling creatures off to the city long before I was born. It wasn't until he caught me trapping a goblin by the woods at the age of thirteen that he used me instead. Young and foolish, I made a deal with him for the money I'd receive after my mother's death a year on from my father's. It was the only way to help Idris when neither Iker nor Illias could find work.

'Faerie blood?'

I turn to Illias as he grabs a vial of iridescent red from one of the shelves. 'Don't touch anything,' I hiss at him, and he immediately drops it, raising his arms apologetically as I manage to catch it between my fingers.

I release a breath, shooting him a stern look as the wax candle flickers above us, the only source of light because Ivarron refuses to install windows. I go to place the vial back when heavily padded footsteps approach from afar.

'Naralía,' a grating voice says my full name.

I glance to my side, abruptly putting the vial away into my sheath pocket, and now face Ivarron. His fine, long mousy brown hair is pushed back, showing off one single green working eye, the other a pale glass sphere.

Revealing his crooked teeth, he says, 'what a lovely surprise.' He picks off the dust from his navy threaded jacket. 'Did you capture the rümen?'

'No,' I state firmly. 'Trapping was bad this morning.'

He narrows his single eye and hums. 'It's a good thing I like you, Nara,' he says, moving one of the rings that adorn his withered hands around. 'Because you just cost me a huge sale today. Rümens are quite popular in the city.'

'Then perhaps you can catch one yourself next time,' I tell him. 'I hear they're attracted to money-hungry swine.'

My eyes catch Illias as he tries to stifle a laugh, then at Ivarron's anything-but-amused face. He takes a few slow steps and stops mere inches away from me. The man is short, at least five inches shorter than me, but even with his small stature he doesn't possesses a hint of fear or cowardliness. 'Don't forget your place with me, girl.' He grinds his teeth. 'You may be my best trapper, but I still hold more power over you.' His working eye moves to Illias. 'And we both know where your weaknesses lie . . .'

My brothers.

Illias, too, tenses at the threat and moves to make a protective shield of his body between me and Ivarron, but I stop him before he can, slamming my arm against his chest, indicating with a head shake that there's no need for him to intervene. My brother may not seem like it, with that loving, nurturing quality to him, but that same quality also makes him fiercely protective. Like a Mother Hen.

Ivarron breathes a laugh, eyeing Illias with disdain. 'I expect you to trap something good tomorrow morning if you want your week's pay,' he says. A grim smile shows up on his face as he looks at me again. 'I hear a water pixie from the north side of Undarion has made its way through.'

Oh, how I'd wish to stab you.

I smile tightly instead. 'You'll get whatever there is to catch first thing at sunrise.' And grab Illias by the arm, not uttering another word as I turn us around. Ivarron's harsh laugh echoes through his house before I storm out of the doors, glad to be breathing actual fresh air.

'I hate him . . . I *really* hate him,' Illias says, fuming. I couldn't agree more, but I also can't deny Ivarron trained me well from a young age and taught me about most critters. 'Damn you, Nara, for getting yourself involved with someone dangerous.'

I huff, not saying a word, and rush him down the streets. Idris once tried to get me out of working for Ivarron. But his roughing Ivarron up hadn't helped the situation at all. The bastard repaid by sending some of his men to find Iker outside the tavern one day. They'd simply left him barely breathing as a warning.

'Nara, are you listening to me?'

'I am, but what can I do about it now—' I pause when I spot a tall figure from afar, wearing a grey shawl that I immediately recognize. 'Shit, Idris,' I mutter, looking up at Illias, who is placing the edge of his hand against his forehead and squinting from the sun.

'What does Idris—oh,' he says casually before realizing what is happening and makes a face, widening his eyes. '*Oh* . . .' He drops his voice to a low tone. 'He looks pissed.'

Indeed, that is true. Idris's usual scowl does not falter once as he excuses himself from the few villagers he was talking to and makes his way towards us. His shoulder-length chestnut hair sways with each solid stride. It's the color all three of my brothers share, in contrast to my golden honey locks – a courtesy of my father's genes.

'Do you think we have time to run?' I grimace, watching Idris getting nearer.

'No,' Illias says. 'But maybe if we pretend to be doing something—and he's standing in front of us, ah, hello brother, fine day—'

'Both of you, home,' Idris grits his teeth, trading glances between Illias and me. His voice low and stern, like always. 'Now.'

Facing Idris or a rümen? I'd choose the rümen again.

By the time we arrive at our secluded cottage on the other side of the village, it's already past midday. There is a light breeze, despite Emberwell normally never getting cold even through the winter months and strands of my hair flick around as I near the grey stone walls. You can make out the steel powder trapped in the mortar between stone walls to ward off any possibility of a dragon. People say it's a weakness for them; however, it's hard to obtain unless you come from the city. Luckily working for Ivarron has its perks, particularly when I steal from him, much like the faerie blood vial in my sheath pocket.

I push through the wooden door, trudging inside. Light encases me from the open windows. My eyes then trace the flower-decorated carvings I have done on each corner of our rickety home. My carving tools, which were a gift from Idris on my birthday a few months back, rest on the floor to one side.

'There you guys are,' Iker says, jolting up from the wooden chair by the fireplace. I frown, noticing he's cradling a pure white rabbit in one of his arms as he waltzes over.

I would ask how, what, when, and why, but I am too afraid of what the answer might be. I turn, following his movements as he goes to stand between Idris and Illias.

Taking the opportunity of having the three in front of me, I look at them – at their features. How Illias's and my soft upturned noses differ from Iker's slightly crooked one, the result of Ivarron's temper. Regardless they all shared that same defining jaw covered in a thin layer of stubble, and what everyone knows us for . . . the Ambrose hands. Strong, rough, full of creativity – even with Illias missing a few fingers and mine with a jagged scar.

'Threatening to kill Kye?' Idris's rage-filled voice drags me back to the current situation. 'Really?'

I keep my face neutral. It's not as if I was going to act upon it.

'You know what it's like to have someone who works with you run up and say that you need to keep your sister in check?'

Well, it seems Kye truly has a death wish.

'If I may.' Illias treads to my side carefully, pointing a finger in the air. 'She's had a rough morning trying to capture a rümen—'

I silently pray for him not to go on, but it's already too late as Idris looks at me with narrowed eyes.

'What?' He raises his voice. The golden tan of his skin, the same complexion all four of us share, pales at the mention. 'Do you have any idea how dangerous those are? There's no cure if they bite you, *Nara*.'

'And you think I don't know that?' My brow quirks. 'I hunt down creatures for a living, Idris. Anyway, why are you so worked up about this now? It's not like we haven't had this conversation a thousand times before.'

'This time you are hurt,' he points out and glances down at my thigh, which I have failed to cover with my cloak. 'And because rümens are lethal predators.'

I know they are. 'I can't just stop,' I whisper, looking downcast.

'Then I'll deal with the consequences of Ivarron if I have to, but you're not working for him anymore.' That makes my head shoot up, brows furrowing. Idris had attempted that in the past, and it didn't end well. For any of us. 'When Mother fell ill, she entrusted me to look after *you*. Explain to me how I can do that when you're out there, putting yourself in danger—'

'Mother may have entrusted you with our safety,' I say, moving in closer and emphasizing my words. 'But you do not get to decide what is best for me and what is not.'

Idris scoffs, shaking his head the way he always does with me. My fist clenches. I am sick and tired of watching him treat me like nothing more than an unruly child. For eight years, he's had to look after us, carrying the burden of both our parents' deaths, when neither was his fault. But not once did he stop to think that we didn't need him to decide everything for us.

'Nara, I think—'

'No,' I cut Illias off but keep my gaze fixed on Idris. 'Time and time again, you have disagreed with me on everything. When I told you I wanted to become a Venator, you shut me down, yet I know for a fact father would have been proud if it meant I was carrying out his legacy.' My nostrils flare and my blood boils. 'I'm twenty-one, Idris. Not a child and *not* the weak little sister you think that I am.'

Silence.

Utter deafening silence resonates in my ears as I stay staring right into Idris's eyes, the swirls of blue and green in his iris brightening against the shaft of light. Those eyes that are the same color as mine. The same as our mother's.

I wasn't going to back down. After all, defying Idris is a habit of mine, but of course, Iker intervenes with a whistle and smiles, slapping one hand onto Idris's shoulder. 'She laid one on you, brother.'

'Shut it, Iker,' Illias says. 'It'd be in your best interest not to get involved seeing as you disappeared all of last night at the tavern and didn't come back until the early hours of dawn.'

'And with good reasoning,' Iker says, covering the rabbit's ear. 'I heard Idris cooked a dreadful venison.'

We all look at him, not knowing whether to tell him that a rabbit is no elk. Idris is the first to sigh deeply, deciding to ignore Iker as he says to me, 'Get that wound cleaned and dressed before it gets infected,' and shoulders past me.

Short curls fall over Iker's forehead as he blows a breath of relief. I glance at Illias, who smiles uncomfortably at me in a bid to lift my spirits. I barely lift the side of my lips in reply, the reality of how we've had far too many of these disputes against Idris sinking in.

Later on that evening, after a tense supper where no one spoke except to fight over the last piece of bread, I wind up in the bathroom. I take off my corset along with the sheath strap, leaving me in a loose white shirt as I set it all on top of the chipped sink.

I exhale deeply, glancing into the mirror and running my fingers along the sides of my body. Although Iker and Illias find it impossible to obtain a stable job, I am grateful Idris and I can provide sufficient funds for food. Some days I still have to hunt so we can have a meal on our plates. Yet, regardless of whether we're starving or not, my natural figure never loses its busty curves.

My hands slowly come down to my thighs until I wince and look down at the injury. I had put herbs and dressed it up after Idris told me to, and of course, Illias had offered to help, but my stubbornness made me storm off with a half-arsed job.

'Hey, Trapper?' Four obnoxious knocks accompanied by my nickname tells me it's Iker on the other side. 'Can you cover for me if Idris asks where I am?'

I roll my eyes, knowing he's going out to try and trick people into giving him money by the tavern.

His knocks continue, with loud whispers of my name over and over again, but I don't respond as I twirl waves of golden hair and weave it into a half-up half-down plait.

I quickly grab my moon carving and turn towards the door. The brass mortice knob cools against my skin as I pull it open and see Iker's hand midair while his gaze focuses on how I tap my foot on the floor impatiently. 'You shouldn't go out,' I say, looking over his shoulder at the rabbit nibbling on its paws. 'You have a new pet to look after, wouldn't want me leaving the door open so he escapes now, would you? Or worse, imagine you eating dinner tomorrow and realizing what's in the stew?'

He blinks, narrowing his eyes with faint amusement. 'Oh, you are positively evil.'

'We share the same blood, so you and me both, Iker.' I pat his shoulder with a smile and walk off, heading outside and into the front gardens that lead up to heaps of woods and greenery.

I stop and take in the unusual hues of purple enhancing the night sky and rest onto the thick layers of grass. I bring my knees up to my chest and wrap my arms around as I lift the carving between my thumb and index finger, studying it under the light of the stars.

Sighing wistfully, I remember how a few years back, my mother took me to a neighboring village. I'd been carrying a carving of the sun I'd made myself before I bumped into someone, and the carving slipped out of my hand. In a rushed attempt to recover it, I ended up with a moon carving instead. I guess the person I'd bumped into must have dropped it at the same time I'd dropped mine and we'd exchanged them by accident.

My mother told me how it was a sign . . . a form of luck. People of Zerathion believe our universe was created millennia ago with the power of the sun and the moon – deities named Solaris and Crello. They believe that the sun always seeks its moon, and when they join, an unimaginable power will surge from them.

My brothers don't share that faith but I do. I want to believe there is *something*.

Minutes pass as I flip the crescent and run my thumb over the letter *R* engraved on the oak surface. My curiosity grows before someone calls out to me. I look over my shoulder, seeing Illias's figure through the window, waving at me to come back inside.

I shake my head humorously at how concerned he gets sometimes, and I dust the dirt off my fingers while rising. When I glance at my carving once more, I breathe a sigh, wondering if I'll ever get my sun returned, as I start making my way back.

Chapter Three

'You didn't steal that bread like last time now, did you?' Miss Kiligra, the seamstress of our village, asks, squinting her hazel eyes at the loaf in my hands.

'Course not, Miss Kiligra,' I drawl. 'That was Iker.' A renowned trickster, he used to dress up as a frail man in need of bread before returning home.

'Oh, you Ambrose siblings are all the same,' she complains, her voice sounding as brittle as a rusted piece of metal as she totters to the back.

After trapping a water pixie by luring it with honey – a sweet substance they gravitate towards – I came to the main village to buy pots of paint for Illias. Miss Kiligra owns a business that provides everyone with almost anything. The vast room of her shop contains an indistinct heap of randomly placed tools of various purposes . . . Huge pans, candles of different sizes, drapes of cloth hanging from windows, there is no logic or order to be found in that mess.

'Now you tell that brother of yours to stop coming by with paint dripping off of him. I don't want him staining the goods,' she says, scratching her long, grey coiled hair as she limps with the paint can in one hand. I chuckle, fully aware Illias won't stop showing up with different colors all over him.

My attention catches a gleam on one of the shelves behind her counter. 'Knives?' I arch a brow in amusement as I hand her two copper coins with a dragon imprinted on each side and study the four small, but nicely sharpened blades. 'Since when did you keep those around in your store?'

Miss Kiligra always tells me off for carrying knives freely. I even gifted her a set once, only to find out she had given them to someone else because she feared someone could break in and use them against her.

A bizarre logic that I've never tried to question her on.

'Oh, haven't you heard?' She leans over the counter, her eyes darting around the room in madness. 'Apparently, a new breed of monsters are lurking around the whole of Emberwell, slaughtering humans!'

My blood freezes. *A new breed? Oh, for Solaris's sake.* 'Where did you hear that?'

'Myrine found out from traders in the city. They say it's worse than dragon shifters or rümen.'

My brows lower as I slowly drop the loaf of bread on the counter. 'Do you think they came from Terranos?'

She shakes her head. 'Some believe the leaders of Aeris might have something to do with it, others, Terranos.'

Right, Aeris. The western part of Zerathion, the land of phoenixes and air creatures. The Leaders of Terranos are who I would believe to be behind it. Run by elves, trolls and the creators of the Screaming Forests.

Staying in a thoughtful gaze, I purse my lips as Miss Kiligra turns back to fixing pieces of cloth. She mutters, 'We can only pray that Solaris and Crello shelter and protect us because all hell will break loose if one of the rulers declares a war.'

I hum, biting my bottom lip. I don't know as much as most people do considering I left education early on. But I understand from what Idris has taught me that Zerathion is the only continent we know of – thus far, containing four elemental lands with different civilians and creatures to each sector.

Emberwell is the only place where mortals reside.

Usually at night, I drift off to sleep thinking about adventures where I would go in search of another kingdom that existed across the Seas of Serenity.

Not even in my wildest dreams can that really happen. Not when our world and other lands have despised one another for centuries.

Once there was a time that mortals were known to be lesser . . . *weaklings* because we have no power. It wasn't until a new reign in Emberwell that the rules changed, and a treaty was put in place by our Queen, Sarilyn Orcharian.

Mortals were to be equals and every territory was to keep to themselves, never crossing borders except for rulers.

Yet one thing we all ask ourselves is what species is the Queen? Some say a sorceress, mighty and powerful. Others think she is a witch, but whatever she is, she saved us because the shifters living among us rebelled at the idea of a treaty. They became ruthless and dangerous, allying with dragons to try and overthrow the Queen, forcing her to create an army of dragon hunters to protect her and her people, the very Venators we have today.

'Nara, are you there?'

I shake my head and my eyes refocus on Miss Kiligra. 'What do these creatures look like?'

'Not a clue.' Her voice drops to a whisper even though I'm the only other person inside here with her. 'No one's lived to tell the tale. Only rumors that it shares most of its traits with a dragon's.'

Waves of doubt come crashing through me, and I try to think of how anyone could be involved in this new creation. 'Are you sure—' My words die in my mouth as terrified screams erupt outside the shop. I can feel the ground quake under my feet and see the necklace beads on the counter jump with the vibrations.

Miss Kiligra looks at me in panic as I turn, rushing to the window. Crowds of people run from each angle, fleeing as if—

'Solaris! A dragon, Nara!' Miss Kiligra shouts from behind, and that's when I see it . . . Dark leathery wings attached to a monstrously scaled body, similar in shape to that of a lizard, fly past.

A few Venators rush through, waving at villagers to get as far away as possible.

I can hear the dragon's harsh growls from here as it suspends in the air, flapping its wings. That's clearly not the biggest dragon I've ever seen, but it is still large enough for the Venators to struggle against it.

Realization hits me all at once while watching in horror as blasts of fire, feral and wild, shoot down on carriages, carts, and anything in sight.

'My brothers,' I whisper.

Immediate worry overcomes me, and I whirl around, glancing at everything inside the store.

I have dropped off Illias by the market stalls, Iker will be at the tavern, and Idris . . . Idris will come looking for us too, as soon as he hears all the commotion.

'Nara.' Miss Kiligra's voice urges as a warning, as if she knows what I am like.

She watches from the counter, quivering and hugging one of her blades as I unhook my cloak, letting it fall to the floor. I yank out the curved dagger from my sheath and give one single nod towards Miss Kiligra as I burst through the doors. All I see is a mess of injured bodies lying on the sides of the street, broken wooden stalls crackling in flames, smoke twisting and disappearing into the sky.

I elbow my way through the crowds, but they push against me, scrambling to make their way in the opposite direction. 'Illias!' My voice is hoarse as I try to locate him. 'Ill—' A man's shoulder connects with mine forcefully, knocking me onto the ground. My knife falls from my grip, and I scurry to grab it when another harsh scream echoes around us. I look up at the sky in time to gasp and roll on my side as spits of fire bounce off the cobblestoned ground.

Breathless, I attempt to get up, but a flash of gold draws my attention as feet quickly trample past me.

A goblet.

Ivarron used to tell me about the dragons and the shifters: there are three kinds that exist. A Merati would be the holder of illusions, an expert in mind games. An Umbrati, the master of shadows. The one attacking our village right now, is an Ardenti. A fire dragon, a bearer of flames. But more importantly, Ivarron told me that all dragons and shifters have one thing in common. Their love for gold. Or rather their obsession with it. Gold has a power to mesmerize, to hypnotize them.

With each second that passes, my heart thunders, and I weigh in on a thought. The dragon needs to be tamed.

Having made my decision, I search for the dagger again, and grasp it before someone's foot knocks it away.

Rising, I gaze at the Venators, steel swords out and flashing, and then towards the goblet. I take off, mentally praying my brothers managed to get to safety, although Idris . . .

I shake the thought off as I swipe the goblet from the ground. Its heavy weight warms beneath my clammy hands, as does the cool metal of my dagger in the other. With a turn of my feet, I sprint into motion – gusts of smoke blend like shadows coating cloudless skies until I reach the other side of the village.

The dragon lands on the ground, dust flies up, and I throw my arms in front of me as a shield. With the dragon's back turned, I lower them, watching it screech and spout its fire across the area while Venators dodge. I stand a distance away as its spiked tail slams across a Venator's abdomen. The propelling force sends them thumping against wooden carts.

My hand trembles, and the fierce memory of my father comes back. I was a fearful child, frozen in place, but after that day, I made myself a promise I would not fear again. I would not leave *defeated* by a dragon. I narrow my eyes, clutching the goblet tightly and square my shoulders, alert . . . no longer trembling.

'Hey!' A man yells. The rough cut of his voice makes me swivel my head only to frown when I see it's the Venator who had been staring at me yesterday. 'Get out of here!' He waves one hand, his copper hair wildly unkempt as he dons a long sharp sword.

My face shows no hint of submission as I raise my dagger skyward and aim it towards the dragon.

From the corner of my eye, I can see the Venator approaching. Still, I inhale sharply, now focusing on the glistening black scales rounding the dragon's neck and throw the blade. It rotates through the air before lodging itself onto the side. The dragon doesn't cry out in pain, nor does it react. I don't want it to. I just want its attention. A dragon's skin is far too thick for simple hunting knives such as mine.

With a slow turn, its slim muzzle bares rows of sharp teeth, a rumble deep within the dragon echoes through the village. Yet its thundering steps don't deter me as my gaze connects with those bright flaming eyes. The dark slit in the middle takes me all in like it's waiting, analyzing what kind of victim is next.

Without taking another second, I lift my hand with the gold goblet firmly held underneath. Puffs of air emit from the dragon's nostrils, blowing back golden waves of my hair. Its eyes land on the goblet, but it doesn't stay there as it focuses on me again, and the strangest thing occurs.

Just like all those years ago when the dragon that killed my father stared straight at me like *I* was the one mesmerizing thing, this dragon purrs, cowering its head at my mercy.

Chapter Four

I drop the goblet, letting it clatter across the cobbled ground. The sound doesn't affect the dragon as it slithers closer. I tilt my head, staring at the intricate scales and the two black horns, which still glimmer even when its broad shoulders block any source of light from the sun. An unnatural urge courses through me as I slowly lift my hand towards the lowered muzzle.

My fingers delicately pause, wary as to what I'm doing though I do not find it foreign. It wants to be touched, tranquilized, but just as I'm about to reach out, a whipping sound of chains wrap around the dragon's snout – a bola weapon.

The dragon thrashes and growls, but more heavy chains come at the legs, arms, and wings, knocking it down onto the ground. I jump back as more dust flies upward and watch, speechless, as Venators hold it firmly in place, giving each other orders to bring the cage carriage in.

They're not killing it?

Why aren't they—

A female Venator suddenly grips onto my upper arm, shaking me as if trying to get me to focus on her instead. 'Are you insane? You could have been killed—'

'Sana.' That same rough voice.

The Venator, who I assume is Sana, lets go of my arm and looks up. Her sharp features soften into admiration before I spin, coming face to face with that dark plated armor fitted on a muscular chest. A strong scent of cedar and sweet spices comes through as my eyes trace upward. No doubt it was the Venator from yesterday, the same one who happened to yell at me moments ago.

His lips are a firm, a straight line as he beholds me with such power and authority. I don't shy away from him as I look into his forest eyes, the way freckles darken against his ivory skin. For a Venator, I imagined scars to coat his face, perhaps a crooked nose even, but this man seems to defy all odds as a perfectly narrow nose graces his face.

He gestures his head towards Sana, and her footsteps sound as she walks away. As he sheathes his sword behind him, twin to another blade, I gaze at both hilts wrapped in fine leather while an ornate red diamond sits on top. A stark difference to my run-down daggers. 'What's your name?' A keen interest in his voice.

Yet I ignore the question, asking, 'What are you going to do with it?' My heart thrums at a vicious speed as I watch the Venators haul the dragon onto a large prison carriage and the cries of children still loom in the distance. I can't understand how not only have I witnessed another dragon nine years later, but I also don't feel the anger of wanting to end its life when I should.

'Well, we don't always kill them,' he says with intrigue masking his features as he studies me. 'Certain dragons we catch; we use them for Venator trials or arena fights.'

I don't respond to that. My father never told me much of his life as a Venator, neither did he want us moving to the city even if he had the money to do so. But whenever he'd visit us – sometimes months later – we'd always be informed of the tests a Venator faced before they'd swear in as warriors. If they passed, that is.

'Now.' The Venator cocks his head, eyes boring into me as wisps of copper hair fall across his face. 'Your name?'

I lift my chin, showing no expression except severity. 'If I say my name, will I get thrown into the dungeons for helping you Venators?'

He chuckles deep and hoarse, though I don't find anything amusing. 'You won't . . . but in theory, I have to ask how you managed to do that?'

'I—' I look back to where I had stood a few feet away from the dragon, no longer in sight. 'I don't know,' I say, frowning as my eyes slide back to the Venator. He stares at me in thought as if prying any further would accomplish nothing, especially when I had no answers myself.

'Lorcan,' he says after a minute or two, extending a hand out to me. 'Halen.'

Flicking my brows up, I survey how despite his face holding no scars, his hand is marred with them. He doesn't hide them the way I do with mine, he doesn't even seem to pay attention to them.

Hesitantly I take his hand in my gloved one and shake – a bit too aggressive on his part. The widened eyes give way, but I don't say anything other than, 'Naralía Ambrose.'

'Ambrose?' His forehead creases in recognition, letting go. 'Was your father . . . by any chance Nathaniel Ambrose, a Venator?'

That piques my interest as I nod once. 'You knew him?'

Lorcan looks to be at least in his mid-twenties, but the red band on his arm reminds me of his high status as a Venator.

'I trained at a young age, so I'm fortunate enough to have met him. He was a known legend. Now I can see where you got those Venator instincts from.'

I huff a disbelieving laugh. My father may have been phenomenal in his line of work, but never once did he teach me to do anything. Nonetheless, those instincts always came naturally to me.

He doesn't take notice of my incredulity, his eyes focusing on me like nothing else matters. 'Have you ever considered becoming one?'

The words take me by shock, and I draw my brows together. Once I turned sixteen, recruitment letters would come through the winter season, and each time they did, Idris would throw them away.

I'm about to answer when the voice I recognize as my brother's comes from behind. 'Nara!'

I turn as Idris, Illias, and Iker rush towards me. All three of their tunics are covered in soot as Idris's hands latch onto the side of my arms, his eyes searching my entire face.

'Are you hurt?' Illias says wide-eyed, huddling next to Idris.

I try to open my mouth to ask the more important question as to whether they are hurt, considering I came out looking for them, but Idris shakes his head, and a simmer of anger tempers his tone as he says, 'We came looking for you at Miss Kiligra's shop, why didn't you stay—'

'She helped us capture a dragon,' Lorcan interrupts, and I look back to see his gaze solely on me. 'I was just asking if she's ever considered joining us. Her bravery is what we need as Venators.'

Illias and Iker finally take notice of Lorcan, as does Idris. He stiffens, letting go of me, and I stumble off onto the side as his unwavering glare – no matter if he's staring at a Venator or not – centers on Lorcan. 'My sister is not interested in becoming one.'

'I think she can answer that for herself.' Lorcan's stare still doesn't stray from me.

Idris shifts his body as if waiting for my response. The many pairs of eyes on me don't make anything easier. Regardless, I puff my chest, exhaling sharply through my nose as I say to Lorcan, 'It's been one of my dreams since an early age, actually.'

My brothers keep silent. I don't look at them, nor do I want to see the reaction on Idris's face. He already knows how I feel about joining the Venators. I'm not going to change my opinion to satisfy him.

Another Venator calls out to Lorcan, beckoning him towards the herds of injured people. He glances down at me, an intense brightness in those green eyes, crisper than any of the spring fields in our village. 'The rest of us leave here at dawn,' he says. 'If you want to join—' His gaze cuts to Idris before they land on me again '—you're more than capable of doing so.'

I frown, taking a step forward as he starts to leave. 'But it's not recruiting season?' I can only imagine how far behind I'll be in training if I join now.

He half turns. 'I know.' A humored smile dances on his lips, one I keep from appearing on mine too as my eyes follow him walking away from me.

'No,' Idris says, placing a pitcher of water on the table. I grab it, passing it to Illias as he pours it into a wooden cup and hands it to Iker.

Soon after we arrived back at the cottage, I wasted no time in pestering Idris to let me join the Venators. His answers were not the least bit approving per usual.

'Why not?'

'You already know why.' He sighs, walking towards Iker's rabbit and lifting it away before it can chew on the boots laid out by the fireplace. I follow around in a desperate attempt to get him to accept as he falls onto a chair and rubs his forehead.

'No, Idris, I don't know why. Your answer is always that it's too dangerous.' I cross my arms over my chest. 'I managed to subdue a dragon. Do you have any idea how hard that is?'

'I wish I could have seen my sister slay a dragon,' Iker says, and I look over my shoulder as Illias smacks the back of his head.

'You didn't even know an attack was happening until Idris dragged you out of the tavern half asleep.'

'What am I supposed to do when the barmaid is in love with me and hands me drinks—'

'May I remind you of Ivarron?' Idris cuts the two of them off as I look at him, watching the curve of his brow go up. Ivarron is the last thing on my mind when it should be the first, after everything we've all been through dealing with him.

'I'll tell him I'll be gone temporarily.' I wince at my own lie, as do the three of my brothers, *loudly*.

'Please, Idris,' I drop to my knees, resting my forearms on his, contemplating what I can say to make him agree. I hate begging, yet here I am prepared to tell him he's my favorite while Illias would likely throw a fit over it. 'This could help you all move to the city. We could start a new life away from this village . . . this tiny cottage of ours. Once I've been sworn in, I could save enough money to pay off my debt with Ivarron—'

'How do you know you'll even become one, Nara?' He snaps. 'Just because you got lucky with one dragon today doesn't mean you'll be fortunate to succeed as a Venator.'

'Unlike you, I believe in myself,' I say, lowering my brows and holding back the coldness in my voice. Still, it fails as I continue,

'Father would have believed in me, mother too, why is it my own brother won't do so much as humor me in this? Why is it my *brother* chooses to give up on me when all I want is this? You may think you could have saved Father all those years ago, and now you fear the same could happen to me, to Illias, Iker, but the difference is you can't change the past, and at least I believe in you for everything. Where is that for me?'

Once more, the cottage falls into quietude. A flicker of hurt shines in Idris's eyes, one where I know I've made it worse.

He slowly rises from the chair, not uttering a word, and, with silent footsteps, walks to the room he shares alongside Iker and Illias. The wood creaks as he shuts the door, leaving me there with nothing but disappointment and sorrow – sorrow because this is all it's ever been.

I stand, turning to look at both my brothers. I watch Iker take a long sip out of his cup, then Illias picking at his fingernails.

'I'll . . .' He starts softly. 'I'll talk to him—'

'No.' I shake my head. 'Why bother, Illias? It's the same thing all the time. I only wish that for once he would act like our brother instead of fathering us.' My bottom lip wobbles, and as Illias takes a step to comfort me, I push past him towards my room and lock it. I hold back every tear that wants to come out, that threatens to slide down each time Idris and I argue.

I tip my head back, closing my eyes, and inhale deeply as I walk over to my wooden chest of drawers. Stars, the sun, and the moon shape the sides while swirls of wood I'd carved fills the other, but the top part has not been touched. Taking out one of my other hunting knives, I begin carving, wanting to forget what happened today. Yet, my hands are unable to as the blade shapes the dragon's wings, the scales, and long swaying tail until nightfall comes.

Until no more ounce of wood is left to carve.

Until the sun emerges from the horizon and dawn awakens.

Chapter Five

I'd left home as soon as birds started singing through trees, while the sky was a coating of blue and gold. Illias and Iker decided to accompany me to the market square so I could see the Venators leave. We knew fellow villagers would wave their goodbyes and thank you's over yesterday's attack.

Somehow when I unlocked my bedroom door, Idris was nowhere to be seen. Illias mentioned he had errands to run; I shrugged and took no notice. It was better that way. I didn't want any more tension between us. We already have enough of that at least twice a week.

'Did you really need to bring your pet with us?' I question Iker beside me, grimacing as the rabbit squirms in his arms. Crowds of people surround the area; some give us harsh looks as others trample over broken carts still waiting to be cleared.

I glare at everyone else, but Iker doesn't seem to take notice of them. 'Dimpy is part of the family now, Trapper,' he says, grinning all high and mighty. 'Deal with it.'

I suppress an eye roll before my eyes catch Idris squeezing past flocks of women in kirtle dresses cheering on Venators. One hand behind his back as he nears me, but the frustration icing my veins from yesterday makes me snap my head to the front, opting to give him the silent treatment. I purse my lips in a mood, watching Lorcan shake hands of fellow villagers far ahead.

'Tell me,' Idris says from behind. Without looking, I know he's smiling – which is quite odd for him. 'Should I call my sister a Venator before the final test, or is it safe to say it already?'

I glance at him with a quizzical frown. Have I started hallucinating from my lack of sleep?

His smile fades as he breathes out, 'I think you should join them.'

The sincerity in that one sentence makes me blink, either fast, slow, or only once. I'm not sure, but it is something I did not expect to hear. 'Are you—'

'I know I'm not Father.' His gaze becomes unfocused as he looks down. *He heard me yesterday*. 'And I know you're old enough to make your own decisions.' He exhales, shifting his eyes to me again. 'But I guess I just saw you as the same little sister who would pester me to read her stories growing up and rebel against anything she didn't like.'

My heart takes in every word, and my face eases into a warm smile at all the memories we've shared, good, bad, even the worst once we lost our parents.

'You'd make a great Venator, Nara. Even if it didn't seem like that at times, I've always thought it.'

Never in my life would I think to hear those words spoken by Idris, and while I keep my smile on my face, it dims when I remember one foe we constantly face. 'What about Ivarron—'

He shakes his head, his shoulder-length hair moving along with it, effectively cutting me off. 'I made a new deal with him. That's why

I wasn't there when you all left for the market square. He still needs a trapper, and I promised I would fill in for you.'

My eyes go round in worry at this new "deal" while guilt aches in my chest over anger getting the best of me when he'd gone and done this for my sake. But the roles have reversed, and now I understand Idris's concerns when it comes to trapping. 'But Idris—'

'I think I know how to trap a few goblins or Faeries here and there.' He puffs a laugh, jerking his chin towards the side of him. 'Illias will help me.'

'Great, I can never get out of these things, can I?' Illias asks miserably, dewy purple paint smears half of his cheek as we all chuckle.

Idris then withdraws one hand from behind him and extends a brown satchel towards me. 'I know they'll provide everything there for you, but I thought you'd want some stuff from home.'

I peek inside the leather interior as he mumbles. He'd put in all the necessities I'd need, including my carving tools and two white tunics. Looking up, he scratches the nape of his neck with a wince as if not sure what my reaction might be. But the slow smile spreading across my lips is all he needs to know as I rise on my toes and throw my arms around him. He stumbles back from my brute strength before reciprocating the hug – something we hadn't done in years.

'Thank you,' I say into the crook of his neck. 'Thank you for believing in me.'

'You'll always love adventure, won't you?'

'I don't just love it, Idris,' I whisper in wonder as we part. 'I'll chase it.'

The words my mother had spoken of on her deathbed . . . for me to always chase whatever bliss adventure awaits me.

Idris's expression contorts into a look of pride before my eyes travel over to Illias and Iker.

'I can't believe you're leaving me behind with Iker,' Illias mumbles, not meeting my gaze like a child.

I shake my head in amusement and pull them both into another hug, ignoring Iker's complaints about squashing the rabbit as I close my eyes. 'I'll see you all soon, I promise.' My throat bobs as I let go, looking at the three standing with nothing more but saddened smiles. I want to take them with me, I want us to live in the city together . . .

Exhaling, I turn towards the parading crowd and start making my way where the Venators are. The urge for tears is replaced with anticipation of a dream I'd been waiting on for years.

I place the satchel over me, careful not to let it catch against my sheath as I move through the crowd. Bodies press to mine once I near horses and carriages, but brittle fingers dig into my wrist, pulling me backward before I reach Lorcan. I turn to see the person holding me is none other than Ivarron.

Not now, not now, not now.

His cruel gaze sets upon my face as he spits out the words, 'Idris may have taken on your role, but don't forget where you truly belong. Did you think leaving this place—'

'I can get you more money,' I say quickly, making him perk up with attention. 'That's all you want, right? Money to cover your wretched gambling problems. It's why you used me when I signed that contract, because you knew I could get you all the money you needed without lifting a finger.'

I subtly glance at where my brothers are as they raise their heads over the crowd, trying to spot me. It won't be long before Idris notices something's wrong, except Ivarron doesn't seem to be making any plans to let go as I stare at him. He looks to be pondering over what I said before, pulling me in closer. I try not to make a face at the dreary, pale complexion of his or the foul odor of alcohol seeping through his shirt.

'It's not just money I want.'

'Then what,' I grit, not prepared to meet his demands.

'They speak of a shifter,' he says, low and quiet. The early sunrise reflects his glass eye as he glances around to make sure no one else can hear. 'A thief that carries all three powers of a Merati, Ardenti, and Umbrati. And that his blood can make anyone immortal without having to see if a bite from one would work.' A wince comes out of me as his grip tightens. 'The problem is that every Venator is after him. They want him dead, but if you capture him and bring me his blood? I won't bother you or your brothers again.'

Voices around us quiet into slurring praises although I know it is my mind losing focus of everyone. Capture a thief, bring Ivarron back his blood, and my brothers won't have to deal with the mistake I made when I agreed to work with him. But a thief who happens to be a shifter isn't simple, and Ivarron knows it.

His hold finally loosens, and he walks backward before I can get a word in, yet the cold gaze stays rooted on me like he knows those final words were enough to convince me.

I stay frozen, watching Ivarron disappear into the swarm of people. I contemplate turning to my brothers, but they don't need that stress, not when I'd do anything for them in a heartbeat.

Turning once more, my expression must look less than cheerless to others as I make it to Lorcan. He's tightening the reins on his horse as his eyes, like fresh clover – ones I feel ever so fascinated by – look me over.

He finishes adjusting the horse as his solid gaze lingers on every part of my face, and a half-grin plays on his lips. 'Did you decide?'

I nod absentmindedly, hoping to forget for now what Ivarron told me to do. 'I already knew my decision a long time ago.'

'In that case,' his voice strains as he mounts the horse, 'you'll ride with me.' That scarred hand of his stretches out to meet mine.

And like how I'd done yesterday, I stare at it like an idiotic fool.

'Unless you'd rather ride with Martin,' he says, and I follow his gaze as he gestures to the Venator in front of him. I frown, following his movements to a guy no less my age, picking his nose and spitting on the floor before wiping whatever residue he has, on his horse.

I've seen worse.

Raising my chin, I say, 'In essence, yes.' And pull my eyes away. 'He seems lovely.' Not a lie. An honest answer because riding with Martin seems easier than Lorcan and his constant intense gazes.

Lorcan huffs in amusement, arching a brow. 'Miss Ambrose.'

I exhale sharply, knowing I shouldn't act stubborn, not to a Venator.

We lock eyes as I grab his hand and haul myself onto the back. A spring of unknown bubbling sensations ride up my stomach towards my chest, seeing that same humored smile from yesterday appear on his lips. I try not to scowl at him as I cautiously wrap my arms around his toned and muscular body, I decide to look at my brothers instead.

A sting prickles my eyelids when they wave at me. Before I know it, my view of them moves farther and farther away as I leave the place I grew up in, and my family, behind.

We ride for hours in silence, passing forests, other towns, and villages where many clap and show their gratitude for everything Venators do. Soon the sun burns bright and hunger coils in my gut, so we stop at an inn on the outskirts.

I rest my forearms against the polished oak table, waiting for the lady who served us to come by with food. I don't say a word as Lorcan scans my face and the single glove I have on.

He wants to ask questions, but before he can open his mouth, the barmaid comes by and places two pies in front of us.

My mouth waters, marveling in the slice I chose with a layer of glazed strawberries on top. Not being able to contain my excitement, I grab the cutlery and dig into it, savoring the sweet fruit mixed with the buttery pastry that melts against my tongue. Hunching over, I devour everything, even the last crumb, until I realize Lorcan is awfully still. I sneak a glance at him and see he's staring at me, blankly with one arm resting against the side of the table and not bothering to hide his pinned gaze.

I glare at him, mouth full, as I ask, 'What?'

His brows go up, but I can tell he's holding back a smile. 'Nothing, you just eat like you've been starved for days.'

Oh . . . that.

'I grew up with three older brothers.' I wipe my lips with the back of my hand. 'Every meal was a battle to get what you wanted.' That and my adoration for food even when we barely had enough for us all to eat during the first few years of becoming orphans.

'What are their names?'

'The oldest is Idris, then Illias, and lastly Iker.' My gaze shifts downwards. I smile and wonder whether Illias is painting right now or if Idris is reading his favorite book while complaining at Iker's constant questions over nothing in particular.

'You really care for them.' He doesn't pose it as a question, more of an acknowledgment.

'Well, they are my family. It'd be strange not to – are you going to eat that?' I eye his untouched slice of pie.

A light chuckle comes from him, he shakes his head as he slides it over to me.

'What about you?' I ask, taking a whole mouthful. 'Any siblings or—' Mid-chew, I stop there and then as his expression changes . . . distant, no smile and something I can't pinpoint prowls his eyes.

'No, I uh—' He clears his throat. 'I grew up with just my father until he passed and I came to the city.'

He looks off to the side, and I can tell that this is not the time or place for me to pry further, especially when I hardly know him, so instead, I ask, 'Are you one of the leaders?'

He turns to me again, this time inquisitively. 'Second in command.'

The side of my lip curls. *So was my father.* 'You must be good at your job.'

'Training since the age of fourteen helped.'

I almost choke. 'Fourteen? I thought—'

'The General saw me fit to join earlier. It's no different than how I saw potential in you yesterday.' He rises, dismissing the conversation as if it's nothing. He looks at the vast number of people dining before inhaling and saying, 'Let's go. I'd like to get to the city before nightfall rather than have to stay somewhere overnight.'

I nod, sealing my mouth shut as I stand and follow him out of the inn into the peaceful warmth of spring. I am so far away from my brothers already; I don't know what to think of it but as we continue on our way, I found myself thinking of them. The wind ruffles my hair. And as more hours go by with other Venators possibly having arrived, we finally pass a stone bridge where the air thickens with heat like midday summer. I'd heard the city was hotter in climate but experiencing it for the first time, it's more intense than I'd imagined.

'Welcome to the City of Flames,' Lorcan throws over his shoulder.

A wry smile adorns his lips while I gaze around in wonder. The sunset casts its orange shadows across streets full of young people as well as elders chatting and laughing. Almost all the women are wearing bright-colored dresses. Even from afar, you can tell the flamboyant layers of red and yellow tulle are of superior quality while the men's tunics glimmer from their fine silken threads.

Everything . . . looks so lively. For the first time, I feel inferior compared to what I'm used to in the village. More streets lead to different sections of markets in every corner I gaze at, and narrower roads of mahogany chalk townhouses mount along steep hills like rivers flowing downward. Pillars hold up other painted bridges above us and as we pass, couples idly stroll by with the faint melodious plucks of violins playing from the western side.

When I focus ahead, my eyes widen as the dark cobbled street leads to a large oak tree, ripe and full of Marigold leaves standing tall amidst the hustle and bustle. I'd carve it as soon as I find material to do so, but the idea quickly leaves my mind once I see in the distance, tall marble gates. Beyond that is where I assume the castle and Venator quarters are . . . my new home.

Chapter Six

Lorcan leads me through the barracks, waltzing past each floor level and darting through crimson hallways lit up with candle wall sconces. Faint noises issue from different rooms, and I can't help but glance around helplessly – much how I'd done when the gates opened to Aurum castle and bright orange flags welcomed me. Venators patrolled the white flagstone pathway while the same gold-flecked trees I'd seen in the main part of the city bordered us.

Lorcan tells me of the four gardens, training grounds, and over five hundred rooms that house all the venators and the staff that work here. I'd have paid more attention if not for the sights of the tan castle, mosaic towers that reach the sky, and the bronze castle gate embellished with the same crest of flames wrapping around a dragon. I almost fall backward with how far I arch my neck to see it as we move on to the other side of the castle grounds.

'Here is where you'll be staying.' Lorcan halts outside a rough-hewn door. 'The staff will provide your training armour, and if there is an issue . . . you come to me.'

I look towards the door and then back into his glowing forest eyes, stern but not cold. When he tilts his head, waiting for me to say something . . . *anything*, I clear my throat. 'Thank you,' I mutter, wanting to scowl at myself over how dense I must have looked staring at him.

The side of his lip curls by a small fraction. 'I'll see you in training first thing in the morning—' He pauses, lowering his voice as he says, 'Miss Ambrose.'

I say nothing as he turns and walks down the halls. His stature and build gives him a grace that flows out of him. Frowning at that unusual thought, I grip the cool metal doorknob and go inside.

Lavender fills the elongated room as my eyes journey to the six single beds. There are three on each side, the oak-panel headboards like ones back home and a doorless archway which I gather leads to the washroom. I bunch my lips to the side, seeing how no one is in here.

Strange, I expected not to be alone.

The last bit of sun stretches across the wooden flooring as I step forward, unbuckling my sheath and dropping it onto the first bed. My carving falls out of it, along with the vial of faerie blood.

Solaris, I'd forgotten to leave that behind.

I rush to it, trying to place it back inside the pocket, when soft footsteps approach from the left corner until they stop behind me.

Seeing as I was initially alone, my instincts to protect myself kick in. As I would have if we ever got creatures such as goblins raiding our cottage back home, my hand carefully glides down to the dagger inside the scabbard.

In no less than a second, I spin, pointing my dagger and glaring at whoever I'll have to defend myself from. However, my expression flattens into wide-eyed embarrassment as I find myself facing a stunned woman.

'Solaris!' She clasps a dainty, deep-bronze hand to her chest. 'Why on earth are you holding a blade as if you're about to stab me?'

'Sorry,' I blurt out, returning the dagger back into its sheath. 'It's just a habit. You never know when something or *someone* might attack.' Each word that I say sounds more absurd than the last.

She laughs, dimples caving her cheeks, and the curve of her upper lip is sharp and prominent. 'If it helps, I don't think there's ever been an attacker or intruder in the barracks before. If there was, we trainees have never known about—' She cuts herself off with a gasp. 'Are you rooming with me? Oh, how wonderful! I've been entirely on my own since the winter months, and it's been ever so dreary.'

I quickly glance at the other beds and trunks in the room. 'There are no other occupants?'

'Oh, there were.' She purses her lips. 'But many didn't want to room with me.' Her solemn gaze drifts behind me to the sheath splayed on top of the bed, and before I can ask her more about what she'd said, her hands reach for my carving. 'What is this?' She examines it and starts to roll it between her palms like some toy. 'It's gorgeous! Did you make it?'

Give it back, give it back, give it back.

'No—' I grab it as it slips through her fingers and retrieve it against my chest far too protectively. An overreaction I didn't mean to have, but it's the single source of luck I've had for years. It felt wrong for someone else to hold it in their hands.

She tips her head to the side, and obsidian coils flow down to her slim waist – thinner than my curvaceous figure – framing her delicate face and high cheekbones. 'What does the "R" stand for?'

'I don't really know.' I sigh, running my thumb over the engraving before putting it away. 'Someone's name, I presume.'

'I'm Freya, by the way,' she changes subjects, and I notice how her dark brown eyes have a ring of green around the iris. She looks to be around my age, albeit a foot shorter than me. 'Don't mind the mess. I was knitting in my spare time. Do you like it?' She gestures to the other side of the room, where one of the bed quilts shines in purple lace with a pile of wool over it; what it is, I can't quite make out. How I didn't notice all of that when I entered baffles me.

'I—' I'm interrupted before I can attempt a compliment.

'It's not my best work— wait, how rude of me.' She lightly taps her forehead. 'I didn't ask of your name or where you're from, although assuming by the choice of clothing, you must be from the outskirts?'

I frown, glancing at my black tunic – a tear at the corner and strawberry pie residue in the middle. In contrast to her purple off-shoulder dress and bodice decorated in lilac flowers, my clothes are not the least bit appealing to the eye. Trying to hide the dirt on my clothes with my maroon cloak, I say, 'Naralía, though Nara is preferred. I come from down south.'

She nods slowly. 'Have you seen much of the city yet?'

'No, I just got here.' I stifle a yawn.

'Well, that won't do.' She places a finger on her pointed chin, humming. 'I'm taking you out for a tour around the city.'

'Are you allowed?'

'For Solaris's sake, we're not prisoners, Nara!' She grins, and I screw my face, fascinated by her bubbly outlook. 'Although this might get me in trouble with . . .' Her words come out as a murmur, not finishing the rest as she waves her hand dismissively. 'Come on. We'll return before curfew.' With the slightest bit of hesitation, I followed Freya out of the barracks.

Time had passed as we made it back out into the lively city. Freya would spin and skip around with her arms extended at the sides when street music drummed loudly. I stared back whenever she'd tell me to join her. I'd never had friends before, nor did I consider Freya to be one already. Still, her cheerful mood was rather . . . contagious. Not at all someone I'd ever think to be training for a role as a Venator.

I was her total opposite and despite my lack of chatter, she still seemed to enjoy guiding me through the city, talking about how it's built along four different districts. The first towards the western side is Lava Grove, where stone townhouses crammed together and outer towns led to the docks that divided our land from the Sea of Serenity and borders of Aeris. Then to the eastern side, streets split into three. One named the district of Chrysos known for its talented tailors and fine jewellers whose gold shone through stained glass windows enticing visitors. Freya quickly declared that she considered this district to house snobby rich people.

She wasn't wrong about my odd clothing, judging by how many stopped to stare at what I wore. I made no effort to stare back since I'd quickly learnt I was not in my village anymore, and neither did I want to make enemies on my first night out in the city.

We ended up walking until night fell, and oil lamp posts began to light up the streets. Freya spoke of everything at a high speed, which I never knew humanly possible. I tried to grasp everything she said as we'd entered the second district: Salus, full of russet brick libraries, institutes, apothecaries, and galleries. Opposite it, separated by a tinted orange river, were blacksmiths and food vendors singing out the prices of their wares, some encouraging civilians to buy a popular brew called Flame Spewer. An unhealthy amount of cinnamon gets poured into the ale before being set aflame. The supposed added ingredient of goblin blood is what makes one belch up fire, and from that, I knew I had to try it.

That is why we're now standing in front of a stall being served. Freya is quickly expressed her worries about how dangerous it might be.

I eye the glowing ember color and flames dancing above the drink as I screw my eyes shut and inhale it down my throat. The heat coats my insides, warming me deeply. When I open my eyes, Freya only looks at me, waiting for the fire, yet nothing comes.

'I think it's quite delicious,' I say to her, licking my lips as I turn and extend my wooden mug out to the vendor. 'More, please.'

The man stares at me, arching a thin brow, and laughs in a horrid boisterous manner. 'I'm almost certain you can't even afford another.' His eyes take in my clothes. 'Let alone hack two of them.'

I guess I will be making enemies tonight after all. 'Well, I guarantee anyone who can't hack them are only those revolted by having to look at your face, you pri—'

'Thank you for the beverage, sir!' Freya smiles, wrapping her arm around mine and pulling me away from the man's livid gaze. The mug clatters onto the ground as I look at him, raising my chin with indignation.

My anger towards the man dissolves as Freya takes me out onto the main square where the oak tree rests, and eateries and taverns encircle us. The city has fewer people at this time, and I'm thankful nightfall isn't as humid as earlier. A soft breeze cools my anger.

I stroll further near the oak tree but pause as I reach the final district I had yet to. The roads silent and dark in comparison to other sections, like they'd swallow up any form of life. Ripped drapes hung off dank stone walls varying in different sizes, and buildings spiralled down in a slope to the center. Filth stains the ground, making me question whether I'm hallucinating as I take a step forward before Freya drags me back and starts walking in the opposite direction. 'Let's not go through there.'

'Why?'

'The Draggards District is sort of . . . rough. People slaving creatures, selling them, brothels and—' She shudders. 'Witches.'

So, this is where Ivarron sells the creatures I capture for him. I wonder how Freya would react if I told her I'm a trapper. 'Witches?'

She nods as I stumble against her hold on my arm, trying to keep up with her small quick steps. 'They don't do anything, but if you ever wander through The Draggards, you might see bizarre displays of eyeballs and dead snakes.'

I lift my brows in interest. The years spent visiting Ivarron's home, I was no stranger to that view. While Illias paled at Ivarron's strange exhibits, I was one to find them normal considering who I was working for.

'You'll also see a lot of people placing their bets already for arena fights between different creatures. So don't look too alarmed when there's a random brawl on the street.'

I glance at Freya's relatively calm state as she lets go of me. Lorcan had spoken of arena fights the day he asked me to join the Venators, but I didn't know much of it.

'Let Solaris and Crello bless you, child.' A mother and her child pass us, both with peaceful smiles.

'Solaris.' Freya bows her head at them.

Involuntarily, I mimic her before going back to the matter at hand. 'Where and when do these fights occur?'

'Outside the castle grounds.' She looks towards the marble gates. 'Twice every fortnight, they hold these fights at Aurum Arena, and hundreds come to watch and make wagers on which creature might win. It's also where we'll face the trial to become a true Venator.'

A deep inhale at the mention of us facing the trial causes my insides to turn. Everyone here had already begun their training months ago. Although Freya didn't question why I'd joined now, I do wonder if I'll be capable of facing the trial alongside others. No matter how hard I believe in myself, I have to be realistic.

We continue walking as Freya forgets the topic of trials and begins to explain her love for trying out new hobbies. But I'm quick to come to a stop when something posted on the side of a rustic tavern draws my attention. Squinting my eyes, I waltz up to it.

It's a washed-out "Wanted" poster and there is nothing but a sketch of a man shaded to darkness, making it hard to see what he might actually look like. A mask covers the top half of his face, and the name *Golden Thief* is written in cursive at the bottom, accompanied by a warning of it being a dragon shifter.

My sudden awareness of the phrase "dragon shifter" brings me to the possibility of *who* exactly it is.

'Oh, you'll see these posters everywhere in the city.' Freya joins beside me. 'It gets rather tedious hearing everyone talk of how he—'

'Why do they call him the Golden Thief?' I ask, not peeling my eyes away from the poster.

'He's known to go around stealing anything of value before leaving a gold coin – a trademark of his.'

My tone comes out nothing more than unimpressed, 'Doesn't sound like much of a threat.' *Other than him being a dragon shifter.* Still, I had to have some confidence in myself for the sake of my brothers.

'No one knows the true reason behind why he does it but some believe he does it to irk sellers so that they can use that gold coin to replenish stock for him just to steal it all again.' Freya frowns to herself as I look at her. 'I can't tell if that makes him a genius or not.'

A witless dragon more like. 'How have Venators not caught him yet?'

'Well . . . because there are rumors,' she says, biting her bottom lip nervously. 'Of someone creating creatures which are killing mortals and by that someone I mean the Golden Thief.'

My forehead crumples, thinking back to Miss Kiligra's rumors. 'I've been told the leaders of Aeris could be the ones doing that?'

'That's what everyone thinks because Aeris leaders and Aerians, in General, are known to be reckless, but take it from someone who's been eavesdropping when higher class Venators hold meetings.' Her face turns grave, preparing herself to elaborate. 'The Golden Thief is a powerful shifter . . . and shifters happen to hate Venators. It's likely a rebellion on his part, and from what I've gathered, he doesn't have any weaknesses that can make it easier to catch him.'

My confidence dwindles. 'But everyone has a weakness.'

She shrugs. 'That's what many assume, except shifters are a lot harder to catch than a full-fledged dragon. Steel powder doesn't seem to work on the Golden Thief, and neither do ordinary traps . . .' Her words trail off into thoughtful silence.

I glance back at the poster – at the word *WANTED* emblazoned on top – and wonder if I'm crazy to even think of considering Ivarron's proposition. Perhaps part of me craved the idea of trapping since that's all I've ever known.

'We should head back.' Freya exhales. 'I'd hate to get you in trouble for arriving late on your first day of training tomorrow.'

Looking at her and the innocent smile shaping her lips, I nod.

Tomorrow . . . tomorrow will be the start of what I've wanted for years.

Chapter Seven

I'm up before dawn, restless from not finding the bed to my liking. It's not that it wasn't comfortable. Laying on the lavish quilts were like melting into a cloud. But I missed my bed . . . my home.

Sighing at the edge of the trunk where I've placed my belongings, I marvel at the sleeveless skintight leather armor that clings onto the thickness of my thighs in a midnight black shade. Scales like overlapping snakes travel from under my breasts towards my neck, where a pin showing the Venator crest of a dragon is clasped. When I arrived back last night with Freya, everything I needed as a trainee was carefully laid out on my bed. The surprise on my face was endless when I'd figured how fitting the training armour was and rather flattering too.

'Nara, Nara, Nara!' Freya walks toward me in the same attire, showing her slim figure. Her black curls are pinned into a half updo with a purple satin ribbon tied around. 'Are you ready?'

I nod, finishing braiding my long tresses before she grabs my hand, a habit of hers that I've already grown to enjoy since my arrival.

She takes me through the same crimson hallways, down to the

ground floor where open double marble doors lead to a mess hall. Chatter echoes through each corner of the grand room, long mahogany tables are crowded by Venators and trainees all sitting down for breakfast. While sworn Venators have different armor with their intricate flame designs, trainees appear dressed in the same garment as me.

My eyes then slide to a stone wall on my left with markings, which I can only gather are names. I try not to let thoughts about what that means cave in my chest as we go grab servings of oats and bread.

No one speaks to us nor looks in our direction as we drop on the benches, eating away. At the same time, Freya expresses her glee over her porridge and curiously stares at the way I rush down every last bit of food in my bowl.

Once she finishes, everyone else seems to rush towards another room located past the mess hall. Sheer gold curtains made of gossamer hang by the large glass windowpanes and weapon racks, full of bows, spears, swords, and more are mounted on the emerald walls.

Like a lost fawn, I follow Freya as everyone grabs their weapons. She picks out a quiver, slinging it over her shoulder as well as a bow. I assume this is her usual choice to fight with. On my part, I don't pick out anything. I'm not sure what to pick, considering there are many I want to choose. Instead, we stride towards the doorless archway at the end of the room that goes out into the acres of fields surrounding Aurum castle. Trainees are already lined up as the heat of the sun radiates across the grounds. Taking in everything, I notice training dummies, targets for archery and throwing knives, before Freya pinches my side to get into formation with the rest.

I frown, although her gaze focuses in front. I follow it to see a partially bald man, older than most of us, perhaps middle-aged, pacing back and forth slowly while Lorcan and other Venators stay still behind him. The man's hands are behind his back as he scowls at each and every one of us. He has the same red band as Lorcan's and others I'd seen at the front gates. But the one distinct thing is his red cape flowing behind him with each step he takes, complementing the richness of his dark skin.

'As you all know,' he begins as the sun bounces off his armor plates, 'with the trial approaching this summer, you are expected to be at the level we think is acceptable—'

'Is that the General?' I lean into Freya. His rasping voice continues on in the background, like all he's ever done in his life is shout.

Freya's eyes widen though it disappears relatively fast as she bites her lip. 'Yes, um, General Erion.'

That's a rather strange reaction. One I'd question her on except the air fills with sudden apprehension, and I snap my head forward to see General Erion standing right in front of us.

Oh.

I stand eye level with him as he stares at me for a few scrutinizing moments before saying, 'So, you're Nathaniel's daughter.' The lines on his forehead protrude. I can't tell whether he's glad I'm the daughter or not. 'My deputy tells me you helped capture an Ardenti.' A quick glance over his shoulder to Lorcan.

'Yes, sir.' I hold affirmative in my tone.

He lifts his chin, and the sharpness of his features doesn't go unnoticed as he chuckles bitterly. 'Let's see if you can last as long as he did.'

So, it is not a good thing for him.

He turns halfway as if he's done analyzing me. I can't help but clench my jaw and say, 'With all due respect, my father was an excellent Venator. I don't think he ever mentioned you being up there, regardless of your title.'

He stops, slowly looking back at me as his mocking smile fades.

I've ticked him off. He can see I'm not backing down, making his eye twitch before glancing at my left hand. 'I don't recall that being part of the livery.'

'And I don't recall Venators being so sensitive about their attire.'

Freya's body goes rigid beside me as General Erion's ears burn bright red. His brown eyes, cold and deadly, narrow and like an animal snatching its prey, he grabs me, yanking the glove off. Deft fingers harden on my wrist as he tilts it around so that my palm faces upwards.

Don't cause more of a scene than you already have – I feel the need to remind myself as I exhale harshly through my nose while some trainees snicker in the background. I don't look at anyone except the General. My brows lower as his gaze journeys the uneven skin on my palm, leading up to my forearm.

'I can see why you kept it covered,' he murmurs with a cruel smile.

With my other hand, I curl my fingers inward, tight enough I might as well cut through flesh. I then peek over at Lorcan. He isn't looking at me, but at my scar, a bleak stare on his face.

Gritting my teeth, I glare back at the General, but as I'm about to pull my hand out of his grip, he raises my arm in the air.

'This,' he says, glancing at the others. 'This! Is a prime example of what could happen to any of you if you don't keep your mouth shut.' He drops my arm forcefully, looking at me one last time before saying, 'Everyone dismissed.'

I clasp my hand as he strolls off alongside other Venators. Pleased with himself and still holding onto my glove, I know he has no intention of giving it back.

Cautiously gazing around me, I see trainees whisper to one another and snickering, while Freya shoots me an apologetic look.

She parts her mouth, like she wants to say something, but I shake my head, signaling it's okay, and walk off.

Using my right, dominant hand, I bend my wrist toward my forearm, holding a throwing knife. I swing it across the field where the target dummy stands and tilt my head in satisfaction at how it almost hits the center.

I try forgetting about General Erion, and though he'd not appeared out here again, anger still curls in side me over what happened.

Except for some of it . . . some of it was directed at Lorcan. I hate that I felt that way, but he'd only stared blankly, and perhaps it was idiotic of me to imagine he'd stand up for me. Why did I think he would, just like how he'd done with my brother?

My chest rises with each slow breath I take. Glancing down at the side table full of daggers, I remember how Ivarron had taught me so much. I preferred using blades even if I'd practiced with crossbows and all sorts—

'Miss Ambrose.'

I still.

Oh, Solaris and Crello, save me.

The rugged voice is one I'd already become all too familiar with . . . *Lorcan.*

Clearing my throat and not looking back once, I reply with, 'Deputy.'

'I apologize for earlier. The General meant no harm. You shouldn't take what he says or does to heart. It's how he is with everyone.'

'I don't take anything to heart.' My eyes focus on the target again, hiding how what I've said is a lie. I do take things to heart at times, but with the General, it's different. He'd found a way to disrespect me.

'If I'm honest with you, Miss Ambrose.' Lorcan's presence seems to get closer. *I do not need this right now.* 'I thought you were ready to leap forward and attack him.'

'I'm no animal waiting for when I'm next provoked.' At least not all the time.

He hums thoughtfully, followed by seconds of silence. I even think he's gone until— 'What caused that scar of yours?'

I close my eyes and inhale. The screeching metal of swords as they clash rings at the far end. 'I'd ask the same about yours,' I say, picking up a double-edged blade. 'It seems mine is hideous to the General. I didn't see him mention your hand.'

'Well, I've never spoken back to him, Miss Ambrose.'

I huff, whirling around to meet his hardened eyes. 'Is the second in command supposed to distract trainees?'

His brow lifts at the use of *distract*, and I realize that must have come across differently to him.

I take a breath, seeing fit that I should answer him. 'A dragon did it . . . right as my father died. Its talon sliced along my arm up to my palm before it fled.' It feels odd saying this. I've never opened up to anyone, not even on my favorite color, unless it were to my brothers.

'A dragon?' His tone sounds more surprised than questioning. 'I suspect that is why you must despise them. Am I correct to assume so?'

Of course, that is it. I'd grown up seeing them as a threat to our land. 'Wouldn't you?'

Something sneaks up on his expression when I ask him this . . . something harsh though it leaves too quick for me to decipher. 'Hate can drive you to extremes, Miss Ambrose.'

'Only if you let it,' I say, studying his face like I want to solve the puzzled expression he had for a second as I add, '*Deputy*.'

He takes a long look at my eyes while keeping his hand against the pommel of his sword. Seeing there's nothing left to say, I spin and go back into my throwing stance, launching the blade. Once again, it lands above the center but as I reach for another knife, Lorcan, not having moved from his position behind me, says, 'Your aim is good, but you seem to use your strength more than skill.'

What an observant Venator.

'Like these daggers can do much harm to an immortal,' I murmur with a frown as I suddenly think of the Golden Thief. Even though I'd stolen steel powder to protect myself in the past so I could repel any shifter possibly lurking around, I now knew the Golden Thief was immune to that. The last thing I want is to be bitten by a shifter.

Shifters may look like us mortals. They can even go as far as hiding their scent from other animals. But everyone knows their bite can turn you into such dreadful dragons unless, of course, your body rejects it – which is almost always. I'd only ever heard the rumors from Miss Kiligra on how most bites killed you in horrific ways. As if your insides were ripping to shreds, and every part of you would cough up blood until there was nothing left to expel.

'Dragons may be immortal,' Lorcan says, making me stray from my thoughts as I look over my shoulder at him. 'But they aren't invincible.'

I know that . . . despite immortality, a steel weapon to the heart, fatal wounds or decapitation usually do the trick.

'But if you want to weaken a dragon,' Lorcan continues. 'Be it a fledgling or an adult, then you aim here.' He points to his eyes before dragging that scarred finger to his abdomen. 'And here. However, when young, their scales aren't developed. It's easier to pierce their skin that way.'

'What if it's a shifter in human form?' The question comes out before I can even stop myself.

'Then . . .' A waft of cedar hits me as he takes one step to my side and reaches his hand over mine. 'You keep your movement fluid.' His gaze sets on the target, never letting go of me as he raises my arm with the blade and aims it. I'm not sure how to feel or react, my instincts usually tell me to punch or kick any man who'd approach me this way, but I can't do that to a second in command.

Lorcan glances at me, and the corner of his lip twitches, making me narrow my eyes. Now I might just kick him, Venator or not. I do not care.

'Only add force when you need to,' he says, soft, in contrast to what he was telling me to do.

For a moment, we stay like that, staring at each other until his name is called out over the fields. He steps away from me, running a hand through his hair. The wisps tapering below his ears burn bright like fire hearths. 'Keep practicing. You already have more potential than most in here.' From his hair, his hand comes down to his jaw, rubbing it as he walks backward. 'And remember . . . we protect those who do not bear the flame.'

The Venator's motto.

My brows lift at that as it takes a second for him to turn his sturdy back on me.

Every dragon carries the power of fire that no other mortal can. Be it an Umbrati who thrives with its shadows of the night or a Merati capable of creating illusions to lure their victims. I'd learned this through Idris's books. Perhaps I'd have known more if I hadn't stopped going to the village school after my parents perished.

'What did you do to have the Deputy smiling so much?' Freya runs up to me, bow in one hand and a quiver on her back, carrying all the arrows. I'd seen her earlier hitting every target with ease. It is obviously her forte.

I shrug. 'He must have had a good breakfast.'

Trying not so much as to glance in his direction, I look toward the target, repeating what he told me as I throw the dagger. It lands straight in the middle, startling me.

Freya laughs incredulously, handing me another blade like it's nothing. 'Lorcan rarely smiles. In fact, I don't remember ever seeing him do it, and I've known him since I was eight and he was just fourteen.'

She's known him for years? I eye her suspiciously. 'Can't be worse than General Erion.'

Freya's body solidifies like water turning to ice. 'Yeah . . . I—I actually wanted to talk to you about that.'

Pinching my brows together, I angle my head down at her.

'He—' She mutters "Solaris" in-between. 'He's . . . my father.'

My blade loosens in my palm, and from the look I must have on my face Freya adds with a wince, 'General Erion Demori.'

Well, that explains the resemblance I'm only just noticing, but the shock still reigns over me. 'I—why didn't you tell me?' I hadn't expected her to last night, but perhaps I'd have kept quiet—no, that is an outright lie, I'd still have said something to the General.

Freya's hands pick at the bow to the point I think she'll break it in half from trepidation. 'I'm sorry, Nara, it's the reason why most people never room with me. They despise my father! And I was so excited to meet someone new—'

'If he's your father and the General, why do you reside in the common rooms of the barracks?'

She sighs deeply, looking back to the open doors leading inside the weapons room, then at me. It's quiet before she says, 'I grew up here never having explored the city on my own terms. My father trained me well, thinking I wanted to become a Venator. Instead, I'd always refuse, up until the age of eighteen when I told him I wanted freedom.'

Despite differences, I understand the feeling of wanting freedom.

'We've never been close, but he made me a proposition: I'd be free to go live my life as I please, and if by the time I turned twenty, I hadn't found a purpose, I was to go back. But this time train to be . . . them.' Her eyes dart to Lorcan and all the leaders starting to sword fight against each other. 'I do not get special treatment, nor would I want it anyway.'

My heart tightens for her as if it has been twisted a thousand times. General Erion didn't so much as bat an eyelid for his daughter when she was beside me. He treated her like the rest of us. I wondered how someone so joyful and bright could have a father such as the General.

I open my mouth, wanting to tell her how who she is doesn't matter to me, but two young men near the bushes on the far right appear to be cornering another man.

'Is everything—' Freya starts, looking behind her when I storm past.

I'm not sure what's willing me to go over, but seeing the way they're pushing him reminds me of the times I'd have to defend my brothers back home.

I stop just a few meters away from them. The two men, one with long ebony hair and the other's ending just below his chin in a dark auburn gleam, swear and move a sword around in the air. The cornered man tries to grab it before he's pushed back.

'Give it back to him,' I order, and they all turn to look at me.

'This doesn't concern you,' says the one with ebony hair. 'Isn't that right, Link?'

The man whose name is Link, the person they'd taken the sword from, doesn't look my way. He seems to be far more interested in the ground, while his golden-brown hair, wavy and layered, moves briskly as he shakes his head.

Rotten bullies.

'And why might it not concern me?' I ask once the two dismiss me as if I'm nothing to them but a piece of useless lint.

This time the auburn-haired man creeps towards me, his pale moon complexion, just like his friend, dulls. 'Listen,' he says. 'I suggest you walk away, princess—' He reaches his bony hand over to my hip and, knowing where he wants to slide it down to, I fist my hand around his index and middle finger, tilting them at an angle it should never be slanted at.

He yelps as his friend comes to his aid who then stops, staggering back when I lift my blade at him.

'Lovely hand you got there,' I say with such calmness you would think we're having a simple conversation. He whimpers, bending over slightly as the bones on his fingers begin to click under my own. 'Would hate for it to break.'

I heard the grass crunch behind me and then Freya appears next to me. 'Oh, my—Nara.'

'Give. It. Back,' I spit, tightening my grip so much that my knuckles turn white.

His sunken face grows paler than it already is as he gestures his head to the other to hand back the sword. Reluctantly, he does as he's told.

'Go.' I motion my chin to Link once he's got a hold of it. His eyes wide, a crystal blue color, he looks at me before bowing his head and jogging away.

As soon as Link's out of sight, I let go of the hand. The man winces, clutching his fingers. His lips thin out, and his eyes, made of grey and moss green, send me a deathly glare, one that screams I've made the biggest mistake ever crossing him.

I don't cower, and give him a hard stare before they both retract, walking away though never breaking eye contact with me.

'Well,' Freya exhales, looking at them. 'That's one way to start your first day of training.'

Chapter Eight

'I feel like we should sit with him,' Freya suggests, glancing towards Link, who is sitting alone at the end of one of the tables playing with his supper. Since I'd helped him last week, Freya mentioned he's a quiet person who rarely spoke to anyone.

'I don't think he wants company,' I comment back, holding onto my plate of venison. Every day so far, he seems to enjoy his solitude during meals.

I don't blame him, I would too.

'How can he not!' Shaking her head, Freya links an arm around mine. 'Come.' She drags me across the dining hall, and even if I am to object, I don't think it'll make a difference because we're already beside his table.

Link doesn't look up, causing Freya to clear her throat. 'Hello.' She smiles. Link's eyes finally drift to her, but he keeps wordless as she says, 'Mind if we sit here?'

Still nothing.

I lift a brow towards Freya, implying how we honestly shouldn't have bothered him. She ignores me, slamming her tray down and pushing me onto the benches with her. 'Link, right? I'm Freya.' Her hand comes out to meet his, yet he doesn't respond to it. I'm wondering if there is a chance that I can run away from this. Again, she clears her throat and points to me. 'This is Nara—'

'I know who she is,' he mumbles, lowering his head. Those golden-brown waves drift over his light tan forehead.

'Oh! Is it because she saved you?' Her smile returns. 'Or is it because she's an Ambrose?'

I smooth the grimace forming on my face as I focus on my food. Despite my father's notoriety, Freya had told me she met my father when she was young and I'd made sure to ask all my questions. Except she didn't have much memory of it other than my father's taunting comebacks to General Erion, something she said reminded her of me.

'So, I took a new liking to painting. Nara told me she adored my portrait of flowers!'

I didn't have the heart to tell her the flowers looked more like a pile of disfigured animals.

'Do you do anything in your spare time? Nara here carves! I asked her if she could carve lilacs on my chest of drawers since they are my—'

'Would you have really broken Adriel's hand?' Link interrupts, and I snap my head up as he looks at me, his finger idly sliding around the rim of a tankard mug. It's like everything Freya was talking about for the last minute went entirely over his head.

'Of course,' I say, thinking back to the two guys who'd cornered him. Adriel and Oran, Freya had said they were called. 'You see, back home, I had an enemy list.'

'An enemy list?' Link repeats like he finds that hard to believe.

Nodding, I say, 'Whoever wronged my brothers or me—' I

pause midway through scarfing down food. '—I'd write their names somewhere and then later threaten them.'

'What did you do if . . .' Freya trails off, and the corner of my mouth flutters upward.

'Well,' I say. 'Once, I broke a man's wrist for stealing from my brother.'

'Solaris!' Freya gasps, her dark bronze skin glowing as she smiles. 'You are wild, Nara.'

'And you never got in trouble for that?' Link's brow curves up.

'I did . . . mainly with my eldest brother.' I drop my gaze as my mind starts thinking about them. A week seems too long without them already. I know we'll write each other letters, and Illias will likely have the longest summaries of what he'd done throughout the day, but it still isn't the same.

With a small intake of breath, I glance up at Link. His lips bloom into a soft smile, and dimples form on both sides of his cheek. It's a smile that showed more with his eyes than anything.

He starts to say something when the mug in his hand rattles as it hits the floor, cutting him off, and whatever tinge of happiness he had before, fades as I see gaunt hands press against the table.

'Seems the new girl has taken a liking to orphaned pigs,' Adriel says as I look at him and Oran standing over Link, both with vile grins on their lips. 'Oh wait . . . aren't you an orphan as well, considering what happened to your father?'

So, these assholes have learned nothing from last week.

'I heard your mother died of a rümen's bite,' Oran chimes in, laughing. His long dark hair plunging past his shoulders.

'That's not true,' I say in quiet wrath as the burning heat of anger grows in my chest.

'Shame, perhaps she couldn't burden herself with looking after a child like you—'

'Adriel, I think you should leave before—'

'What are you going to do Freya, tell your father, who doesn't even acknowledge your existence?'

Freya's shoulders sink low at Adriel's words, and I eye the knife to my right. I picture grabbing it then holding it to his throat.

'It's not as if the General would disagree with us,' he jeers. 'We all saw how he treated her the other day.'

My hand now hovers above the knife without them noticing, and I stare at it, wanting to wipe the smug look off their faces.

'Hey, how did it happen?' Adriel's voice doesn't sound like he's concerned. It sounds taunting again. 'Was it a witch? Are you cursed?'

Clenching my jaw, I clutch the blade harder, ready to dart forward, but a whistle and a musical voice cuts in. 'If it isn't oat head and dry as a toast at it again.'

My gaze shifts up at where a man, grinning, wraps his arms around the shoulders of Oran and Adriel. His dark hair is cropped and crimped like fresh waves as his eyes slide to me, warm brown and inviting, like the smooth shade of his and Freya's skin. Only that she is slightly more bronzed.

'What is it you want, Rydan?' Adriel tries pushing away, but Rydan keeps a firm grip.

'I'm simply here to stop you both from being mauled to death by this lovely lady. Hello there.' He looks at me, speaking in a sultry tone. I jerk my head back, bemused as he returns his gaze to Adriel. 'Let the people enjoy their supper unless you are truly starving for some deer, then I suggest you join my table. I am considered great company in more ways than one.'

'You're disgusting.' Adriel manages to pull away.

Rydan chuckles, crossing his arms over the dark training armor. 'You'd be surprised by how many here say that of you.'

A bitter frown comes from Adriel, but Rydan doesn't step down. 'Let's go,' Adriel moves away, bumping his shoulder against Oran's chest and glaring back at me.

I need to start making a new enemy list.

Rydan turns to us. His eyes travel down to the knife, making me draw my arm back away from it. He'd seen me wanting to use it.

We don't exchange any words as he shoots me a *you're welcome* wink and strolls away from us, leaving me with a permanent scowl. 'What just—'

'Rydan Alderis,' Freya breathes, watching as he goes up to another table and leans against it with that same juvenile smile. 'Many think he joined for fun since he doesn't take anything seriously and enjoys irritating everyone, especially Lorcan.'

'How does Lorcan react?' A question not needed to be asked, but I couldn't help it.

'He tends to walk away once Rydan calls him Lorcy.' As she says that, it's like we wished him into the mess hall as Lorcan appears by the entrance. Hand on his pommel, his calculating eyes stare at everyone before Rydan springs forward to reach him.

Whatever Rydan's saying, Lorcan's jaw tenses. I'd even go as far as thinking he wants to use his sword on Rydan, but soon his gaze catches mine. He doesn't seem to shy from it, reminding me of the first day I saw him after killing that rümen. His lips stay in a firm line as he continues ignoring Rydan, and something odd flickers in my gut, but I push it away, breaking eye contact.

'—With the Queen coming over in a few days and whatnot.'

I come to my senses upon hearing Freya in the midst of another conversation with Link.

'The Queen?' My brows tangle as I look at her.

She clasps a hand to her mouth. 'Solaris! I'd forgotten to tell you! The Queen comes by certain days and sees us during training. Most of the time, it's to hold meetings with my father, but it's always ever so frightening.'

I'm not sure why I'd thought I wouldn't meet the Queen so soon, but a cluster of anticipation does form inside of me. 'Is she nice?'

'More like intimidatingly beautiful.' Link sighs, playing with his food. The encounter with Adriel and Oran looks to have put him back in that shell of hiding away. I'd still not forgotten the mention of him being an orphan. But unlike my brothers and me, I don't think Link has *anyone* at all.

'It's true,' Freya exhales dramatically, placing her elbows on the table and cupping her cheeks. 'But I just tend to get nervous either way.'

Pursing my lips as I stare far ahead, I ask myself if the Queen would say anything about my father. He never spoke ill of her when he'd visit us, but again, he didn't tell us much of anything.

Later that night, when Freya had decided she wanted to try out carving, I'd lent my tools and left her to work on the sides of oak wood in our room, while I'd cut up a piece from her old dresses. I punctured holes through it with my hunting knife before placing my cloak on and walking out into the gardens near the stables, where a pond lay bare surrounded by bushes and blue iris flowers.

It's not like I'd planned to leave my room at first, but boredom had crept up my spine, and I'd figured why not come out to trap frogs.

I wasn't going to keep them; Solaris forbid how Freya would react to me bringing back a frog, but . . . I'd long needed to have the feeling of something familiar.

As candlelight from inside the barracks filtered through the grass and the night stars bloomed iridescently, I bend down near the edges of the pond, picking up rocks and stones. Frogs prefer shelter, so that's why I'm building them a small cave.

I place the cut-up dress to one side, which I tied into a knot at the end as a form of net. Scavenging with my bare fingers, I gather some mud before finding a worm and placing it inside the towered cave.

Wiping my hands against my corset, I slide off onto the grass and bring my knees up to my chin, waiting and waiting . . . and *waiting*.

Until the patter of wet feet sound inside the cave I'd built, and a frog's singing croaks deepens from within.

Grabbing my net, I take off some of the rocks and set my eyes on a frog no larger than my fist. I scoop it up, making sure its weight won't fall through some of the small holes I'd made as I lift the net eye level and smile at my success. Everyone knows capturing any animal is hard enough. Yet, they seem to gravitate towards me, much to my delight when it comes to smaller, friendlier creatures too.

'There's always something new every time I encounter you.'

Oh, shit.

Spinning and almost tripping on my cloak, I face Lorcan's curious gaze.

'Do you always happen to appear everywhere I am?' I raise a brow, aware I'm coming across as defensive.

'I'm on guard, and I just so happened to see you exploring the grounds on your own.' His hands are behind him as he tips his head to the side. 'I thought I'd check you hadn't gone mad, and here you are covered in mud sitting in a pond.'

I frown, but he doesn't give me time to quip back. 'What's in there?' He points to my hand and the lavender silk net.

'A frog.'

He didn't expect that answer. He chuckles, reminding me of how Freya had said she'd never seen him smile before. 'Do you hate those too?'

'No.' My frown deepens. 'I—I was going to let it go.' Feeling the need to set the frog free, I lower myself to the ground, shaking the net as it hops out. The glossy skin, like colors of the forest, are visible even in the night as I watch it disappear. The water ripples across the pond as I stand, facing Lorcan again.

A crease forms between his eyebrows as he looks toward the pond then at me. 'Might I ask why you trapped it in—' He nods at the net. '*That*?'

I glance at it in my hands. 'I used to be a trapper.' *Or still am . . .*

'And you miss it,' he states, the same curiosity now dripping from his voice.

'I've done it since I was thirteen. I'm not like you, I'm not used to this since a young age.'

His eyes drift down to his sabaton boots, letting out a soft disbelieving laugh. 'You'd be surprised by what I've been used to before.'

I angle my head slightly. Before arriving in the city, I'd not asked much but now I *want* to know things about everything, *everyone*. 'And what is that may I ask?'

'Well, if you must know, Miss Ambrose, I was homeless after my father's death. My mother had died after giving birth to me, and by the time I came to the city, the General found me on the streets, barefoot and malnourished.'

A whoosh of air leaves me as I try to hide the shock on my face. I didn't expect him to open up like that . . . All at once. 'I'm—I'm so sorry,' my words stumble over each other.

'It was a long time ago.' He dismisses it, but I can sense a kernel of anger for one second before it vanishes. 'You should head inside. I'd hate for an attack to occur and for it to have been my fault because I was . . . *distracted*,' he muses, and I glower at how he's thrown back the word I'd said on the first day of training.

Raising my chin, I ignore his request to head inside and instead say, 'Freya tells me there's never been an intruder in the barracks before.'

'*Freya* . . . wasn't here for two years. There hadn't been attacks for years prior, but as of lately, shifters have become more unpredictable.'

I just about jolt over the word *unpredictable*. 'Even with steel powder?'

His head motions over me. 'The walls all contain it, but that doesn't mean they can't infiltrate the fields, where there's less of it.'

'Or maybe they're becoming immune,' I say in a quiet murmur. If the Golden Thief is unaffected by it, who's to tell if others of his kind aren't? *Who's* to say he hasn't breached past the castle walls before?

Lorcan regards me silently, intrigued by my response. After a while, he nods. 'Maybe, Miss Ambrose.' With that, he looks off past the barracks and to the castle towers, turning to walk away.

'Wait,' I call out to him in a rush. He stops, russet hair lightened by the moonlight brushes below the neck of his armor. Once he turns to me, I say, 'I know about the Golden Thief.'

He studies me carefully, almost like he had put up a shield that not even the sun goddess Solaris could shine through.

'I saw a poster in the city,' I add, chewing on my bottom lip. 'Is he really that hard to catch?'

'Supposedly,' he says, looking at me through lowered brows. 'He's smart in his own ways, but there is one thing we've come to know.'

'What's that?'

His lip twitches, and satisfaction rolls off him. 'He can't fly.'

That only makes me question more. 'Why not?'

'He's been doing what he does long enough for us to track him, and he's never once flown, not like other shifters we've come across.'

I frown. There'd have to be a reason he can't fly. Dragons have always known how to on instinct from birth. Perhaps he sustained an injury in his wings that didn't heal. But that only opens up more questions about someone who is supposed to be powerful, holding all three dragon powers and immune to steel.

'Why does everyone say he has no weaknesses, then?' I ask. 'Surely being unable to do the one thing he was born to do can help us.'

'Except what he lacks in flight he makes up for with all the power and agility he has.'

A sharp sigh expels out of me, I hadn't meant to do it so loudly, but the Golden Thief is already testing my patience.

'I once saw him.' Lorcan's gaze suddenly appears miles away. 'A few years back in one of the districts. I'd used a spear on him, but his reflexes were faster. He grabbed it mid-air, broke it in half, and threw it, before it pierced my armor and through my chest.'

I don't say a word. I only stare at him blankly in shock. The Golden Thief is known as someone dangerous; yes, everyone thinks of him that way, but what is his purpose in stealing if he is likely the one creating those new creatures?

Is it a distraction? If it's not rulers from different lands, then what is the Golden Thief's endgame in this?

'We'll catch him,' I say, at last, a sudden determination in my voice. 'I know we will.' *I just have to figure out the Ivarron part.*

'I hope so, a threat like him—' He pauses, wincing and looking away like the whole ordeal is too frustrating. 'Just be careful . . . shifters aren't the only dangers in Emberwell.'

He means the new breed.

'I will be,' I say, although I don't sound the most convincing.

'Good.' He nods before bowing his head. 'Then I'll leave you to enjoy the rest of your night, Miss Ambrose.'

'Nara,' I correct. 'You can call me Nara.'

He smiles, a white and beautiful shine against the night. 'Goodnight, Nara.'

Chapter Nine

Walking through hallways, I falter on my feet, seeing Rydan lean against the wall. I'd meant to express my gratitude over the other day during supper. Still, in truth, I was avoiding his possible irritating tendencies Freya had spoken of.

Sucking in a breath, I stroll towards him. At the same time, his head turns, and his gaze latches on me.

'Rydan, right?' I ask as he faces me front on. He nods. 'Can we talk?'

'We may,' he replies curtly, yet his eyes shine with amusement.

Ignoring it, I clear my throat. 'I want to thank you for what happened the other day in the mess hall.'

He purses his lips as a frown warps his features, like he has no clue what I am talking about.

'Adriel and Oran?' I prompt, refreshing his memory which seems to work as his expression smoothes, and he clicks his fingers with a nod. 'I just thought you didn't need to . . .'

'I was simply making sure you didn't ruin my dinner by

bludgeoning those two,' he concedes, and now it's my turn to frown at that. I wouldn't have bludgeoned them. I'd have scared them, perhaps cut them a little, so they knew their place—I pause on that idea, not needing to get into what could have happened.

'Well, thank you either way,' I say. He doesn't reply. His eyes stay on me with slow and careful blinks. No smile present, but you can see he wants to by the corner tilting a tiny fraction. A beat of silence goes by, and I walk backward, hesitating whether I should say something else but seeing as there is nothing, I whirl to face the other way.

I hardly make it past a few steps before he's saying, 'You know, I saw how you defended Link that day.'

I turn back around. Rydan pays no attention to me, just his fingernails this time as he adds nonchalantly, 'Have to say I was impressed.'

'Did you expect something else of me?'

'Despite hearing you were related to Nathaniel Ambrose, I expected you to suck, yes, so now I have even more competition.' He drops his head with a dramatic sigh before glancing up at me. 'I suppose it'll be more thrilling this way.'

Anger suddenly dominates my mind, and I bite my tongue, not wanting to give in. But I can't. I blurt out, 'I've managed to trap thousands of creatures before, killed a rümen firsthand without any remorse, stood in front of an Ardenti with nothing but a goblet. What makes you think I can't do any of that to you in this little competition of yours?'

Three blinks, three blinks, and then a smile grows on his lips, beaming like sunrays on his warm bronze skin. 'Wow,' he breathes, and the questioning frown on my face doesn't leave as he starts clapping slowly. 'I mean, I was kidding about the competition, but you're unmerciful. I like it!'

I keep quiet. Not even a laugh comes out. I'm sure I'm also glaring at him.

'Well, aren't you just a doll to be around?' He wiggles a finger in my face. 'Look at that smile.'

Such regret I have for thanking him. 'Are you always like this?' I slap his hand away.

'Like what?'

'Childish?'

He tilts his head, looking upward in thought. 'Certain days, I can be an adult.' Soft brown eyes dart back down to me. 'Others . . . I choose not to. Or even some days I do both, I call it multi-tasking.'

That is just . . . I truly have no words.

Rydan smiles innocently at the concern written all over my face and pats my head, walking past but not before a whisper comes from him, 'See you in training. Don't forget to keep your competitors close, Ambrose.'

I glance over my shoulder and glower as he salutes, disappearing into the corners of the dark hallway. Part of me is glad he's gone. The other is dreading the idea I'll be seeing him every day and possibly for years if we both swear in as official Venators. After a few minutes of us talking, he already seemed like a right pain in my existence. Although, I've managed to live under the same roof as Iker for twenty-one years. I should be used to handling men like him.

'Nara!' I jolt at Freya's squeals as she appears in front of me, linking her arm with mine. 'Excited to see the Queen tomorrow?'

Shit, the Queen. 'That's tomorrow?'

Freya nods rapidly as we fall into step, down the halls. 'I told Link how I am still petrified. I've seen her since I was a child, and yet I feel like heading straight to the toilets each time she comes. Do you ever feel that way when you get nervous? Or do you not get nervous? You seem like the type not to get skittish.'

I fold in my lips to hide a smile – the smile I dared not show Rydan – because, during my short time here, I've become fond of Freya's ingenuous talks. Although I find it difficult adjusting to any friendship, I feel the most at ease with her, and even Link. Luckily, I haven't driven them away. And when I'd finally told Freya I was a trapper, she only gasped and hugged me before saying how "marvelous" that must have been.

'If I'm honest, I do get nervous at times,' I tell her. 'But I'll let you in on a secret.'

Freya's doe eyes go wide in anticipation as I whisper, 'You just have to imagine your worst enemy running through the streets being chased by a rümen . . . *naked*.'

She tips her head back with a laugh. 'Oh, you are absolutely strange, Nara, and I adore you for it.' She hums with the remnants of a smile still on her lips. 'Except one issue, I have no enemies.'

'Then,' I drag the word. 'We'll have to introduce you to some.'

'Bested you once again, Link,' I pant the following morning, extending my palm out to him after we've been at it in hand-to-hand combat. Ever since Freya and I sat with him for meals, he's grown accustomed to us. He rarely speaks, but neither do I in comparison to Freya.

He wheezes, clutching his chest as he takes my hand, and I help him up. 'How did you learn to fight like that?'

'I didn't.' Except that I did with Idris. He never classified it as learning to fight. It was more of when we weren't arguing; he'd show me counterattacks. I assume it was his way to teach me how to defend myself despite how protective he is. 'Shall we go once more?' I reposition myself in a fighting stance, raising my dominant fist in front of my face and the other by the side of my head. Full of energy, I bounce around.

Link's eyes go wide. A hesitation on his part as he scratches the nape of his neck where the armor meets him. 'I think . . .' he says before his eyes travel to the other side of the field. I observe how he's now staring at Freya, drawing her bowstring back as she focuses on the target. 'I think I will take a break instead,' he continues shyly just as she shoots it.

I drop my fists and narrow my eyes at him. 'Alright,' I say, unable to hide the suspicion in my voice as Link lowers his gaze and stumbles over his legs. He jogs towards Freya, and I tilt my head at them both.

I smile over Freya's bright laugh echoing the training grounds as soon as she sees Link. However, I can't help looking to the far right of them where Rydan is cutting the air with his sword rather dramatically.

I scoff, crossing my arms at his foolishness until weapons and chatter fall silent. Even Rydan stops what he is doing and turns to the entrance of the weaponry room.

One by one, everyone turns to look that way as the Queen steps out. I inhale sharply as my eyes journey the square neckline and cap sleeves of her samite dress, showcasing her deep mahogany skin. Thick layers of gown flow behind her, creating a lake of pure gold silk, her coal-black hair cascades in waves down her bodice. A gilded crown fitted with glittering jewels sits atop, resembling flames as they come to a point. Intimidatingly beautiful, Link had said, and he is not wrong. The Queen, Sarilyn Orcharian, as everyone knew her, excels in elegance. Not a doubt about that.

One thing that consistently causes my curiosity to reign high is how the Queen has never wed, not from what I'd learned. All I know is that there is no family heritage either, only her.

Beside her, stand Lorcan and the General along with another woman dressed in a cool orange-toned kirtle, whom I imagine is her lady-in-waiting. Venators follow behind, guarding the Queen's every movement.

The Queen makes a hand gesture towards us all, and already I can see trainees resuming what they were doing, this time showing off whatever skills they might have. Adriel and Oran start sword fighting from the left, and anyone can gather that they are trying immensely to impress the Queen. She does not even peek their way as I roll my eyes at them and stroll to where the practice dummies and daggers are.

My hand grabs a double-edged blade, so scalding to the touch that any sane person would drop it. I don't as I divert my sight to the practice dummies ahead – the warmth of spring in Emberwell bats against my eyelids as I close them.

Inhaling with all my strength, I envision the target, and parting my feet, I open my eyes, flinging the dagger. I go again, each time faster and stealthier, getting lost in the way it doesn't once miss the center.

Focusing ahead, I reach for another dagger but find I've used them all. My shoulders droop with a sigh, but I sense a presence around, causing me to turn. My gaze immediately fixates on a round pendant of pure gold with what looks to be three rivers intertwining over a compass – one down the middle, another across, and the last diagonal.

Realizing the pendant rests on that glowing mahogany skin, I lift my eyes to meet the Queen's. Her lips are painted with a sheer gloss and her facial features are so sharp yet so soft.

I've always been told how delicate my face is, with my button nose, freckles and that if I smile, I smile with my cheeks. But beyond it all, I am a torrent of winds. Somehow the Queen is all of that.

'What's your name?' She asks. Her eyes, almost obsidian, and voice radiating that same grace, while her lady-in-waiting stares at me.

I consider imagining what I told Freya to do when nervous. This was the first time I'd ever witnessed the Queen in the flesh rather than hearing about her through word of mouth. Now she is here asking me a simple question. Thankfully, I'm used to hiding my nerves. 'Naralía,' I answer, drawing in a breath as I add, 'Ambrose.'

Alert yet with amazing poise, she tilts her head. 'Ambrose?' She looks towards the General, parting her lips like waves of shock have gone through her. 'You are Nathaniel's daughter?'

A nod towards her as her eyes slide to my face. As always, I find Lorcan's gaze on me.

'The Deputy saw to it that she joined us soon after helping us capture the Ardenti,' The General says from behind the Queen's shoulder. He doesn't even try to feign the begrudging tone in his words. One might say he hates me more now than the first day of training.

'Well, Erion, it's not as if you didn't do the same with Deputy Halen twelve years ago.' The Queen swings her head in the General's direction, a speck of humor in her voice that does not bide well with him as he turns stiff. 'But an Ardenti?' She glances back at me, the humor now settling into wonder. 'Remarkable for someone who's never trained before.'

I try not to wince at that. Knowing I helped was one thing, but everyone seemed to speak of it as if I killed the dragon. I hadn't touched it, not even used any form of weapon, yet it yielded at my feet. 'I just want to carry out my dad's legacy, Your Majesty.' I curtsy, and my eyes slit in response to the General's malicious gaze as I send him a look that says, *I will endeavor to be what my father once was.*

'We should head for that meeting, Sarilyn.' He glowers.

'Yes,' the Queen says slowly. 'Let's.' Not once does she take her eyes off me. 'I trust I will see you at the arena fight next week, Naralía?'

'Of course.' I bow once more as she turns to walk off with her Venators and the General.

Her gown brushes against the grass as Lorcan passes by, hands behind him as he whispers, 'You seem to catch everyone's attention.'

I angle my head up at him. 'Well then, I hope I don't distract the Queen, either.'

He shakes his head with a smile. 'I'd sure hope not, Nara.'

My mouth parts but right when I want to say something, he's already following after the Queen.

A frown then stiffens my expression, seeing Adriel and Oran opposite me. Their stares hold nothing friendly as they pause their practice. My nails curl into my palm, not cowering from them. The jealousy of the two pretty much melds with the air, yet I still do not submit, which is what they'd want me to do.

They nudge each other with cold glares as they go back to practicing, and I to prying out the blades from the practice dummies.

I jerk upright from my bed, having had a nightmare, hair strands matt to my face as I swallow my harsh gasps. I'd not had such a dream in a while. The same one where my brothers and mother hid in the corner of my cottage, shielding each other. And the dragon, a distant haze of what I can remember, right in front of me before Idris shot that arrow. By the time it had fled, my father had bled out . . . it was too late.

Calming my breathing, I sit up on the silk sheets of my bed, but among the quietness and soft snores of Freya sound asleep, I know I won't fall into slumber again. I've been like this since I'd arrived. Not one day have I slept well.

Huffing, I conclude that perhaps I need fresh air or to trap frogs again.

Freya doesn't wake as I get up and slide into my boots while hooking a cloak over my nightgown. Bending as I reach for the net I'd made, I slip past the door and down the sconce-lit halls until I'm outside, staring up at the moon. It's a shade of orange this time, a rarity but a beautiful sight, nonetheless.

I make my way to where the ponds are, but pause for a moment when the bushes nearby begin to rustle. Scrunching my forehead, I scan the gardens. I see nothing but thickets separating different sectors within the castle walls like a maze.

The noise stops, and carefully, I continue my path, nearing the pond, but as I let the net fall from my hands beneath me, I hear footsteps approach from behind. Before I can turn, an arm wraps around my waist, and a grimy hand covers my mouth, causing me to grimace at the grotesque feeling.

Alarm prickles my skin as I try to pry the person off and kick while I'm hauled backward, but the bones of the slim arm digging into my abdomen quickly remind me of someone.

Adriel.

Chapter Ten

Knowing who the culprit is, I continue thrashing in Adriel's arms. Fury blazing in my veins brings me to clamp my teeth down on his hand, and he curses, letting go of me.

I spit the horrid taste of his sweat onto the grass and spin round to face him. He's holding his wrist with his palm stretched out, glaring at me. He lunges forward, but I grab his shoulders, kneeing him in the groin.

His legs tumble as he barely makes a sound between a groan and a yelp of pain. Whatever his game is, his plan, his end point to this, I'm not going to play it. I draw my fist back, about to strike him, but the blow doesn't hit him. It hits *me*.

The side of my face falls first onto the grass, scraping my cheeks and temple. From the burn in my thigh, I imagine I scraped that too. My head spins, and I try to gain back control, but as my eyes flicker up at Adriel, I realize he isn't the one that hit me.

Oran now stands beside him. The moon's orange hues gleam off his ebony hair looking as if the tips burn in fire. 'For someone who acts all tough, it sure doesn't look it now,' he sneers.

I attempt to get up, but he kicks me back down as I topple onto my stomach. More scrapes prick my skin, and raising my head, I squint my eyes at the pond.

'Why should the Queen take an interest in you?' Adriel's voice is cruel, like blades sliding along my skin. I ignore it as my arm, without meaning to, stretches out where water meets land.

'You'll just end up like your father.' Oran laughs, and I lower my brows. Fury turns into a white rage as I stare ahead at the pond and concentrate on it. My fingertips sting, no longer hearing Adriel's or Oran's taunts. It's like the world slows down as the light of the moon blooms upon the waters.

When my senses come back, Adriel and Oran's words diminish as singing croaks of frogs blaze, and not one but hundreds of them swarm together from the pond like an army. They pounce, jumping past me, and head straight to Adriel and Oran.

They yell out an abundance of profanities. And as I look over my shoulder, their shadows show them stumbling to the barracks, shaking their arms and legs as the frogs continue to leech onto their armor.

What in Solaris's name . . .

Widening my eyes and sucking in air sharply, I wait on the ground for a minute or two until carefully rising to my feet. I gaze back at the pond in disbelief because I'm not sure what just happened, nor can I muster an explanation for it.

And just as quickly, I no longer see Adriel or Oran *or* any frogs.

A commotion comes from some of the Venator's posts, and I imagine they heard screams, meaning soon they'll be approaching.

Limping and not wanting to deal with any of them, I stalk back inside while darting my gaze everywhere. That rage over Adriel and Oran floods me once again, as I search to see where they might now be.

With my jaw tensing, I mutter to myself as I cross the hallway how not only are they on my enemy list, but if the frogs didn't get them, then I will make sure I do. I will start with breaking their fingers, then their toes, then their—

My chest collides with a hard surface, and my feet sway backward. I was too engrossed in my thoughts to realize where and who I could walk into.

Glancing up, I meet with Lorcan and his furrowed brows.

'Nara—' he pauses, barely touching my elbow. 'You've been hurt,' he says, his eyes finding the possible injuries forming on my face.

Turning away, I mumble, 'it's only a few scrapes.'

'How did that happen?' He steps a little too close, and I stare at him in silence. I don't want to mention Adriel and Oran. I'm not one to go asking for help. I'm used to doing the opposite of that.

His gaze sweeps over me again and my shoulders tense as his expression shows me nothing.

By then, I suppose I must answer him. Except he moves his hand to my lower back and glances behind him before turning me around and, to my confusion, walks us forward.

'What are you doing?'

He keeps his steps steady, his eyes focusing on the hallway. 'Taking you to the infirmary.'

'I can head to the infirmary myself.' I stop, sliding away from his touch.

He studies me with doubt. 'Will you, though?'

I stare up at him through squinted eyes. Truthfully, I won't. I need to pursue Adriel and Oran first.

At my refusal to answer him for the second time tonight, he sighs sharply and places that same hand on my back, guiding me away from the corridors and instead towards the stairs by the entrance.

'This isn't the way to the infirmary,' I grumble, putting pressure on the ground to halt our movements. It doesn't seem to work, and we begin ascending the creaking stairs.

'I know,' are the only words he says as a slight smile pries the side of his lips – a smile I can't help but keep my gaze on.

His chambers.

He's taken me to his chambers on the top-level floor . . .

Oh, this is outrageously wrong.

Lorcan opens the door, strolling in first, and waits for me to enter. Once I do, I stay put, taking in what I can so far see. I know the General rooms in a different wing within the palace walls. It's why I first questioned Freya on it, but Lorcan's quarters is a view I'd dared not imagine.

An armoire sits to the left beside the enormous bed of blood-red silk covers, where terracotta curtains hang loose and a window just above the bed frame. The walls seem to follow the same color scheme, as lamps project their golden flames onto it. On the other side, an open doorway leads to the bath chambers in crimson and white marble.

All my life, I've bathed in wooden tubs. I never had the privilege, even with our father being a Venator, to wash as a king or Queen might.

I lightly shake my head, enough for Lorcan to notice as he drops his baldric of weapons atop a chair by a dressing table. He comes over and guides me to the sink before gesturing for me to sit on the countertop, but I stare, vigilant and stubborn in doing so. This is still . . . *wrong*. What if someone had seen me enter? They'd think I'm wanting to seduce the second in command into giving me the position of a Venator without the trial.

Lorcan takes a deep breath, pinching his lips together. Something that reminds me of what many would do when getting impatient with me – mostly, it reminded me of Idris.

Exasperated by my own mulish thoughts, I march over. I feel his gaze on me as I unfasten my cloak and place it to the side before not so graciously getting up onto the counter.

I bunch my knees together and raise them to my chin. Lorcan stays soundless but tilts his head with sharpness as if I'm making it more difficult than it should be. Rolling my eyes, I drop my legs, so they dangle.

That makes him smile – hardly but still a smile as he reaches for a cloth next to me. Candles scattered down the sides of the bath flicker while he wets the cloth. 'Are you finally going to tell me what happened?' He asks, bringing the cloth up to my temple. I wince when it collides with my skin. He pauses but then continues.

'Are you going to tell me why you took me here and not the infirmary?' I try and focus on the lattice-tiled walls.

'You didn't seem keen on the infirmary.'

'And you think taking me to your chambers would make a difference?'

He sighs, and I tap my knee impatiently before he says, 'Either way, you'd protest, Nara.'

I would, but that doesn't tell me anything I need to know.

'I tripped and fell,' I answer in a whisper after a minute of silence and after a minute of him cleaning my cuts.

'How does someone—' The word lingers off his lips like he knows it's a lie '—who used to be a trapper . . . trip and fall so easily?'

'You'd be surprised to know I've had my fair share of tackles, sometimes even against a mere branch on the ground.'

His laugh is soft and gentle as he drifts his scarred hand over my left thigh. 'May I?'

'May I what?' I ask, shooting him a glare and pressing my palms against the thin cotton material of my nightgown.

'There's blood seeping through.'

I frown, but my chest hollows at the thickness in his voice and at his eyes dropping to my leg.

'Oh.' Nodding, I pull the nightgown up. Slashes, short and staggered, enhance the redness of where I fell onto the ground.

As soon as the damp cloth hits the cuts, I inhale sharply. Not for any pain, but for the touch of his skin on mine as his thumb swipes the sides.

Again, this is soulfully wrong.

'You don't have to . . .' I cut myself off at the distinctive rasp in my voice.

'I don't mind.' His stare now travels from where candles glimmer on the top part of my exposed skin, under my collarbone, to my eyes.

My veins pulse with unfamiliarity. 'Well, you should.' *I'm not sure of what I'm even saying.* 'You're a Venator. This isn't part of your duty.'

He's so close that I don't know whether to look at his eyes, the dark green hues in them, or his lips, straight . . . *defined.*

'My duty is also to help trainees.'

'I don't think it's necessary to help me after some minor scrapes. I get them all the time; it'd be a nightmare for you.'

He flashes another smile, but it disappears just as fast. 'You really intrigue me, Nara.'

A confession that makes my cheeks burn.

'I intrigue a lot of people.' I try to control my breathing. 'Usually they are always bad.'

He shakes his head slowly, not wanting to pry his eyes away from my rising chest. 'You intrigue me in a different sense.'

'And what sense is that?'

'In the sense that I ask myself . . . why is it—' He swallows hard, the tip of his finger now grazing the side of my uncovered thigh '—that I always find myself so drawn to you?'

I inhale a gasp, and for the first time, I have no snarky comeback, no need to slap him away like I would with anyone else.

The skin on his hand is uneven to the touch as he brings it to my hips, and his head dips down to my neck. 'Do you have an answer as to what that could be?' His breath is warm against me, heating not only my exterior but also deep within my stomach.

I *don't* have an answer. I don't have anything because this isn't something I'm used to. I've not once felt a kiss nor the touch of a man.

'I don't think this is allowed, *Deputy*,' I manage to say with ragged breaths, going back to that formality between us though we are far from that right now. The palms of my hand fly out to meet his chest – the tight leather armor.

'It's not forbidden,' he whispers onto my skin.

'Then—' My eyes shutter closed '—perhaps it should be.'

'And why would you want that?' That hand, *that rough hand,* takes comfort in drawing circles along my thigh, getting closer and closer to where I've never allowed anyone.

Tipping my head back, my body shivers, yet sweat coats me. He drags his lips towards my shoulder but at that moment, just when his hand finally slides between my legs, I return to my senses and startle myself into reality. I clasp his wrist and lurch backward, hard enough that I slam against the mirror.

All movements stop, but I keep my eyes closed, and a heartbeat later, I no longer feel the warmth of him on my skin. 'Nara,' he says. 'Have you . . . ever done anything?'

I yank my eyes wide open and stare straight at the confusion contorting his expression. His brows knit together, and it's a look that makes me feel instantly judged.

'Does it matter if I have or not?' I push his hand away, letting my defensive side take over as I jump from the sink. Gone are the strange sensations of his touch, and gone is the need that had laid rest in my stomach.

Many times, I have had similar opportunities, to find love, find something with a person, but Idris's protectiveness and my infamous fearful ways drove everyone away. And right now, I am not looking to be someone's enjoyment.

Lorcan shakes his head, frowning to himself. 'No, it doesn't—'

'Then good,' I say with a temper to my tone. 'Because I assure you what just occurred in here will not happen again.' Picking my cloak off the floor, I storm past him to the other side of the room.

'Nara.' He exhales, following behind, but the desperation in his voice has me whirling back around.

'I have a question for you. Do you do this with every new trainee? Take them to your chambers and try to seduce them into having sex?' *Defensive, I am acting defensively again.*

A muscle in his jaw flutters, and his eyes harden. 'I did not mean—'

'I think it's best I leave,' I cut him off firmly as I step back when he tries to approach me. 'Thank you for your concern about my injuries, but I can take it from here . . . *Deputy*.'

Clutching my cloak up to my chest, I don't regret anything as I walk out and rush down the stairs before he can come after me.

Once I get to my room, I close the door behind me and lean my back against it. Freya's still sound asleep, unaware of anything while I'm here reliving it all. I'm not used to being intimate. I shouldn't have even let Lorcan take me to his quarters. He's a high-rank deputy, and I'm a trainee.

I can't afford a distraction. Not when I'm so close to achieving what I've always dreamed of becoming.

Chapter Eleven

We all line up as soldiers in the weapons quarter. Night had fallen the next day, and sightings of a dragon surfaced nearby. Venators made sure streets were cleared of people, windows shuttered, and now the General is parading the room, giving out positions to trainees. For many, this is another mission, for me, it's my first.

'Ambrose, Farron.' The General walks towards me and Link, a wicked smile as he looks at us, rolling up the parchment. 'Patrolling duty around the central.'

Detesting the choice, I glower, opening my mouth with a million protests swirling my tongue but Freya cuts in.

'Father—' she pleads, but his sharp stare makes her lower her head.

'I suppose you can be on patrolling duty as well,' he says coldly. 'The Draggards District ought to be your . . . comfort.'

Cruel is one of many words I'd use to describe the General. How can your own father throw you in where witches and ruffians live?

Hardening my gaze, I lower my tone, 'She will not patrol—'

'When do we depart?' Freya asks, and I glance at her with a quizzical frown, but she does not turn to me. She keeps her head down like she already knows better than to defy him.

I, of course, never learn.

Unyielding hatred churns in my gut as the General dismisses us with a smug smile, and everyone grabs their weapons in an orderly fashion. Freya turns to me, sighing, and mutters, 'it's okay,' before heading to the wall of bows and arrows.

Link goes with her, and I huff out a breath as trainees fill the room, and in the middle of it all, I see Lorcan adjusting his weapons across his back.

Irritated, I march up to him and grab his upper arm, making him glance down at me. 'Patrolling duty?' I ask incredulously, dropping my hand. 'After everything, you're going to give me that position?'

He exhales roughly from his nose. 'You just joined. It's what the General thought most appropriate.'

It seems like Lorcan had quickly left behind what had happened last night, or it looks like he has. I know he wanted to apologize; I could see it in his eyes earlier today, but I just focused on training, on getting through the day until now.

'But you said I had more potential than some—'

'This is different, Nara.' His voice struggles to gain control as his nostrils flare. My breathing comes in harsh upheaves, and his gaze slowly drifts to my chest, watching its movements. He sighs, rubbing his forehead. 'I did try getting you out of that position beforehand.' The words this time sound softer. 'But the General had the last word, and I couldn't do anything about it.'

'You are his second in command,' I say tightly, my face inches away as I look up at him. 'If you made an exception with me joining the trainees this late, then you can make another without the General's input.'

Lorcan's face is like a blank wall crumbling over my words.

Voices in the room drone out, and weapons hissing as they're sheathed don't register in my ears. I know Lorcan wants to say something, even if he can't seem to. He only opens and closes his mouth. His stare is hard and painful to look away from, but as he goes to part his lips once more, Rydan cuts through inbetween us. 'Lorcy, I was thinking, me and you – the best of the bunch – team up and fight these—'

'We're not teaming up,' Lorcan deadpans, tightening his jaw as he adds, '*Ever*.' His eyes flutter towards me one last time before turning away, with Rydan nagging behind.

He slows down, broad back tensing as he stands beside Adriel and Oran who glare at everyone on the side. Whatever had happened with those frogs, they don't seem fazed anymore, but their hatred towards me is felt, during the day, during meals, and even now, without looking, I can tell.

'Patrolling duty,' I mumble, shaking my head as Link and I stand in the central part of the city where the Marigold tree glows. 'It's obvious the General gave me the role out of spite.'

'At least here it's less dangerous,' Link says, keeping a tight grip on his hilt. His eyes lift to the starry sky. 'Well, I hope it is.'

Nerves, that's what I've picked up on with Link. He always looks nervous wherever he is . . . whenever we speak.

'May I ask, what made you join the Venators?' It's a genuine question for someone who feels more comfortable where no danger lies despite it being the opposite of a Venator's duty.

He looks at me like no one has ever asked him that before. After a minute of silent pondering, he says, 'I had no place to go.' His voice a faint whisper. 'My parents died due to a rümen's bite when I was five, and I ended up in five different orphanages around Emberwell until my eighteenth birthday.' He shrugs, circling his foot along the pathway. 'Training to be a Venator seemed the easiest choice rather than have to live on the streets. Sadly, it turns out it's harder than anything I've done before.'

And it is. Not once have I thought differently. 'When I first became a trapper,' I say when it goes too quiet. 'I stumbled upon my own net trap once.'

Link cocks his head, a spark of curiosity in his blue crystal eyes.

'I was good for a thirteen-year-old, but it wasn't easy.' Nor when I'd come back with no money from Ivarron's. 'And when I was fifteen, some of my brother's bullies deliberately made me jump into a well, and though it took me hours, I managed to climb out of it. But . . .' I exhale softly. 'What I'm trying to say is that every choice someone makes, whether it's easy or hard, will challenge you in some way.'

'And how do I change that?'

'You challenge it back,' I say. 'You *do* something.'

At that, Link smiles, as do I, but his is one I've not seen reach his eyes before. He turns away with it still lingering on his lips as my eyes scan the city and the uphill streets leading into the districts. Then there's movement – sharp and of reds and yellows up ahead of the Chrysos District.

'Did you see that?' I tap Link's arm, squinting my eyes for anything strange to appear again.

'See what?' Link whispers in alarm, his body locking into place.

I focus through the darkness, any sound, anything to catch my eye, but . . . 'Nothing.' My brows draw together as I step forward, tilting my body to the side. 'I'm just going to check it out. Do you want to come?'

'Um—I—' He shakes his head, downcast, and I nod in silence, understanding him.

Leaving Link behind, I take off past the central and other trainees patrolling. I think of Freya for a moment as I enter the narrow paths of Chrysos. How even though I'd insisted once we'd left the barracks that I switch with her, she still declined. She's strong. I know from the way she trains she can withstand anything.

My footsteps echo on the empty paths. Wooden panels cover the windows of the townhouses and stores Freya had said contained all the highly tailored clothes and expensive jewels.

I slow down when I see no sign of anything and look to my left at the tawny-colored walls decorated in swirls of paintings – most of them different versions of the sun and moon, representing Solaris and Crello.

We don't have much of this back at our village. It is all breathtaking artwork. Illias would adore it. When I see my brothers, I'll tell them of this, of the beauty that is the city.

Craning my neck, I gaze at each piece, then I see one of gold paint, sparkling like gemstones flowing down from a pair of hands onto the continent of Zerathion. Two other hands, holding Solaris's arms, emit silver spirals of power.

My hand reaches out to it before I see a quick shuffle from the corner of my eye, making me jerk to attention.

I touch the blades across my thigh and stay alert, staring into nothingness.

But another patter of feet behind causes me to whip around and squint my eyes when I don't see anything.

What the—

Patter, patter, patter.

I turn again. This time my gaze falls to the ground as a creature no less than two feet tall rocks up on its tiny round trotters. I can't see any legs as a coating of thick orange fur lines its plump body, darkening into redder tones at the neck – if it even has one – and rounded large ears.

'Hello, Miss!' His wide, glossy black eyes blink twice, practically taking up half his face.

I frown, not knowing what to make of this. 'You talk?' I had not seen a creature of his kind before, though pixies, goblins, and all sorts speak, this one is new to me.

'My friend taught me!' He grins, revealing small fangs, but then falters in a fit of nerves as he notices all the blades sheathed at my thigh and the Venator symbol on my attire. 'He also told me not to talk to ven—venny—veh—' He stumbles backward, panic struck and unable to pronounce the name. I advance intending to catch it. My mind is fiercely intrigued by this creature, but as I near him, he dashes in a waddle-like run.

For the love of Solaris and Crello.

I yell after the creature, racing down the street as it makes a right turn towards the other storefronts. He's fast on his feet, I'll give him that.

Reaching that bend, I watch the creature make a dip into another road where it's a dead-end. I grin as I follow and corner him.

He whimpers, staring at the four walls. As he faces me, he tucks himself in, forming a ball where I can only see bright orange fur. I pause, narrowing my eyes, unsure of whether I should react or not as the creature starts rolling around.

'You are murderers, murderers, murderers!' He growls, but it sounds like baby's gurgle as he slips past, in-between my boots. 'My friend won't like you wanting to murder me!'

Alright, that's enough. My eyes follow the creature whirling in circular motions before I slam my hand down as it tries to scurry away. I grasp onto his back, and unlike most animals, his hair is soft and plush, comforting like a blanket.

Unfolding from his cocoon, I bring him eye-level as he swats his arms and paws around, like he wants to hit me. My face twists, glancing at the top part of his head where leaf-like flames appear out of nowhere, fluttering upwards. 'What *are* you?' I ask, but he doesn't answer. He blinks those round black eyes and, with such speed, escapes my grip, scattering up my arm. He tugs at my braid, jerking me back as he slides down from it and rushes past me.

Scowling, I jog out of the dead end, but the creature's long gone. I groan at his escape. I needn't have bothered in the first place, but the thrill of trapping still seems to entice me.

I shake my head. I know I wanted to go with Lorcan and the others into the forests just outside the city to help trap or kill whatever dragon lurked. This creature is the closest to an adventure I could have been today—

A loud clash to my right makes me snap my head in that direction, forgetting everything for a moment.

Trinkets knocking together follow from the jeweller's. The only store without any boarded-up windows. I still can't see anything through it except displays of necklaces, and then a dark silhouette sweeps by.

Someone is in there.

The hairs on my skin tingle and stand. Whether it is anticipation or worry, I can't decide. Slowly, I make my way over, careful not to make a sound as I notice the latch on the door has been broken.

Sucking in a breath, I push through and stumble inside the room aglow with the light of a thousand stars stars coming through long, glass-paneled windows. Thousands of rings and necklaces glistening in all kinds of colors lie on top of mahogany counters. And right there . . . right there in the middle with his back to me is a man dressed in a tight black leather jerkin hugging his well-built figure.

A single candle to the left casts his shadow on the wooden walls, tall, intimidating, *fearless*. And almost as if he can sense my presence, his head turns first, then his whole body.

My eyes narrow in on his raven mask – one that covers the top half of his face and the one I'd seen sketched across wanted posters.

The Golden Thief.

Chapter Twelve

I stand still, staring at him. I don't know what I expected to happen when I saw the Golden Thief, but I certainly didn't *expect* it to be tonight.

Despite the mask, you can tell he's young. Then again, all shifters are immortal. Illias always said shifters stop aging after they turn thirty. The Golden Thief seems to be at least a few years older than me.

His short tousled hair, of a dark onyx color like ink on paper, swishes as he tilts his head, surveying all of me. My first thought is that he looks like someone I'd carve; the cut of his jaw, the shape of his full lips. But it's his dark amber eyes that draw me in the most, against the hue of black smudged shadow under them. Almost as if they are decadent pots of melted gold, entrancing enough to make anyone surrender.

I swallow. 'You're the Golden Thief.'

'That I am, what gave it away?' He grins, flipping a gold coin between his leather gloved fingers as he leans his back against the counter.

I don't respond.

'So serious.' He pouts, clearly goading me. 'Tell me, is that common for Venators?' His eyes survey my garment.

'Tell me,' I repeat, narrowing my gaze. 'Are you the one creating the new deadly breed?'

'Is that what they're saying now?' His grin never falters. 'Interesting.'

I don't like that answer. I don't like it one bit.

'What else are they saying about me?'

I stare at his face, trying to grasp something beyond the mask and the glittering mischief in his eyes. Everyone says he has no weaknesses, but I don't believe it. Lorcan had shown me a shifters' weak points: eyes and abdomen.

'How dangerous you are,' I reply. My hand silently slides to my thigh, and a hateful smile stretches my lips. 'But all I see is a lousy thief of a shifter.' *I'm pushing it. I'm beyond pushing it.*

He chuckles deeply, unaffected by everything I say. 'If I'm so *lousy*, then the Venators would have had my head on a stick by now.'

I focus where his heart lies. I can't kill him, I need his blood, but the question is how do I get it?

'Careful with what you say.' My gaze locks onto where his abdomen is as my hand unsheathes one of my blades. 'It might just *happen*.' I cock my arm back as I hurl the dagger from my grip so fast and effortlessly, flying in a sharp straight line. But the Golden Thief seizes it with one hand, inches away from piercing his jacket.

'Now that's not playing fair, Venator.' He tuts. 'Here, I thought we were just getting acquainted?'

I pay no attention to his last teasing words. 'And you think having powers is fair?'

Sighing over my glare, he rolls his neck in such a dramatic way. 'No, you're right. Powers are just another means to inequity against mortals.'

Again, I go back to staying silent because I can tell he didn't mean any of that.

'How about we do this—' The Golden Thief throws the knife in the air and catches it before pushing himself off the counter '—since you seem so keen on . . . hurting me, I won't use any powers, and if you manage to strike me right here.' He gestures a finger to where I'd thrown the blade. 'You win, and I won't steal. I'll even let you capture me.'

A definite lie. 'Why would a shifter, who's supposedly dangerous and a likely killer—' A pointed glance '—willingly offer himself up for capture?'

He shrugs coolly. 'Life can be so dreary without a little entertainment.' He walks up to me, and I stand my ground as he extends the tip of the dagger outward. 'So, what do you say, Venator? Care to have some fun?'

I don't have to weigh my options out. I know this could buy me time, or maybe I'm stupid. Everyone thinks the Golden Thief is smart, cunning. He might be setting me into a trap right now, and I'm accepting it of my own accord.

'What happens if you win?' A raise of my brow.

'Then you let me walk out of here with all the jewels I want.'

Then I won't let him win.

'I don't have all night,' he drawls as I gaze at the blade, then at the side of his lip curling up. 'I'd like to get out of here before dawn.'

Narrowing my eyes, I make my decision, taking it from him. A silencing second passes as I slide out another blade, keeping the other snug between my fingers and whirl, swinging my arm. He throws his forearm up, shielding himself. And as I move my other hand towards his neck, he snags me with his right arm.

I withdraw my hands away from him and step back, puffing my chest, *up, down, up, down.*

He angles his head, studying me and my next movements, all with a devilish smile on his face.

This is his fun, his . . . *entertainment*.

That drives me to thrust forward, aiming the knife high to his abdomen, but he dodges it, causing me to tumble and almost hit the ground.

Frustration travels up my spine as I tighten my grip on the blades and turn—my braid spinning in a swift motion along with me.

I launch another dagger at him. He jumps out of the way as the blade lodges itself into the wooden walls.

He winces, shaking his head. 'Almost had me there, Venator.'

Taunting, he's taunting me.

Darting towards him, I swipe the blade, left, right, up, middle, but he's astute, veering his body, so I miss.

At each pounce, he chuckles. At every moment I nearly get him, he laughs harder.

All I see is red. *He is trying to piss me off.*

Leather burns and tightens from my hold on the handle as I twist, directing all my movements to his face. He whips to the side as my dagger slices across him. The force causes such stillness that for one solid heartbeat, his jaw tenses, sharp and straight.

I notice that below his mask, where the light from above highlights his deep golden tan, a bead of blood trickles down his cheek.

I'd managed to cut him.

I smile at that as he brings a hand up, wiping the blood onto his glove. 'It's a good thing that won't scar.' His eyes flicker to me dangerously. 'I happen to like my face.'

'A conceited asshole,' I say, not bothering to hide the derision in my voice. 'How lovely.'

I lunge swiftly, but he catches my wrist, then the other, ready to jab. 'I admire your bravery Venator, truly—' He mocks, the corner of his lip flitting upward '—but do we really have to try with the face again?'

I huff in annoyance, drawing back my knee and jerking it into his groin, but he blocks that too by moving his leg in front.

He puckers his bottom lip, but the playfulness never disappears. 'Now that just hurts my feelings.'

'I didn't know a murderer could have such things as feelings.' I should be afraid, but I'm nowhere near fearful of him.

'Did no one ever teach you not to judge so soon?' He lilts, the deriding tone never faltering as he pushes my knee down. I grunt, breaking free from his iron grip and pace backward with my knife still raised at my side. He watches me with amusement once more and curtly nods as if waiting for my next attack.

By now, I imagine he knows all my tactics. I don't even think I have any. I just want to get *him*.

Kicking my leg up as I charge, he grasps my boot. I glare, lashing out my arm as he drops the leg. Not shocking at all as he grabs that too and the other arm after that. His eyes focus on my left palm . . . *the scar.*

'Ruthless,' he mutters, staring at it with a tantalizing smile.

Raging heat explodes in my chest, and I pluck my hands away. I take this time to use my foot behind his and sweep him off the floor. For the first time, I'm successful, but he takes me down with him. I land on top with my palms and the blade flat on the ground beside his head. My legs then come at either side, straddling.

'If you wanted to bed me, Venator, you could have just asked politely.' He chuckles in satisfaction. I only yell my fury, pressing my knife to his throat.

He doesn't flinch, his eyes brimming with a sense of thrill.

A dragon.

A dreadful shifter.

The very beings I despise.

But like before, his reflexes are quick, grabbing my wrist and then my waist as he flips me over. The blade falls from my grip as he says, 'Sadly, for you, I'd have declined that offer.' His amber gaze glimmers like the animal that he is, toying with his prey. 'I'm not one to sleep with Venators.'

'Get off me,' I say through my teeth as his hand slides down the side of my leg.

'Gladly.' He's up in a matter of seconds, snatching my blade before I can as I roll onto my front, scrambling to my feet. Turning, I reach for another dagger, but I feel no curve or sharp edge when I pat it. I dart my gaze down to my thigh, noticing they're all gone. And as I glance back at the Golden Thief, he dangles two of them in his right hand.

He's taken them.

A thief, a nuisance of a thief.

Panicked, I lunge for anything in sight, crystals, pendants, and hurl it at him. Each time with anger pumping through my body and mind.

But the Golden Thief snatches them all mid-air, placing each in his pocket. 'Well, you're just making my job easier here.'

'You repugnant—'

Noises come from outside—Venators. This is my chance.

I go to shout for aid, hoping they'll hear me amongst their prattle. But in a flash, the Golden Thief swallows up the distance between us, pressing me against the wall, and pins both my wrists above my head with one hand before the other clasps over my mouth. His body shoves up against mine, too close that I can't even kick him where I'd so badly love to.

My chest connects with his abdomen as I thrash against his grip. *I get nowhere.*

The Golden Thief waits for the Venators' voices to die down, shushing me further as I try to speak but fail to.

'I'd say a pleasure fighting you since I've *clearly* won, but I'm not so sure you'd agree.' A half-smile plays on his lips as he lowers them, so his mouth is level with my ear, and I can feel them graze against my skin. His whisper sounding like nothing but a perilous caress, 'I'll give you a word of advice, though . . . next time you want to fight a shifter, use something far better than those petty blades of yours.'

I muffle a curse word at him, wanting to bite down on his gloved hand, but the grip is so tight that leather is the only smell drifting over me.

'Now, if you'll excuse me,' he says. I lower my brows. 'I have some stealing to do.'

I gasp for air as he lets go. I'm not going to let him steal. Not a chance. So, I try to take my hands off the wall. Except I can't.

Why can't I—looking up at my wrists, through the starlight coming through the skylights, I gape at the black ripples of shadow around them gleaming with specs of violet dust, like chains to the wall.

He's used his Umbrati powers.

Oh, he did not just do that. I don't care if he'd won or not. It's cheating.

Walking backward, slow and with a pert smile, he dances around, grabbing different kinds of beads and jewels. He raises them to the side of his ear, showing me each one and shaking his head at the others he puts back down.

Now I want to kill him. I want his death to be slow and painful.

He comes over, pressing a necklace of lapis lazuli against the top part of my armor, pursing his lips like he's mulling things over.

My mouth parts, seeing an opportunity to shout for anyone except—

'Ah!' He cuts me off, taking the necklace away. 'You know what will happen if you try to yell for help.'

'Dragon pig,' I spit, pulling at his magic restraints.

'Foul mortal,' he murmurs humorously, eyeing my predicament.

Stepping back, he heads to the counters again. When he looks to be done, he flips that coin he'd had earlier on and places it atop. 'Until never, Venator.' He bows with such grace that I find it hard to believe as he turns to the door.

'Aren't you going to try and kill me?' Bold and outrageous of me to think about giving him that idea.

The Golden Thief stops and glances over his shoulder. The subtle smirk plays on his lips as he says, 'How boring it is to *kill* if I'm not hunting you down instead.' At that, he walks out with the jewels and gold, leaving me still tied in his shadows.

It goes silent with only my harsh breathing over those words, and then . . . I start tugging and pulling and shouting.

Seconds pass, giving him more time to escape. A grunt bubbles out of my throat as another minute goes by. I strain my hands to the point my shoulders hurt as I pull and pull.

After a few more tries, to my relief, the shadows disintegrate, releasing my wrists. Without another thought, I lurch towards the door, staggering into the streets. I glance at every corner and up at the roofs, but the Golden Thief is long gone.

I had him. I almost had him.

Another part of my subconscious tells me I didn't, not at all. He knew what he was doing, and the thought angers me more.

Exasperated, I drag my hands down my face, as clamors resurface, echoing the far streets from the central. *They're back.*

Dashing, I make my way out of the streets where I'd fought that creature, and the jeweller's where I'd faced the Golden Thief until I see the exit of Chrysos. The first person I spot is Lorcan, waving in Venators to come through as I run to him.

'Lorcan!' I inhale, trying to catch my breath. He turns at my voice, grabbing my arms as he looks me over. 'I—' I'm about to mention the Golden Thief, but I pause as Venators call out to one another, giving orders of clearing the infirmary. 'What's going on?' I look back at Lorcan.

'There was an attack,' he says, exhaling. 'A rümen.'

If Lorcan wasn't holding me right now, I'd likely fall.

A rümen, not a dragon. I can't tell what is worse.

'One of the trainees didn't make it.' Lorcan shakes his head. Copper strands mattify to his forehead with forest dirt. His hands not letting go of me. 'The other was bitten.'

Deaths . . . either way, one or the other would die. 'Who?'

Lorcan doesn't need to answer my question as more yelling comes from behind some Venators. Lorcan's head turns as Rydan stumbles on his feet, as well as someone else beside him, both trying to hold up a battered and bloodied man. His leg bent in ways it shouldn't be, and leather armor ripped open, revealing skin.

Crusted mud clings onto his hair, *auburn, unmistakably auburn.*

Solaris, it's Adriel.

A few more haul in a body, limp, lifeless in their arms. His head down, but I recognize those long spindly dark locks.

Bile sticks to my throat. This means that Adriel was bitten, and Oran . . . Oran's the one that died.

Chapter Thirteen

I wait outside the infirmary double doors, crossing my arms over my chest as I watch Lorcan talking in hushed tones with another Venator. Sana, the woman who I'd seen the day of the dragon attack at my village. The strain on her fair neck apparent as she tries not to raise her voice, making me wonder why she looks so mad.

'I'm going up to our quarters. Are you coming?' Freya asks, coming into range and blocking Lorcan and Sana out.

I blink, shaking my head. 'Yeah, um, I'll be up soon.'

She nods, half exhausted as she strides off. As soon as we returned, Freya looked sick to her stomach. According to her, she isn't one to handle death, despite witnessing far too many throughout her youth. I suspect it has to do with her mother's passing when she was three years of age. Freya has only spoken of it once, but the dullness in her eyes when she explained it was more than enough to know it pains her, like any death of a parent would.

As I straighten up and uncross my arms, Lorcan dismisses Sana. He walks over, stopping a few inches away.

'How did it happen?' I ask. Why of all people, them? I want to say, as if he'll have the answer.

'Most of us split up, heading into different sectors of the forest,' he recalls, glancing down at the floor. 'After a while, there were screams and—there was nothing we could do.'

'Did you kill the rümen?'

He shakes his head. 'Disappeared before we arrived.'

Back to its herd, I suppose. Just as how bees have a Queen, rümens drift back to their leaders.

My shoulders ache from how stiff they are. Nothing can save Adriel from this bite. It is only a waiting game now for the venom to seep into his system, rendering him blind after the first twelve hours. And then, slowly, all his organs will shut down. Oran's death was at least quick. He didn't have to suffer.

Lorcan is silent, as am I, for what feels like seconds, minutes, hours. My desire to tell him I'm glad he is okay replaces itself with stubbornness – stubbornness because of last night. And almost as if he can sense what I'm thinking, he expels a long breath saying, 'About yesterday, I'm—'

'I know,' I say, so soft I can't recognize my voice or myself.

His long stare causes something unexplainable to pull inside me, wondering what would have happened if I hadn't stopped that hand, his fingers touching me. I don't like that I'm thinking about it. I don't want this feeling.

'Nara, I just—'

'Deputy,' the General interrupts us. The oil-lit lamps flicker onto his rich brown skin. 'A word.' His icy gaze frisks over me to Lorcan.

Lorcan ducks his head for a second, turning rigid before he looks at me and follows the General out of view.

I tip my chin up towards the ceiling and sigh. Freya will likely be asleep by now, exhausted from the day. Still, the reason I had waited outside the infirmary was that I had the intention of going in to see Adriel.

As strange as it is, that I'm ready for forgiveness. I don't have the urge to shout how it was their own doing even if they'd done me wrong, tormented Link, and Solaris knows what else. I'm aware it could have happened to anyone else, me included if I'd gone in their place. Nonetheless, this is what we all signed up for. To be a Venator no matter the hardships, no matter the deaths.

Plucking up the courage, I turn to the double doors and enter into a room full of cots of those ill and injured, white linen curtain barriers between each one. I scan the beds and walk to the end of the room, sliding the curtain. My stomach twists into a rope and I wince as I survey black blood oozing through bandages covering the middle section of Adriel as he lies there. As I drag my gaze up, four fresh deep cuts slice diagonally down his face like the claws of the rümen attacked there first.

'Come to gloat in the hour of my death?' Adriel croaks. Nothing in his words sound welcoming as he hisses air through his teeth, trying to sit up.

I nudge forward but keep my distance. 'I've come to show mercy.'

'Why?' His frown across his gaunt face is expected. 'Shouldn't you despise me?'

'I do,' I say. If I was feeling kinder, I'd scrap his name off my enemy list too. 'Except I've always been told to forgive even in times I wouldn't want to.'

'I don't need your forgiveness.'

'And I'm not asking you to take it,' I say, harsher than I intended to. Adriel looks away, unbothered, to which I huff out a breath and shake my head. 'I forgive you, do what you will with that.'

I don't expect any type of reaction, so I turn and take my leave when his voice – the voice of a scared, dying man, says my name. I glance back at his hollow and blanched face. He looks terrified.

'You should know . . . the rümen that attacked us,' he says, lowering his head. 'It wasn't a normal one.'

My breath tightens in my throat. I was not expecting that.

'It looked—' He hacks a wet cough like blood is clogging his throat. 'It looked like a dragon. It had the build of one, but its tail was thinner, its eyes entirely black, and it's like it couldn't see?'

Could it be . . . could it be the new breed?

I try my best to keep a blank face, but the words of the Golden Thief ring in my ears, 'Is that what they're saying?' He flashed that confident smile, but thinking back, why would someone who everyone spoke of as the one creating this breed act like he didn't know of it himself?

'Why are you telling me this?' I whisper.

'Because one of these days, you might be the one lying in these beds nearing death,' Adriel says. 'Or far worse.' He lowers himself back down, resting his head to the side, intending not to speak further or for me to question more.

Every knot tightens inside me as I glance around at Venators who have possibly come back from other missions.

I take a few steps back, taking one last look at Adriel before quickening my pace out of the infirmary and closing the doors behind. I freeze in the moment and eyes widen as I stare ahead, detached from everything.

'Nara?'

I glance to my left, where I see that Lorcan has returned.

'Are you alright?' He inclines his head with a frown, the General nowhere to be seen. 'You've gone awfully pale—'

'What do you know of the new breed?' The words rush out of me as I let go of the doorknob and face him.

My question at first startles him, then he lowers his brows. 'Nara, that's not something I can discuss with you.'

'Why not? Isn't it our job as trainees to know what is going on instead of hearing rumors from others?'

'It is something we are trying to figure out,' he says with cold authority like he doesn't want to talk more of it. 'Once you swear in as a Venator—'

'*If* I swear in as a Venator.' It's not that I don't think I can pass the trial. Adriel's warning is more important, and it pulses through my mind, repeating over and over. *Or far worse, or far worse, or far worse.*

Lorcan heaves a deep breath, rubbing that marred hand over his forehead, dried mud still coating it. 'Just don't worry about those rumors. Focus on training and passing the trial.'

'But what if it's not—' I stop myself before I can say the Golden Thief, remembering that Lorcan doesn't know I've seen and fought him, only to have him escape.

'Look, I think you should get some rest,' Lorcan says as I clamp my mouth shut. 'It's been a long night.' His wall is up again, scorching with fire that I can't touch or see through. He makes a move past me and I spin without thought.

'Wait, Lorcan,' I call out to him, but the minute he tilts to face me, I hesitate. I left the jeweller's without thinking straight, and I was ready to tell Lorcan then and there about how I'd tried to fight the Golden Thief, but what difference would that have made? My need to catch him lies with Ivarron. The Venators have other plans. 'Thank you for trying to get me out of patrolling,' I say weakly, but I still meant my gratitude.

He nods curtly as he resumes striding down the hall but not before hesitating and looking towards the left like he wants to turn back.

But he does not.

My eyes blink as I release a breath, listening to Lorcan's steps down the hallway, growing more faint the further he walks.

Standing by the foot of my chest of drawers, I cradle a letter from my brothers. Days after Oran's and Adriel's deaths, the arena fight had come round. Everyone in the barracks went on with their days, their training. A few others carved both names onto that stone pillar in the mess hall, while each night, I'd questioned if their deaths were fated or something more.

Snapping out of that thought, I gaze at the parchment paper, ripping it open. I'd not expected a letter so soon, compared to other trainees, but I know my brothers – Illias most of all – would have wanted to send me one straight away.

I smile, focusing on the cursive words:

Nara,

As usual, Iker is the one writing this though I am the one telling him what to put down. If only you could see his face right now, it's priceless.

A soft chuckle departs from my lips, Illias had never learned how to write, but Iker was magnificent with pen and paper.

It's been a strange time here without you around, Idris yells at us more frequently, and I suppose it's his way of missing you. On the other hand, I've completed two paintings. One I gave to Miss Kiligra, which she threw away since she'd heard scary stories of paintings coming to life to attack you. And another to Ivarron after we failed at trapping a goblin.

Strangely, he asks about you, wondering when your return might be and frightening as always, Idris tends to hold back from pummeling him. I still curse you for getting involved with Ivarron, but I suppose I also thank him for strengthening you.

Nevertheless, we hope everything is going well there. It's nice telling everyone our sister is training to become a Venator just like father. And as Idris says, go chase that adventure you have always wanted, Nara, you deserve it.

See you soon,
Illias, Iker, Idris.

I fold the letter, smiling brighter as I hug it to my chest before putting it away. Reading it has only emphasized how much I miss them. Ivarron, however, is the one person I do not miss. I know why he asked when I'd be back, it's definitely because he is interested in the Golden Thief's blood more than me.

'Just to inform you, Nara—' Freya walks in, raising a hand. Her violet cloak matching the day gown she's wearing. '—I am no fan of these arena fights, they make me queasy and nervous, but since it is your first time, I've agreed to come with you.'

I pin my lips to stop myself from chuckling at her clear annoyance. 'You don't have—'

'Now, quick.' She darts forward, looping her arm around mine and under my cloak. 'We don't want the carriage waiting on us.' And at that, she rushes us out of the room.

Chapter Fourteen

Aurum Arena is nothing like I imagined. In truth, I'm not sure what I had imagined it would look like. But it certainly wasn't this.

The discordance of crowds gathered at different levels drifts into a large arena opened up to the sky. Freya drags me to sit beside Link on the stone benches which run down in concentric circles towards the sanded pit. My gaze centers on the balcony across the arena, where the Queen leans her back against a beige-pillared throne.

Even shielded from the mid-morning sun, her golden gown shimmers as she turns her head to speak to Venators in each corner. The General sits on a smaller throne next to her, overseeing everything as he glares towards the pit.

'Did you guys know the Golden Thief robbed one of the stores in the Chrysos District the night of the rümen attack?'

Blinking, my head snaps to the left at Rydan, forcing us to scoot further as he drops by Freya's side.

'How did you find out?' Freya asks. 'And since when do you come and talk to us?'

'Since now?' He says, making a face of disbelief. 'And Frey-Frey, I know everything. Besides, he left a coin behind and strangely a necklace.' My eyes go round as he sighs pensively. 'Sir Longford was not happy his jeweller's was broken into.'

At least Sir Longford didn't have to deal with an arrogant dragon prick that—

'Imagine coming face to face with the Golden Thief.' Rydan leans back, smiling. A shadow casts over half his face, darkening his warm brown skin. 'I'm not sure if I'd shit myself or ask for him to sign one of his posters.'

I refrain from rolling my eyes. The Golden Thief would likely love the second idea.

'Solaris, I'd freeze on the spot,' says Freya, slumping her shoulders and gazing around.

'I'd run away.' Link shudders. 'He's too dangerous.'

I snort at that last part, causing them all to turn their heads at me. Clearing my throat over their sudden frowns, I say, 'I don't think he should merit from a grand title like that. You know what is dangerous? Someone not liking strawberry pie.'

They all blink like I've gone mad. Perhaps, but I don't want the Golden Thief winning, even in our conversations.

'So, you think shifters aren't dangerous?' Freya asks slowly.

'Of course, she won't think that,' Rydan drawls. 'She once killed a rümen without remorse, stood before an Ardenti—' He grins, throwing back what I'd said to him after he'd irked me. He really is a nuisance. '—Caught the attention of the Queen with her impressive knife skills and is the daughter of the one and only Nathaniel Ambrose.'

Heads turn at the mention of my father, and I look away, but a pair of hazel eyes further down meets mine. A woman no later than her mid-forties in layers upon layers of thick tunics. Amethyst crystals clip back her vicious and beautiful black curls as she narrows her gaze, tilting her head like she knows me, yet I've never seen her in my life.

A frown creeps onto my forehead as she breaks off our stare and I return to Rydan still going on about what I've done. I shoot him a tight smile. 'I'll show no remorse by throwing you in the pit.'

'Now that would be classified as murder.'

Shrugging, I answer, 'A murder with a worthy cause.'

He twirls strands of Freya's curls in his fingers, and she flicks his hand away, but he doesn't seem to notice as he regards me with a contemplative gaze. 'Is that the same thought you had for Adriel and Oran?'

I tense at their names, as does Link. 'I forgave them,' I mumble.

'Wow, Ambrose, I never took you as the forgiving type.'

'I don't intend to make it a habit,' I grit. But I didn't want to stoop to Adriel and Oran's petty level. Idris had always taught me to forgive, and I'd always disobeyed. For once, it felt good doing it on my own.

A long pause between the four of us breaks out, that is until Link smacks his lips and says, 'So, Chrysos District . . . Golden Thief. You went up that way, Nara. Did you witness anything?'

'No.' I tuck my lower lip. 'Well, except for an odd little creature.' Not a complete lie, at least.

Freya smiles. 'What kind?'

I describe the orange fur-coated critter and how I'd wanted to trap it. By the end of it, the three are gaping at me.

'What?' I give them a wary look.

'You tried to capture a Tibithian?' Link gawks his blue eyes at me, and it's the most expressive I've seen him be so far.

'What on earth is a Tibithian?'

'They're the rarest form of creatures!' Freya's voice takes on a rather excitable edge. 'All are born from elemental fire plants near Helland volcanos up north.'

My brows lower, gathering that piece of information and recognizing how the lands of Zerathion separate into what they deem the four elements. Emberwell, fire, Terranos, earth, Undarion, water, and Aeris, air. History tells that when Zerathion was created, the power of the sun and moon fell onto a small island named the Isle of Elements. It is situated at the center of our continent and parted by the Ocean of Storms and Sea of Serenity.

And every year, a festivity named Noctura falls on the day of the summer solstice, where we celebrate the release of magic, it projects up into the sky, supposedly to help all of our lands maintain their elemental balance. When young, I'd watch the bright colors of yellows and oranges glimmer like stars, coating the velvety night, with my brothers, eating and dancing along our village market square. This year is different though because I likely won't celebrate it in my village, I'll be celebrating it in the city.

'They're supposed to aid the fields and crops, which is why no one captures them,' Freya carries on, and I blink out of my thoughts. 'Save for certain people living in the Draggards who enjoy slaving any creature, be it good or bad.'

That must be why Ivarron has never told me of these Tibithians, though he usually never cares for any creature.

'I'd like to know how one got to the city,' Rydan says. 'Maybe I could befriend it, so it brings me food.' He pats his stomach.

Freya gasps, frowning at him. 'Solaris, no! They are sweet—' Her words drown out as soon as the crowd's cheers increase and all our heads whip to the pit. People start exchanging gold coins with each other until the Queen raises her hand, and shouts become whispers.

'Oh my,' Freya breathes just as gates groan open from both ends, and I suck in air when two dragons emerge into the pit. The crowd's silence becomes ecstatic once more as roars bluster like a storm sweeping from the grounds towards us in a breeze. I look at the long thick chains attached to their hind legs, preventing them from flying up but still allowing them to move around, to *fight*.

That is where I'll be facing my trial, on that same ground, be it against dragons or something more.

I chew on my bottom lip, staring at both, each circling the other. A low rumble vibrates the grounds, and then velvet specks of shadow wrap around one of the dragons. An Umbrati.

My gaze instantly cuts to the other dragon, much smaller in size compared to the Umbrati. Its body is leaner and sharp at the head, where large fiery eyes glare at the Umbrati's muscular physique.

Female . . . the Ardenti is a female.

Not only is it that, but the scales, faded colors of reds, almost feathery in nature implies it's young. And when it opens its muzzle, projecting fire, I recognize the dragon.

It's the one that attacked our village. The one Venators captured because of me, and if the Umbrati is older and a male then— 'It's an unfair fight.' I turn to Freya with wide eyes, she simply frowns back. 'The Ardenti is a fledgling, barely an adult compared to the Umbrati. It will lose.'

Freya glances between me and the pit as people around jeer at the Ardenti. 'The arena fights are never fair, Nara. They won't care even if it were a young whelp,' she answers, slightly wincing, knowing there's never a choice.

I wonder why I care that this feels wrong, but I do.

Whirling my head to the two dragons, I lean forward, anticipating what could happen next, what skills the Ardenti might use against the Umbrati. They pounce at each other as chains rattle and dust sand into the air. Their tails thrash, making it harder to see which has the upper hand. It's clear they had been riled up beforehand. Their primal rage dominates the whole arena.

They topple, with the Ardenti latching its maw onto the neck of the Umbrati. For minutes it's a constant back and forth as the Umbrati manages to throw the other dragon off.

The crowd shoots up from the benches, waving their gold as the Ardenti gets up on its hinds, shaking its head. The Umbrati darts to the left, rounding and spewing black shadows from its mouth like sharp blades. The Ardenti successfully dodges each one, making me almost rise just to peeve off those betting against it.

The feeling is short-lived once the Umbrati catapults into the air. All eyes lift, watching the chain take the strain as it flaps midair and dives towards the Ardenti.

It happens so fast that the Ardenti doesn't have time to veer out of the way as the Umbrati's claws come out and slice through its wings, pinning it to the ground.

'Oh, that ought to hurt,' Rydan winces. I pay no attention to him as the Ardenti yells out a painful cry, allowing the Umbrati to clamp razor-sharp teeth onto her neck. Blood, so much blood, pours onto the pit as the Ardenti stays rooted to the ground, and the other backs away with a snarl.

I stand too fast as the Ardenti tries to rise. Her torn wings slowly opening, but still, she falls back down on her side, blowing puffs of smoke through her nostrils.

Shaking my head, I stare past everyone's grumbles and murmurs. My face frowns painfully as the Ardenti's eyes flutter to a close.

Concern bangs at the surface of my ribcage as my fingers fiddle with the border of my thin cloak, tightening and wringing it in-between.

Get up, my mind frantically tries to communicate, *fight*.

I say it over and over again, *get up, fight, get up, fight*, and I don't stop until the dragon moves its head and its large serpent eyes open and it finds me in the crowd. She *looks* at me, looks at me as if she recognizes who I am from that day at the village. And in that crucial second I vehemently repeat, *fight*.

A bawl from within her slices through the air as the crowd's riotous noise starts up again. The Ardenti takes off, pushing itself from the arena walls to gain speed and move atop the Umbrati.

The Umbrati shrieks, releasing shadows as the Ardenti sinks its claws into its chest, and bears her muzzle down to where the heart lies.

A wet crunch like bones splitting echo off the walls, and then there's stillness from the crowd. The Ardenti raises her head through the dust, stretching her neck as a roar followed by flames of fire unfurl across the air like a call of victory.

The Umbrati doesn't move, doesn't flinch.

Dead, it's dead.

'Is it over?' Freya asks, and despite not glancing at her, I know she had her eyes closed the entire time.

'Yes,' is all I can say in a stunned breath. 'It's over.'

Not a minute after Freya exhales, the crowd complains and yells, having lost money on the Umbrati as some start leaving and others get into disputes. My eyes slide from the pit to the Queen. While the General holds his regular cruel gaze, the Queen's is blank. Thoughtful, I'd even say, as she just stares at the Venators hauling the dragon back down towards the dungeons.

I don't quite notice what's happening around me anymore. Nor do I hear Freya and Link shouting my name until the third or fourth time. They start descending the stone steps, and I glance at the pit a final time, with the memory of the Ardenti. All my life I've never cared if someone had said a dragon died, so why did I want to help this one? Why does an ache of sorrow shoot through me even for the Umbrati's death?

I'm making my way down, squeezing past people when someone clutches my wrist and jerks me back. I twist, gazing up at the woman who'd stared at me before the fight. The crystals in her hair glow a darker shade that makes it look almost blue.

'Naralía Ambrose,' she says, her voice delicate and sweet, but her hazel eyes narrow and distressed.

I try and twist out of her grasp. 'How—'

'I knew your father,' she says, and shock swamps me. 'He spoke of you.'

I attempt to speak yet find myself mute as she expels a shaky breath and glances at everyone still heading out of the arena.

'Meet me today by the Draggards,' she says, her voice faint and low. My joints stiffen at the mention of the Draggards. 'There's a tavern called the Crescent Eye.' Her grip hardens but not enough to cause pain. 'Ask for Leira, and they will inform me of your arrival. I promise I mean no harm.' She lets go, ducking her head as she pulls her tattered cloak up and blends through the crowd, leaving me no chance to say whether I'll meet her or not.

Because one way or another, if she'd known my father, then she knows my curiosity is just like his.

Chapter Fifteen

Hours after the arena fight, I find myself exactly where I knew I'd be.

The Draggards district.

Any sane person wouldn't trust someone who'd mysteriously mentioned their dead father and asked to meet in the district where no one dares to ever enter. But the entire day, I'd kept quiet, thinking of how she said she knew him, how he'd spoken of me.

Therefore, once I'd made up my mind, I explained to Freya I needed fresh air out in the city. She'd nodded with a smile and resumed with her newest passion: *poetry*.

So here I am, at the mouth of brothels, subjected to judgemental stares from people as I walk past. I'm all too familiar with those looks, so they did not bother me.

Streaks of golden sunlight carve the grime-cobbled roads which are full of stalls selling meats still dripping in blood, herbal medicines, and . . . creatures of all sizes in cages.

Heart hammering, I slowly make my way through, trying not to glance at them. I keep one hand on the sheath at my waist and cover it with my cloak. But a nasally voice, old and frightened, calls from the sides, 'Help me, please help me!'

Don't look, don't look, don't look—

'Shut up,' someone says before muttering, 'filthy Goblin.'

I suppose not looking is out of the question now.

Clenching my fists, I spin on the heel of my boots and spot a vendor banging the small cage. It rattles as the goblin falls onto its bottom. Its bat-like moss green ears flap over its obsidian eyes, covering the hook of its nose.

I storm up to the vendor and he turns. He's taller than me, and his belly protrudes from below his linen shirt. 'How much for the goblin?' I jerk my chin towards the cage.

Guilty, for the first time, I feel guilty that I'd captured these creatures, and this is where they ended up being sold as slaves or who knows what else. I'll set it free as soon as I pay the seller, but I don't have much on me. As a trainee, we don't get the payments a true Venator would.

The man lets out a nasty phlegm-like laugh. 'Why would you want a goblin for?' His rotten grin revolts me. 'I think you're lost, sunshine. Why don't I point you in the right direction back to the brothels?'

Oh, I'll break his hand, then cut it off and feed it to the goblin.

Glaring with such maliciousness, I reach for my dagger then stare at his stocky fingers caked in dirt. I'm about to lunge at him, but a firm voice from behind stops me.

Why does everyone stop me!

'That's not how we speak to people, Tig. You should know that by now.' The man now stands beside me. I sneak a side glance up at the dark hairs curling below his ears and at his black cloak which is like mine. 'Learn to be more respectful unless you'd rather end up in one of these cages.' He smiles mockingly towards Tig. 'Though I doubt that'd be humiliating enough for you. I'd much rather see you being chased by a rümen.'

I swallow the laugh prickling my throat.

'Archer,' Tig mumbles. 'Always a delight when you visit.'

'I'll take the goblin. He must tire from seeing your face every day.' Archer hands over some copper coins and, despite Tig's grumbling hesitance, he takes it. Turning to me, Archer narrows his brown eyes with a glint of humor. 'Nice dagger.'

My gaze shoots down to the blade still tucked inside my fist. The edge isn't sharp, neither does it shine like a knife should, but it's one I've had for years and it's still fit for purpose.

I sheath it back in, staring up at him. Strange . . . for whatever reason, it's as if he looks like everyone I've known in my life merged together.

'What is your name?' He asks, a smile rippling from his lips.

'I'm—' I pause just as my attention snags on a wooden sign behind him at the far end of the street. *The Crescent Eye*. 'I'm sorry,' I say, looking back at him. I do not have time to talk with people I'll likely not see again. 'I have to go, I—thank you.'

'You have nothing to thank me for,' he says, and I draw in my brows at the familiarity of him. 'Enjoy the rest of your evening.' He bows, and I nod another thank you before rushing past him towards the tavern.

Reaching the doors, I peek over my shoulder only to see Archer gone, as well as the cage where the goblin was held.

I can't tell what type of person Archer is. Whether the goblin is safer with him, I'll never know.

Pushing back that thought, I forget the goblin and everything else as I set foot inside the tavern. Sweltering heat from drunken bodies fills the crimson room, their brays of nauseating laughter and brawls among the tables. Nothing but drabs of brown ripped dresses and men in ragged tunics that blend with the entirety of the vast Inn. Such starkness to the bright shades of clothing in the center of the city.

A tankard is hauled across the tavern, splattering mead on the walls as I make my way to a barmaid at the edge of the bar. I ask for Leira, and the woman doesn't smile, doesn't react. She just bows her head, extending an arm towards the back of the inn, and leads me through a beaded curtain doorway.

The barmaid silently leaves me by the entrance, and I take a breath. Guttural noises from the tavern become muffled as my gaze shifts to every corner of the dim room full of shelves stacked with herbs and oils, likely for healing. But there's no windows nor paintings in this barren place and I wonder if I should have come at all.

A clatter drags my eyes to the center of a small oak table, where Leira stands behind it. 'Naralía,' she breathes a smile. 'You came.'

I don't answer. Her smile fades as she approaches me and places one hand on my back, signalling me to sit on the chair.

She lights a candle and settles herself opposite me, resting her arms against the table. Beads and all sorts of bracelets dangle from her wrist as the flame flickers between us.

'You live here?' At last I ask.

'We reside here most of the time, but my wife, Aelle, owns a cottage far out of the city.'

I reply with a slow nod, gazing off to my right at the shelf of books above a mahogany counter, all bound in leather, before I look at the one out in full view. The same violet amethyst Leira carries in her hair is embedded in the core of the book.

Amethyst, a crystal many spoke of as a witch's symbol. And that book isn't an ordinary one, if not a grimoire. 'You're a witch,' I say, gazing back at Leira all too warily.

Her eyes move to where the grimoire is, and she sighs. 'I understand you're cautious of me.'

'It's not every day I get a witch asking in a secretive manner that we meet in the Draggards.'

It's not every day one accepts that offer.

She chuckles despite my mistrusting tone. 'I understand. As witches, we're often depicted to be dangerous though, if we used any magic—' Her stare, empty as she looks away. '—We'd be better off dead.'

My face hardens in concentration at the candle. I've heard how rare witches are—that they use their magic to enchant any mortal, and if it is witnessed, they'll be hanged.

'It's not true, you know. What they say about us enchanting mortals.'

My eyes dart up through furrowed brows. 'Did you just read my mind?'

She shakes her head, drawing her bottom lip in. 'No, we can't read minds, but we can feel emotions, influence them even. And based on your apprehension followed by the idea that everyone thinks of witches as manipulators, it's not hard to guess that was what you were thinking.'

Now I have the urge to hide all of my emotions.

Shifting on her seat, she says, 'Millennia ago our ancestors—witches called Exarees—were guides and protectors to shifters after they helped the Exarees against the raging wars with—'

'Sorcerers,' I cut in. 'I know the history.' Sorcerers and witches had feuded for centuries before the treaty. Sorcerers wanted to rule Emberwell, the witches did not agree, neither did the shifters. And after the witches and shifters won, not many sorcerers survived.

It was said that now only a few remained alive, residing in other kingdoms.

'So, you know of the Rivernorth bloodline. The previous rulers of Emberwell that were shifters.'

Again, I try not to let it show on my face, the surprise of never hearing that name. I know there was a ruler before the Queen but who? I've never been told. 'No,' I mutter.

'I thought so,' she says, talking more to herself, as she leans back.

'And how do you know?' I ask, narrowing my brows. 'Witches aren't immortal.'

'I know because my sister,' she says, cautious, 'fell in love with a shifter over twenty years ago. He'd lived through the era when the treaty was forged, lived to see the fall of the Rivernorths. All killed, which means someone else had to take the throne.'

'The Queen,' I say with the single thought that'd popped into my mind. 'Did she . . . kill them?' I'd wondered what her story was, *what* she is, if she has held power and lived for over three hundred years.

'It's a possibility,' Leira hums. 'But the true extent of what happened is not known. That side of history is buried deep within Emberwell, I've only known parts here and there thanks to my sister.'

'And where is your sister now?'

A speck of sorrow shines in her hazel eyes as she holds my stare. 'She perished.'

I can't sense emotions, feel them like Leira says she can, but I *felt* pain in those two words. 'I'm terribly sorry for your loss,' I whisper, hiding the grimace I feel for repeating a phrase I've despised hearing from others in the past.

Her thankful smile is weak and sealed. 'You know, sometimes I prefer to imagine she's somewhere else still alive, perhaps in one of the other lands of Zerathion. Then I remind myself how impossible that is when we can hardly step into other lands without the possibility of being killed or enslaved.'

'It's hardly fair that other leaders can cross kingdoms as they please.'

Leira nods. 'Except for the only ruler who has never once made an appearance in any other land, the king of Terranos.'

The Elven king.

'Why?' I ask. I'd thought previously that the Elven king despised Emberwell too much to ever visit. For all I know, it could still well be the exact reason for him never crossing territories. He is the one whose land is known to hold the darkest, most fearsome place . . . *The Screaming Forests.*

I shudder, remembering the times I'd come close to the borders when trapping and days where Idris would pick me up when I was a child and had wandered near there.

'It's something I'm still trying to figure out,' Leira notes. 'Aelle and I thought perhaps he is the one in charge of those new creatures.'

I frown at the mention of the new breed. 'What about the Golden Thief?'

'That boy?' Her brows rise. 'He may be the only known shifter to carry all three dragon powers, but it's doubtful he's the one causing havoc other than robbing every store out there.'

Just don't worry about those rumors, Lorcan had told me, but it's all I can do. 'Well, did your sister ever say? She knew a shifter, why—'

'Because even then she was secretive, she held onto many things and—and we'd fought too much, too often until she left one day, and I didn't see her for many years. I had to hear from someone who knew the shifter, that they'd both been found dead near a forest up north.'

I shut my mouth, slouching back onto the chair. The candle wavers amongst my movements. And then, after a minute of silence, I ask, 'How did you know my father?' My voice is unrecognizable.

Leira loosens a defeated breath, running a hand through thick obsidian curls. 'A year prior to his death, we'd met when another Venator had accused me of stealing. Your father swooped in and saved me. He'd always spoken about how he didn't agree to many aspects of being a Venator. And that day as a token of my appreciation, I invited him for tea, and from then on, he made sure to visit once in a while.'

A lump forms in my throat, but I smile, picturing how he'd likely had made a quippy remark during that time.

'Your father was a man of great curiosity, NLaralía,' she continues. 'Whenever he thought there was injustice, he'd say it, but he also managed to lead so many to victory as a Venator that he was a legend among us all.'

I laugh under my breath, gazing down at my hands. 'He was far too modest with it though.'

'Not when it came to the love of his children.'

I look up with my heart pressing so hard against my chest, as Leira's eyes darkened in pools of fear.

'There is something that you should know about your father though,' she says as my saddened smile flattens into a straight line. 'Weeks before I'd received the news of his passing, he'd become frantic, telling me there was something unsettling in Emberwell until, on the day of the Venator trials for the new trainees, he'd spotted me from the crowds and told me he'd figured it all out.'

She pauses as if waiting for a reaction from me, but I say nothing; my face is solid stone.

'Confused, I'd questioned him,' Leira notices how tense I am as everything she says comes out carefully. 'But he'd only said that when he'd return from his visit to his family, he'd explain everything . . . Except he never did.'

That was his last visit to us. That was the week he died.

'Naralía,' she exhales, closing her eyes and wincing before she opens them and meeting the blue shades of mine. 'I think your father's death was not an accident.'

Accident.

The word I knew she would say and something that she knew herself I would disagree with.

'My father,' my voice quietly vexed, 'was *killed* by a full-fledged dragon. He was *attacked*.'

'But during that time—'

'I was there.' A flicker of irritation in my tone. 'I was there when my brother shot an arrow through that dragon's back. I have the thick scar running down my palm and my arm from that *day* as a reminder.'

'But dragons—'

'I witnessed him die, Leira! I witnessed the dragon in front of me. I—' My hands pull back my hair as I shoot up from the chair. Leira rises, chary of my reaction, and slowly walks towards me.

'There is something off involving Emberwell,' she says, the lines of her forehead creasing. 'I mean the history behind it, these new creatures? It can't be a coincidence that your father died right when he'd discovered something.'

I shake my head, and I sway on my feet. 'Coincidence or not, he died in a dragon attack, nothing more.'

'Wait, Naralía—' She reaches for my wrist as I'm about to turn, and as soon as her touch connects with mine, her pupils fade to complete white before the words come out of her like a trance:

'The sun blooms again for she has found her moon,
Death, reign, and resurrection commence,

But he who shall bear thy wicked bite,
A beast no less, though a heart of gold—'

I snatch my arm away from her grip, and she stumbles back with a sharp inhale as if breaking through deep waters. Her eyes return to colors of greens and browns as we stare at each other. Frowning, I hold my wrist to my chest, and she remains speechless. Whatever that was, she sang it like a lullaby, a soothing melody, but the words were chilling.

Still keeping my wrist to my body, I rush out through the curtain door. I careen past the tables of people seated and out into the streets, never turning to see if Leira tries to follow me or not.

Stalking back into the barracks, my pulse beats alarmingly fast. I'd acted too harshly, leaving Leira when all she wanted was to aid and inform me of things I deserved to know. But for nine years I've seen in my nightmares how that dragon clawed at my father, *nine* years I've carried this scar as a reminder of that day. Telling me that it might not have been the case, challenges the beliefs I've had for so long.

'Nara.'

I freeze near the corner of the empty hallway, scrunching my face as I mentally curse, knowing who is behind me.

'Nara, you do realize not moving doesn't make you invisible, right? I can still see you.'

Huffing out a breath, I spin towards Lorcan's stoic stare, his lips in a firm line though I can see the faint tug at them.

It just had to be him.

'I didn't see you at supper.' He takes two strides and our chests almost touch. His leather against the soft linen of my tunic. 'Where did you go?'

As always, he is so observant.

'I was picking up wood,' I lie. He lifts a brow.

'Wood?'

'Yes.'

Narrowing his eyes, he glances down at my empty hands. 'And where is that wood right now?'

I give him a long unblinking look. If I weren't so caught off guard, I could have made up a better lie than wood. 'I couldn't find the right type.' I hold my head high. 'Carving requires special wood most of the time, now if you'll excuse me—'

'You carve?' He asks, ignoring how I was preparing to push past him.

'Yes.' I square my shoulders. 'Does that surprise you?'

Something flickers in his eyes before moving his gaze elsewhere. 'No, not at all.' He clears his throat, and that unknown flicker is gone once he looks at me again. 'What do you like to carve?'

At the question not many ask, my body relaxes, and I lean back onto the wall. 'Everything,' I breathe a wistful sigh. 'I like knowing I made something, be it small or grand.'

'And have you carved anything since your arrival here?'

'Yes,' I say. 'Flowers for Freya on her chest of drawers and—' I conceal my smile. 'The Marigold tree on mine, the one just at the center of the city. I thought it was beautiful from the moment I first saw it.'

It's quiet while Lorcan's stare remains as if he can't decipher me. 'You are so . . . *intriguing*.'

There's that word again. 'Intriguing because I like to carve wood?'

'Intriguing above all,' he says, taking another step so that his cedar and spice scent mixes between us.

I straighten. 'You've said how intriguing I am twice now.'

'I guess I have,' he says, so low that if we weren't this close, I wouldn't have heard him. It's hard not to focus on his eyes, now like emeralds shining among the sconces or the russet strands falling over his brows.

'So, do you use knives or other tools to carve?' His voice is still quiet, still so deep.

'I have a set. Whittling knives, chisels for bigger woodwork, but um—' I unsheathe the blade from my waist, lifting it between us as a barrier, but he doesn't step back. '—This dagger is one I've always used to carve smaller objects.'

He laughs through his nose, staring at it and then me. 'You look like you're more ready to stab me with it than carve.'

Well, I have tried to stab with it before.

I shake my head. Words don't seem to fall from my lips as his hand lowers the dagger for me and doesn't make any plans to let go of my fist. I feel every bump, every uneven surface of his skin from the scars on his palm and fingers, shortening my breath with each swirl of his thumb against my knuckles.

'Run out of ways to answer me back, Nara?' He murmurs, deepening his gaze.

I scowl. 'I didn't see the need to answer back to such a stupid remark.'

He chuckles, smoothing the hard lines I always see when he's out during training, the laidback stance that people rarely witness. 'Have you always been one to talk back to superiors?'

'You don't seem to mind it.'

His other hand comes to my waist, and I almost gasp at the touch . . . *almost*. 'I don't mind when it's from a particular adventurous blonde.'

A sensation flares in my chest as his gaze roams over my face and at my fuller curves. 'Deputy,' I warn, and his eyes snap up.

'Miss Ambrose,' he retorts with a faint smile.

'Would you want a repeat of that night?' I raise a brow because the day I stormed out of his chambers is a memory that doesn't stop coming up.

He shakes his head. 'Most certainly not.'

'Then good, glad we can agree on—' I say before I'm stopped as Lorcan's head whips to the side and swears under his breath.

I don't see anything for a few seconds. Then I realize why Lorcan is moving away from me.

The General, along with a few other Venators, come into sight, muttering to one another as they walk down the hall.

I look to Lorcan, wanting to ask how on earth he knew they were coming but the frustration emitting off him suggests not to.

'Deputy.' The General inclines his head as he comes to a halt along with the rest. There's something so malignant in his gaze as he runs an eye over me. 'I hope we haven't interrupted anything.'

Lorcan doesn't look at me, acts like I'm not there, so stepping up, I tell them, 'I was just leaving.'

The General tilts his head as two other Venators dressed in their leather armor stare me down, and like a stupid girl, I wait for Lorcan to acknowledge me.

He does not even flinch.

Bowing my head, I whirl around and don't bother to look back and just as I turn the corner, not far out of reach, I hear the General say with a sigh, 'Do we need to have another talk?'

My steps falter. It's the first time the General sounds . . . fatherly. Freya had told me he acted more as a father figure to Lorcan than her. Perhaps this is one of those moments that he is showing that side.

Whatever the situation is between them all, I'm still not fond of the treatment he gives Freya, and as Lorcan mumbles something incoherent to the General, I hurry my footsteps again.

By midmorning the following day, I'd gotten up before the heady sun rose. I trained until Link could no longer stand my constant adrenaline, and then I explored the city once more. Passing academies where priestesses teach children, entering the clothing stores I couldn't afford, and lastly, a library in Salus District that if Idris were here, he'd adore.

The building has just a few people roaming by the tall ancient shelves, smears of vibrant orange paint brighten the stone pillars in every corner, and with just one single floor, the room stretches out far and wide. At first, I set out for Generalized books, letting my fingers glide among the wooden edges . . . The light streams through dozens of long windows, but as if a beam focuses on a particular book, I come across one to do with the history of Zerathion.

Leira's words are still fresh in my mind, and I've not stopped thinking about it the entire night. I thought of going back there, but I wasn't sure the outcome would benefit me. I'd soon enough rush out of there again at the mention of my father.

And while I tried desperately to forget about him and what she'd said, I'd toss in my bed and think of the Rivernorth bloodline instead.

Tragic for a reign to fall and have no one remember the legacy. But I suppose there's a reason for it, and shifters who still live since then are likely to know.

I wonder if the Golden Thief is one of them.

Sighing, I grab the book, worn and used. I flick through the pages and paintings depicting different variations of Solaris and Crello. No one knows what they looked like. Some imagine two beacons of light; others agree that they are exactly the sun and moon. While my mother used to think it was two goddesses.

She would tell me the tales of how Solaris and Crello spent so long wanting to share time and space. Then as twilight fell, dawn would wait, the two stealing glances at one another, wishing and yearning. And when they finally joined, life, power, *death* became their creation.

'So, not only does she threaten people, but she also likes to read.'

I snap the book closed, glancing up to find Rydan's childish grin.

'Every day, I'm learning more about you, Ambrose,' he muses, folding his arms as he leans against the shelf.

'Have you been spying on me?' I attempt not to raise my voice as a frown stiffens my face.

'Of course not. Who do you think I am?' He asks, taking offense, but before I can answer how that is precisely what I imagine him to do, he says, 'Look, I wanted to beat this man who is an all-time champion drinker of the flame spewers, and then I saw you enter the library, which to me was suspicious.'

I make a face, holding the book to my chest. 'You thought me entering a library . . . was suspicious?'

'Well, you constantly have this murderous charm to you, so perhaps you were on your way to slaughter someone in here.'

I take a deep breath, utterly done with him already. 'Maybe I was.'

He lowers his arms, moving closer with such eagerness. 'Really? Who?'

'A prat named Rydan Alderis. I lured him in here on purpose, and now I have him right where I want him.'

His brows wriggle together, looking down at the spot he's standing in, then all the bookshelves, and lastly, the ceiling. 'I see no trap that will kill me.'

'I do wonder how you've managed to survive this long as a trainee,' I say, shaking my head slowly in disbelief.

He shrugs, lazily waving a hand. 'Dragons fear me, and Lorcy adores me too much, that's why.'

'Clearly.' The constant avoidances from Lorcan prove that perfectly.

'You know Ambrose, there's another reason I came here. I actually have a confession to make.'

I quirk a brow, hoping the sudden sigh and shake of his head doesn't mean he will tell me a confession that's relatively Rydan-ish.

Placing a hand to his chest he starts, 'I feel that you and I have this deep level connection that not even Solaris and Crello could have. It's like you are the cheese to my grape, the—' He slows his words down as his gaze wanders to someone waltzing past us, disappearing into the next set of shelves. 'Pie to my—'

'Were you checking that man out while telling me how much of a connection we have?' I ask, quelling my smile.

'I did say I'm a great multi-tasker.' A proud smile drifts over his face. 'Does it make you want me?'

'No, it makes me want to hit you.'

He purses his lips thoughtfully. 'Everyone always says that to me.'

The urge to roll my eyes proves difficult to resist, but it passes when I hear whispers and the name Golden Thief on the other side of us. I shift on the spot.

'Have you ever thought what it'd be like to spend the night with him?' A woman's voice says. 'I heard he's stunning. I mean have you seen the posters?'

My nose scrunches in disgust, much to Rydan's confusion, before the friend gasps and I hear the patting of clothes as if she hit her. 'He's a criminal and a dragon shifter, Lillian, how can you think of such things?'

'Oh, you can't tell me you haven't thought it before! I for one never cared for what he is. A wanted criminal makes it all the more thrilling, and besides, I heard crystals allure him.' Lillian's voice lowers enough to sound sultry. I pray I don't gag at whatever else she has to say. 'Perhaps I could tempt him with some on my brea—'

'Solaris, save you,' the other sighs, ironically saving me before both erupt into obnoxious giggles.

'Who are we eavesdropping on?' Rydan leans in, his eyes shining in excitement.

'No one,' I deadpan, pushing his face back as I place the book on top of the shelf.

Rydan rubs at his nose as Lillian and her friend don't speak another word. Their footsteps drift further away.

Hearing her swoon over the Golden Thief makes me wonder if some thought him different or harmless. Many might have tried to capture the Golden Thief, maybe even attempted it with gold and all sorts of precious jewels as bait.

But I'm still intent on delivering what Ivarron has tasked me to do. I just need to lure the Golden Thief into a trap myself; I'm known to be good at that.

'Why do you look like you are planning something?' Rydan inquires of my frown.

I smooth out my features and smile. 'That's because I'm still planning on ways to kill you.' *And how it is time I use my skills in trapping on an insolent thief.*

Chapter Sixteen

A week.

I had a week to think about it all, from traps involving ropes to nets and arrows. One might say I was a lunatic to do this on my own, defy the General and the duty I've taken upon myself to train as a Venator.

Although, I've always been one to defy. And each night so far, I'd snuck out with all the equipment from the weaponry room, careful not to be spotted as I went into the most prestigious jeweller's store.

I started to believe I was just as bad as the Golden Thief, breaking into stores. Even so, I took comfort in the idea it was to catch him. But rigging the place and setting down a jade crystal amid it all, had done nothing to coax him to enter.

Every day, I waited for hours, placing the crystal near windows, hoping just as the moon bared its light, it would attract the Golden Thief.

But no, the Golden Thief never appeared, but I continued because I knew sooner or later he'd have to come.

Leaning against the wall in the store's backroom, I position a steel quarrel on the stock of my crossbow. I hold it up by my shoulder, keeping all my senses open, and just soon enough, boots thudding against wooden floors cause me to swing in the other direction.

It's him. It has to be him.

I'd unlatched the roof windows, anticipating he might come through them.

Keeping quiet, those same footsteps sound until they stop, replaced by the sharp noises of necklaces and beads clanging together.

I creep past the curtained doorway, and for the second time, I'm looking straight at the Golden Thief.

Same black jacket, same mask and the raven hair that's short yet cascades over where his brows are hidden beneath.

A week I've waited, but a week worth waiting.

The Golden Thief looks me over with the same mischievous glimmer that never goes unnoticed as he stands behind the counter holding the crystal I'd laid out atop a box of treasures. Other jewels and gold beam under the silver light of the moon.

'Drop it,' I order, aiming the crossbow at him as I step into the central part of the shop.

'I'm guessing the term *until never* doesn't seem familiar to you,' he says, raising his gloved palms before me and dropping the jade crystal into the wooden box. 'Ready for round two?' He goes on, grinning as his head motions to my crossbow. 'At least I see you've taken my advice with those blades you had last time.'

My fingers settle on the trigger. 'There won't be a round two because I have already won.' *Solaris, I despise how at ease he acts.* Needing a form of reaction, I fake a smile and continue, 'I've set up traps so that if you step on a particular flooring board, you'll activate it, try and guess which ones they are.'

Like a puzzle I'd set out the traps so that when he'd step on one, an arrow would shoot from the corner towards his head. Another at his abdomen.

He whistles. 'It sounds like someone hates losing.'

'I don't *hate* losing,' I grit out, albeit it's a dreadful lie.

His head cocks to the side, and I figure he knows I am lying too. 'Well, now that you have me here, what is it you want, Venator?' His voice an alluring tease. 'To send me to the dungeons? The stocks so everyone can throw tomatoes at me? Or better yet, witness the Queen sentence me to a beheading?'

'Quite frankly, I'd love all of those, but . . . I want answers.' *And your blood.*

'Answers?' His voice lilts with curiosity. 'You're here to question me?'

I nod, never once letting my fingers off the trigger.

'Alright.' His side lip perks up. 'Since there's not much I can do, what is it you seek to know?'

I shift, wanting to frown at how easily he's giving in, but then I'm reminded how there are so many things I'd ask, I'm not sure where to begin. I want to know why he can't fly when shifted or why he's immune to steel powder. All signs point to him having nothing to do with the new breed, and I believe so, which is why the question to leave my lips instead is— 'What do you know of the Rivernorths?'

Something slips past the Golden Thief's gaze; be it shock or anger, it's hard to differentiate. 'What a peculiar question to ask, Venator.' He's back to smiling. 'I'm assuming you must think I was there.'

'I wouldn't put it past you. For all I know, you could be over five hundred years old.'

'Five hundred is such a grand number. Imagine how much I could have stolen if so.' His eyes widen in humor.

Impatience burns through me. 'Just answer the question.'

'Why don't you guess my age instead? Make it a fun little game.'

'I'd rather not.'

'I'll guess yours first then.' He crosses his arms, humming. 'Eighteen? Nineteen?'

I'm going to pull the trigger sooner at this point.

'Twenty?' He points his index finger at me, but I show nothing. 'Twenty-one—'

'Yes,' I sigh sharply. 'Now, will you tell me, or do I have to pierce this arrow through your skull to get my question across?'

'Are you always such a killjoy?'

My silence and raised brow are answer enough for him that he expels a breath. 'Fine, I'm only twenty-five, so the answer to your question is no, I did not witness it.'

Twenty-five, not even past the stage of never aging. He must have learned how to steal from his youth to be so well known for it. 'But you still know of them, that means—'

'I know the history. What others of my kind have spoken of. The question is, why am I to tell *you*, a Venator who imprisons or kills us, something that has been kept in the dark for over three centuries?'

'Wouldn't you want to know if you were me?' Maybe I'm heading into a dead end. *Maybe* Lorcan is right when it comes to rumors. I keep hearing so many stories that it's hard to distinguish truth from lies.

'Well, if I were you,' the Golden Thief chuckles a rich melody. 'I'd first and foremost stop trying to harm such a talented thief.'

'A highly *questionable* thief,' I correct as my eyes wander over the mask alight with the night sky. 'What is the purpose of that mask anyway? Anyone is likely to recognize you without it.' His presence and amber eyes would give it away, but I don't want to say that.

'You'd be surprised how daft people can be,' he says as I narrow my gaze. So, he clarifies with a sigh, 'It makes me look good.'

I roll my eyes at how vain he is. 'Hardly.'

'What a jealous Venator,' he croons, rounding the corner of the counter. 'I'll have you know I can easily make anyone fall to their knees for me. Man, woman . . . troll.'

My throat tightens as my mouth becomes dry.

He stalks towards me, unperturbed by the crossbow aimed at his heart or how lucky he is to miss the floorboard where a quarrel would shoot. And if I wasn't still holding the weapon, I know he'd be just inches away from me, like our first encounter where he'd pushed his body against mine.

The tip of the arrow touches his jacket as he leans forward, and the edge of his lip slowly curves up. 'And I thoroughly enjoy it,' he whispers it like a soft stroke against my skin.

I grind my teeth so hard, pain shoots up my jaw. 'You haven't made *me* fall to my knees.'

He cranes his neck, a suggestive look in his gaze of golds and browns. 'Not yet, at least.'

'You're such a pig,' I hiss.

'And you have such a dirty mind.' He backs away, chuckling. 'Did you think I meant something else?'

I don't answer, blood rushes up to my cheeks at the sheer embarrassment, but I still manage a glare.

'I already said I don't involve my pleasures with Venators.' He steps on the floorboard, but nothing goes off. Why— 'I'd rather stop stealing—wait, no, that's a lie. I would never do that.' He smiles to himself, shaking his head.

'It seems you might just have to, though.' My smile is tight as my gaze darts to the corner where my trap had failed, but too quick my eyes are back on the Golden Thief. 'After all, *I'm* the one who has the upper hand here.'

'Are you sure about that?' His eyes shift towards the floor. 'Why do you think I haven't set off any of your traps so far?'

What?

My hand almost slips off the crossbow as he chuckles at my expression, undoubtedly surprised. 'Maybe you should ask the question: do I work alone?'

My eyes turn to slits, but my pulse rate fails me as he adds with a whispering taunt, 'The answer is *no*.'

And all it takes is one second for me to have the crossbow in my hand.

The next . . . *patter, patter, patter*, and it's gone as a familiar bright and orange fur sweeps past me, knocking it out of my clammy palms.

I blink, stumbling on the spot. My hands are still mid-air as if it was a force of wind, and I have to bring my focus back. And when I do, I look at the Golden Thief. He's smiling with his hands behind his back, before my gaze falls to the ground.

'Sorry, Miss!' That same creature – a Tibithian – I'd chased the night of the rümen attack, with its canines peeking through. 'But my friend here told me to disarm all the traps; otherwise, it could hurt him! And I don't want my friend getting hurt.'

This can't be real.

I'm hallucinating.

He knew. He was one step ahead . . . Again.

My head snaps back and forth between the creature bouncing on its feet and the Golden Thief, my crossbow in the hands of the Tibithian.

Fury overwhelms my spirit, and unsheathing my dagger, I raise it high enough that I lurch towards the Golden Thief, aiming for his face.

He doesn't react any differently. It's like he expected this from me as he twists me, causing the knife to fly out of my grip. My back to his front, he brings my hand behind me and the other gets trapped when his arm comes around my middle. I jerk my head in an effort to hit his chin. Instead, I find that I'm looking up at the coolness of his smile.

'You really love the idea of cutting my face, don't you?'

'Oh, I dream of it,' I answer dryly, fidgeting against him.

'That's quite obsessive of you, Venator.' He breathes a laugh. 'Have you thought about getting help with that?'

My lips thin with a flash of irritation as I lift my boot and stamp down on his. He grunts, but there's still an undertone of laughter as he releases me, and I spin to face him just as my gaze cuts to my blade.

I make a move for it, but the Golden Thief stops me as he raises a finger, shaking it twice.

'You know.' He strolls behind the counter. 'It's impressive how committed you are to capturing me. I mean, trying to lure me in with a crystal? Setting up traps for a week?' Amusement flares up in his eyes. 'It was fascinating to watch from the roofs, wasn't it, Tibith?'

'Very!' The creature nods one too many times, and my brows rise at the name.

'Tibith?' I practically scoff back at the Golden Thief. 'A Tibithian named . . . Tibith? How original.'

'Are you insulting my naming skills, Venator?'

Tibith gasps, his voice a child's squeak. 'That is very rude of her, Dar—I mean Gold—Gold—den Thief.'

The Golden Thief briefly nods towards Tibith before looking at me. 'So, seeing as *I* have the upper hand.' He lifts a few necklaces, lacing them through his fingers. 'It's time I asked a question. What is the *real* reason you want to capture me?'

'Doesn't everyone want to?' Some for the wrong reasons, Lillian springs to mind.

'True, but you're alone, I don't see you've brought reinforcements, and while I must admit your bravery intrigues me, it's also bold of you to want to do it on your own. Therefore, there must be a reason of some sort.'

I let my stare linger on him, deciding what to say or how to phrase it, when his contemptuous smile is one I'd like to wipe off his lips.

'Shall I return another day when you have the answer?' He mocks.

My glare hardens without saying a word, and when he clicks his tongue towards Tibith, he grabs the jade crystal, walking over to the door.

It's then I blurt out, 'Your blood.' My eyes snap closed with a grimace. 'I need your blood.'

'My blood?' He asks, his voice causing me to look again. 'Well, that's new.'

He leans against the entrance as Tibith hums in agreement. 'Why do you want my blood, Venator?'

Because I owe a debt, because I want to protect my brothers, because . . . In some way, I have the need to prove myself. 'I made a promise to someone I'd get it,' I reply softly, lowering my head.

Though in reality it was short-lived, heavy silence feels like it's going on for hours until he says, 'Then I guess you'll have to break it.'

My head shoots up just as he's grabbing the doorknob. The Golden Thief didn't sound harsh nor any hint of his usual mockery, but it doesn't stop my vexation.

'I hope you rot in the cells one day,' I say, no hint of cowardice in my voice. His hand stills, as does Tibith.

'And I hope they make room for you too.' He smirks over his shoulder before waving the crystal in the air. 'Always glad to have an accomplice at my side.' And once more, just like our first encounter, he leaves, this time with Tibith. However, he's not used his powers to leave me tied up, and I'm not running out to catch him.

Chapter Seventeen

'Someone seems angry,' Rydan says as I look up from the dining table. He drops onto the bench alongside Link. Freya then grabs the piece of ripped parchment from my hands where I'd vigorously written the same name until there was no capacity left to add more.

'You've put the Golden Thief down on your enemy list?' She questions with a frown. 'Solaris, I know many despise him, but I didn't think you would.'

I scoff incredulously and nod. Dealing with the Golden Thief twice already has proven I do, very much so.

I hope you rot in the cells one day.

And I hope they make room for you too. Always glad to have an accomplice at my side.

Screwing my lips at the memory, I grab a chunk of chicken and bite into it. He already has an accomplice, which makes more sense as to why no one's able to trap him.

'I don't understand why so many despise him.' Rydan flails his drumstick around. 'He's practically a king.'

'A king of thieving,' Link counters, spooning some pottage into his mouth.

Please, not even the role of a jester would suit him.

'And a king I'd happily allow to choke me,' Rydan says dreamily through a full mouth of food, causing the three of us to stop what we're doing and stare – stare like we were hoping we'd not heard right.

'You are simply the strangest person I've met, Rydan.' Freya shakes her head, muttering, 'I can't believe we are the same age.'

'I have no regrets in what I say, Frey-Frey.'

'Rydan.' Lorcan appears from behind, and it'd be a lie if I said I hadn't felt my heart lurch, seeing him.

Rydan doesn't take even a second to stand, dropping his drumstick as he turns with a grin. 'Lorcy,' he says. 'Care to join us? We were just discussing how I want to be—'

'Why weren't you at training this morning?'

Thank Solaris Lorcan cut Rydan off before the topic of being choked by the Golden Thief made its way into the conversation.

'I didn't need to train.' Rydan shrugs. 'I'm already well skilled.'

'Are you now?' Lorcan questions him flatly.

'We can spar right here to prove—'

Lorcan lifts a palm, silencing him. 'That won't be necessary.' He then looks towards me. 'Nara.'

I blink, stiffening. He'd not sought me out in almost two weeks, not since we'd spoken by the hallways. We'd only stared at one another each minute I trained, every moment I threw those blades at the practice dummies, and when the Queen visited again.

'Can we go for a walk?' He asks, one hand on his pommel like always. 'I would like to talk to you about something.'

I nod and feel Freya's hand squeeze my arm. Her nerves are obvious enough I don't need to look at her.

Rising from the bench, I follow him out of the mess hall and fall into slow steps beside him. He's quiet, even as we reach the gardens, and the night greets us warmly.

'What is it you wish to speak of?' I ask, letting my hands roam across the leaves on the bushes beside me.

'I feel that I owe you an apology.' He stops opposite the pond, and I frown. He adds, 'For everything. I know how much becoming a Venator means to you, and I've only pushed my luck by letting certain emotions get through.'

My hand stops fidgeting, and I pick off a leaf, letting it fall freely. Of all things, I did not expect an apology.

'You should know it is never my intention to make you uncomfortable.'

'I know,' I say, lowering my gaze at the fresh-cut grass, the smell reminding me that summer is right around the corner. 'I just—this is all new to me, this life, away from my brothers, away from my previous tasks as a trapper.' When I look up, Lorcan's eyes fix on me attentively. 'In some ways, I have always been sheltered. I think that's partly why I always craved something more, why I'm so focused on becoming a Venator.'

'Sheltered because of your brothers?'

I shake my head, but in part, he's not wrong. 'My eldest brother, Idris, he . . . he was always protective of me, and in turn, it's what kept me so isolated.'

'I can see why,' Lorcan says. 'Emberwell isn't the safest. He was merely doing his job as a brother. One can only wish for such a family.'

I stare up at him, pensively. He'd lost his mother and father as well.

He'd even spoken about never having any siblings. Still, there's an odd presence in his eyes, fury blazing upon those green forest colors.

'I know,' I say. 'I would never trade my brothers for the world. Everything I do, it's for them.'

He gives me a peculiar look, causing me to ask, 'What is it?'

'Nothing, it's just you don't often see siblings being so close with one another.'

I chuckle. 'Oh, we've had our fair share of arguments—' Brawls and food fights between Iker and me. '—But they're family, I imagine anyone would do the same.'

He takes in my words, looking ahead as a breeze skims the sharp contours of his face. My gaze journeys the leather armor, the same material as my own but his accentuate that strength in his arms, legs, torso . . .

'How did you get those scars?' I ask with a tilt of my head once my eyes land on his hand.

He looks at me, his forehead narrowing. I prompt, 'You asked me how I got mine. Now I want to know your story.'

Nodding carefully, he brings his hand in front of him. The jagged lines, zig-zagged and overlap, lightening under the moon. 'An animal attack,' he says.

'I hope you don't take offense, but your hand is coated in scars. That animal must have truly mauled it.'

He laughs quietly, turning his palm over. 'I was young. I'm just thankful I came out alive.'

'Was that before you took the Venator trials or after?'

'After,' he says. 'I took part in the Venator trial when I first came here at fourteen.'

'Right, I forgot you were an exception.' I raise my brows, kicking the grass. 'So, what is the final test like?'

No one tells me much of it, even my father had only gone as far as mentioning how difficult it is, and that not many come out alive.

'It changes each time,' Lorcan inhales, 'but it usually involves showing your survival skills . . .' He trails off as if perhaps recalling his own trials. 'Leaders of other kingdoms come to judge alongside the Queen and General.'

Except for the Elven king, I want to say but refrain, thinking of Leira. And when I open my mouth to change the subject, our attention turns to the bushes as a rabbit flitters out.

It twitches, springing over to us, then rests by the edge of my boot like it's waiting for something.

Lorcan lets out a small laugh. 'You seem to fascinate everything.'

I stare down at the rabbit circling me, then nod back up at Lorcan. 'Sometimes I fascinate the wrong things.' I'd said a similar phrase to Lorcan the night I'd run out of his chambers. Wherever I go, I can never shake off any creature or vile person.

'Do I count as that wrong thing?'

My gaze falls on his lips as he smiles, and I wonder what it'd be like to be kissed, how it would feel sharing something so intimate.

Forcing that out of my mind, I look at his eyes. 'Depends. Are you a dragon?' Even with my slight chuckle, I can't help but imagine the dragon at the arena. How I'd wanted to help her. How, despite my efforts to capture the Golden Thief, I hadn't informed the Venators of our encounters. Many would say I'm a sham. Why should I get the title of a Venator? Why should I keep this all from Lorcan?

'Wouldn't it be ironic if I were a Venator as well as a . . . shifter.' Mirth tints his words in contrast to the shame in my chest.

'Lorcan,' I say a pitch higher as his smile dims. 'I have something to say about the Golden Thief. I—' Pausing, my brows scrunch together as I glance at the ground, rumbling beneath my feet.

The rabbit scurries back into the bushes, and ripples swirl across the pond like someone has skipped a rock. Lorcan is scanning the dark cloudless sky when bells ring in the castle towers.

Warning bells, shouting and—

An explosion coming from outside the castle walls, and shouting from the people in the city. Smoke hits the air followed by screeches above. Even the screams of people from there resound to where we are.

It's an attack.

'Shifters,' Lorcan whispers as I snap my gaze back to him in horror. He pinches his lips together as if trying to keep his emotions contained. Glancing at me, his expression is no longer relaxed as he says, 'Get to the armory, *now*.'

I don't protest as he rushes to the stables, and I race inside, passing the commotion of Venators gathering longbows and spears.

My eyes shift from every corner of the room while Venators push me back as I then make my way through the weapons and yank the sword free off the wall.

Daggers are already sheathed at my thigh, and I assume Freya and Link have left since they're nowhere to be seen.

I can't imagine the fear Link must have right now, and I can only hope tonight doesn't end in any casualties, but my mind can't rid itself of that idea.

Inhaling a deep breath, I follow everyone else outside as the gates rise. Distant shrieks echo from every part, and the night air whips at my hair as I charge through the city towards the chaos.

Chapter Eighteen

Streets are filled with blood, people and families running to where there's a shelter as shifters dominate every area. Some turned into full dragons, others like a mortal.

Cries of terror cleave through the night, and Venators swarm the streets, slicing at heads, *hearts* . . .

I'd once made a promise to myself not to fear dragons, shifters, any kind of creature that could cause harm after my father's death. But my trembling hand on the hilt of my sword betrays me.

Forcing out a breath, I remind myself of the times Idris taught me to fight, the moments he'd tell me to get up even when I wanted to stop. And then, of Ivarron's words the first time I'd hesitated to catch a creature: *'Fear can enter when you open that door, when you embrace it and let it roam free.'* I'd looked up at him like any thirteen-year-old would, not knowing what I'd be getting into as he handed me a blade and said, 'You don't always have to close that door, Nara. But you can choose to ignore it and prevail.'

Ignore it and prevail. Ignore it and prevail. Ignore it and prevail.

I repeat, I memorize, I *engrave* that memory in my head, even if it was Ivarron that had said it.

The leather warms under my fingertips as I harden my grip on the sword and bolt past the Marigold tree. A shifter from the side charges towards me, and those minutes of fear I'd had before, leave once I thrust my sword through her chest. Blood spurts from her mouth as I slide it out.

I haven't killed her, but I'd managed to weaken her, and having the higher ground, I take out a blade from my thigh and flip it through my fingers before ramming it into her heart.

A groan tears out of her as she falls backward, and I blink, watching the blood trickle from the dagger onto my hand.

For half a heartbeat, guilt threatens at how I'd wanted to protect a dragon at the arena only to kill a shifter now. But I swallow that guilt quickly, allowing no remorse to break through, just how I'd felt with the rümen weeks ago.

Screaming snaps me out of my stupor as I whirl my head to the left at another shifter fighting off a Venator against the floor near the end of Chrysos District. Except the shifter is overpowering him, and the Venator isn't just anyone. It's Link.

'No!' I shout, rushing to get to him, but spits of fire crash in front of me, and I stumble to a halt. I look up at the sky as a row of arrows fill the air, striking shifters.

I must get to Link, I must get to Link, it's the one thing on my mind as I run down the path, trying to get to the edge of where the fire ends.

A chilling cry cuts across as I turn my head back for just one second and catch sight of Sana. A shifter in dragon form slices its talons across her neck while she lies on the floor, and crimson splatters along the cobbled stones.

By reflex, I squeeze my eyes shut and shake my head. I couldn't save her. Even if I wanted to, I wouldn't have gotten there in time.

And I'm not about to do the same with Link.

So, picking up my pace, I dart to the end, passing the fire, and head to Link, still battling the shifter. I throw the dagger mid-run towards the back of the man, managing to hit him right in the spot I needed to, and with a jerk of his body, he drops to the ground, knees first, then face.

Panting, I reach Link's wide-eyed stare as he pats down his body, checking for injuries. 'Go find Freya.' I yank the blade free from the shifter and pull Link up.

His eyes grow wider as he nods brokenly, and I hand him his sword. He staggers off down the other direction as I'm ready to rush through more crowds. But a huff behind me and daunting flaps of wings sends shivers through every part of my body.

Ignore it and prevail. Ignore it and prevail. Ignore it and prevail.

I twist around slowly as the dragon lands in front of me. The puffs of air from its nostrils brush my hair. Flames rise all around the dragon, encasing it until I can no longer see any scales, and as the bright blaze dies down, out comes a man with long, ragged dark hair and a face pale as ice. He's shifted back to his human form.

Fingers crack and click, drawing my gaze to them. Despite how hard it is to catch shifters, something always gives away who is human and who isn't. Twin tattoos on their hands, of the power they are born with. A Merati's symbol – three lines with two arrows on each one, the first meaning illusions, the second manipulator of emotions, and the third dreams. While an Umbrati shows a spiral, and just like the man in front of me, his Ardenti tattoos are of whorls of fire.

Instinct reels in as he nears, and with sharp precision, I swing my sword. He twists, causing me to miss, and his lips peel back into a vicious smile as he unfurls his palm, igniting flames.

'What a wild thing you are.'

I launch my sword at his arm, to stop him before he can use that power.

He laughs as he throws a shield up with the fire. I widen my eyes when I see what he's about to do, I dip under him just as he sends a fireball towards me. I twirl, seeing an opening, and don't waste a second shoving the sword through skin and chest. He cries out as I tear it from him but much to my panic, he carefully turns, holding onto the blood surging like gushing waters.

'You missed my heart,' he snarls, and I don't have the chance to duck or strike again as his hand comes out to my neck, slamming me so hard against the stone walls that I see stars.

The force and pain rock my sight; I drop the sword and grab his arm to push it away.

'There's something about you that—' A vile reek of alcohol from his breath causes me to grimace. Everything seems to be blurring as he tilts his head and says, '—I can't quite pinpoint . . . it's almost *mesmerizing*.'

'Wish I could say the same about you, but I'd rather gouge my own eyes out.' My throat closes as he presses his palms tighter.

'Well, aren't you a vulgar mortal,' he trills, kicking the sword further away. 'Maybe you'd benefit a bite from a shifter.'

My scream of anger comes out as he seizes my arm and his fangs lengthen, shooting me a horrid grin.

He can't bite me. He can't.

I'm trying to free myself, but he only pulls harder, locking me in place and lowering his mouth to my wrist.

No, no, no—

Small, ragged breaths throttle out of the shifter as the curve of his canines never sink in. He releases me as I choke out a gasp, and looking up, I furrow my brows in heavy confusion, noticing a black shadow wrapping around his neck.

Violent specks, a chain of some sort, the same that—

Oh, Solaris.

Stumbling away, the shifter turns his back to me, and I step out of the way to see the Golden Thief standing there, with Tibith to his side covering those large eyes. Not daring to look.

Dangerous eyes bore into the shifter, like nothing I've ever seen from the Golden Thief before. It's almost murderous with a hint of his familiar derision as he holds his gloved hand out, focusing all his power to strangle the man.

In turn, the shifter wheezes, clawing at his own neck. 'Darius, what are you doing here?'

My shocked gaze goes back and forth between the two. *Darius . . . the Golden Thief's name is Darius.*

'It's a little hard to go around stealing when an attack has broken out.' The Golden Thief – Darius – says, his palms closing as if tightening that magic. He smirks. 'And a bite? How low do you have to stoop, Hake?'

'Stop—please,' Hake begs.

Darius narrows his eyes, never seeming to loosen that shadow grip on the shifter. 'Why should I?'

In the second that Darius doesn't make any move to let go of Hake, I glance at the sword on the floor and dash for it.

I rise, and with a blood-curdling cry from my lungs, I plunge it into Hake's heart. A nauseating grunt of pain releases from him as the shadows disintegrate into dust. The sword was that sharp; I could feel it go through tissue, cut through arteries.

Retracting the blade, blood glistens off the weapon, dripping as he slumps down.

Short of breath, I look up to Darius's brows rising, and he nods slowly at the stiff body on the floor. 'Well then. It's a good thing I never liked him.' Amber eyes shift to me. 'However, I'm starting to think you enjoy all our encounters being this way, *Venator*.'

Chapter Nineteen

My brows pucker. I don't say a word while staring at . . . *Darius.*

Such an ordinary name. Why did I think it'd be any different? Did I just adopt the idea that his name was simply Golden Thief, or did I not want to believe it could be normal?

'You can stop covering your eyes now, Tibith,' he drawls, his eyes on me, burning in gold under the beam of moonlight.

Tibith lowers his hands, blinking as he looks at the shifter and the blood-stained sword in my hands. Gasping, he points at me. 'She killed him Gold—Gold—den Thief!'

I glare. *He was going to bite me!*

Darius hums in amusement, the corner of his lips curling up to show his carefree smile. 'She knows my name now, Tibith. I don't think there's a need for any formalities.'

'Does that mean I can call you Darry again?' Tibith asks, hopeful, his large ears flapping rapidly as Darius nods, looking up at me.

'So . . . aren't you going to thank me then, Venator? I did just save your life.'

I straighten, cautiously, with the sword prominent by my side. 'Why did you do it?' Too stubborn to thank him. His arrogance and playful tone make me not want to.

He chuckles, moving toward me, but I stop him with my sword, Hake's blood, clotting and drying on it. Darius's eyes dart to the blade's tip, and he smirks. 'Not the thank you I expected.'

'Answer me,' I demand. '*Darius.*'

His smile wavers, and then he takes me by surprise as he pushes the sword away. I try to lift it again, but his right arm comes around my waist, and the other grabs my wrist with the sword still there, pinning my arm behind me.

I struggle in his arms, wanting to set myself free. I glare up at him. The noises and screams start dying down, yet there is a humorous speck of light in Darius's features.

He's enjoying this way too much.

'Let go.' I clench my teeth. 'Let go, or I—'

'Will try to stab me?' He smiles, and I scoff at him. 'Because I don't think you are in a position to do that.'

'That is because you are being unfair—' I grunt out my words, tugging at my arm, '—*again*.'

'Darry,' Tibith says from the ground, but Darius's gaze is rooted to mine. 'We need to go!'

I release harsh breaths from my nose as we hold our stare.

It looks as if he's about to say something, but he never does as he steps back, snaps his head to the side, and catches an arrow right before it strikes his head.

I follow where the arrow has come from and find— 'Lorcan,' I whisper.

Exhaling as I bring my sword around, I see he's at the entrance of the street, armor shredded at the sides and jaw set firm as his narrowed stare on Darius turns severe. Notching another arrow, he aims it again, firing one after another as he strides towards him.

Air draws out of me, watching Darius snatch each one, his playful smile never faltering.

'It's another murderer!' Tibith yells in panic, curling up into a ball and rolling in circles just as Lorcan abandons the bow and arrows, lunging at Darius. They both slam onto the ground, sending a jolt of shock in me as Darius throws his arms up, shielding himself from Lorcan's hits.

Tibith knocks into barrels, rocketing towards Lorcan as if flames are spreading in his wake from the speed.

I have to do something, I have—

A screech, like a squawking crow, jerks me to the right as another shifter launches himself at me. He swings his arm around, and I duck, coming under him as I twist, curving the sword into his back and all the way through to the other side.

He yelps, collapsing, giving me a clear view of Lorcan and Darius tackling each other. But as I rush over to them, Darius shoots a ball of flame from his palm, startling Lorcan, then elbows him in the face, causing him to fall onto his side.

As Darius gets off the floor, he murmurs something too low to hear. I figure it is one of his irritating comments with that grin of his.

He whistles at Tibith to stop kicking Lorcan's boots, and I shoot Darius an irked expression before running up and kneeling to grab Lorcan's arm.

'Are you hurt?' Lorcan asks, propping himself up on his elbow and scanning my face. I shake my head, sheathing my sword as my breaths come abnormally shallow. Looking up, I find Darius and Tibith no longer there.

'Darius,' I say absentmindedly, staring into the dark alleys of the city. 'The Golden Thief—that's—that's his name.'

When Lorcan doesn't answer, I slide my gaze to him. His expression is unclear as he pins his lips together. It's hard to know what he wants to say, and even worse, as padding of footsteps echoes the narrow streets, I whip my gaze to the shifter charging our way.

Alarmed and knowing my blades are scattered elsewhere, I go for the next best thing. My sword won't be fast enough to hit her, so I scramble to get the bow and arrowheads at the side of us.

Notching one, I whirl, aiming with precision. I'm still on the floor with Lorcan behind me as I draw the arrow back and release it just in time as she shoots a shadow blade from her hands.

It strikes her heart, and I expel a breath of alleviation or worry. Either feel far too similar right now.

'Nara,' Lorcan grunts in a low tone, a pained one that triggers a sense of dread in my gut as I look at him.

He's clutching the left side of his chest, and slowly, it hits me.

Red, darkened blood leaks down from his hand, not anyone else's, not mine, *his*.

I'd managed to dodge the shadow magic from that shifter, but in the process, it'd struck Lorcan.

I drop the bowstring, shock zaps at me as I stop him from falling unconscious. 'No, no, no,' I whisper, pressing my hand onto where his is. Blood now soiling my fingers. 'We need to get you back to the infirmary, we need—'

'It's not deep. It'll be fine,' he says with labored breaths while attempting to stand. I rise with him and grab him by the side as he sways.

'I don't believe that,' I mutter, lifting his arm over my shoulder.

The barracks are in an absolute state as I stagger in, trying to keep Lorcan upright against my shoulder while everyone heads to the infirmary. Some drag in unconscious Venators, and others, I can hear the screams of pain from the other side of the room.

'My chambers,' Lorcan breathes. 'Take me there.'

I let my gaze slip to meet his staring down at me, weak and flickering. I'm hesitant to agree, but with the number of injured people crowding the infirmary, I huff, directing us to the staircases by the entrance.

At that second I turn, Freya tumbles in with Link and Rydan. Soot covers them head to toe, yet I almost cry out in relief that they've made it back unharmed.

Freya notices me, eyes widening, when she spots Lorcan by my side. She mouths the words 'go,' and I nod at the reassurance of her smile.

I push Lorcan and me towards the stairs, tiring out by the time we get to the higher levels of the barracks and burst into his chambers. Kicking the door closed, I let go as he drops onto the edge of his bed.

'There's some neem paste in the cabinets. It'll help the healing,' he says, inclining his head to the bath chambers.

I nod, still thinking the infirmary was a better option. I've only cured injuries on myself or Illias and Iker. Idris usually handled all his wounds himself, it was a matter of pride.

Searching the cabinets, I can't process anything that's happened tonight. I can't even think straight as I fill up one of the wooden bowls with water and find a half-empty jar of green neem paste.

By the time I walk out with the equipment in my hands, Lorcan has stripped the top half of his armor. I stop and glance at his upper torso, lean and sheening with sweat.

Heart freezing and mind struck with the sight, I shake my head and stroll over to him. He glances up through his lashes as I stop in front of him, his legs part as he presses his palms at the sides of the bed.

My eyes zero in on his chest but what surprises me is the scar on his right, twin to what now is bleeding after that shadow blade.

I'd used a spear on him, but his reflexes were stronger. He grabbed it mid-air, broke it in half, and threw it before it pierced my armor, my chest, and through to the other side.

Lorcan had said it that night outside in the gardens. And while I'd seen how Lorcan was fast, agile like no other, Darius's reflexes were far too good, and this scar is the result of that.

I avoid staring at the circular mark for long and position myself to dress his wounds, reluctant in doing so as I dip the cloth into the bowl. Lorcan's stare doesn't help my awareness of the position I am in right now. Which is why I look away and begin cleaning the wound. His silence eases around the room as his body tenses whenever I dab the cut.

Annoyingly, he is right, it's not deep, but he's lost a vast amount of blood. I drop the cloth back into the bowl, placing it on the floor before grabbing the neem and swiping two fingers into the thickening paste.

'I can do it—' Lorcan winces when I slather it on carelessly and then manages a slight chuckle. 'Always such a brute, Nara.'

'I don't care.' My tone is sharp though my sigh shows the concern tugging inside me.

With a murmur, he says, 'I didn't think you'd worry this much.'

'I'm not worried.' I try to find the strength in my voice, but there is none when I can't seem to lie.

He doesn't say anything to that. We don't say anything for a while, but I know he's looking at me . . . staring at every movement of my hand.

I inhale once I'm done, knowing I have to step back, yet I can't.

Setting the vial aside on the bed, I wipe any neem residue on the cloth. My gaze then wanders to the scar. Surprisingly on the other side, he looks to be healing well enough already. But that scar.

Drawn to it this time, my fingers reach out to caress the corners, the red pigment contrast to the rose tint of his skin.

'Nara,' he grinds out as if my touch scalds him, but I don't stop. I focus on the way the oil lamps burn bright, and sweat trickles down his forehead.

My breath shakes, sliding my fingers away from his scar to the hard muscle of his abdomen. I flicker my gaze to his lips, betrayed by how close I am to him.

Allowing myself to pry my eyes from the sharp curves of his cupid's bow, I stare at him.

I can't look away this time. No matter how much I want to, I'm tangled in the branches of his forest gaze.

He's breathing hard.

I'm breathing hard.

And for one second, he's staring at my lips. The next, they're on mine, smothering my gasp.

I'm frozen, unsure of what to do. My eyes are still open as he goes slow, parting my lips with his own, and I feel shivers running down my legs. He knows this is new to me, but a natural urgency takes over my body and my eyes close, melting into him.

He lifts me and places me on his lap, my legs on either side of him, as his hand curves around my back, the other sliding to the nape of my neck. My palms travel to his chest, aware of his wound, and the gentleness of the kiss evaporates as his tongue glides along the bottom of my lip.

Everything I thought my first kiss would be, didn't prepare me for my body's reaction, how I crave more and more as he tilts his head. I push further against him, taking my hands off him only to dive them into his hair.

My pulse flickers with trepidation at the unknown, and at every minute, his fingers caress my thick, full curves.

He whispers my name more times than I can count. A yearning in the syllables, *Na-ra*, sends a pulse of heat to every part of me, causing a sigh to come from my lips against his.

'I think kissing you has healed me completely,' he says, his palms skimming along my thighs.

My eyes still closed, I breathe a laugh, mid-kiss. 'Maybe it's time we stop then.' I don't want to stop. I don't want to stop at all.

He shifts my body closer to him so that our hips join, and I swear a groan escapes him. 'I don't think I want to—' He kisses me again.'—But then you, here on top of me, isn't helping what else I'd like to do.'

'And what else is that?' Experienced or not, I knew enough for that "else" to mean things beyond a kiss. Yet I want to hear it from him.

His lips curve into a smile over mine. 'If—'

The door to the chamber hits against the wall just then, and my eyes fly open. Abruptly, I pull back, stumbling away from Lorcan and covering myself as if I were the one shirtless when I'm not.

My face pales as I look at the door where the General keeps a firm grip on the doorknob.

He saw me on top of Lorcan, he walked in on— 'Sorry I—' Shame floods me at how I'd let myself go for the second time.

The General snaps his head to me, staring long and hard, without a word leaving his lips.

'Erion,' Lorcan addresses him, not as the General and not as someone of authority. But the General doesn't even sneak a glance his way.

'I'd advise you get back to your chambers, Miss Ambrose,' a curt order the General.

I cut my gaze from him to Lorcan as he closes his eyes and exhales a frustrated sigh. Biting my tongue, I slowly look back, realizing there's no winning against the General, and Lorcan wouldn't—won't defy him.

The General doesn't budge from the doorway, but I maintain a fixed stare on him as I walk past and out of the chambers.

Chapter Twenty

It took a few days for everything to return to normality. For most, this was just a blip in their life. Others had lost homes and lives. And the wall carved with names of the deceased Venators grew in numbers.

Even the Queen's proclamation over the castle balcony that one day, shifters will torment mortal lives no more, didn't settle people's spirits.

'Something seems to be bothering you lately,' Rydan says beside me with Link next to him, as we stop patrolling near some jeweller's fixing the cracked doorways to their shop.

A lot is bothering me lately. The Venator trials, the Golden Thief or Darius in this case. The knowledge that something is hidden deep in the city of Emberwell, these new creatures . . .

'How do you know what bothers me and what doesn't?' I ask Rydan as I look at him. 'Last I checked, I barely even know you.'

He ignores that statement and hums knowingly. 'Is it Lorcy?'

A dip in my chest unnerves me, and my brows curl upward, ready to become defensive towards that idea. Rydan, though, beats me to it as he carries on, 'It's certainly obvious he's lusting for you—'

'Rydan!' I whisper harshly, wishing we weren't in public so I could smack his head.

'Maybe Nara is facing the stress of the Venator trials approaching.' Link tries to be amenable, smiling awkwardly at me.

'I think that is more you, Link,' Rydan looks pointedly. 'You go pale whenever the General comments on it.'

'No, I don't.'

'You almost spilled your guts onto the training grounds when the General said 'dragon."

'I'd overeaten that day.'

'You're stuttering right now—'

This is getting ridiculous.

I shake my head, ignoring the two, although grateful the attention has been taken off me. Gazing straight ahead, I look towards the city center when three men get out of a carriage by the stables.

Paints of all colors coat the dark green tunic, and my eyes widen in hope.

Can it be?

'Illias?' I say, and when he spots me from afar, I realize it's truly him. Illias, Idris, and Iker. A grin stretches across my face as I shout this time, 'Illias!' I sprint towards them, bumping into the occasional civilian and yelling out apologies.

I take Illias by surprise as I drag him down into an embrace, squeezing him around the neck.

They're here. They're actually here.

Not a dream or something I'm imagining after everything that's happened. *It's them.*

'What are you all doing here?' I let go and rush to hug Iker, then Idris.

While Illias and Iker are all smiles, Idris's hard stare lingers on me, the missing glove over my scar and the Venator attire, as I step away from him. His hair passes his shoulders now, but his face . . . the darkness under his azure eyes makes it known he's tired.

I pray Ivarron hasn't been as hard on him as he had been with me most days when I was trapping.

'We wanted to surprise you,' Iker says, and I pull a face at the grumpiness of his tone.

'Did we come at a bad time?' Illias questions, glancing at the central, his gaze widening over the Marigold tree and the castle walls up ahead.

Certain roofs burned down during the shifter attack. I assume that caught his attention, along with the broken planks and debris lying around.

Word never gets out much from the city to the smaller villages. Near the south where we are from, the only gossip ever received is from Ivarron or Miss Kiligra hearing things from the nosey neighboring towns.

'No, you came at the perfect time,' I say, not needing to worry them with any shifter information, smiling the most I have since I first came here, before looking behind me. 'Link, Rydan!' I gesture my hand as they approach us. 'These are my brothers, Illias, Iker, and Idris.'

They all incline their heads at one another as Link stays staring at Illias in admiration. Color creeps up onto Illias's cheeks as his gaze wanders off to the sides. And as Link doesn't drop his gaze once, I cock my head to the side, holding back another smile until Rydan steps in, opening his arms far and wide. 'Ah, my future brothers-in-law, lovely to make your acquaintances.'

Just like that, I'm back to scolding.

'In-laws?' Idris asks unamused, glancing at me and then at Rydan nodding.

'Yes,' he says, coming up beside Idris, and draping an arm around his shoulder. 'I plan on marrying your sister. Although she keeps saying no to me, but the way I see it, she's playing a treacherous game of love while trying to get me jealous using Lorcy – I mean Lorcan.'

I exhale roughly, wishing I'd not introduced Rydan to my brothers. It should have been evident from the start he'd say something like this.

'Who is Lorcan?' Illias asks, frowning before it smoothes out into a look that tells me he realizes something. A look that means Idris won't like this at all.

Rydan heaves a loud sigh, shaking his head. 'My common enemy in this love affair—'

'Lorcan!' I blurt out by accident and far too eager as he appears from behind them. The timing is not perfect, I must admit, not when everyone's heads whirl to him and Idris stands tall and strong – his usual stance of vigilance when it comes to me.

Lorcan's gaze shifts to me, and flashes of his lips on mine slide into my memory, forcing me to bury the tightness inside my chest.

'Idris.' Somehow the air has been pushed out of my lungs, and my voice is tremendously high. 'This—'

'We've met,' Idris cuts in, staring Lorcan down. *Dear Solaris and Crello, save me.* 'I remember you. You were the one who told Nara to join the Venators.'

Lorcan sends him a curt nod. 'I saw potential.' He looks my way. 'Couldn't let someone like her get away.'

I don't think he's talking about my role as a Venator, not with that starkness in his gaze.

You let me get away the other night are words I'd say if we were alone right now.

'Do you plan on staying for the Noctura festivities next week?' I clear my throat and change the subject as I glance at Idris. His frown deepens, still looking at Lorcan.

Illias looks to answer, but Idris quickly interjects, 'Occupying an inn for that long will cost us far too much in the city. We'll leave before the week is over.'

Right, and I can't even help cover any of the costs.

Nodding, though anyone can see the disappointment in my eyes, I plaster on a smile. It's the first time I'll be celebrating without them.

'I can help.'

I stop blinking, and in silence, we all cut a gaze to Lorcan.

He waves a hand, and I try not to look Idris's way. 'You can let the innkeeper know you're my guests. It'd be an honor to have the Ambrose's here for the festival.'

'Lorcy, this is the most I've seen you talk—'

'If it makes Nara happy.' Lorcan cuts Rydan off with a sharp stare. 'Then I'd be glad to help in any way.'

My heart knocks against my ribcage. If it makes *me* happy. 'I can't accept your offer to pay for my brothers, Lorcan, it's—'

'I'll make sure to repay you for your kindness,' Idris says, and I look at him in puzzlement, as do Iker and Illias. Knowing how prideful Idris can be, I'm surprised he's not declining Lorcan's offer.

Lorcan nods deeply and appreciatively as he says, 'That won't be—'

He trails off as whistles signal for them to join the other Venators gathering nearby. Lorcan excuses himself, as do Rydan and Link, and they all head back to patrol the city.

I watch as Lorcan strides past the moving carriages and people chattering in bright orange dresses that swish across the ground. For a second, I continue staring; Lorcan looks over his shoulder, a subtle glance, and then he is gone.

I face my brothers again, hoping they didn't hear the sigh under my breath. I walk up to Iker who is still pouting.

'What's wrong with you?' I grin, ruffling his chestnut curls. He shakes me off.

'He's just annoyed that Idris gave Dimpy over to Miss Kiligra to look after,' Illias snorts, and Iker jabs his arm.

Of course, he'd be annoyed at that. Miss Kiligra would likely run away the second the rabbit hopped around her cottage. 'Come on, let me show you around the city.' Or what's not been destroyed.

We spend the evening walking through the city, entering the Salus District. Thankfully we find that the libraries have been salvaged. Illias smiles as I lead them down narrow paths filled with paintings embellishing the walls. And then we sit down for food at a tavern.

Illias had subtly mentioned how Ivarron was keen on them visiting me, which meant he was hoping for some news on Darius.

I've seen him enough times now, and each time, he's escaped one way or another. I've become tired of it, hating the idea of admitting defeat because I never have done over anything before.

'Gosh, I've missed Nara scoffing down her food like there's no tomorrow,' Illias remarks as I finish my stew.

I wipe my mouth with the back of my hand, laughing. 'At least here I don't have to fight Iker over the table for the last piece of bread.'

Iker furrows his brows, scoffing at that, and I turn to Idris, expecting him to laugh, except he doesn't. He's been quiet most of the time we've been catching up.

'Where's your carving?' He taps his sturdy fingers against the wooden table, staring at my waist where my sheath strap would normally be.

'Back at the barracks. I haven't felt the need for luck,' I mumble, keeping my eyes on my tankard. I feel a ripple of guilt. Even if the carving is a small thing that others at my village saw as a joke, it's been my source of luck for so long.

I'd stopped carrying it around since . . . since the night Adriel and Oran were attacked.

Idris places something in front of me, wrenching me from my thoughts.

I lean closer, grabbing what seems to be a hilt made of sleek ebony wood, but no blade is attached. 'What's this?'

'A gift.'

'A gift for what?'

He rolls his eyes and huffs. 'A gift because I know how much you've needed a new dagger, and despite this one not being useful for carving, I thought it'd be a good time to upgrade to something more suited for a Venator.'

I jump as he presses something underneath the hilt, and a blade shoots out at both ends, barely a forearm's length.

'There are no designs on the hilt since, knowing you, you'll want to personalize it yourself.'

I stare, gob smacked at the sheen of the newly sharpened blades. 'How much did this cost you?'

'He made it himself,' Illias says, sipping on his mead.

Idris shakes his head at Illias as if he wasn't supposed to admit that. Idris's modesty never fails to impress me.

'You did?' I ask, my tone relatively soft. I remember Idris carving and working on weapons since the moment I'd learned to walk. He'd befriended our village blacksmith, and I'd questioned why he never took on that role instead of a woodcutter. For him, creating weapons reminded him too much of Father.

'It took a few sleepless nights to get the device working, but I got there in the end.'

That's why he looks so fatigued.

'Idris.' I take a sharp inhale, not knowing where to start. 'Thank you . . . for everything you've done for us, for me. You didn't need to do this.'

We've always fought the most and have never seen eye to eye, but his loyalty and love is something I've admired from a young age.

His lips crack into a smile. I know he wants to tell me it's nothing, that he'd do it for anyone, but he keeps it to himself.

'How come you get a gift, and it's not Yule yet?' Iker moans, rubbing the sides of his head. 'All I get is earache from Idris about letting Dimpy shit on his bed.'

Illias chokes on his mead, sparks of laughter burst out of him, and Idris can't help chuckling at Iker's banter.

I'm so happy that they're here after all these weeks. I have never gone more than a day without them, and I can only wish that one day they might move out here with me.

After leaving my brothers to stay at the inn, I stroll down the moonlit pathways while holding the blade Idris gifted me. I smile, tracing the indents on the wood, already thinking of ways to carve something into it. Perhaps the sun again, or my brothers' names entwining between leaves of the Marigold tree I adore so much.

Whichever option I choose, the thought is put to a halt. My smile vanishes as I notice a figure resting its body inside a crescent-shaped hole on the wall, overlooking the other side of the city.

Walking closer, orange fur scurries in front of me, and the figure is revealed to be Darius. One leg dangles off the moon, and the other is pulled back with a hand draping over the knee.

He leans his head against the curve, tilting it slightly to look at me. 'Hello, foul mortal,' he greets, a dark smirk dancing across his lips.

I press the button on the hilt and lower my brows as twin blades slide out at the side. 'Dragon pig.'

Darius remains calm and chuckles. 'Always a warm welcoming with you.'

'Hello, again, Miss!' Tibith waves, drawing my gaze down at him and his round frame.

I'm doubtful whether to smile back or frown questionably.

It doesn't look like I can do either as he turns and crawls up Darius's leg and plops himself on top of his knee.

'What are you doing here, *Darius,* stealing again?' Already he has me wound up tight.

Between the shadows of the night and the oil lampposts in the empty street, Darius straightens off the crescent as Tibith slides down with a slight noise resembling a cheer.

I'd step back if I wasn't so stubborn, as Darius emerges into the bright moonlight. I don't let him see the slight jolt of surprise in my body at the sight of him not wearing a mask.

Stopping a meter away, the breeze ruffles his raven hair, as he studies me with his kohl-lined playful eyes.

I always knew his features had the power dominate anyone. That carved jaw – a dangerous weapon for someone who is already lethal, ready to summon every power at his command.

'I'm here to make a deal,' he says, darting his gaze to my blade. 'That is, of course, if I can get through a conversation without you trying to stab me.'

'You make it impossible for me not to.'

'How so?'

'For starters, everything you say vexes me.'

'That's not a valid reason, Venator.'

Perhaps it's the cool smile or the tease in his voice, but I already want to swing at him. 'Alright, how about the fact that every time we meet, you play unfairly.'

He laughs, crossing his arms over his jacket. 'As do you. If I recall, you even placed traps to capture me.'

Traps he knew about and disarmed so easily, he made me look witless. 'That's different.' I quell my anger.

'Different how?'

'I *had* to place traps to protect myself. Besides,' I shrug, 'I could have succeeded in capturing you. It's just the first time I was caught off guard.'

He narrows his eyes and smiles. 'And the second time?'

'Well, you cheated there too with that orange fur ball of yours.'

'I am no orange fur ball!' Tibith scampers up Darius's leg before resting on his shoulder. 'My name is Tibith, Miss!'

'I know,' I say with a straight face. 'I haven't forgotten when we first met.'

'It is not my fault, Miss. I must protect Darry first,' he says, crossing his arms.

A loyal accomplice, how lovely.

'You know I hate to admit it, but you're a somewhat special Venator,' Darius says, pointing at me and then placing Tibith back down on the floor. 'Most mortals fear me.'

'Really? I've heard a few that think differently.'

Excitement flickers in his eyes, gold turning to honey brown. He *knows* what I'd meant.

Rydan, Freya, and even others speak of him in whispers they think no one can hear. To my utmost frustration, the name *Golden Thief* follows me everywhere.

'Well, some happen to be fans of my work,' he says, taking out a gold coin from his pocket, tracing it between each leather-clad finger. 'But *you.*' His movements stop as his gaze roams over me. 'You wanted to catch me as part of your own efforts that didn't involve the Venators.'

The grip on my hilt loosens, knowing I have branded myself as traitorous towards the Venators, unworthy.

'And after days of thinking it through,' he goes on. 'I decided I'd give you exactly what you want from me.'

His deal.

'You're willing to give me some of your blood?' I ask, lifting my brows, doubtful since he'd told me to break my promise of ever getting it.

He nods, to my amazement. 'In exchange for something, of course.'

Of course. My lips peel back into a wry smile. 'And what is that?'

'First tell me why you want my blood, and then I'll explain.'

I keep staring at him then Tibith as he rocks on his feet, tilting his head to each side like he's also waiting for the answer.

An answer I haven't told anyone.

Several seconds pass, leading into minutes. Some categorize my obstinance as tiresome.

'Is she frozen, Darry?' Tibith inquires with a tweet to his voice.

Darius noises his agreement, looking at Tibith. 'Would explain why she lost against me the first time. She's always freezing.'

Oh, please.

'It's *said*,' I finally say with a sharp tone, prompting Darius to look at me. 'Your blood grants immortality if ingested. And a man I'd worked for as a trapper told me to bring it to him in exchange for—' I sigh '—freedom.'

'Is being in the city and part of the Venators, not freedom enough?' He asks, and I understand why he says that. For a shifter, freedom isn't an option.

'Freedom for my brothers,' I answer quietly, lowering my head before shaking it as I meet his stare again. But all there is, is silence slamming down a width between us.

He angles his head, and something in his gaze stirs unrecognizably. I speak again, controlling that firmness in my posture. 'I've told you the reason. Now tell me what your demands are.'

His expression is gone within a second as he gives me a knowing smile. 'I want you to steal something for me. The pendant the Queen wears. I'm sure you've seen it on her by now.'

I recall the faint memory of when I was training a few weeks ago. The Queen had approached me, and the first thing I'd laid eyes on was a gold pendant with rivers overlapping a compass.

But the idea of stealing from the Queen . . . I shudder at the thought of failing and being thrown in the dungeons.

'Can't you do that yourself? You're known as the greatest thief, even possessing immunity to steel powder.'

He chuckles under his breath, flicking the coin on the tip of his finger as it spins, its gold light reflecting onto his skin. 'I'm not immune to it.'

My eyes jerk wide in shock.

'I've simply taken it in my drinks for years so I've built up a resistance.'

That must be why many shifters are gaining confidence in their attacks. Maybe it's Darius showing them that resistance.

'But even then—' He catches the coin in his glove mid-air. '—It's more thrilling to see you steal it rather than me.'

I glower at his grin. He's giving me an impossible task, much like Ivarron had done. 'Why is it you wish to steal that precise pendant?'

His brows rise slightly like I've asked the most ridiculous thing out there. 'Are you really questioning a thief as to why they want something stolen?'

'Good point,' I expel a sharp breath. 'So, if I get this pendant—which, by the way, is a dreadful mission—'

'It is.'

I shoot his mocking face an exasperated look. 'You will give me a vial of your blood?'

'Vial, jar . . .' A thoughtless motion of his hand. 'Whatever pleases you.'

I pinch my lips together, narrowing my gaze at him with the thought sinking into my mind. *Get the pendant and I get his blood in exchange.*

Another task I can't believe I'm getting myself into.

'Then,' I take a deep breath. 'I'll have that pendant within your reach soon enough.' My voice gives nothing away, but I'm not sure I believe my own words and certainly not *his*.

As I pass him to get away, he grasps my forearm. Our bodies meet, and my hand grips my blade. 'Hang on.' His voice is almost a whisper by the side of my head, I can almost feel him smiling against it. 'You know my name. It's only fair I get to know yours now.'

Slowly looking up at the closeness of his eyes glittering like golden stars, I pluck my arm from his hand, detesting the thought of even giving him my name. He backs away, and the insufferable mischief in his countenance makes me think of a nickname I'd once given to my father's mare. 'Misty,' I say.

'Misty? Who named you, your father?'

'No.' I glare at him. 'My mother.'

'You don't look like a Misty.'

'And what do I look like then?'

He hums in thought, circling me slowly and pursing his lips, then starts murmuring names and whether he likes them or not.

I tap my foot, tiring of this game.

'Goldie.' He stamps his boot in satisfaction. 'I think you look like a Goldie. Wouldn't you agree, Tibith?'

'Goldie, Goldie, Goldie!' Tibith sings before gasping. 'Just like her hair, Darry!'

'Exactly like her hair,' he says.

'Are we done here?' I ask flatly, impatient, *infuriated.*

He steps aside, extending his hand out to lead the way, and he bows at the waist with that surprising natural grace.

I make sure to lift my dagger in his line of sight, not intending to retract the blades as I walk off.

'Oh, and Goldie?' He calls once I've made it halfway down the street. I twist around. 'I never got that thank you for saving your life the other night.'

I smile through gritted teeth and mimic him with a curtsy back. 'Thank you ever so much for being so kind as to spare me from a bite.' I turn again but not without hearing his smooth laughter bouncing off the walls as I mumble, 'Pig.'

Chapter Twenty-One

I consider my inability to sleep as part of my routine now. And realizing the extent of what Darius has requested me to do . . . it rocked a part of my mind so completely that the only solution was to go to the stables and pet the horses.

Clad in a white nightgown and cloak, I run the brush along the mane of a white mare. 'If only I had your job,' I whisper, tilting my head as the horse gently nudges my shoulder. 'At least you wouldn't need to worry about collecting a vial of dragon blood.' Or stealing a pendant, or my brothers finding out, *or* the trials.

'Nara,' a surprised voice and one I can recognize in a heartbeat. Lorcan walks in, pulling on the reins of his horse. 'I didn't expect to see you at the stables.'

Ignoring the flutter in my chest, I keep my eyes on the mare and mutter, 'Where did you expect to see me?'

'Out in the gardens, trapping worms.'

I hear the lightness in his voice and sense a smile on his face.

'Frogs,' I correct him with an exasperating sigh. 'I'd be trapping frogs.'

'As a previous trapper, I thought you'd trap anything.'

I turn and catch the scent of cedar on him. Clearing my throat, I say, 'A worm only needs water for it to resurface. A rabbit needs fresh vegetables. Deer are attracted to salt and apples, and a frog ironically love worms and seek damp areas.' He nods with a stare I'd pass as impressed. 'I've captured almost every living thing during my life, but as a trapper, animals weren't a priority compared to creatures.'

He stays quiet. I don't think he knows what to say, maybe because of the coldness in my voice. He might have offered to help my brothers, *for my happiness*, but what about me? Maybe it's all my frustration coming out, when I open my mouth without thinking. 'Do you regret what happened the other night?'

His brows furrow, jerking his head back slightly in shock. But I can see it . . . I can see that he knew this topic would come up. 'The General just doesn't want me distracting—'

'You didn't answer my question.'

He sighs, deep and tired, running his hand over his face. 'No, I do not regret one second of what happened, Nara.'

His answer tugs my heart strings so much it feels like a real ache. He doesn't regret it, but do I? He's the first I've ever kissed; I hate to think I might be well and truly scared.

My breath locks in my chest as he breaks the distance between us. Staring down at me and in a low voice, he adds, 'And I haven't stopped thinking about wanting to do it again.'

Then why did you not defend me in front of the General, I want to voice but can't.

Despite how much I want to become a Venator and follow in my father's steps, I'm already failing before the trial. Lying, working with a shifter to steal from the Queen. I can't even bring myself to tell Lorcan, despite the fact I almost did the other night.

Lorcan tries to divert his gaze from me, taking slow breaths like he wants to resist, and at that moment, I realize I don't know enough about him. Sometimes I think he avoids me or gives me the sense he's holding back.

My teeth sink into my bottom lip as I shake my head. 'I should go,' I whisper, dropping the brush into a bucket. I move past him, then hear footsteps on the wooden floorboards behind as he whirls me around to face him again. He grips onto my elbow, his green eyes flaming in the torchlight.

'Do *you* regret it?' He inches closer, but there's something brewing in his voice, like the question is at once both painful and hopeful. The desperation within his words sears my heart.

'No,' I breathe, still not knowing if I do. His sigh of relief is followed by a crashing of his mouth on mine.

Unlike our first kiss, I'm not shocked into it as he cranes his neck, allowing more access for his tongue to slip in and claim each second they intertwine. My heart thrums, sending me into something I'm not in control of as I bring my hands up to the leather covering his chest then slide them up around his neck.

He's soft and tender enough, like he's guiding me. His forehead presses against mine, and my breathing levels down to a heartbeat as he breaks away, saying, 'Come with me for a meal at the castle tomorrow—' His voice hoarse '—with the Queen.'

I raise my brows, surprised by the invitation that seems to have come out of nowhere, nonetheless I'm intrigued. 'The Queen?'

He nods. 'She thinks of you as highly skilled for a trainee.'

If she saw how unskilled I really am against Darius, then—

I blink at the sudden thought of how unskilled I am when it comes to him. *Idiotic dragon, ruining everything.* Shaking my head with a pensive frown, I ask, 'Won't the General dislike the thought of you inviting me to a meal?'

'The General dislikes a lot of things.'

'Dancing around the question again, Deputy?'

He huffs a short laugh, tipping his head back for a second. 'It doesn't matter what the General thinks when it comes to the Queen.'

True, the Queen has final say in matters regarding the Venators at the end of the day, and I want to say yes, I *have* to say yes. Dining with the Queen means I'll be closer to the pendant—to figuring out how to get it.

I wonder if perhaps Lorcan's invite is fate gifted by Solaris or Crello, though pitiful of me to think that. It's stealing. If anything, I should be punished by the two deities. Unless I'm already to be punished for all the countless things I've done in my life.

Drawing in a breath and seeing it is my only chance, I accept. 'I will see you tomorrow then.'

The edges of his lips rise at my answer, and I slide past him. 'And—' I spin as Lorcan – having stayed in the same position – looks over his shoulder at me. 'Thank you for also helping me with my brothers earlier.'

He dips his chin in a nod. 'You don't need to thank me, Nara.'

'But I want to.' I sigh, and I see that as my cue to turn and walk out of the stables, not knowing how I'd be able to sleep again.

Despite the anticipation of attending a meal at the castle, it came swiftly. I'd mentioned it to Freya within hours of what happened at the stable.

Sitting at the foot of my bed, and blushing at the memory, I cough, as Freya runs her hands through my hair.

She'd insisted on helping me fix it, although there was no need since I'm still in the sleeveless leather attire. But I accepted regardless since I've never had a friend, no one to help me get ready, not even my mother would do my hair. Sometimes she'd brush it, complaining how my long locks always got tangled when I'd climb up trees to look at the world.

'Your hair is golden like the sunsets over Emberwell, Nara,' Freya says, amazed as I stare at her in the mirror, kneeling behind me.

I smile. 'My father thought the same thing. He'd always compliment it even when I'd show up with mud caked on it.'

She looks up, glancing at our reflection, and chuckles, shaking her head. 'If only my father could give me one small compliment . . . at least once.'

My smile withers at the misery hidden behind her words. For the cheerful person that is Freya, it's hard to get glimpses of her hidden sorrows.

'Your father is blind not to see what a wonderful daughter he has,' I say, and her hands cease within my locks as she looks at me with a tilt of her head.

'You're the first person to ever say that to me.'

'And I won't be the last.'

A smile traces her lips as she resumes pinning my hair back in places. It's quiet for a minute or two before a question pops into my mind, a question I've never even thought to ask my brothers despite knowing their answers.

'Can I ask you something, Freya?'

'That's unusual,' she snorts, her mood rising again. 'You never like asking me questions.'

I chuckle then drop my gaze to the floor. After a second, I inhale and say, 'Have you ever experienced being in love with someone?'

I've wondered about love before, but I didn't want to know what it felt like. I cared more about trapping and protecting my brothers, except now, I've grown curious since my time in the city.

Freya sighs as if thinking it over for a second. 'Well . . . once I had a lover, during my time away from this all. He was my first for many things.'

I twist to face her. 'What happened?'

She raises her brows, grabbing my shoulders, and turns me back around. 'We never truly loved each other.' Her fingers collect the sides of my hair. 'I was searching to find myself, and he didn't care for that.'

My lashes lower, flittering over my skin as I wring my fingers together. It's not an answer I expected from Freya. It makes me wonder how one knows the difference between love and false feelings.

'I don't regret it, though,' she adds. 'It taught me a lot. Now I just hope I meet the right person.'

I don't have an immediate response; actually, I don't say anything at all. The concept of love is something I find uncertain.

'All done.' Freya pats the sides of my arms. 'Now, these are my favorite hairpieces, and I usually don't give them out to anyone! But I must say they look gorgeous on you, Nara.'

I lift my gaze to the mirror, lightly touching the violet crystal pins as they shine on each side of my hair, pulling it back into a half updo. Waves plunge down, resting by my waist as I gasp at how she's made my hair go from a matted mess to . . . well, *delicate*.

I turn to her, almost gaping. 'It's yours I—'

She lifts her palm. 'Keep it. I can always find myself a new favorite hairpiece—trust me,' come the words when I frown skeptically.

Recognizing Freya's constant habit of changing her likes and dislikes as well as her hobbies, I mouth the words, *thank you*, and smile as I stand.

'Nara?'

I turn with a hum as Freya's gaze focuses on the window, the golden sunset caressing her dark bronze skin like glistening jewels.

'Do you think the sun ever wants to stay up there in one place?' She asks, taking in steady breaths. 'Or do you think every time it scorches its heat down on us, it's saying how badly it yearns to reach the moon?'

I've never thought of it that way. 'Are you saying that for the sake of Solaris and Crello or because of you?'

She lifts a shoulder. 'Maybe both. I've always loved the history behind our religion. Sometimes I pray to both Solaris and Crello over my future and what it holds.' She draws in her lower lip. 'If I have a purpose or not.'

A long moment passes as she never takes her eyes off the window. It's something I consider that I used to do when I was young, wishing for something greater to come for my brothers and me.

'You don't need to try out every hobby to find your purpose,' I say. 'Sometimes it lies within oneself and in parts of our minds where we've not dared search before.'

Freya doesn't smile, doesn't respond, doesn't move. But her hazel eyes glisten with appreciation before returning to look outside the window.

I leave the room with my words echoing inside my head as I walk down the hallways towards the stairs. I wonder if *I've* found my purpose. If whether being a Venator is that purpose. It's been my dream for so long, yet things are so different to what I thought they would be.

'Lorcan,' I say, breathing a smile as I take the last stair. He stops talking to another Venator, dismissing him as he strolls over. His eyes drift over my hair, the crystals, and then he smiles.

'Permission to compliment, Miss Ambrose?'

'I can't promise I won't roll my eyes.'

He chuckles, holding out his palm. I hesitate before puffing a breath and taking hold of the scars and his calloused touch.

'Then I'll take my chances,' he says as he leans in and whispers, 'you're exquisite, Nara.'

Swallowing the wild warmth of his words, I do manage to roll my eyes, but the smile making its way onto my lips betrays me once he leads me out of the barracks.

Chapter Twenty-Two

Never in my life have I seen a feast so grand as to what has been laid out upon the long table. If I'd felt discomfort entering the palace as it beamed with gold and white marble décor, then I most definitely am on edge now.

Lorcan's demeanor had changed almost in the snap of a branch once we'd entered the dining hall, and the Queen and General led me in silently. The Queen politely showed me to a chair made of delicate oak. Then for half an hour, it was silent, wordless, no form of communication with one another.

'Are you not hungry, Naralía?' The Queen finally asks, sitting at the far end in an oversized red velvet chair. There are no paintings or ornaments in this vast room or in any of the hallways I'd gone down, only mirrors and filigree ceilings.

I run my hands over my knees a little too vigorously as I stare at the Queen sipping on her wine. The fine goblet, gold just like her dress, just like the pearls in her gown, and just like – the pendant.

Realising the impossibility of such a question I answer with, 'I am always hungry, Your Majesty.' And bow my head, ignoring Lorcan and the General's eyes on me from across the table.

She laughs, her obsidian curls bouncing with the rhythm of her voice. 'Then eat. No need to be afraid of us.'

Afraid, no, wondering how to steal from you, yes.

I put on a weak smile, turning to the food in front of me as I begin helping myself to all sorts of meat, bread, platters of cheese, and tarts. Without much thought, I pick up my fork and eat, ravaging each bite.

'Solaris,' the General mutters. 'Child, if you carry on eating like that, you'll choke. Did you never learn table manners?'

I gulp a piece of chicken down and slowly look up at the General's face twisting with aversion. Setting my fork on the side, I say, 'No, I did not, but I'm sure I'd learn quicker than you would with how to be a father to Freya.'

'Watch your tone,' he snaps, his glare smoothing out as a wicked smile creeps in. 'I can see how you are Nathaniel's daughter; you can't keep your mouth shut just like him. At least now, he forever will remain . . . *silent*.'

My stomach plunges as his words sting more than anything I've endured, but anger quickly sweeps in, and I open my mouth to spout my wrath towards him. Except Lorcan clears his throat before I can go any further. I could, he knows that, but his pointed glance stops me, reminding me who else is in the room.

I return to my food, picking up the fork just as the Queen changes the subject. 'Any news on the thief?'

Hoping I don't give any thing away in my face, I try and carve at my chicken. I *have* news. I've seen him too many times now—

'Four reported jewellery stores have been robbed as of recent,' the

General replies. The sounds of chalices and servants bringing further food to the table clink and pound in my ears.

The Queen murmurs pensively. 'Has anyone seen him?' the Queen muses.

Yes, too much for my liking.

'Nara has.'

My fork clangs onto the plate as I look up at Lorcan.

'She even knows of his name,' he continues, cutting his meat. '*Darius*.'

I knew when Lorcan asked me to dine with the Queen, it wouldn't go how I'd wish. It's also why I was hesitant for Freya to tidy up my hair.

And now as the General and Queen share a dry look, they don't seem shocked by the information. Although despite this, they still turn to me, curious for whatever explanation I might have.

'A shifter,' I say softly. 'Said it while the Golden Thief was—' I cut myself off as I focus on my lap and remember how he saved me.

'Protecting you?' Lorcan suggests for me, his tone sounding forced.

I lift my eyes to him, but he looks away just as the Queen chuckles. 'It seems that the thief has taken a liking to Naralía.'

'That is *not* the case.' I shake my head then realize who I'm speaking to. 'Your Majesty . . . He despises what I am just as much as I despise his kind.'

Betrayal echoes in the back of my head. I'm betraying what I am trying to be.

The Queen gives me a long look as she purses her lips. 'Well,' she breathes sharply, tightening her smile. 'It's only a matter of time before we catch him.' Her gaze flickers to the General. 'One of these days, he will slip up—'

'Do you plan on killing him?' I blurt out, surprised by my own question. Ivarron had said how they all wanted him dead. It's what I'd believed since the start, that if they caught him, he'd not last a day in the dungeons. He'd be sentenced to death in a heartbeat. Now I'm not so sure they want that.

Everyone in the room pauses as I brace myself, watching the Queen cock her head to the side. 'I'll see to it when the time comes,' she says casually, but her eyes continually stare like she is studying every inch of me. Interior and exterior. 'Although we do believe he is a leader for the shifters.' Directing her attention to Lorcan and the General again, she adds, 'He might be of use for catching the rest of his kind—'

I drown out the rest of the conversation, focusing on my plate. He might be of use? Would that mean torture if they caught him? If they ever managed to. Despising him is one thing. I know I do. He's a pain, but he can give me what I want, and from what I've witnessed so far, I'm starting to believe he isn't a leader, simply a lone thief with a furball as a sidekick.

And telling them I know more than just his name could jeopardize everything.

'Have you invited Naralía to the Noctura Ball, Deputy?'

Blinking away my thoughts, I glance up as Lorcan freezes at the Queen's question. He sets his goblet down while clearing his throat. 'I haven't had the chance to discuss it with her.' His eyes never leave my face, but I have no idea what they are talking about.

I lean forward, glancing at the Queen. 'I'm sorry, Noctura Ball?'

'Every summer solstice,' the General interjects, 'the Queen invites the leaders from other kingdoms to come and celebrate here in the castle along with other people of high class.' His eyes narrow on me, as he lifts his goblet. 'Commoners, however, do not attend.'

I grind my teeth as I glare at him, but the Queen says in a humorous drawl, 'Erion, aren't you forgetting she is not a commoner? She is a trainee.' Grinning, she plays with her pendant. 'An Ambrose.' When she notices me staring at it, she lets go, adding, 'You are more than welcome to join us.'

My gaze drifts to meet her dark eyes, almost onyx. A ball . . . an occasion where I will not fit in, not in the slightest. 'With all due respect, Your Majesty, I was planning on celebrating with my brothers since they are here visiting me—'

'Then bring them too,' she cuts in, leaning back against the chair as she waves her hand.

'Sarilyn—' The General tries to say in protest as my wide eyes jump between them. Lorcan's expression mirrors mine.

'In honor of Nathaniel.' The Queen's tone has lowered an octave, imbued with authority. 'I am inviting them all to join me at the ball. Whatever objection you might have, Erion, I do not care for it.'

The hall fills with rising tension, momentarily cooled by the breeze flowing through the curtains and the fading light from outside. My shoulders stiffen at how the Queen's words tick the General off as he shakes his head, pegging me with that harshness in his eyes.

Attempting to clear the strange atmosphere, I say quietly, 'I do not have a gown for such an event, nor will my brothers have anything suitable.'

'You needn't worry about that, Naralía. I'll be sure to have Miriam, my lady-in-waiting, help your brothers, and as for you—' She emphasizes, staring at my hair. 'Once supper is over, I'll have someone fetch a seamstress to measure you.'

I nearly choke at all her offers and kindness. It's hard to believe she's capable of such cruelty as the Rivernorth's demise.

'I—' Looking over at Lorcan, his intense stare pierces through me such that I have to take a deep breath when I gaze back at the Queen. 'Thank you for the invitation, I'll be sure to tell my brothers.' It's all I can say, knowing that declining an offer from the Queen would be foolish.

Her lip quirks, the shine of them painted in rouge. 'Now.' She rests her elbow on the arm of the chair. 'Tell me more about your brothers.'

I perk up at that, my heart full just by thinking of them as I begin telling her their names.

Chapter Twenty-Three

Lorcan and the General retreat to the barracks as soon as the meal is over, leaving me alone with the Queen and the seamstress she'd promised to beckon at such short notice.

With the seamstress scowling at me to stand straight, I can't stop staring as the Queen lounges on a plush settee with orange cushions, near the yellow gossamer curtains, colors of Emberwell – bright, fiery and warm.

I watch the seamstress as I straighten out my arm then at the Queen. 'What will the dress be like?' I ask as she swirls the goblet in her hand.

'A surprise.' She grins. 'Noctura Ball, everyone is notified to dress in colors of the fire. It's in honor of the lights that the Isle of Elements will project.' Taking a sip of wine, she points at me. 'But *you*, darling, will dress in something that will enthrall anyone who walks through the palace doors.'

Enthralling? I never thought the day would come when the Queen would treat me far better than most. 'Why are you being so kind to me?' My voice skeptical. It's not as if my father spoke of her as if they were once friends. 'I'm only a trainee, not even a true Venator yet.'

She lowers her goblet, her smile sharp. 'Am I not allowed to be kind to my warriors, Naralía?'

I blanch. 'No, of course, you are. It's just—'

'I know how much Nathaniel adored his children,' she interrupts, and I try to hide my wince at the memory of my father and how I miss him. 'I'm only returning my kindness for his youngest, who seems just as passionate about her duty as a Venator.'

The urge to scoff at myself is almost irresistible when I know passion means nothing, given I'm working with a thief – a dragon, a shifter, an . . . *idiot*.

Nodding slowly instead, I glance at her neck, and then my lips bend into a smile. 'That's a wonderful pendant. I couldn't help but notice it.'

Her hand clasps over it as she tilts her head. Swallowing, I add, 'Is it a family heirloom?'

'No,' she answers in a curious drawl. 'More like a gift given to me.'

'I suppose it must be important to you then,' I say, the words trailing off at the end as the seamstress mutters for me to stop fidgeting again.

The Queen's lip twitches. 'It's quite frankly useless to me.'

'Oh,' I say, puzzled by her answer. 'May I ask why you wear it then?'

'I wear it the same way you are wearing those crystals in your hair.' She rises from the settee, waltzing over to the other side of the room as her gown sweeps behind her.

Deep in thought, I trace my fingers over the crystals. Mine aren't useless to me. They're Freya's. But the Queen seems to have brushed that question off in her own way.

After setting her goblet down, she turns and comes towards me, unclasping the pendant from her neck. 'This pendant, Naralía.' She moves it between her fingers, gold shining over her almost ebony skin. 'Holds a certain history to it.'

Nearly entranced, I study the pendant and the three rivers atop a compass pointing north.

The Rivernorths.

Perhaps her acts of kindness are a cover for what might have happened. Remaining calm even if I already know about the history, I act unsure. 'With the treaty?'

A light chuckle. 'More than that.' She retreats to where she'd set her goblet down, placing the pendant around a mannequin's neck.

And at that it takes me five seconds to scan the room. I can't guarantee she'll remove the pendant again, but it's too much risk to do anything—

'Hold still!' The seamstress hisses from her bent position by my knees.

I scowl back, but the Queen, taking no notice, says, 'You know of the wars before the treaty, don't you?'

I snap my head up at her as she grabs her chalice and turns to walk back to me. She raises her hand, motioning for the seamstress to depart. The seamstress bows, then glares over her shoulder at me before shuffling out of the hall.

I answer, 'Yes.' I stand slightly taller on the stool against the Queen, yet no height can match her powerful stature. 'The Exaree witches and shifters against the sorcerers.'

I'm reminded of my talk with Leira that led me to flee from the tavern, and the eerie words she told me.

The sun blooms again, for she has found her moon—

'A witch and a shifter always go hand in hand.' The Queen

tears me away from my memory of what Leira said. 'Once a witch bonds to a particular shifter, they're allies, confidants, and helpers, which is why the sorcerers never stood a chance, not even the most powerful.'

The Queen exhales a sad, distant sigh. Leira mentioned that shifters helped the witches, and that they felt emotions from others. However, she'd not said they were the type to bond. And the Queen . . . hearing her now explain this, I consider how she despises shifters, has an army of Venators at her disposal to get rid of them, while a witch is to be hanged or burnt at the stake if they dared use their magic.

'Are you a sorceress?' The question sounds so absurd once I ask it, but the Queen only chuckles, flitting her gaze downward.

'I am . . . though one without power.'

A wave of shock pours over me. For a while, I've wondered what the Queen was and why she'd lived this long. I knew she couldn't just be mortal, but her answer opens more questions, wonders, and curiosity. Why is she without power? Did she fight in the war? Does it have to do with the Rivernorths?

But my questions remain unspoken as she looks at my arm. 'My, what a scar you have there.'

I bring it to my chest, an instinct to hide it even if I am standing in front of the Queen.

She doesn't seem bothered nor wonders why I'm hiding it as she asks, 'How did you get it?'

I look at the deep red mark from my palm up my inner forearm. 'A dragon,' I say quietly.

Hiding what had done this was never the answer but the longer I stare at it, the more I think of the day my father died. It may be a distant memory; I can hardly picture the dragon anymore. However, I still can't accept that day.

'I see.' The Queen breathes. 'Well now you are here training to make sure that never happens again.'

I bow, letting my arm drape to the side, keen to still hide it. 'Of course, Your Majesty.'

She raises her chalice, a flicker of a smile that almost seems furtive before she says, 'As you know, we protect those who do not bear the flame . . .' And drinks from it.

The following morning, I rush down the stairs, fiddling with my hands in front of me while reciting the Venator motto, *'we protect those who do not bear the flame.'*

A phrase I should focus on instead of wondering how I am to steal from the Queen.

Saying it once more, I drop onto the last step and stop, slowly drawing my brows together when spotting Lorcan and a few Venators coming out from the weapons room with spears and chains.

'What is going on?' I stroll up to Lorcan, eyeing the other Venators who pass me holding spears and chains.

'Sightings of dragons have been reported up north,' he says, bringing my focus back to him. He sighs, a deep sound that sends sparks of emotions through me. 'I have to leave for a few days.'

A weight presses on my chest, and it's as if someone pushes me back as I see a flash of a memory—when my father used to say his goodbyes.

'Look after everyone for me, Idris,' he'd say when I'd hide in the corner of the cottage, staring as my brother would nod back in a solemn motion.

Turning my head away, I blinked rapidly. 'For how long?' I forced myself to look at him.

'We hope to be back before the ball—' he begins, but another man, flipping a knife as he saunters past, calls for him to follow.

Lorcan's expression is tentative as he looks over my head then at me. 'Goodbye, Nara.' He whispers it out like he knows he doesn't want to leave, and I understand that this is what a Venator does; what we *all* have to do at one point.

'I have to leave, Lía.' My father's words push through once more, to when he'd lower himself to his knees so that he could meet my eyes. *'Try not to get into too much trouble.'* He'd chuckle with all the brightness in his heart, ruffling my hair.

'Try not to be too adventurous while I'm gone,' Lorcan says, and I blink again as I focus on his lips, stretching into a smile, one I can't reciprocate.

He leans in, but I turn my cheek just as his lips brush my skin, and he lets them linger there – my breath heavy with the resemblances of the past and now. Lorcan must think I didn't want a kiss, that I didn't want anything. He rears back, and I don't look at him as he walks away.

Chapter Twenty-Four

It has only been a matter of hours since Lorcan left. I'd trained, listened to Rydan explain why he was the greatest, and then to Link asking me questions about Illias. It's the most I'd heard him speak, but with my head elsewhere, it was hard to act enthusiastic.

'So, are you going to tell me about this Lorcan guy?' Idris probes as we stroll through the streets of Chrysos. After explaining how they were to come with me to the Noctura Ball, Illias was the one most excited out of the three. Idris's grunt of annoyance told me he'd despised the idea of a ball.

I shrug, staring down at the ground, hearing Illias and Iker going at it far ahead of us. 'What is there to tell?' I reply to Idris.

Pleas to the side of us make my head snap to the left. A Venator and a man in tattered robes clasping his hands together as he says, 'I beg of you, just until next week, I promise I'll have the money.'

I frown solemnly. It's the day of tax collections. We'd experienced that day before, the fear of never having enough to pay, the worry of being left on the streets or far worse.

'I know you, Nara,' Idris cuts in, interrupting my stare at the man. 'Illias knows you, Iker . . . well, he knows nothing most of the time, but the three of us can tell something is going on that you won't say.'

My sunken mood was the likely giveaway when I met up with my brothers in the city today. Expelling a breath, I look up. 'Idris, whenever I've told you something in the past, you've either argued with me or given me the silent treatment. Why should I tell you about a guy you'll likely want to scowl at, even if I mentioned it was just a friendship?'

My raised brow makes him frown. 'I wouldn't do that.'

'You would, and you know it.'

He rolls his eyes, as Iker and Illias make their way towards us. 'Look, Nara,' Idris sighs and I turn with curious eyes. 'I want you to know that even if he was more than a friend or—' he finds it hard to say the next word '—if you are in *love* with him, I'm always going to be there for you. Feelings such as these aren't supposed to be battled alone.'

He doesn't see it, but for a second, my eyes go round, not for the use of the word love but because I'd not expected for him to say it so . . . achingly. Once, he'd had a lover but she was taken by a illness too young, the same illness that took our mother as well.

'I only want what's best for you,' he goes on, his blue gaze like mine, glosses over. 'And sometimes my judgment when it comes to people can get in the way of that.'

Idris has never spoken this way to me. We've always argued instead. Stunned, I attempt to respond, but Iker and Illias reach us, and I spot Freya, shouting my name from the other side of the street.

She darts our way, her cloak catching between people as I smile, saying, 'Freya! I never introduced you to—'

'Solaris, don't tell me these are your brothers?' She pants, placing her hands on her hips and smiling at each of them. Then with a squint of her eyes, she starts pointing, 'Iker, Illias, and—' Her head tilts for a second. '*Idris.*'

Surprised she'd guessed them all right, I nod before her smile widens as she says, 'Oh, I've heard such wondrous things about you all! I know Iker loves to write. I once attempted to, though sadly, I'm an awful writer, and then I know that Illias is an artist and—'

'Are you always this excitable?' Idris questions, and I inhale a breath, mentally cursing him for his coarseness, though often I am just the same.

Freya clears her throat, the smile disappearing from her lips as she stares him down and turns to me. 'I see what you meant by grumpy.'

I smother a laugh, and despite Idris's disapproving gaze, Freya doesn't yield. She raises her brows in a challenge, keeping her chin up.

Idris narrows his eyes, baffled, yet it glistens with something else, something *unexpected*, just as Iker snickers. 'It's true, Idris is—'

'Misty!'

My smile wipes itself off my face and eyes grow wide.

No, no, no.

Begging that it's my mind playing tricks on me even if I know it is not. The whole group turns to look behind them, my stomach bubbles with confusion and shock.

Darius, in broad daylight, striding towards us as he nods at each stranger passing him.

How is he—

'There you are,' he says, gesturing his hand at me with a huff. 'It's been such a pain trying to find you, Misty, truly.'

My gaze jumps from Idris to Illias to Iker. Then Freya squinting her eyes and biting her lip as if she can't figure out who Darius is.

What in Solaris is going on?

'Misty, our old horse?' Illias asks, looking at me to see whether he'd understood like he usually does, but not this time.

'Old horse?' Darius jerks his head back with a frown twisting his lips. 'No, no, that's her—'

'Will you excuse us for a moment,' I cut in, as I clutch onto Darius's arm, dragging him away before my brothers or Freya can say a word.

'Strong grip you got there, Goldie.' He laughs, letting his feet drag before I push him around the corner of the street.

'How is it possible—' I shove him against the wall '—you're walking around so freely, and no one is noticing who you are?'

He leans back, kicking his leg up with a casual smile. 'Power of illusion. Right now, everyone around me except you, believes I am someone completely different, sort of like a mask or glamor.'

I've lost all patience. Of course, it's a Merati power – tricksters of the mind. 'And you choose to steal from places without a glamor?'

His eyes shine with roguish charm. 'I'm more memorable that way.'

Ugh.

'Alright, then.' I cross my arms over my chest. 'Let me ask you this then: what are you doing here?'

A dangerous coquettish grin plays off him as he lowers his leg and steps away from the wall. He walks past my shoulder, and I turn with him as he spins, saying, 'To give you this.' Between his index and middle finger, he holds out a note.

I pluck it out of his hands and unfold it. I can just about make out the name Havenwood Tavern and Draggards scribbled down. 'What's this for?'

'It's where I want you to meet me tonight.'

'Tonight?' I shake my head at the insanity of him. 'There is no way will I go anywhere just because you tell me to.'

'It's not a choice, Goldie.' Humorously smirking down at me, he waits a few seconds for me to say something, but a man carrying trinkets and posters in his hands, limps down the road.

'Help us capture the Golden Thief, and we will win a mass of awards from the Queen!,' he yells, sprawling them across the streets, his withered hand shaking, as he passes a poster to Darius with a smile.

'We will catch that thief, don't you worry, sir,' Darius cheers, as the man continues down his path. Darius looks at the poster and nods. 'Whoever the artist is, they're incredible at their work, not a single fault,' he mumbles thoughtfully. 'Even my mask is perfect.'

Unbelievable. 'You're loving all of this, aren't you?'

Huffing a laugh, he folds the poster and tucks it into the pockets of his breeches. 'You mean having people say they will capture the Golden Thief right to my face? Sure, but seeing your face turn red whenever I'm near you is more *enjoyable*.'

Exasperated by his irritating wink, I look to his side and then at the other. 'Where's your little friend?'

'Stealing bread for himself.'

I press my lips together into a scornful smile. 'Nice to see you taught him all your tricks.'

'Only the best.' He grins before another person walks past, carrying jasmine flowers in a basket. Darius looks over his shoulder, pinching one without the lady noticing. He turns towards me and extends it in front of us. 'Here.'

My fingers stretch out to grab it as my brows close together. 'What's this for?'

'You always smell of jasmine.' He shrugs a shoulder, still grinning. 'Take it as a form of my *appreciation* for your help in stealing a prized pendant.'

I scowl at the apparent sarcasm in his tone before raising my brows as I scrunch the flower in my fist and then let the petals fall to the floor.

He watches in humor. 'So terribly rude, Goldie.'

'You're insufferable.'

Chuckling, he closes the gap between us, lowering his head so his eyes align with mine. 'Likewise,' he whispers. His eyes are a shade darker during the day, yet they still glisten in the light. 'But at least I'm civil.'

'Civil?' I repeat with incredulity, standing on my tip toes and leaning into his face. 'If anything—'

His sigh cuts me off, dramatic and full of contempt. 'Goldie, if you're going to give me a reason as to why you think you're in the right, I don't want to hear it. I'd hate to then counter that with why you're actually in the wrong.'

I shake my head, completely lost. 'I still don't understand how people fear you, honestly.'

'Because I'm capable of a lot of things when it comes to protecting myself and Tibith and those who are—' He runs his eyes over me. 'Assets to me.'

Oh . . . Now I understand.

'So, is that why you saved me from a bite?' I ask, and at the use of the word *bite,* any form of amusement or derisive comments leave him as his jaw stiffens. I tilt my head and continue, 'Because I'm an *asset* in your little quest for this pendant?'

'Well done, Goldie.' The words come out harshly, matching his attempt at a smile. 'Earned yourself a little point there Didn't think you'd ever catch on.'

I clench my fists, blood boiling in my system even though I knew that would be the answer. If it was for any other reason, then I'd have to think he actually *had* some sort of heart.

'You know,' I start quietly, but my underlying anger is clear as day. 'I've despised a lot of people in my life, those who came after my brothers, ridiculed them or hurt them in any way, but you?' I look up at the cold, knowing gleam in his eyes, coaxing me to say it. 'I hate *everything* about you as a person and as a shifter. And I promise you, once I get the vial and you get your stupid little pendant, I will hope to Solaris I never see you again in my life.'

'And what a great promise that is,' he whispers with menace. 'I'll see you tonight, *Goldie.*'

I make a low sound in my throat, pushing past him to get away, yet once I'm at the end of the street, I don't know what wills me to look back, but I do.

He hasn't moved from where he was standing, his eyes fixed on the floor. I don't even think he's looking properly until his head whirls to me. And for the slight moment he meets my gaze, the seriousness fades as his lip quirks to form that arrogant smirk.

I roll my eyes and turn back around then feel myself slowly frowning at how that smile seemed forced, not like the ones he always shoots at me.

'Who was that?' Freya asks, her voice oddly entranced as I halt, not realizing I'd made it back to where the group was still waiting for me.

Staring at me as if I've committed a crime – though I'm about to – Illias and Iker tilt their heads, narrowing their gaze while, Idris watches me carefully.

I shake my head. 'Nobody important.' Looking over my shoulder again, I don't see Darius and assume he's gone the other way. But with the thought of his strange reaction, I turn back to my brothers and puff out a smile, wanting, *needing* to forget it. 'Shall we continue?'

Chapter Twenty-Five

I stand outside Havenwood tavern, scrunching the piece of paper Darius gave me into my satchel. Two drunken men stumble out of the wooden double doors, jeering at one another. The foul stench of old mead and heat wafts past me like a gust of humid air.

Darius just had to send me to the Draggards of all places.

Annoyance boils inside of me, and I push past the doors into the hectic tavern. I dodge a flying tankard as it splatters across the walls behind me and huff, coming up from it.

'Hello, there, pretty—'

I lift my hand to the slurring man crossing my path. Cigar and ale reek from his breath, and I shove him out of the way. His swears and insults are drowned out by the fiddle playing. But none of this matters once I see glistening raven hair, a leather jerkin, and a flirtatious grin aimed towards the barmaid.

Slamming my palm against the countertop as I reach him, his head whirls around to me, staring down at my unamused face.

Perching his hip against the counter, he says, 'Care for a drink, Goldie?'

No. 'What are we doing here?'

'We—' he emphasizes, '—are on a mission.'

I look at him with a bored expression. 'We?'

I curse the unwise part of me for coming here.

'Well, by we, I mean mostly you.'

Staring at him, like I've heard wrong, I wait for him to say otherwise. He doesn't, so silently, I turn to walk away, but his hand snakes around my waist, twirling me back to him.

He's tall and sturdy. I give him that.

'Where are you going, Goldie?' He murmurs with a smirk.

I try to squirm out from his hold. 'Back to the barracks! I'm already having to help you steal a pendant – from the Queen might I add –' I raise a brow. 'And I'm not going to help you steal something else. Now let go of me.'

He does, and I huff, dusting my cloak off as if he's messed it up.

'Come on, it will be fun,' he cajoles. 'It'll be great practice for the real thing.'

'The real thing wouldn't happen if it wasn't for your blood.' My lips pucker with vexation as I glance around. 'You know I could easily cut you and drain it from your body.' It would have been simpler to do that from the start.

I look back at him, and his brow rises with delight. 'I think you've unlocked a new kink in me, Goldie.'

I tut in disgust. 'What do you even want to steal that requires us to be in a tavern?'

His arm slides across the counter, his face a meter away from mine as he cocks his head over my shoulder. 'See that guy over there.'

I turn, looking at a table in the far corner of the tavern. Men surround it, watching a game of backgammon, with one in particular, staring at the players with an intense frown.

'Name's Tarron Gurn,' Darius continues. 'Owner of this place though he loves to take money from his workers to fund his considerable greed.'

I glance back at him and scrunch my nose into a smile. 'Sounds just like you.'

He huffs a laugh from his nose, not at all offended. 'He has a backroom, guarded by many of his men, and no one's allowed through except the women he invites back there.'

From the way Darius says all this, it seems he's stolen from him before or at least thought of doing so.

'He's a tricky man to get hold of, but he'll approach you if he's interested in you.'

'So, you want me to get his attention?'

He nods. 'He has valuables in that room, including an emerald crystal, worth a lot of money.' His brows rise as if for emphasis. Everyone around us continues drinking and dancing, unaware of who is in front of me right now. 'So, are you in, Goldie? Or are you going to try to walk away again?'

My brows squish into an offended frown. I look to my right as a barmaid slides a tankard across to someone, but I snatch it off the counter before he can grab it. He yells something at me as I turn to Darius and shout, 'How dare you break my friend's heart!' Launching its contents all over him.

His eyes widen as he wipes his face with his glove. People turn to us; some even stop dancing. Darius glances around and chuckles as he leans in with a whisper, 'What are you doing?'

A smile lifts at the side of my lips. 'Getting his attention.'

I reach for the another tankard and do the same, before he can react. 'And that—' I say, shaking off the mead from my fingers. 'Is for you just being you.'

He's wholly soaked as he rubs the pad of his thumb along his bottom lip and chuckles.

Smug, I flick a brow up and turn my back to him, moving toward one of the chairs near Tarron.

Tarron's eyes focus on me as he runs a hand over his beard, and all I do is sit and wait.

Barely any time passes as I look up to a standing Tarron before me. Sconces gild his long blonde hair, and half his face is shadowed before he sits down opposite me.

'That was quite a scene over there.' He gestures to the bar. I don't look as I lean over the table and smile.

'He had it coming.' There is no lie in that.

He chuckles, tapping his dirt-filled fingers on the surface of the table. 'I've never seen you here. What is your name?'

'Misty,' I answer without missing a beat, and he frowns. 'My mother loved out of the ordinary names.' If he's about to reply, I do not let him as I brush my fingers over his wrist, and flutter my lashes up at him. 'What's yours?'

His eyes shoot down to my hand, and then he gives me a crooked grin. He sees that as a sign I'm interested. My pulse quickens with excitement and adventure. Flirting is something I'm never good at.

Tarron starts to ask me more questions about where I am from, if I would like a drink, and then talks about how proud he is of this tavern. I attempt to look interested, my hand on his, laughing at the slightest joke he makes, then biting my tongue when he mentions that women shouldn't be Venators.

After a while, I tire of this not going anywhere. I lean over the table, and my eyes skate over to Darius's eyes on me, his jaw looks tense as I whisper in Tarron's ear, 'Shall we get out of here?'

Tarron's smile grows hideous and vile. His response is to rise from his chair, gesturing for me to follow him.

As Tarron pushes open a backdoor, Darius watches me disappear with Tarron.

Chapter Twenty-Six

Darius is right. As soon as we enter through a backdoor into a gloomy hallway full of gruff men, Tarron leads me into another room at the end.

I glance at the candles scattered along the desk, bookshelves encrusting the stone walls, and a decanter. There is a bed to the left, large enough to fit five kings, and as my gaze searches for the crystal, I don't see it. Gold dragon crested coins spill from a pouch on the desk before Tarron blocks my view with a silver chalice in his hand.

He hands it to me, and I smile. 'Is this where you live?' I ask, trying to buy time.

His brittle laugh makes my skin crawl. 'Yes,' he says as if I should be impressed.

I nod slowly but don't drink the wine from my chalice. Awkward tension rises in the air as Tarron nears me, his green eyes feasting on me like I am his dinner. I dodge him, moving out of the way as his hand comes to my waist. 'Why don't you show me around?'

He looks startled, letting out a short chuckle. 'Or I could show you something else if you want.'

Disgust swirls in my gut. *No, thank you.*

I place the chalice down on his desk and tip my head to the side as I stroll toward him, trying to be swift and seductive. 'How about—' My fingers tiptoe up to his arm, '—you close your eyes, and I surprise you instead?'

His eyes glaze over with lust, turning wild as I take his chalice and down the wine inside it. I unlace the top part of my corset, then pause and raise my brow for him to close his eyes.

He obeys in a second, and I smile, lifting the chalice as I strike him in the head with it. The bed dips and creaks as he thumps down onto it.

Thank Solaris for that.

I look around cautiously and drop the chalice as I run over to his desk and search through drawers. Coins rattle against the wood before I switch to the bookshelves, wondering if they're hidden somewhere amongst the books.

Trying to reach the top shelf, I step back and slam straight into the chest of someone.

I spin to face Tarron, wide awake.

My eyes jump from the empty bed to his furious face.

'That was quite some surprise.' He rubs the side of his head. '*Misty*, if that is even your real name.'

I should have hit him harder.

'What are you, a thief?' He has me backed against the bookshelf. I eye the door and amuse myself with the idea of hitting him in the crotch. But he grabs me by the elbow and wraps his other hand tight around my waist. It blinds me with pain as his arm digs into my skin. 'You want to know what I do to thieves like you?'

Air from my lungs cuts off, and a low gasping sound emits from my throat before his mouth is on mine. His tongue is like a lizard's, flicking in and out of his mouth, as I try to press my lips together to block it out.

I press my hands against him, fighting off the taste of alcohol on his lips.

He jerks away with a grunt, and I slide my dagger out from my sheath, raising it in front of me to warn him not to come any nearer.

He dabs his bottom lip with his finger, then draws it back to find blood. 'You bit me!'

'I'll do much worse,' I spit as I inhale every bit of air back into me. As he flies into a rage, I look to the door. Darius bursts through as planks of wood break off, and behind him, I am shocked to see all of Tarron's men lying unconscious on the floor.

Show off.

Darius notices my lip; it must have Tarron's blood on it. With that, he's a mass of wrath and fury as his stare drifts from mine to Tarron's.

'Who are you people?' Tarron demands. I keep my blade out, in case he tries to attack but his face slowly pales as if he's about to pass out. He fumbles backward, stuttering as he whispers, 'The Golden Thief.'

Darius must have dropped his glamor.

'No—please,' Tarron begs; saliva splutters out of his mouth as he looks between us and crouches onto the floor. 'Please don't hurt me. Take whatever you want, money, jewels, anything!'

Darius hums and smiles, delighted that his name inflicts that much fear in someone he's not yet touched. He stalks forward, his smirk a warning that he is not one to mess with as he keeps his composure. Yet as the seconds drag, I wonder if he's waiting to strike.

'What I want—' He lowers himself to Tarron's level '—is for you to shut down this tavern, pay every barmaid in here what they deserve, and then leave the Draggards for good.'

So, Darius wants more than just the crystal. He's seeking justice.

'And—' Tarron swallows. 'And if I don't?'

Darius raises his hand to the side of Tarron's face. What would seem to be a sensuous move isn't, as a flame ignites from Darius's gloved finger. 'Then, I'll make you wish you complied.'

Tarron winces, crying out as the flame makes contact with his skin.

Darius withdraws his finger for a moment. 'Now apologize to the young lady.'

'I'm—I'm sorry,' Tarron whimpers as he looks at me. The burning panic pinches around his eyes, but I stay still, not uttering a single word as to whether I accept it or not. It's best I keep it to myself.

Darius stands up and reaches for a wooden box hidden between books on the top shelf. He opens it and takes out an emerald crystal, the shape of my palm.

I pull a face. He knew where it was this whole time.

Oh, how he aggravates me.

He walks over to me, throwing the crystal up in the air and catching it before he grabs me by the elbow and stops to look back at Tarron. 'One last thing,' he says, eyeing Tarron up and down with a mischievous smile that spells trouble in every way possible.

Cackles and whistles swarm the air throughout the tavern as Darius and I watch Tarron walk into the center of the room *naked*.

My face contorts into a tight wince, and I look at Darius. 'Was that necessary?'

He nods, drinking his mead. 'Always.'

'So, is that how everyone fears you? You make them strip and embarrass themselves in front of a crowd?'

He chuckles, mouth closed, and shrugs. 'Most of the time, but people tend to spread other rumors. Frankly, I love hearing the ones where I turn into a raging dragon beast and slaughter them.'

Frankly those rumors are pathetic. I roll my eyes and study him. 'Well, would you?'

'Only if it comes to it.' He winks at me, and I frown. 'Like I've said before, Goldie, it's not fun killing someone if I'm not hunting them down.'

'And who have you hunted so far?'

It takes him a moment for my question to hit him. He looks straight ahead, partly lost within himself. 'Everyone except the people who deserve it the most.'

I don't realize how close we are until his arm brushes my chest. 'And what is stopping you from hunting them?'

'Nothing,' he answers and takes another swig. 'Killing just doesn't seem satisfying enough.'

I don't know why that answer surprises me or why I want to know who else he wants to hunt, but I do.

His gaze falls back on me, and his eyes rove over my face. I'm startled when his thumb grazes over my bottom lip. 'Did he hurt you?' He's not asking, he's commanding me, in the softest manner possible, to say yes or no.

The touch of warm leather has me breathing out heavily. 'What does that matter to you?' I say in a taut whisper, aiming the best hostile stare I can muster at him.

His thumb stills before he yanks it away. 'You're right. It does not.'

A weird moment drifts by us, and I shake my head, changing subjects. 'You know, I still don't understand why you just couldn't have done it yourself. You incapacitated his men easily, knew where the crystal was, and scared Tarron within seconds.'

'You also accepted my task with ease; otherwise, you would have put up more of a fight or not even showed up tonight.'

I glower. 'What's your point?'

He places the tankard down on the table out in front and narrows his eyes at me. 'My point is that you crave something else that isn't included in the title of a Venator.'

My back tenses and I act impatient and flustered by the idea that he might be right. 'May I remind you that I am only doing all of this for my brothers. You don't know me, and you never will, so stop making assumptions.'

His lip kicks up. 'I don't have to know you to see that deep down . . . you hardly even trust your own people.'

I laugh scornfully as a form of defense. 'I'm leaving.' I shoulder past him, clenching my fists to the side as I ignore catcallers.

'Goldie,' Darius says, and stupidly my body turns before my mind can decide not to. I dread what he will tease me about next. 'I find it incredible how you weren't afraid to throw a drink in my face or trick Tarron into taking you through that backdoor.' He slowly grins. 'Too bad you're still that rude Venator who tried to capture me.'

I try desperately not to smile. 'There will never be a moment in the day when I don't want to throw a drink in your face,' I say, and then disappear into the crowd.

Chapter Twenty-Seven

My sword clashes against Link's, sending him back onto the grass. He groans, sweat clinging to his golden-brown strands. 'Do you always have to go so hard?'

'Sorry,' I mumble, pulling him from the ground as the sun warms the skies in a tangerine light. 'I guess I'm just on edge with the trials coming up.'

'I find it hard to believe you're on edge about that.'

Truthfully, it's because it's been three days since Lorcan's departure. It left me somewhat out of sorts. I hate admitting that I'm worried because then it means I care more than I should. And yes, I know I did or . . . do, but that is exactly why I didn't want to involve myself with anyone while I'm focusing on becoming a Venator.

Except that is out of the question now I'm helping a thief – a thief who is a shifter.

'Missing Lorcy?' Rydan strolls up to us, two blades in each of his hands as he wiggles his brows at me.

A slight roll of my eyes. 'Here to irritate us, Rydan?' I ask.

'You didn't answer the question.' He grins, and I scrunch my nose at him. 'If it helps, I too miss him dearly. Especially when he raises his voice at me.'

The dramatic hand on his heart says otherwise, or potentially he *does* miss Lorcan just to annoy him.

'There's nothing to worry about, Nara,' Freya says from the ground, sitting cross-legged. Picking off the grass and toying with it in her hands, she hums. 'Venators go on missions all the time. It's how Lorcan met you, isn't it?'

It is, but it doesn't mean it's safe. Our village was under attack by a dragon when I initially met him. Not that I don't have faith in Lorcan, Solaris knows I do, but it's something I've always feared since my father's days as a venator, when he'd leave us. Whether we'd receive word from someone else that he hadn't made it or if he'd appear through our cottage doors, safe and sound.

'You know what you should be worried about?' Rydan lilts, swinging his swords in a circular swooping motion. 'Those creatures lurking around.'

I lower my blade, my whole face blanking. 'The new ones?'

He nods rather chirpily as Freya asks, 'How do you ever find out all of this?'

'We live in a place full of Venator leaders talking about their daily missions. It's not hard to eavesdrop on certain conversations.'

'What—' Link starts though his voice sounds relatively small before clearing his throat. 'What did they say?'

'Two new deaths just off the west side of Lava Grove.'

Deaths. Why are we never informed of this? 'Is that all they said?'

One of Rydan's shoulders rises as he pouts in thought. 'That's all I gathered, though it's odd, isn't it?'

'What is?' Freya probes, a worry line on her forehead.

'How there are so many deaths, yet their bodies seem to disappear completely, and everyone just . . . forgets about them.' Rydan shudders, but the words leave me in a loop of pensiveness. 'I'd hate to encounter one like Adriel and Oran did.'

I don't think many would want to encounter said creature; on the other hand, I do.

While Freya sits in the mess hall dining away, I'm up in the chambers, sitting on my bed and staring at the door, thinking, processing, wondering about the creatures.

A trainee is a trainee. They don't have as many rights as a sworn-in Venator would, but knowledge of these creatures – of these deaths is something I firmly believe we need to know in order to protect ourselves.

I had weighed up my options while plaiting my hair to the side and placing my double-ended blade against my sheath.

One, these creatures seem to prey on human flesh at night, which means now is the time they'd surface.

Two, Adriel said it looked as though they were blind, just like a rümen, and everyone knows their weakness is at the nape of their neck – the softest part of their scales. If it is anything like a rümen, I can weaken it.

Meaning, I'm setting out to trap one.

Outright irresponsible of me to do so, and perhaps I'm acting upon impulse simply because it's a form of adventure for me, which is why I'm so prone to accept anything no matter the difficulties.

Gulping in a breath, I shoot up from the bed and swing the door open, only to freeze as Lorcan stands there, fist in the air as if about to knock.

Oh, my Solaris.

'You've returned,' I breathe. Relief stirs inside of me, yet awkwardly, I don't know whether to hug or kiss him. I choose neither as he lowers his fist and nods.

'We managed to hunt down a few fledglings—'

I hold back from widening my eyes, my chest pounding. Fledglings are just the equivalent of barely a child.

'Is something wrong?' he asks.

I blink from my stupor and shake my head in a lie. Something *is* very wrong because the knowledge of fledglings being hunted down makes me . . . *distressed*. I don't like it, even if, as a future Venator, that is what my duty holds.

With a short nod, his other hand from behind him comes out, holding something dark and leathery. 'Well—I picked up something along the way.'

Taking a good look, I stare down as he unfolds his palm, showing me . . . a fingerless glove.

'I tried to return your old one, but I figured you deserve a newer glove.'

For the scar I always try and hide.

Wordless, I'm not sure what to say as he dips his chin in askance. I glide my hand up from the side and give it to him. I'm aware of my whole body, breathing too harsh, then too soft, and lastly uneven as he places the glove on my hand, letting the tips of his fingers deliberately linger on my skin for a minute longer.

My eyes flicker to the leather extending up to my elbow, and I half-smile as I wiggle my fingers. The leather stretches as I close and open my fist.

'Were you afraid that day?' Lorcan asks. He points to my glove. 'The day this happened?'

'I was,' I confess, making his eyes narrow slightly.

'Was?'

'I made a promise to myself I wouldn't be.' I sigh, dropping my hand to the side. 'I don't like the idea of being afraid of anything.'

The candles from the hallway light the feathers of his russet hair before he nods slowly. 'Well, you must fear something at least.'

'Just because I don't like the idea of fear doesn't mean I don't have it. I just don't like showing it.' Or telling anyone of them. I tend to hide emotions, though, oftentimes I've let it get the best of me, if not always. Particularly anger. I turn the question around. 'What do you fear?'

'Losing,' he answers after mulling it over for a second.

'At what?' I muse. 'Sparring against Rydan?'

Not even a hint of laughter in his face, my joking expression fading as he avoids my eyes. 'Losing things I've valued in life.' He sighs sharply from his nose. 'I've already lost a lot. Some things to certain situations and others to someone—' He pauses with a wince.

'Someone?' I repeat, prompting him to try and say more.

His gaze meets mine in a fierce forest blaze. 'Someone you could consider family.'

The way in which he says family unnerves me. Nonetheless, I lean the side of my body up against the door frame and say softly, 'Family or no, we all lose something at some point. It's whether we grow from the pain or carry it with us for the rest of our lives.' Mine was always the latter . . .

That intensity in his eyes leaves, dialing down to his usual calmness, until he looks at my thigh strap and chooses to change topics. 'Are you going somewhere?'

I straighten up. 'No, I—'

'Trapping frogs?' His voice is a flicker of humor.

'Something like that,' I murmur. 'But I realize it's getting late—'

'Since when has that stopped you?'

Since a likelihood of death.

And now I realize it truly is stupid of me to go out searching for a dangerous creature.

It never stopped you before, a small voice in my head says, but I now know the risk goes beyond trapping a criminal or a rümen.

'I'm just exhausted from all the training,' I answer vaguely. Part of which is true.

'I see.' The edge of his lip turns downward. 'Then I will leave you to rest, Miss Ambrose.'

I hope my grimace isn't noticeable at the formal title with which he addresses me. There are moments he does it teasingly, as do I, moments where I've said it to him in a bid to stop anything going further, but now it's almost done in disappointment.

'Wait,' I say just as he turns to walk away. He faces me again, and I wave my gloved hand. 'Thank you for the glove, it—' I take a breath. '—it means a lot.'

He gives a curt nod, hesitating on his feet before leaving me as I facepalm at the way I can't handle a situation with someone I actually, for once, like.

Chapter Twenty-Eight

The days went by quick, and the Noctura Ball came around, and its vision was remarkably breathtaking. Having been inside the castle, I'd never entered the throne room, and now, with the violins playing, people flood the hall, dancing in bright orange and yellow dresses.

Queen Sarilyn, wearing a beautiful billowing red gown, looks on from the golden marble dais. It's strange not seeing her in her usual colors, and I notice that she isn't wearing the pendant.

The gown she had gifted me is a delicacy I never thought I'd be able to wear, a world away from my usual tunics, corsets, and leggings. Layers of gold in glistening silk droop down to the floor, trailing behind me just like the off-shoulder sleeves, draping freely and showing my arms as I move them around to touch the sweetheart-cut bodice.

My hair cascades over my back in a half up half down that Freya clipped earlier with pearls and thin braids entwining within strands. Idris was the first to gape at how different I looked. He didn't know what to make of it, neither did he fancy the fine yellow tunics he and my other brothers had to wear.

All in all, I liked the change, the feel of the dress, my rose-stained lips, and the shimmers Freya had dusted over my hair.

And now, loitering by the golden pillars of the hall, Iker mumbles how bored he is to Freya and Idris, while Illias makes no comment, staring straight into the middle of the floor. I follow his gaze, finding that it's not the floor he's focusing on. It's Link.

Unable to help my smile, I turn and nudge him. 'Ask him to dance.'

That jerks Illias out of his daydream as his wide brown eyes shift to me. 'Nara, I can't possibly do that—'

'There's no harm in trying. Besides, I know Link, and I'm sure he'd be thrilled if it's you asking him.' Link had shown a keen interest in my brother since the moment I introduced them, along with the million questions he'd ask me, mainly about Illias despite his denial.

'As long as he is no Kye—'

'He is most definitely *not* a Kye.' My brow lifts. Kye never deserved my brother's love.

Illias beams at me, bending down to kiss my cheek before rushing into the crowd. I chuckle softly, watching as he approaches Link and bows. Even from here, I can see Link's cheeks flush crimson, as he accepts my brother's hand.

'Solaris.' A soft gasp escapes Freya, rushing to stand beside me, and in a whisper, she grips my gloved wrist, saying, 'Rulers of other kingdoms are here.'

I screw my forehead, searching the crowd before looking back at Freya. She jerks her head to the left as the ruby jewels in her updo shimmer much like her dress. 'That's the Sea King, ruling all of Undarion and its water creatures.'

Subtly turning to look in the direction where Freya points, I watch as a few people of high class laugh alongside a man with short, white-frosted hair. Skin kissed by summer in a dark bronze gleam, with a crown made of lapis lazuli shards atop his head.

'I've only spoken to him once, before I left my father,' Freya says. 'But a word of advice, don't tell him Selkies are better than Mermans.'

Now I want to.

'Oh, and those.' She moves her gaze to the other side of the throne room. 'Phoenix warriors of Aeris.'

I gulp as I stare at the three warriors, all women with their sleek ebony hair braided down to the waist. Red armor coats them with the crescent of a gold phoenix on their chest plates.

They look wild and spiritedly beautiful; with their rose-tinted skin and an ethereal shimmer to them. Outshining the entire place, the one in the middle locks her gaze with mine. Sharp features contour her face despite her smile, then someone else comes into view, and my body ignites.

Lorcan, in his Venator armor, except this time, donning a red cape and showing that he is the second in command.

He stops in front of us, blocking the sight of the Aeris warriors as he beholds me. 'You're magnificent,' he exhales, like he is genuinely out of breath.

My heart speeds in my chest, but I can feel Idris's gaze on us, causing me to say unequivocally, 'You know I'm not the biggest fan of compliments.'

Lorcan doesn't take notice of Idris. His lip quirks into that white shine of a smile. 'Well, I like giving them to only one person in this very room.'

Idris coughs, moving closer. My heart now races, even more, this time with worry over Idris's instant protective mannerisms.

'Idris!' Freya jabbers out, hooking her arm around his and attempting to lead him away. 'Have I told you how fascinating it is that you make weapons?' She looks over her shoulder at me with a small smile, and I titter in appreciation.

'Once or twice,' Idris grumbles.

Freya scolds him. 'You don't have to be so moody about it you—'

'Deputy Halen,' a woman's voice with a slight accent says as Freya walks away, making me swirl my head to meet with the Aeris warriors.

The one who'd looked at me and smiled stands in the middle of the other two, shaking hands with Lorcan as he says firmly, 'Hira, a pleasure seeing you here again.' He turns to me. 'This is Naralía Ambrose, a Venator trainee.'

Her gaze traces over me, slow enough to make one feel intimidated but not with ill intent; but rather with her deep curiosity. I always assume people will recognize my last name and correlate it with my father, but instead, she asks, 'I suppose we will see you for the Venator tests?'

My mouth parts, but I'm not sure how to reply. In just a few months so much has happened. Now meeting an Aerian – a phoenix isn't something I could conjure even in my wildest dreams. All I had ever heard is that they live an immortal life, but that didn't mean they aged wisely in phoenix form, and at some point, there's a rebirth from ashes. Hira's firm lines around her lips, the taut expressions which are yet edged with natural charm, tells me she's possibly hundreds of years old.

'She's one of the best to succeed,' Lorcan gloats, even if my confidence had dwindled lately. His gaze drops to my hand and the glove I'd not taken off, before the corner of his lips crease upwards.

But on Hira, her smile doesn't quite reach her deep-set fire eyes.

'Then we look forward to seeing her there.' She and her peers excuse themselves, waltzing off. I know that rulers dislike one another, yet now that they are forced to be civil, Hira's reaction to the trials makes me wonder if she agrees with them.

Freya doesn't. I always knew that. She tells me how it saddens her to even kill a dragon, but if she mentioned that to the General, I don't want to know how he'd react.

Wanting to rid myself of these trial thoughts, I tilt to speak to Lorcan when something in my periphery catches my attention. I turn to face the dance floor, and thinking my eyes are deceiving me again, I squint, holding in a curse word as Darius breaks through the dancing crowd. It was just how he appeared that day with my brothers. Grace and elegance shadow him as he waltzes in our direction, dressed in a blood-red tunic with gold thread bordering the sides.

With a cheery smile, he brings out his hand to meet Lorcan's, ignoring my stupefied countenance. 'Archer Fipps, a merchant from the city—'

Archer.

While Lorcan greets him back, a frown creeps up on my face recognizing that name – wait.

The memory of the time I'd gone to visit Leira at the Draggards comes back at full speed:

'That's not how we speak to people, Tig. You should know that by now.' The man – Darius – had come up beside me right when I'd wanted to take that goblin, to free him.

'Archer,' I remember Tig mumbled back that day. *'Always a delight when you visit.'*

Piecing it all together, I realise it was him. He'd used his Merati powers, just how he'd done recently in the Chrysos District to everyone except me.

Blinking back into focus, I look at him and the gold chips that glisten in his eyes, which he's allowing only me to see. 'An exquisite evening, don't you think?' he says to us.

My lips snarl, wanting to shout every insult in the book at him. How does he have the nerve to show up when the Queen, who'd said only the other day that we would catch him soon, stands in this very same room? Even if a Merati can trick you and do everything Darius is doing right now to everyone around him, the tattoos are always a giveaway. They never disappear, no matter what, although whenever I've been around Darius, he'd always worn gloves, except tonight he isn't, and there is no sign of any tattoos? Can it be because he holds all three powers? None of it makes sense.

'What part of the city are you from?' Lorcan asks, and I can sense the slight suspicion rising in his voice.

Darius doesn't falter, not even a little bit. 'The south.' He then chuckles. 'But those dragons can be a right old nuisance, can't they?'

I cough out a laugh at the same time he says that and clear my throat as Lorcan and Darius both look at me. 'So, Archer Fipps?' I crane my neck, staring at Darius. 'Who named you, your father?'

'No.' He purses his lips, hiding the smile that wants to break out. 'My mother.'

Annoyance bubbles in my throat before he slants his head and that smile finally comes through. 'What is your name, Miss?'

Solaris be damned.

It's inevitable. I'd hid my name from him for as long as I could, and now, he sees an opening to figure it out.

I want to tell him to stop grinning and to leave me alone. But I can't, and sensing Lorcan's eyes on me as if wondering why I'm taking so long to answer, I give in, hating every second. 'Naralía,' I mumble bitterly.

'Nara-lee-ah,' Darius stretches out my name, rolling each syllable off the tip of his tongue. 'A name one might consider royal.'

I consider quipping back despite knowing that it will not help if Lorcan notices something is off – that's if he hasn't already, when the tempo of the music changes. It's lighter, and people's excitable chatter gravitates to the dancefloor.

Darius's gaze wanders to the crystal chandelier shining down onto the center of the floor. 'Do you mind?' He says, returning his gaze to Lorcan and holding out his palm for me.

I don't even glance at Lorcan. I scowl and grind my teeth in answer to what Darius is suggesting. 'Yes,' I say, grabbing Lorcan's hand instead and feigning a smile. 'He minds.' And without looking back, I let Darius's outstretched palm hang there as I take Lorcan with me to the center of the hall.

I regret it, however, the second I stop and face Lorcan's inquisitive gaze. I'm not one to dance, I can hardly move in this dress, and Lorcan's question does not help.

'Is there a reason you declined to dance with that man?'

Looking to the side, I watch Darius stroll to meet another woman beaming at him as she accepts his hand far too readily. 'I'm not up for dancing with strangers,' A feeble tone slips out of me as I flit my stare back to Lorcan.

He lowers a brow in caution as both of us stand still. 'But that's what this dance is all about.' He gestures to everyone around us and the women twirl, leading off to a different partner.

Stifling a groan, I shake my head. 'This was a mistake, I don't know this dance—'

'I'll guide you.' He closes the distance between us, and my chest seizes up as he lifts his palm.

Watching others use theirs to lightly touch their partners, I reciprocate. The smooth and soft music serenades the hall as Lorcan nods once and begins circling, our hands still touching, leather against his calloused skin.

'People are staring at us,' I whisper as we bow together. Everyone always had a habit of staring at me in the wrong way, in the *judging* way, but these seem more like looks of awe.

'They're staring at you,' he says with a curl of his upper lip, and I look around in surprise. 'You are the only person in gold. Archer was right; not only is your name like royalty, but so is your appearance.'

I get an overwhelming drop in my stomach at the mention of Archer, and I steal a glance over Lorcan's shoulder. Darius doesn't take his eyes off us while he dances with that woman. Quickly snapping my head back to Lorcan, a tight smile blooms on my lips. 'What is this dance again?'

'A tradition everyone does on the night of Noctura Ball. We switch partners on the beats of the drums.'

My breath squeezes from me when his arm wraps around my waist, and the other grasps my hand, and he switches me into a different position.

'Though I'm reluctant to let you go,' he murmurs.

'Then don't.' And I mean it, hoping he continues to dance with me, so Darius doesn't get the chance. But he chuckles, moving us now in almost a square, one step, two steps, three—

'That's not how it works,' he says, while I'm busy trying not to tread on him. 'Unless there's another reason why you are so hesitant to switch partners.'

My eyes lift to meet his cautious gaze. 'Like I said, I don't like the idea of dancing with someone I don't know.' Or, in this case, an annoying dragon.

Lorcan doesn't look convinced. He parts his lips to speak, but the drums beat twice, and he lets go of me. 'Spin to your left,' he whispers as another woman in a blood-orange tulle dress swivels towards him.

Numbly, I do the same, partnering up with someone new – I have no clue who he is. But he smiles, repeating all the previous movements I did with Lorcan. I don't know if I'm doing all the steps correctly and oblivious to the small mindless words of *what is your name?* that each person I switch to asks me. I'm only focusing on who is drawing ever closer.

Darius.

Our eyes lock in-between every partner we whirl towards, and I swallow with my heart in my throat. With each twirl, I bow to a new stranger, the music flowing, the Queen watching me through narrowed eyes until . . . until I'm facing the roguish expression of Darius.

'You look—' His gaze roams over my gown as we bow, and then he smiles. 'Hideous.'

I roll my eyes as I raise my hand to his. The tips of my fingers – not covered by the glove – feeling the warmth of his skin.

'No compliment towards me, *Naralía*?'

Never.

'*It's Nara*,' I reiterate as we turn. 'And I will never compliment someone like you. Your head is already big enough. I'm surprised it doesn't drag you down.'

He chuckles brightly as we switch hands and glide the other way. 'You're right. Tibith sometimes has to hold my head upright.'

I have to give it to him. He doesn't care about such insults. Life seems like a breeze, no wonder he's always ready for fun. 'What are you doing here anyway? Isn't this too much of a risk?'

'I've taken a lot of risks lately, Goldie.' Another bow and specks from the chandelier flash upon his features. 'This just happens to be my wildest one yet.'

I frown at the way he says that, without a hint of his familiar, mocking smile. Trusting someone who is on the path to becoming a Venator is a risk. But I have already taken too many risks myself, and it all began because of Darius. 'How do you even know this dance?'

He grips my waist, bringing me in, and my chest knocks against his, too close for comfort. 'I know a lot of things, unlike you.'

An icy shard of anger impales me. As we begin moving to the music, I clamp my heel down on his boot, hard enough to dent the white marble beneath it. It's no mistake; I wasn't being clumsy . . . I did it on purpose. And his strained groan makes me smile, until his eyes dance with mirth, nodding as if admitting he deserved it.

Something that's been on my mind comes up when I glance at his hand. 'Why don't you have any shifter tattoos?'

Amber eyes flicker to my hand. 'Why are you covering up your scar with a glove?'

Hesitating, I remember he'd seen it the day I fought him, but I quickly recover. 'Why do you care if I cover it up or not?' He's deflecting why he doesn't have tattoos, and I know I won't get an answer anytime soon.

'Because the dark leather doesn't favor your gown.'

I make a face, albeit an irked one, at his self-amusing words. 'You're—'

'Handsome?' He grins. 'Thank you, Goldie.'

I scoff at his arrogance. It's like he wants me to despise him.

'Ambrose!' Rydan says cheerfully, appearing to the side of us when the drums sound. 'I know the woman is supposed to twirl to a different person, but I figured I'd switch it up.' He presses his lips into a smile, placing a hand to his chest. 'You are most welcome.'

I've never grinned so much or been so pleased to see Rydan approach me. Eager to switch, I lurch forward but Darius blocks me as he turns and offers instead, 'Why don't you dance with someone more desirable? Nara, here, is anything but that.'

Oh, he did not.

Fury singes the arches of my ears as I go to protest and insult Darius back, but Rydan narrows his eyes. 'You seem familiar—' His gasp cuts his words off as if he's solved something. 'Wait, you are the flame spewer champion, aren't you!'

I glance at Darius as he chuckles with obvious pride. It's despicable how he is out here fooling everyone, and I'm the one providing that support for him to carry on. I deserve to be exiled and thrown into the Screaming Forests.

'I've tried to beat you a few times but always fail,' Rydan shakes his head in amazement. 'You have impressive willpower; those drinks burn tremendously.'

He is part Ardenti, I want to say but bite the inside of my cheek.

'Because of who you are,' Rydan continues, raising a palm. 'I'll accept you dancing with Nara—'

For Solaris's sake! 'Rydan!' I practically gape, but he's already sauntering past us.

'What?' He shrugs, walking backward as he whispers, 'He's a champion.'

'Well, he's not wrong.' Darius's laughter swirls from behind me as I watch Rydan stop by Lorcan and begin pestering him away from his partner. A quizzical frown warps my forehead as I whirl around to Darius and bring my palm up to his. 'Did you use powers on him or something?'

'Of course not.' His confusion matches mine. 'That's all *him*.'

'Right, how can I be so sure you're not just tricking me? We shouldn't even be dancing still,' I hiss, my eyes darting around the hall.

'Look, Goldie, as much fun as it is tricking mortals, I've not once used any Merati powers on you apart from when I saw you at the Draggards. Besides, shifters weaken the more they use their magic, and even with some resistance to it, the steel powders trapped in these walls—' His smile turns tense. 'Well, let's just say I'm running on a limited timeframe here.'

Learning things about Darius always surprises me. Not because of our constant disagreements – more me than him – but because he's perceived as untouchable, invincible, and too dangerous to catch. Yet he has the same weaknesses as any dragon. The difference is he's just learned the smartest way to avoid capture. 'Is that why the attacks in the city have gotten worse, because you've helped shifters build resistance too?'

He tilts his head, something glistening in his eyes. 'Perhaps, but I'd only decided to join my kind a few years ago. I don't like following what some choose to do.'

Such as the attack on the city. He was stealing, not involved. This is why the Queen is wrong when it comes to her assumptions on him as their leader, and the rumors of him being behind the new creatures.

We stay quiet for a few minutes, the music crescendoing with the violins, followed by a soothing melody as we circle at what seems like a slower pace than all of those around us. His eyes dust over with golden hues from my dress as he observes me, every second, every moment.

So, I say, 'The day we met, you said how boring it is if you are not hunting me down instead.' Our hands fall to the sides and he grabs my waist. 'Why did you never kill me when you had many opportunities to do so?'

He angles his head, the tips of his fingers light as a feather on my hips. He spins me around so my back is to his front, my hand curled in his by my side and my head falling back onto his chest. 'If I had killed you, I wouldn't have anyone to annoy anymore.'

An involuntary laugh escapes me. 'Is that truly the reason?'

I can feel his lips curving into a smile near my neck, the warmth of his breath caressing my skin. 'There are plenty of reasons, some that have me wishing the opposite. But the truth is—' He spins me back around, his eyes tracing my lips. 'You drive me *mad,* Nara.'

My breath comes out jagged and slow as we turn. 'I feel the same way when it comes to you.'

His amused hum rumbles deep within his chest.

The music starts to slow, we repeat each step, our eyes fixated on one another as we dance in silence.

'The Queen isn't wearing the pendant tonight.' At last, I sigh, catching the sight of her on the throne. Crystalized gold encases it as the General stands to her side. 'It's too dangerous.'

'All the better then.' A tug at his lips before he's grabbing my hand and waist.

Pushing him slightly away, I huff up at him. 'Do you not understand that me stealing from the Queen is punishable by death?'

He pulls me back in and chuckles, tightening his grip on my hand as we grace the dancefloor. 'You had no problem accepting my offer, Goldie.'

I have no response. He's right, I accepted, just as I had at Havenwood Tavern. In a low torturous whisper, he says, 'I never took you as someone who'd back down.'

I shoot him a cold hearted glare. I know what he is doing, and I loathe that it's working.

I'm not one to back down easily. I never cower. I follow through even if I fail, *even* when I am on the brink of giving up. I know there have been changes in me since living in the city, with the creak of the gates in my chest opening to new things . . . new experiences. But as far as not backing down, especially for my brothers, that's the one thing that stays the same.

'Fine,' I say. 'I might have an idea where she has it.' As clapping ensues and the music halts, Darius steps back. Everyone bows to signal the end of the dance. And as I bow to Darius, I lift my gaze, looking at him beneath my brows, adding, 'Wait for me by the entrance and *don't* talk to anyone.'

The side of his lip curls, giving me that smile that says he knows he's won, and I walk the other way, attempting not to draw any attention to myself.

Chapter Twenty-Nine

When the joyous parades of people clink their chalices and go forth with the celebrations, I make a move to the entrance of the throne room. I'd waited around cautiously for a good five minutes, watching Link and Illias talk by the walls; Iker, flirt and fail with a girl, while Freya distracted Idris, although his irritation was clear as day, as was Lorcan's displeasure with Rydan's continuous nagging even after the dance had finished.

Weaving through guests, I arrive at the foot of the latticework doors which are already open. I step out into the hallway and look to my right, where Darius leans against a pillar. With a coin flipping between his fingers, he smiles, turning his head to me. 'Took you a while, Goldie.'

'Let's just get this over with,' I mutter, walking past. It takes him two seconds to fall in beside me, and I peer up as the light from the throne room gilds his skin, disappearing as darkness shields the corridors in the ensuing silence.

His slight side smile hints that he knows I'm looking at him, so I divert my gaze elsewhere, but as we turn a corner, he pulls me back.

Startled and wide-eyed, I stare up at him as he presses me against the wall and places my arms around his neck. 'What are you doing?' I whisper, but it's ineffective when he hushes me and slides a hand around my waist, pulling me closer.

I catch sight of a Venator guarding the hallways as he walks down our path. The moon shines through the double-hung windows, casting an iridescent light against Darius as he sends the Venator a single nod. 'Evening.'

Resisting the urge not to hit Darius, I see the Venator laugh at our position, not perceiving us as any kind of threat, merely two . . . *lovers*.

'You should really give me more credit for always saving you.' Darius lowers his head to mine in a drop of a whisper once the Venator heads off into a different sector of the palace.

'I'd rather give credit to a rümen,' I say flatly, sliding my hands down to his chest and pushing him off as I spring away from him as far as I can.

'Or perhaps to that guy,' he says, trailing after me again. 'Lorcan.'

I stop, carefully turning on my heel, but I don't utter a word. He widens his grin. It's an infuriating grin.

'Oh, come on, Goldie, I saw the way you were looking at him.' He chuckles bitterly under his breath. 'You were practically undressing him with your gaze.'

And that's enough of that.

Pivoting back around, I eye each door, the ones I'd looked at when I was last here and the areas I'd tried to memorize by heart.

'I get it,' Darius says into my ear. 'A man can be just as desirable as a woman. In fact, my first male sexual encounter was when I was—'

I exhale sharply and whirl to him, pointing a finger at his chest. 'You want to know who isn't desirable? *You*.'

His gaze is challenging. 'Now that's a lie.' Lips part, and then he breathes a laugh inclining his head so it's inches from mine. 'In fact, I can guarantee that you'll think about me, even dream about me tonight when you are lying in bed.'

He smiles as if he can sense how his words have made my stomach clench, my palms sweat, and my breath shaky.

'The only time I think about you is when I want to punch you,' I say, and his smile turns dangerous and seductive.

'So, you do think about me?'

My face flushes. That is not what I meant.

His fingertips touch the curls of my hair, tucking them behind my ears as he leans in to whisper. 'How about we change that vulgar expression of yours?'

I glare, facing the front, and when I try to answer, he's already speaking into my ear again.

'Imagine you're in that throne room, no one is around, no one will be able to hear for miles, especially not the sounds you'd be making as I bury my face between your thick thighs.'

I suck in a breath, and pressure that I'm not familiar with builds right between the spot he's just mentioned.

He rears back to look at my face. His golden eyes flash with lust before he tries to hide it by laughing it off. 'See? Even someone like you finds me desirable.'

That ends my trance, and I glower. 'You're sickening,' I lie as I turn away, but not before sticking my tongue out at him as if I were a child myself. I pat down my chest, wiping away the sheen of sweat, and desperately try to forget what he's just said. And by the time we've stormed certain areas of the palace, my mind wonders if anyone has realized I'm not there.

'Here,' I reply with a blunt tone as I halt by a door, the same one the Queen took me in the other day.

Darius surveys it warily like he's not sure whether to believe me or not. I jerk my head at it again, each minute just wanting to get out of here, to see my brothers, to *breathe* for a second.

He hovers his hand over the brass knob. Flame designs flash bright when the moonlight hits the doorway, and then Darius opens it.

The door creaks, and I'm puzzled that it isn't locked. I feel the worry in my gut that this is a trick, that the Queen knows, and she expects this exact thing to happen:

Us – trying to steal the pendant from her.

'Wait.' I grasp his arm, tugging at him. The need to get us out of here begs me to say it, but as he looks over his shoulder, the only thing that spurts out of me is— 'What did you do with that goblin?'

He quirks a brow at where my hand is. 'For a Venator—'

'Trainee,' I say with impatience, not realizing this is the first time I've ever corrected him on that.

'*Trainee*,' he amends, vaguely amused. 'You seem to care a lot about the welfare of creatures.'

I let go. 'I don't.'

He tips his head back, laughing, his throat moving with the vibrations of his voice. 'You're also a terrible liar.'

'You can read minds now or what?'

'No.' He looks down at me with a darkened gold gleam in his eyes. 'But I can hear your heartbeat speed up when you lie.'

I clutch my hand over my heart, feeling it thump rapidly beneath my palm. *How many times has he listened to my heart?*

'And to answer your first question,' he lilts. 'He's safe.'

For a moment, relief floods me to my core, then I think about how I never used to care about creatures. I despised them, caught them, and sold them off to Ivarron. But ever since that dragon they captured in my village, things have changed.

Darius ignores my silence and goes inside, and I don't stop him. Instead, I swallow any worry and follow. The draft from the windows blows the honey-colored curtains across, creating shimmers onto ornaments and the settee where I had seen the Queen lounge.

My eyes scan the room and lock onto the gold pendant twinkling around the neck of the mannequin.

Darius has spotted it too and slowly moves towards it. Skillful fingers unclasp the pendant before he holds it up and it twists and turns in all directions like a beacon of light . . . a river flowing its course North. Admiring it on the Queen, I can say that it intrigued me, but up close in Darius's hands, it fascinates me.

It's still too easy, though, and I can see Darius knows that too by the way he frowns like he'd expected there to be more to it.

'Did you know the Queen is a sorceress?' I ask, my voice softer than I'd anticipated like it's still in awe of the pendant. I don't know what caused me to say that, but it was out before I could think it through. When Darius doesn't answer, I flick my eyes to him and rephrase: 'Do *all* the shifters know?'

He stares ahead, thinking my question over as he slides the pendant through his fingers. 'A few.'

Leira didn't know much, she only told me what her sister had once said, and her sister had been with a shifter.

'She's a sorceress without power.' I tilt my head, acknowledging the little information I'd gotten from the Queen. 'Why?'

Both brows lift as he looks me over. 'That's a question you should ask her, not me.'

'But you know why, don't you?' I press, starting to get agitated.

'Maybe I do, maybe I don't.'

Frustration coils up in my chest. 'Just tell me.'

'I'm not up for a history lesson right now, unless—' he flicks the words right off his tongue, enticing and full of wonder. 'You think of the Queen differently to what a Venator does?'

Testing me. He's testing my loyalties to the Queen. I ball my fists, knowing my answer is uncertain. I've already proven my loyalties do not lie with her by helping Darius, but do I trust the Queen? That is an entirely different question I've not explored. 'You got the pendant,' I grumble, choosing not to mention Sarilyn again. 'Now, give me what I need.'

He winces. 'About that, Goldie.' He flicks a finger up to his lips. 'My blood doesn't grant immortality.'

If the world around me didn't just shake, then I'm certain it's the anger trembling inside of me. 'What?' A hiss of breath seeps out of me.

He strolls around the room, dangling the pendant from his hand, clueless I am tracking his every movement. 'Sure, it possesses healing abilities like any other dragon blood, but if you wanted that, you could just go to the illegal markets in the Draggards and pick up a vial yourself.'

A lie, that's what it all was.

'So, all this time, you've been tricking me into believing you had what I needed?'

Pausing, he now looks at me with a pert smile. 'Well, I didn't *make* you believe. I just never said if I did or not.'

The fury now pumping through every one of my blood vessels makes me lunge at him with my fist in the air. But he snatches my wrist, crossing it between us and not lowering it as he huffs in mockery, 'What did I say about the face?'

That just makes me want to strike him even more, *arrogant ass*. 'I knew I shouldn't have trusted you!'

Even with his arm restricting us, he still holds me and leans in. 'Did you ever trust me to begin with?'

'No . . . I didn't.' I try and slide out of his grip, but he makes it impossible.

'That's because you *hate* me, don't you?' A taunt, a ridicule over the other day.

'With a passion.' He finally releases me with a smirk as I stumble backward.

'Well, Goldie, it's been wonderful working with you.' He saunters over to one of the windows. 'Feel free to scream for any Venators to come, although that won't help your case if you don't want to be trialed and hanged.'

'Have you always been this selfish?' I rush up to him, lifting my gown a little. His leg is just over the ledge when he wraps the pendant around his neck and stares at me – a soul-purpose stare.

'I've been worse.'

'Solaris, I despise you.' I shake my head, my words sharp and full of grit.

His eyes flicker to my lips, and then he lowers himself to the side of my head. 'I know,' he whispers. 'But do you despise me that much to take me down with you . . . *Naralía?*'

My lips are unmoving. *Yes*, is the answer I want to form but can't bring myself to say it.

The night air brushes my hair back as he jumps from the ledge and vanishes. I brace my hands against the ledge and peer down and see him wink up at me, but he'd not transformed. He's not using any powers to escape, all because . . . because he can't fly.

And I'm not going to yell to anyone for help, or inform on him, because he's right: I've helped him, and another side of me can't rat him out.

I skulk into the throne room again, laughter echoes the walls, but I don't make sense of it as I focus on Illias. He's smiling, content with Link. I can't imagine the sorrow they'll feel when my brothers leave early in the morning, to head back to see *Ivarron*.

'Where were you?' Freya cuts my thoughts off, furrowing her brows in front of me. 'Do you know how hard it is to please Idris—'

'I'm sorry, Freya. I just—I need some fresh air.' I glance at the open balcony overlooking the city.

As if she notices how out of it I am, she touches my shoulder consolingly. 'Would you like company?'

I shake my head, taking a step to walk past her. 'I'll be fine.'

She latches onto my upper arm, and I swivel my head to meet her stare. 'But you're *not* fine, are you?'

She looks at me as if she can see right through me and . . . *read* me.

I thread my fingers under hers, plucking each one off as I sigh. 'I'll tell you everything soon, I promise.'

Worry skims her features, but she nods reluctantly, and I saunter to the balcony.

A breeze hits my chest as I look over the ledge, trying to think of how to tell Ivarron that I don't have what he wants; that I've failed, even when I hated the idea of that the most. I stare back into the palace, watching my brothers, though Iker as usual has disappeared. I then wonder what I will tell Freya and whether she'll be annoyed I hadn't told her beforehand.

A groan rises to my throat as I rest my forearms on the stone ledge, thinking about all my misfortunes. The night blossoms with swirls of purples and blues and I just wait, wait for when the Isle of Elements will unleash that power into the air.

'I saw you didn't switch partners.'

I jolt, turning my head to Lorcan who leans by the entrance, stoic and fierce.

My brow lifts. 'You danced with Rydan.'

'*He* tried,' he clarifies, stalking towards me and finally smiling. 'I've never met someone so persistent.'

I chuckle, shaking my head in silence. Sinking my teeth into my bottom lip, I gaze out beyond the palace walls, the city bright and cheerful. From here I can hear drumming sounds and feel the excitement the children must feel, twirling and dancing over the summer solstice, praying for good fortunes Solaris and Crello will bring.

'Look,' I say quietly, staring up at Lorcan. 'Balls, parties like these aren't my thing. I've been used to celebrating with my brothers back in our village, never this.'

'The thought overwhelms you.' An observation rather than a question but it's not that. I'd always craved an adventure, but this . . . isn't what I'd expected. In some shape or form I still feel *trapped*.

'It's just new to me,' I lie, and without meaning to, I place my hand on my heart, remembering Darius's words. 'I suppose if I'd grown up the way you did, I'd be more used to it.'

'Age does not matter. I may have been younger than you are now when I first came here, but I still had a difficult time adjusting.' His brows draw in. 'I still do.'

I snort. *I find that hard to believe.*

'Maybe one day you'll take over my position.'

My eyes widen so vast that he chuckles. 'Someone has to take over when I make it as a General.'

Second in command, which is what my father was. I'd be honoring his title, but did I want it anymore? It's the first time I've been so unsure of something.

'You'll make a great Venator, Nara,' Lorcan's words soften, much like his expression as he clutches my hand on the ledge. Shame paves a line along my skin. Would he still think the same if he knew I'd helped a shifter steal from the Queen?

He rubs his thumb against mine, slow, steady, causing my stillness to grow, my aching desire to run miles. And as his head lowers and his lips brush mine, I tip my head back.

'Sorry,' I whisper, puzzled by my actions. 'I—'

'You don't need to apologize, Nara,' he says and steps back.

This whole moment is suddenly awkward and most of all annoying. Lorcan smiles down at me, pressing his palm against my cheek.

'I will see you inside,' his words are light and calming, as I nod.

When he goes back into the hall, my shoulders hunch and I groan in misery, resting my head against my forearms.

Then the cheers from the city seem to get louder, and as I lift my head up to the sky, spirals and streaks of fiery colors burst through the dark clouds.

I perk up as childish excitement flickers inside my stomach and I smile in awe, reminiscing the times I'd spun around with Illias, laughing as dust shimmers resembling snowflakes fell onto us. Now an upper balcony shields me from it, but I can still see the gold specks landing on the ledge.

My palm comes out to catch a few and I think of the wishes I'd made every year on Noctura night. It was always a tradition, whatever wish you made, Solaris and Crello would someday grant it.

I close my eyes, focusing my breathing in tune with the warmth of Emberwell and the sounds of distant cheers as I think of a wish.

When I have it, I smile and make one.

Returning inside the throne room, I blink as I find Iker half confused, half aware coming from the entrance. I careen past a few people before reaching him. 'Iker?' Tilting my head in suspicion I glance at his hand in his pocket. 'What do you have there?'

He furrows his brows, looking at me then down at his hand as he slowly drags out a glowing emerald stone.

Recognizing it, I gasp, leaping forward and gazing around the hall to check if anyone has noticed. It's hard not to when its cuts refract its brilliance across the entire floor. 'How did you get that?' I hiss, mouth half open as I urge him to place it back in his pocket.

'What?' He sounds just as startled. 'I—' Another frown. 'A man gave it to me.'

'A man?' Remaining calm seems impossible when I know exactly *who* that man is.

His head bobs but even then, he looks doubtful. 'The conversation was a bit hazy, but he told me to hand it to the trapper whom you worked for before coming to the city.'

'Iker,' I say slowly but commanding. 'What else did the man say?'

Iker hesitates with a perturbed expression as he tries to recall. 'He said—' A pause, biting his lower lip. 'He said it's one of the most expensive crystals one can get, but it will help us with our freedom.' He frowns at the end as if he himself doesn't quite understand. 'What does—'

'Did he mention anything other than what to say to Ivarron?'

He nods, pursing his lips. 'Just that . . . the rumors about the Golden Thief's blood are a myth and to accept this token as a form of payment to release us and that if it's still not enough he will personally take matters into his own hands.' Expelling a breath, he goes on, 'Shit, I must have drunk something weird. That was the weirdest conversation I've ever had with anyone – and trust me I've had plenty, you know me—'

Iker's words drown out. I don't look at him. I don't think I look at *anything*. Ivarron wanted Darius's blood. He'd entrusted me to get it. And for the sake of my brothers I'd not backed out. I'd taken the request as if he were asking me to go trap a creature like he would on any other day.

And Darius . . . a chord of guilt plucks at my heart. He'd lied about his blood but then done this? Why did he go through all that trouble? Why didn't he tell me the day we were at Tarron's tavern?

In some way it's like he wants me to hate him, despise every ounce of him, and he succeeds every single time but then what was his purpose in this?

'—Let's hope Idris doesn't ask any questions over this now, you clearly seem shocked,' Iker's words draw me back to the real world, and I look at him as he sighs.

'Who wouldn't be?' I answer, absentmindedly. One can only be astonished by news like this. If Darius had tried to use his powers on Iker it'd clearly not worked. Maybe it'd been his weakened state from putting on a glamor for so long, but either way I'd have found this out. 'Just . . . just hide it away from everyone and take it to Ivarron as soon as you get back.' I turn the other way once he nods in silence. My hand still shines with gold dust as I search for everyone else.

'Trapper?' Iker's hesitant voice pulls me back and I twist, watching him scratch the back of his head. 'Who is the Golden Thief?'

A wicked smile dances across my lips. I wait a few seconds then say, 'A dragon pig.'

Iker bunches his brows, not understanding my answer and I can almost hear what Darius's reply to me would be . . . *foul mortal.*

The sun gilds the hall, setting soft strokes of yellow upon the throne. I stare mesmerized at it before a large hand spans across my middle, then the other slides up my neck.

I exhale deeply through my nose, biting my lower lip as I drop my head back onto someone's chest. My hand drifts up to caress his hair, wanting his mouth to meet my own. When I turn to look at him, it's Darius.

His hooded gaze lands on my lips, and the corner of his lip kicks up. 'Have you ever fucked in a throne room before?'

I've never done anything.

Regardless, I shake my head, unable to form a word.

I want to tell him I miss the contact of his hands on me, yet I still can't seem to speak.

He reaches to touch the side of my face, and I shudder, pressing my hand against his. Closing my eyes, I wait for him to feel me again – to have his fingers run over my curves and take me on that throne.

I can sense his lips graze mine like a feather as he whispers, 'take off your dress.'

My smile is a whisper of its own. 'Make me—'

A branch thwacking across the window outside my room has me scramble awake, and I rise into a seated position. My hair sticks to my neck, and I pant, clutching onto my nightgown over my chest. It was a dream . . .

A dream where I was in the throne room like he'd said earlier. 'Prick,' I mutter, and Freya seems to hear it as she stirs awake and sits up, yawning.

'Is everything okay?' She asks, half asleep, her curls all over the place.

I nod. 'Just a dream I had.'

One that Darius messed with.

I will blame it on his stupid Merati powers. What he had said back at the castle clearly was a way to mess with my mind.

Freya, being half-delirious, smiles with her eyes closed before plopping back down. I shake my head and chuckle, letting my head rest against the pillow as I stare at the ceiling and hope I don't dream of Darius again.

I did not dream of Darius again – thankfully – but the contentment from being with my brothers this morning dwindled as soon as they waved me goodbye from their carriage. And then the General waltzed up to me, and said the Queen wanted to see me.

Unsettling nausea rose in my throat the second he'd said it, and now with palms sweating, legs aching, I feel smaller than ever, standing inside the throne room.

It's nothing like last night, where hundreds swarmed the grand hall, instead it's me and the Queen . . . alone.

She taps her fingers on the arms of the throne, and the echoing of her nails blasts in my ears like drums. She's no longer in red, the gold samite clings to her ebony skin so gloriously that I understand why she didn't wear it last night. I can never outrank her in that aspect. She is grace and beauty driven with power even if she can't physically project it.

'Do you know why you are here, Naralía?' She says after what feels like a century of painful silence.

I swallow nothing but dryness. 'I was hoping you could inform me, Your Majesty.'

She chuckles, rising from the throne. She walks down the dais until she's feet away from me. 'Something was stolen.'

My heart drums.

'A pendant,' she adds, 'and since you were the last to see me wear it, I'm wondering if you might have an idea as to where it is?' Her head tilts, obsidian eyes infiltrating every part of me, waiting to see if I'll confess, because that's what she wants. She knew all along. Of course she did. The door wasn't locked. She'd purposefully not worn it and watched me the whole night, had me dressed—

She dressed me in gold . . . knowing it's favored by the Golden Thief. Yet she saw who I was dancing with; glamor or not, we weren't discreet, so why didn't she act upon it then?

Exhaling slowly, I stare at her, not balking this time, which takes her by surprise as she straightens and frowns. She begins toying with the gems of her bodice, examining me before the doors creak as they grind open, and a small voice comes through. 'Your Majesty, Magda is here—'

'Tell her to wait,' the Queen says, her eyes rooting me to the spot. 'Naralía and I have somewhere to be.'

Chapter Thirty

I swallow the persistent retching in my throat as the foul stench of death and mould from the cellar-like dungeons wave over me with each step. In some way, I knew the Queen would bring me here. I had a hunch as she hadn't spoken a word, and I'd trailed behind her the deeper we went underground.

Fire torches on the walls illuminate the narrow paths. Prisoners hiss insults, though the Queen ignores them. I try my best not to hurl up the breakfast I'd had at the rise of dawn.

'Why are we here?' I ask. My one thought is that if she is taking me down here then I might never come out again. This might well be my next home, a well-deserved one.

The Queen doesn't answer. Her steps never falter and instead she says, 'Naralía, do you know why we hold trials for trainees?'

'I've always assumed it's to see who is capable of becoming a Venator warrior.'

Her surprisingly gentle laugh echoes off the bricked walls. 'And to test one's loyalties.'

I give a slow nod despite she's not looking at me, and feel a tightness in my chest, constricting my every breath. What loyalties have I shown since I arrived at the city? None. I have failed even before the trials.

With a shuddering breath, I scan the paths leading towards other cells. Some go even further underground, making me frown as we pass. When we turn a different direction, I spot tattoos, two of them on each hand. They belong to a man crouching on the ground – a shifter.

Lifting my eyes from the chains on each wrist and the ones at his ankles, his gaze meets with mine. Haunting dark eyes follow my movements until I reach the end of his cell, then others of skin and bone come into view.

A sickening place I never thought I'd find a shifter alive in. Freya hadn't mentioned whether shifters were put up for arena fights, but then again, I've only attended one.

'Tell me, Naralía.' The Queen stops and turns to face me. She places her hand atop an iron lever. Dread digs its way into my chest. 'Why is it you want to become a Venator?'

'To honor my father's legacy.' That's what it's always been for me since the moment he perished. Now it's more a lie than anything else.

The Queen dips her chin. 'And do you feel as though you are doing that?'

No, not at all.

And she can see it too, feel it within her that I'm not honoring my father.

'Why are we here?' I repeat, sharper and with no cowardice.

The Queen simply smiles, pulling on the lever. 'To see where your loyalties still stand. The Golden Thief or me?'

My head turns to the creak of iron gates dragging up. There at the end, resting through the dimness, is a dragon, rattling in chains. It doesn't take me even a minute to recognize it's the one from my village, the one I'd so desperately wanted to win in the first arena fight I'd attended.

As if she remembers me, the dragon lifts her head. Soft vibrations rumble the cracked ground, and I crane my neck, gazing at the thick horns just starting to grow on her.

I return my gaze to Sarilyn and say, 'I have no loyalties to the Golden Thief.'

'Prove it,' she practically whispers in a taunt. Her gaze travels down to my sheath strap and the few daggers I'd placed there early this morning.

Hesitant, I look to my left where the dragon cocks her head, purring through her snout. Knowing what the Queen is implying, my chest heaves, and I choke in my throat. 'She's only a fledgling.' A painful plea in my words as I turn back to the Queen.

Her cold, ruthless face is not the one I'd seen when she smiled and laughed during the dinner we had. 'As a Venator you'll be expected to hunt as far as hatchlings.'

A horrid sickness twists in my gut, rising to my mouth. I swallow at the thought.

'Oh, come on Naralía,' she huffs, like I'm a child needing guidance. 'Is this not the dragon from your village?'

I can just about manage a nod.

'Then kill it,' she orders.

I step back with quivering legs; I'm surprised I'm still standing. 'I can't.' I could before. I killed, even shifters, but this? Everything? It's all changing for me with every rising morning I wake up in Emberwell. 'I—I can't.'

Sarilyn grips my wrist and raises it, grabbing the blade from my sheath. Forcing it into my palm, she says in a controlled, calm tone, 'Kill *it* or you leave me no choice but to set forth a punishment.'

I breathe hard through my nose as I stare at her. Chains rattle in the background but I don't dare look at the dragon as she snarls. An act I consider protective. 'Then punish me,' I say through clenched teeth, startling the Queen. She contemplates my defiance, as cries and taunts ring out from other prisoners. And then the Queen releases my wrist, with a smirk creeping upon her gold-flaked lips. 'And what would your brothers think of that?'

I clutch onto the dagger. *My brothers.* She's using them against me, knowing how much I love, care, and would do anything for them. She walks around me, her gown scraping over the rocks. 'So let me ask you again, Naralía.' Stopping behind me, her curls brush past my cheek as she says in that same provoking whisper, 'The Golden Thief or me?'

Staring at the blade, I curl my fingers around the handle and then glance up at the dragon. Fetters are at her front and hindlegs, but the bonds around her snout prevent any use of power. She's defenseless . . . young.

So young.

When I look over my shoulder at the Queen, I want to say no again, to disagree and run, but I can't ignore her threatening words against my brothers.

I force myself forward. High above me, the light from the arena filters through iron bars. The dragon's murmurs deepen as I close in on her lying in the shadows of the dungeon.

I once stood in front of her like this and she'd yielded before me. Now here we are again. Her wings tuck in tight behind her and serpent eyes glisten with fire as she studies me, my blade, and the way it trembles in my grasp.

Maybe she knows. She's not thrashing around or trying to get away with the little movement her chains allow. She's just . . . staring at me. A soft exhale from her nostrils blows tendrils of my hair, and a strong need takes over me, and I extend my hand towards the scales on her underbelly, still growing and fragile, easy for anyone to stab through. The dragon's head bows, as I spread each finger along her leathery touch. Like armor it shines when she moves, and as my hand travels to where her heart is, I raise my head to gaze into her eyes.

I feel a thrumming connection as if waves of understanding transmits between the two of us. It's foreign, indescribable, but above all . . . powerful?

She does know. Not maybe, not wondering, not possible for it to be otherwise. And the worst is how her eyes tell me that she accepts it.

'I'm sorry,' my whisper is so low, I don't think she hears me.

I lift the blade. Steel blazes under my palm, and she cocks her head to the side, the chain denting the scales of her skin.

'Forgive me.' I register how in this moment, I want to escape, take my brothers, and see what else there is in this world.

The dragon thrums soothingly, a sound so many would run from, to me it's what I imagine peace as.

Curling my other palm over the pommel, I inhale like I've come up from water in need of air. I look at her again for one, two, maybe three minutes. The time is endless, but then those glistening eyes, fire and gold, youthful and peaceful give me that same understanding as before, of what I'm about to do.

And with a nod I thrust it into her chest, into her heart.

She roars out a cry as I squeeze my eyes shut. Strangled gasps burst from my lips, feeling the blade go deeper. When warm thick liquid pools onto my hands, I let out a wet sob. I pull the dagger free from the dragon, and drop it. I keep my eyes closed at the thumping of the body hitting solid ground. A wind drifts through the dungeons – this prison cave and the dragon, soundless, her chains no longer creaking.

'That wasn't so hard now, was it?' The Queen calls out, her voice tormenting. I can envision the smile on her face.

I slowly twist around. With my head lowered, my breath heaves from me as if I've been running. 'Why didn't you capture the Golden Thief?' Forcing myself not to look at the dragon and at what I've done to her, I focus on the Queen.

Her narrowing eyes lock onto me in wicked amusement. 'I wanted to test something out on him first.' With lips slightly parted, she lifts her chin. 'And he proved exactly what I had suspected, the second he entered.'

Before I can ask what that is, she's already turned and walked away. I stare down at my bloodied hand and the dagger on the ground. A sharp guilt consumes me.

I barge back into my room. Freya jumps up from her bed, clutching her chest. 'Solaris,' she says out of breath. 'Nara what—'

'I need you to cover for me,' I say, rushing to my chest of drawers and bending down to open it. The first thing I grab is my old sheath and double ended blade before flipping the pocket over to find the faerie blood as well as my crescent. Taking it out, I squeeze it in my crimson stained hands and slowly exhale. 'I won't be long.'

Once I left the dungeons, I only had one thing on my mind. I'd kept to myself, distant and dazed while the Queen smiled, letting me know where our trust stood.

'Hold on,' Freya says, but I'm already making my way to the door. 'Cover for you? Where are you going?'

'The Draggards,' is all I answer with and just as I pry the door open, Freya rushes over the beds, slamming it back closed.

I look up at her and the unsettled furrow of her brows as she says in a low warning, 'Nara—'

'Please?' I beg, my voice weakened by the flashes in my mind of the dragon and the blood and the way the way those eyes glanced at me—

'I can't,' Freya mutters, and I frown, about to question her when she lets go and says with all seriousness, 'because I'm coming with you.'

I open my mouth, not knowing what I want to say but she beats me to it. 'And on the way, you're going to explain everything that's been going on.'

Chapter Thirty-One

Weak, a coward, cruel, those are a few of the words circling my mind with what had occurred back at the dungeons. I want to throw up. I want to erase it, but I can't.

And telling Freya everything, from the deal with Ivarron to Darius and the necklace, caused a stiffening tension to permeate the heavy air. She'd listened attentively to every word, watched how I scrubbed at my hands to get the blood off, and how I needed to see Leira. A witch, a friend of my father, and someone who believes his death was no accident.

I glance down at the herbal tea Leira had made after I rushed inside and through the herds of drunken people. The strong whiffs of lavender steam off the cup, and the tea ripples as I take a sip. Freya stands in the corner, resting against the wooden wall, and bites her nails, still ruminating on everything I had told her.

'Trying to get ahead of the Queen can easily go wrong, Nara. You saw what she did to you today.' Leira sighs, shaking her head, almost too angry at what I'd explained.

I place the cup on the table. 'She might be the reason my father died.' I'd chosen to believe otherwise. And certain things still don't add up. A dragon killed him. Whether it's pure coincidence or she threatened him too, I'm at a dead end. 'And . . . she knew about Dar—' I stop myself. 'The Golden Thief.'

'But from what you've explained, she wanted your loyalty at all costs—'

'No, she wanted to see me *vulnerable*.' I realize the words came out testy. I take another sip – gulp it more like.

Leira's hazel eyes gaze at me with sympathy. She clutches my hand as I set down the tea again. The candle wax melts between us, and flames flicker onto her bronzed skin. 'It's not your fault.'

My eyes sting. Maybe it's the candle burning them. When I speak, my voice is a weak whisper. 'If I hadn't helped the Golden Thief—'

'*If*,' she cuts in, 'you hadn't helped him. She would have still found a way.'

I sag against the chair, exhaling deeply. Sneaking a glance at Freya, I see her staring at a grimoire in fascination. By the other side of the room, Aelle, Leira's wife, cuts fresh flowers, placing them in jars. I remember that Leira mentioned they both resided in a cottage outside the city. Maybe that was their escape from this.

'Do you still see the Golden Thief?' Leira's question makes me look at her.

'No, I don't. I'm not sure I'll ever see him again.' I frown, eyeing the candle. Seeing him would mean he's a step closer to getting caught, especially after Noctura. As infuriating as it sounds, Darius is right; I no longer want him captured. He helped my brothers. But that doesn't mean I've stopped my dislike for him—

I straighten on my chair as a thought materializes, and I peg Leira with a stare. 'There was a shifter there, in the dungeons. He—he'd looked at me, and maybe – maybe he knows more than anyone.'

A slight crease forms on Leira's brow, and her lips pucker to the side. 'Why would she keep him in the dungeons? What purpose does that shifter serve for her?'

That's what I'd questioned when I was down there.

Freya's voice cuts across the room, 'Because she's likely to use him for one of the trials.' Leira and I turn our heads to her. It's the first she's spoken since we left the barracks. She averts her gaze, nervously fiddling with the hook of her cloak. 'I heard my father speaking to Soren, another Venator, of how the trials were to be set harder this time. With less than a month to go, I'd imagine that could be why he's there. Whenever shifters are caught, they are usually sentenced to death. I imagine that would be the same if they caught the Golden Thief.'

'No,' I immediately say. I'm quick to recall what the Queen mentioned at the dining table. 'She thinks he can lead her to where most if not all the shifters reside.' I notice Leira's eyes are on Freya, analyzing her, as I had seen her do earlier. There is no judgment but still hard to read what she's thinking.

'And I suppose you want to speak to the shifter down there,' she says pointedly, dragging her gaze from Freya.

'It's a start.' It doesn't take much to know my intention. And with Leira's ability to read emotions, I'm sure she can feel my desperation.

'It's also dangerous.'

'Anything can be dangerous, Leira.'

I've risked a lot by now. If talking to the shifter gives me access to whatever secrets lie beyond Emberwell and the Queen, then I'm willing to do it.

Leira sighs heavily, and the chair creaks as she rests her back against it. She can see there's no chance of convincing me not to go. I imagine this makes her think of my father as she looks at the table with a reminiscent smile. Out of my brothers and me, I am the one that takes after my father the most. It was never just the hair or other physical features. We both always followed our curiosities until it got us in trouble, and we possessed a fearless passion that drove us to adventures.

I want to mention him again, ask more of what he spoke about before his passing, but Leira, without a word, gets off the chair and walks to a shelf on the side, rifling through all kinds of jars. Bracing my hands on the table, I rise, wondering what she's doing. Her thick curls bounce as she rises on her toes to reach something, and with a victorious hum, she turns towards me.

'Here.' Her voice sounds breathless as she passes a vial containing black dust. 'It's ash from the Helland volcanoes. If the shifter is in any pain, this will help, and in return, you can gain answers from him.'

I smile in appreciation, and look down at the vial. I had run out of here once, not trusting what Leira had told me, yet circumstances have changed. And remembering that shifter, its eyes close to the color of this ash, I picture his tattoos, two spirals meaning an Umbrati. 'Leira?' I run my thumb over the glass and glance up at her with a question I've been dying to ask. 'What does it mean if a shifter bears no tattoos?'

I'm not sure what comes first, the jerk of her head or the rapid blinking. 'That's . . . that's unusual.'

'Why?'

'Because it means that twin witches performed magic to remove them.'

'Twin witches?' Freya suddenly exclaims. Her reaction is exactly like mine. My extent of knowledge regarding witches isn't vast, so I had not thought of this.

'We haven't heard of any twins in a while.' Leira nibbles on her bottom lip. 'It's dangerous and forbidden as they are the strongest among us, only *they* can remove shifter tattoos, but it's painful. And unless there is a particular reason for it, witches won't just remove them willingly.'

My eyes narrow into a frown. What must have Darius's reasons been to remove them? 'So, it's uncommon?'

'Extremely,' she says. 'If a witch gives birth to twins now, one is likely to be taken away.'

I wince at the horrible truth before Aelle approaches us and rests her hand on Leira's back. Her auburn locks, plaited with similar crystals to Leira's, drape over her shoulder. 'We should head back before it gets late,' she says to Leira. She shoots me a warm smile.

Leira nods with affection as Aelle walks off, after bidding us goodbye. I grip harder onto the vial, then put it away into my sheath after Leira looks at me as if she's struggling whether or not to bring something up. Then she says softly, 'Nara . . . do you remember the last time you were here, what I'd said before you left?'

An unknown force presses against my chest; I feel it with each heavy breath. The haunting lullaby she sang to me. I've not forgotten it since that day.

The sun blooms again, for she has found her moon,
Death reign and resurrection commence,
But he who shall bear thy wicked bite,
A beast no less, though a heart of gold . . .

I nod at Leira with distant eyes, still remembering how I'd yanked my arm away before she could finish.

'Well, sometimes,' she says, low and timid as she creeps forward. 'And not often, we have visions, but unlike a seer, we tend to forget them quite quickly.' Sighing, she adds, 'What I want to say is, fate is a hard thing to tamper with, and what I saw might be long forgotten, but the words that remained have not stopped repeating themselves inside my mind.' She latches onto my gaze. 'The one to bear the tides and stars is your path, Nara . . . your destiny without doom.' Her fingers splay across my heart, and I know my breathing has stilled. 'The *key* to freedom.'

Stunned into silence, I stare at her as she withdraws her hand and wishes me good luck with the shifter. I'm trying to make out a word, a sentence, anything normal, but Freya's beginning to tug me by the arm into the tavern. We make it outside, where the narrow streets and buildings hide the evening sun. I root myself to the floor just by the doors and stand behind Freya as she glances at the busy streets ahead. With all that Leira and I have told Freya today, and seeing her standing with her hands on her hips, I wince, suspecting she will be mad.

'Freya, I—' I start, but she whirls to face me and raises her hand.

'Look, I still don't understand much of anything but . . . I know that I can't stand one more single dragon fight or killing, I—' She takes a deep breath, closing her eyes then opening them. 'For the longest time I've not felt like I belonged here. I'd rather escape than become what my father wants me to be. I just want you to know I'm on your side, for anything, and if it means helping you talk to this shifter then I'll do whatever it takes—'

I throw my arms around her before she can finish, sending her tumbling a few steps back. 'Thank you,' I whisper and close my eyes because I never knew how much I needed her support. I've never had such a loyal and brave friend in my life before.

She smiles, and her arm hooks around my elbow. 'Who knows, maybe helping you might be my true calling.' We bump our heads together in amusement, then get going. 'Now I need you to guide me through everything again because how on Solaris almighty did you form a friendship with the Golden Thief?'

I chuckle quietly. 'It's not a friendship. It's more hatred and a strong desire to scratch his face and watch him cry over it.'

Freya stops and fixes me with her widened gaze. 'That's quite specific.'

'Exactly.' My smile is psychotic. 'Now come on, the Draggards isn't a safe place to be, and we've been gone too long—shit.'

My legs stop working as I spot unmistakable copper hair, armor, and the eyes of strength and green forests.

Freya tries to get me to move, but it's like I'm weighed down by pillars as Lorcan notices us whilst strolling through the crowded pathways. 'Nara.' He nods at me then looks to my right. 'Freya. What are you both doing here?'

'We could ask you the same thing.' Freya's grip on my arm tightens.

Lorcan's lip twitches with a hint of a smile over Freya's interrogatory tone. 'Some are reporting a possible shifter around here.'

'Right, that makes sense,' Freya mutters to herself. Luckily Lorcan doesn't notice my eyes growing wide as I wonder if that possible shifter refers to *Archer*. The Queen knows it was Darius I danced with at the ball, but I don't think she's mentioned it to anyone.

'Any luck?' I ask, attempting to mask my apprehension.

'Not yet.' He glances behind him at three other Venators eyeing some people – likely witches – with disgust. I almost crumble and have the urge to treat these venators the same, even if I am training to be one.

'Well,' Freya chimes in, her throat straining as she's able to jerk me with her. 'We should go, training and whatnot—'

'I was hoping I could talk to you?' Lorcan doesn't move from his position, staring at me, *only me.*

My eyes slide to the crest on his chest, a dragon wrapped in flames. A sting reverberates through my heart, and though I want to shake my head to rid the memory of the Ardenti, I simply can't.

I look at Freya. Her face is a grimace of worry before I nod at her that it's fine.

She clears her throat, flitting her gaze between Lorcan and me. 'I will—I will wait for you over there.'

I'm struck with silence as Freya leaves. Feigning coolness, I ask, 'Have I done something wrong?'

He huffs a laugh, shaking his head. 'Formalities seem to return fast for you, don't they?'

I keep my face neutral.

Defeated, he sighs. 'I just want to make sure you're okay.'

My calm front fails me, my shoulders droop, but I try to put that impassive wall back up. Lorcan, from the start, has shown how much he cares for me, but how can I tell him that nothing is okay? How can I say it without mentioning everything that's happened? He's killed hundreds of dragons and spoken of fledglings, while I can't bear the idea of what I did today.

'Other than feeling hungry, I'm . . .' I lie, trailing off as he looks at my hands. I mildly panic, wondering if I've gotten all the blood off, but when I drop my eyes, I realize he's noticed I don't have my glove on. I'd not worn it this morning. In truth, it'd slipped my mind. Hiding them within my cloak, I force a smile. 'I'm doing great for someone who will face the Venator trials soon enough.'

With a vague frown, he lifts his eyes at me: 'As a favorite contender to pass them all,' he adds.

My stomach churns, and I desperately want to touch my chest to calm my heartbeat. He sounds more convinced than he looks, and not wanting to give away anything more about how I feel towards the trials, I head past him. 'I should get back to Freya.'

His arm quickly grabs my midriff, wrapping around it and stopping me from walking any further. A touch so cold, that even through my leather attire, it freezes me. I look at him. His gaze is resolute, as he says, 'If anything is ever wrong, Nara, you can always tell me.'

Everything is wrong.

And perhaps he can see that, see through me even if I am always the person who hides their emotions well. But I can't tell him now. He's a Venator who's served for years. Why would he side with me?

'I know,' I say, quiet while removing his hand. I know he doesn't believe me as I walk off without looking back even though I can feel his gaze following my every step.

Chapter Thirty-Two

Over the next few days, Freya and I planned what I would do to talk to the shifter. She concluded that it'd be our best option if I went during an arena fight, since everyone else would be focused on what was happening out in the pit. I knew whatever we chose to do was a risk for us – a risk for me, where I'd be opening fresh wounds from what I'd faced with the Queen.

And last night, while I lay in bed, clutching the blade Idris gifted me in one hand and in the other my crescent, I thought of my mother.

She once said you can have the clearest vision of what you want from your future and the steps you plan to get there, but the more you visualize it, the more it will likely change. She believed destiny had a role, that we aren't supposed to know what comes at us in life, so if we are to plan what happens next, destiny changes it, and it becomes unknown again.

My life right now is unknown again.

I clench my fists as I pass the cells, exhaling in need to calm myself. Freya had the vital task of distracting some Venators before

I snuck down here. Even though she's not close to her father, the Venators were keen to know how to get into the General's good graces from their one and only daughter.

Hearing the racket from the arena dripping through the walls of the dungeons, I still myself. The pathway narrows the further down it goes. I close my eyes, the fabric of my tunic sticks to my back, and I shake my head, clearing my mind of the dragon.

When I slow my breathing, I open my eyes and carry on, never glancing to the sides and trying to ignore the cacophony of prisoner misery. I slow my steps as I draw closer to the cave where the dragon was being held, and to my left, I stop, turning to face that same shifter. He's on the floor, his hair rugged and outgrown, knees up to his chest, and the same chains rest on his wrists and ankles.

I move closer, and from his bowed head position, he looks up. I swallow as I take a good look at the blood, seeping from where his chains lie. They must dig deep into his skin.

Inwardly, I shudder, but the shifter tilts his head, and a smirk on his pale lips appears – pale like the rest of his gaunt figure.

'Well, this is new,' he says, dark eyes narrowing as if to see me better. 'They must have granted my request to have someone desirable torture me instead.'

'I'm not here to torture you,' I keep my voice easy, but his comment makes me rethink whether I want to do this or not.

He laughs like he doesn't believe me, until he stops, and his gaze focuses on me too long that I shift uncomfortably. 'I recognize you.' He points at me, the chains dragging across the floor. 'You were here not long ago . . . with the *Queen*.'

He's curious, but I know he doesn't trust anything right now. Why would he?

'She's not with me,' I say slowly and his brows lift. 'If that's what you're wondering. I actually came down here without her authorization, hoping you can give me answers.'

'Why would I do that for a mortal I do not even know?'

'Because I have something that can help you.'

'And what could that possibly be?'

I take out the vial of ash from my sheath and hold it under the crackling fire of the torchlight. 'It'll help any pain you're feeling. All I ask for is information in return.'

The single strand of hope that he holds helpful information about the Queen hangs by a thread. He might just as easily know nothing.

He stares at the vial in my hand for a few minutes, then looks at me, tipping his head back, half-bored, half-amused. 'Aren't you a Venator?'

'Not exactly.' He chuckles doubtfully. I'm starting to believe I was never one to begin with.

The shifter rests his forearm on top of his knee, his clothes shredded and dirty before he clicks his tongue and says, 'Seems like an unfair deal to me.'

'I can get you out,' I blurt out as he starts looking away. If I have to beg, I will. 'I just need time.' I can already imagine Freya shaking her head at me for even suggesting I get a shifter out.

He regards me silently, the spark of curiosity firing up again inside his eyes. 'You're right. You're not a Venator.'

Hearing those words forces my limbs to lock. It's the first time I've heard someone else say them out loud. He reaches his hand out, motioning his head to the vial. The only thing separating us are the steel bars which cast shadow lines onto his face as he moves.

I retract the vial to my chest. 'First, the answers.'

His lip curls into a half-grin. 'Smart move.'

I get straight to the point, knowing I can't stay down here

for long. 'What do you know of Sarilyn Orcharian and the Rivernorths?'

His eyes widen, and he blows out a breath. 'It's been so long since someone asked me of the Rivernorths.'

My gaze narrows. 'How long?'

'Centuries,' he answers. 'They were a bloodline that dated to millennia before my time. Shifters so powerful everyone believed that they were born of the moon coming from the northern rivers of Emberwell.' He swirls a finger over the dusted floor, drawing a circle and lines. 'They controlled the oceans, the light, and skies. Zerathion thought them to be invincible. Normal weapons, steel, poisons of sorts couldn't kill them.'

'Yet the Queen managed,' I say and notice once he lifts his finger, he'd drawn out the same symbol that was on the pendant. Three rivers and a compass pointing North. This means there aren't just three dragon types because the Rivernorths were a fourth.

'Sarilyn grew up thinking she was mortal. Back then when Aurum Rivernorth ruled as king, he enslaved humans, used them as servants,' he says. 'Witches provided for shifters, bonded with them like no one else could, and around that time, sorcerers detested it. They wanted a new leader and to overthrow the Exarees.'

'And so they ended up fighting wars against the witches. Where does Sarilyn fit into this?'

He lifts his index finger, implying that he's getting to that. 'When she was young, soldiers including me were sent to a village by orders of Aurum to gather mortals. She lived with her parents and a brother, but that day—' Wincing to himself, he glances at the floor and the Rivernorth symbol. 'When we were capturing civilians, her family fought back to prevent their children from being taken. It resulted in her parents and brother brother being slaughtered by a shifter in front of Sarilyn.'

My hands curl around my throat as if to stop any nausea. Slaughtered in front of her by a shifter. The very beings she despises.

'What happened at that moment,' he continues, but I'm staring at the bars. 'Unleashed something within Sarilyn. We all witnessed her magic destroy the village with flames, and then escaping before we could do anything.'

'A sorceress,' I whisper. 'What happened after?'

'We searched among sorcerers for Sarilyn, but when years passed, we presumed she was dead.' He rises to his feet, stretching to his full height. He's unnaturally tall but I do not show any fear. 'Until a girl . . . grown, beautiful and kind came to the castle. She claimed to be a witch, here to help against the upcoming battles as well as with trading. Immediately she caught Aurum's eye, and months went by without anyone realizing who she truly was.'

She was out for revenge. 'How is that possible?'

'When she escaped that day at the village, she found a woman named Sybil, a sorceress like her, who taught her everything. Sarilyn has always been a smart person, but . . .' He trails off, shaking his head.

'But what?' I step further into the light of the dungeons, agitated by his pause.

His eyes cut to mine with cruel amusement. 'She was never able to fool Aurum.'

'He knew it was her all along?'

The shifter nods. 'She couldn't kill him, but we know she wanted vengeance either way. The only problem was that she fell for him.' He pauses as soon as he sees my expression fall, and it's as if my body liquifies. 'She fell for the one person she despised the most.'

I shake my head slowly, not able to grasp what the shifter is saying. My mind spins at the vision of the Queen in love with the man she ended up murdering.

'Of course, Aurum, only having loved himself, played her just how he had intended. And one day, he led her to where he had captured Sybil without her knowledge. Before she could realize what was happening, he killed Sybil as punishment.' The shifter paces in his small area of confinement, my eyes tracing him and the chains scraping against dust. 'He showed Sarilyn how cruel he could be as she fought him back with her powers, but he was prepared to end her life too.'

Aurum killed everyone she'd loved, and killed the love she'd felt for him along with it. 'But she survived it,' I say, knowing where this has all led her to now.

'Even in her weakened state, she did. She fled, and the cold, heartless Sarilyn emerged from then on.'

My eyelids lower solemnly, and I channel the pain she must have felt, to lose everyone she loved, to be betrayed.

'What no one expected was for her to come back at the time of the war with a crafted weapon that could kill the Rivernorths so easily.'

I snap my head up at him and blanch, only to see his bleak and distant stare.

'I saw it happen,' he says, voice gruff and low. 'On the battlefield, how she gained the upper hand on Aurum with all her wrath, then finally plunged that sword through him. I then *watched* how she proceeded to murder the entire bloodline, children included and shifters, with the help of mortals she'd trained at her disposal.'

My heart instantly recognizes how that was the start of what one day would be the Venators. She'd formed them from the beginning.

'After that, the treaty was formed, the war stopped, and we all had to bow down to the new leader of Emberwell.' The shifter waves a hand, but the bitterness in his scoff is clear. 'You know the rest.'

I do, at least I think I do. Huffing, I ask, 'How did she craft that weapon?'

He snorts in remembrance. 'We called it the Northern Blade. But before that, when Aurum killed Sybil, Sarilyn spent a long time in Terranos, right before the Screaming Forests were formed by Dusan, the Elven king.'

I straighten at the mention of the Elven King, and the shifter notices, parting his lips and wetting the corner of them. 'You've heard of the stories about the Isle of Elements, haven't you?'

I don't answer, but my expression conveys that I have. It's where the festivities for Noctura come from, the release of its magic. Without it, who knows what our lands would be like now.

The shifter makes his way towards the bars, adding, 'How it contains the power of Solaris and Crello. Grants what you desire . . . and more.' His head now tilts, getting a better look at me. 'The only ones who have access to it are the Elves. So, whatever happened during that time she spent there; the Isle of Elements played a part.' He waits for a reaction before shrugging. 'And according to others, that's how she lost her powers, obtaining that very sword before the supposed Elven King cut all ties with the kingdoms, creating the—'

'You don't know what might have caused the Elven King to do that? Did the Queen—'

'Possibly,' he says, knowing where my question was heading. 'But no one wants to go through that forest, you're as good as dead. And once you cross the threshold between Emberwell and the Screaming Forests, shifters, witches, and whomever else become powerless.'

Powerless? I've always assumed the creatures that lie within the forest are what makes it so dangerous. But for a shifter or a witch, being unable to use their magic is just as perilous.

'Besides, many times, we almost went to wars against other

kingdoms just because of Aurum – because he wanted more power than he already had. He *wanted* to reign over every land.' He sighs, wrapping his fingers on the handles.

'But where is the sword now?' I don't even really know why I'm asking, but if she has it, there might be more to it that even the shifters don't know.

'Last I heard was that twenty years ago, Sarilyn had someone destroy it.'

I frown at the number. Why did it take her that long before she decided to destroy it? I want to ask the shifter exactly that, but a screech of gates opening and closing come from a different direction of the dungeons. Assuming it's Venators, I know I can't stay here any longer. I look back at the shifter, handing him the vial of ash. 'Here, it will last you until I come up with a way to get you out.'

He glances at it as I wait for him to grab, snatch, pry it off me in some way, but he just smirks. 'What if I tell you I want something more?'

'That wasn't part of the deal,' I say, shaking the ash for him to take it. Annoyance colors my voice as I look left and right, hoping no Venators appear. I panic, as his fingers close around my wrist and jerk me forward.

'I've been in hiding for centuries, and when they finally captured me, I didn't care what they might do to me, but—' He drops his head to my arm, inhaling '—strangely, you draw me in. I don't know what it is.'

I focus my glare on him. 'And you never will, so let go.'

He doesn't. He laughs as I pull at my arm and struggle through the bars. For a shifter that should be weakened from the chains, he still possesses an unnatural strength.

I tell him to let go again. He ignores it, pressing his nails into my skin. I wince and drop the ash. He's a lunatic; he must be. From what he's seen throughout centuries to being locked up, what else has he got to lose?

I use my other hand to grab my blade from the sheath, but I'm limited in movement. With my knuckles crushing against the cool steel and alarm pulsing through me, I find the hilt and tear it free.

It's a blur of seconds where I'm unaware of what's happening as the force knocks me back and I trip. I never hit the ground as hands catch me around my waist, and I watch my crescent carving flip in the air and fall. Something else then crashes onto the floor. All I see are shards and fluorescent red splattered everywhere before the shifter yelps like an animal having just been struck by a weapon.

My ears ring. I'm baffled as I stare at him, whimpering and clinging onto his arm in agony. When I look at the trail of red liquid leading up to the shifter, I also realize I'm still in someone's arms.

I raise my head, and it hits the chest of Lorcan. *He's here.* He's staring down at me with confusion and possibly anger tormenting his features. I don't see Freya nearby and wonder if he's come from a different part of the dungeons.

'Lorcan—' I start when he moves past me, and I swivel, watching him bend down.

When he stands and slowly turns, my heart beats sporadically. He's holding my crescent carving. He flips it over and notices the engraving of the letter *R*. A sharp breath leaves him, shocked, confused, as his thumb glides the markings.

I reach out for it, and he still doesn't take his eyes off of it as I grab it away from him. I repeat his name, but a low groan from the shifter's cell finally snaps Lorcan out of his trance.

We both look at the shifter, coiled up on the floor, panting and wincing in pain. His hand squeezes his other arm so tight that veins bulge underneath his skin.

'What did you do to him?' Lorcan rasps, treading carefully, with all the blood sprayed everywhere. I follow behind, shaking my head because I hadn't done anything. My eyes scan the shards and then stop at the label stuck to the floor.

Faerie blood.

The vial I've carried around since the day I stole it from Ivarron's home.

I jump as the shifter's pain echoes off the walls. Lorcan grabs me by the arm, spinning me round to face him.

'Wait for me in my chambers.' His voice isn't soft; it's authoritative.

I can't seem to get my words out. I'm just shaking my head, trying to understand everything as the shifter continues his agonizing cries. 'What? No—'

'Nara.' He presses his palms flat on my shoulders, his expression stark. 'As a deputy, I'm *ordering* you to wait there.'

There's enough finality in that command that I stare at him. He's not Lorcan right now. He's the second in command of the Venators army, doing his duty.

I step back, and his hands slide off me. I look at the shifter, then Lorcan again, then sprint away. Holding the crescent to my heart I get to the entrance and spot where Freya is still talking to the Venators. I try and catch her attention so that we can get out of this horrible place.

Chapter Thirty-Three

I didn't wait in Lorcan's chambers.

I didn't follow his orders.

Instead, I ran to my room and threw the sheath, my crescent, and the blade all onto the bed.

Freya and I came back to mayhem. While Link and Rydan were still at the arena, Venators passed us on the way out, scurrying towards the dungeons. I knew why and worse is that *I* was involved in it.

I glance at my wrist, running my fingers over the fresh bruises, then drop my hands to fiddle with the ends of my clothes. I've played out every outcome that could happen today. Lorcan appearing should have been up there, but it wasn't.

'It will be fine, I'm certain it will be,' Freya mutters under her breath, pacing back and forth at the foot of my bed. 'Lorcan has a soft spot for you. He has since the beginning; he can't be mad! You can just tell him you wanted to explore the dungeons. You are always in the mood to explore everything—' She halts then looks at me in concerned panic. 'How are you so calm!'

'Trust me, I'm not calm.' I just hide it too well.

Freya sighs, her shoulders sinking as she walks over and lowers herself to her knees. 'At least you managed to get all the information from that awful shifter.'

I shake my head. Freya's hand rests on top of mine to stop the constant fidgeting. If I wasn't so worked up, I'd thank her for preventing me from ripping a hole through my clothes. 'It's only opened up more questions, and Leira was right. Going against the Queen is too much of a risk.'

'When have risks ever stopped you?' Her voice is delicate and sweet. It's comforting, like that of a mother's love.

I tug at my bottom lip with my teeth but end up smiling. 'Never,' I whisper. 'It's why I always used to get into trouble with Idris.'

Freya chuckles light-heartedly. 'I can imagine. He kept arguing with me on the night of Noctura when I told him he was worse than a grumpy old man.' Her laugh fades into a meaningful smile. 'You know . . . I'm glad you're my friend, Nara.'

Words lodge in my throat. Freya is the only friend I've ever had, and I'm grateful to have met her. I don't think anyone else would do what she's done.

Loud raps thud against the door, and Freya jolts, placing her hand to her chest. I close my eyes and sigh as a gust of air flickers through my hair, as Freya rises to open it. Slowly getting up, I hear the voice I've heard a thousand times. 'Can I speak to Miss Ambrose in private?'

Lorcan looks at me with an expression I can't decipher. The same expression I encountered when we first met. One of his hands is behind his back, the other holding the door as if he's worried Freya will close it on him. I glance at her, nodding, and for a few seconds she hesitates. She wants to stay, possibly defend me in the most dramatic way, but Lorcan and I have shared moments I never thought I would with anyone. I have to face him.

My brows rise towards Freya, and I mouth the words *don't worry.* She straightens, huffing a sigh as she glances at Lorcan, and then decides to walk out. Lorcan steps into the room, closing the door and locking it behind him. We gaze at each other in silence for minutes. He knows I won't be the first to speak, not when I'm so mulish. His hand goes to his forehead as he breathes roughly from his nose, and at last, he says, 'I should have known you wouldn't wait.'

'Forgive me for not waiting inside your room for hours until you returned,' I say, perhaps a little too sarcastically.

He shakes his head, a muscle flittering under his jaw. 'Do you know how dangerous the dungeons can be if you're not given authorization? If the General had caught—'

'What?' I step forward, a hint of irritation in my voice as I remind myself that the outcome could have been worse. 'Revoked me of my rights to become a Venator? Lock me up in the dungeons themselves? Because I'm certain he would enjoy that.'

My gaze wanders to his other hand still behind his back and then up at him shaking his head once more. He sings my praises to other leaders, believes I can pass the trials, but how am I supposed to tell him something I'm not sure of myself anymore.

He doesn't answer my mocking questions. His voice is a low whisper as he moves closer to me. 'Why were you down there?'

Never have I seen such darkness in those green eyes. It's as if worries cloud them. I don't back away from him and mutter, 'You said it yourself once; I'm adventurous.' I cock my head, clearing my throat. 'Will that be all, Deputy? Or must I give a reason for that too?'

I'm aware of how cold I'm acting, and his sharp chuckle tells me he notices. 'Always so defensive, Nara.'

I don't provide an answer because it's true. The same way he puts his walls up, so do I, no matter how regretful I feel afterward, especially with him.

'I do have another question, though,' he says, and it's so quiet, yet with him standing so close, I can hear my every pulse beating in my ear, my throat, my chest. 'Where did you get that vial of blood?'

My veins freeze. I picture the shifter curled up on the floor in agony. 'I—' A deep pause. 'I took it from a trapper I used to work for He had a thing for collecting various magical items, and I suppose faerie blood was one of them.' It's hard to imagine the blood I took from Ivarron could have reacted that way upon the touch of the shifter's skin. 'I forgot I still had it with me,' I say, and Lorcan's slow, cautious nod prompts me to add, 'Is the shifter—'

'He's weak but alive,' he answers bluntly before I can finish. I wish to ask more, but it'll only raise suspicion. I don't want to see that shifter again, and he didn't care whether I freed him or not. But the blood reaction . . .

I refrain from saying another word and cross my arms over my chest, waiting for him to leave. It's minimal, but a flash of struggle crosses his eyes. Struggle and torment with himself.

He walks to the door, and shame fills my chest; I fear it will burst. By the time he raises his hand to unlock the door, he stills for what feels like many contemplative seconds. 'Nara,' he sighs my name before turning around, his head hung low. 'The carving of the moon . . . tell me about it.'

I look at him with caution, not understanding why he is bringing that up now. His eyes lift at my silence. He reminds me of a child getting reprimanded. 'Please?' His pleading voice makes my heart stop.

I start softly, like I'm still not sure if I should be answering him.

'When I was young, I used to carry around a carving of the sun.' I say, as Lorcan's gaze stays put. 'One day, I bumped into someone in a rush who dropped the crescent. We ended up picking each other's, and from then on, I've always carried that crescent as a form of good luck.'

'So, this . . .' He brings forward his fisted hand, the one he kept holding behind his back. 'Must belong to you then.' Peeling his fingers away, shock grips at my throat. White oak carved into the shape of the sun.

My carving . . .

'It was you?' I breathe, rushing to grasp the carving. Tears well in my eyes as I touch the wooden rays with my index finger, recollecting the memories of my mother. It's the first carving I'd ever done with her help. 'You kept it all these years?'

'I always wondered why it was so special.' Lorcan looks at it then his eyes are on me, purposeful and fierce. 'Now I know.'

Because I'd carved it.

I'm at a loss, nothing . . . yet everything comes at once. It's odd, strange, peculiar. I still remember the words my mother told me when I tried to yell after the person who'd dropped the crescent. That it was a sign from Solaris and Crello, two souls crossing paths. Iker always made fun of that idea, but I always believed.

With my fingers on the carving, I look towards my bed and the crescent. I glance at Lorcan. 'What does the *R* stand for?' A question I've wanted to know the answer to for so long.

'My father's name,' he says, and his stare twists pensively down at the sun. 'Rayth . . . he is the one who carved it.'

My heart skips, and my eyes widen as I retract my fingers from the carving. 'I didn't know your father was a carver.'

He laughs, but it sounds sad, distant. 'There's a lot you don't know.'

He's right. There is a lot I didn't know about from the start; yet he's found something that tethers us together. So many thoughts race through my mind; why was he in such a rush that day? Did he keep it for the same reasons I did?

He sighs as if he's about to apologize, but I'm the one who's constantly lying to him. 'Nara, I—'

'No.' I shake my head. 'I'm sorry for the way I've been acting lately it's just—there is so much going on. I'm not used to talking to people about my problems, I—'

'You know you can trust me, Nara.' His words take on a sweet melodic tone, enough to make me believe. Except despite everything, part of me still finds that hard, because of who he is.

I give him a weak nod, then Link bursts through the doors, nervously apologizing when he sees Lorcan is with me.

Lorcan's smile doesn't quite touch his eyes. 'It's best I leave.'

I don't reply. My hands simply clutch onto the carving.

He leans in. His lips press onto my cheek, but I can barely feel the kiss against my skin as he withdraws and walks past Link.

'Wait,' I blurt. Lorcan turns halfway at the door as I walk up to him and grab his hand, placing the carving inside his palm. 'I still want you to have it.'

He looks at it, wearing a cheerless expression before he leaves and I feel . . . hollow almost.

'Did I interrupt something?' Link asks cautiously.

I shake my head and smile. 'Not at all. Is everything alright?'

He rubs the back of his neck. 'Since there is no one else I can send a letter to, I was hoping you could help me write one for Illias.'

My face glows with joy at his request. 'There is nothing I would like more than to help you write that letter.'

Chapter Thirty-Four

Leaves crackle under my boots as I walk deeper into the forest. Talk of dragons causing havoc here had made it back to the Venators, and just before nightfall, most were out hunting.

The hope that we don't find any dragons, grows the more we move through these thickets. I thought that if we did, I could convince Venators not to react. Or with luck, I might luck, find the dragon first.

I do not want a repeat of my village, nor can I endure another second of pretending I'm ready for the trials. Solaris how I'd laugh at myself in the past if I knew the more I'd spend time in the city, my hatred for dragons would lessen.

'Why are you frowning?' Rydan asks, sword in hand in case of an attack. 'You finally got a mission that doesn't involve patrolling.'

Because the General and Lorcan are too occupied elsewhere to give out the orders . . .

And though I've not seen Lorcan as much during the week, despite our moment together after the dungeons, he's become distracted.

'Must be because you haven't stopped following me since we left the barracks,' I grumble as I watch the ground for any marks or potential hazards where one might trip up at night.

Rydan chuckles and then exhales dreamily. 'Ambrose, it's okay to admit you're trying to run away from our love, I get it; I mean, I'm such a great warrior, even Lorcy is intimidated by me.'

Well, now I know Rydan would get along with a certain self-obsessed shifter.

I look over at him, one brow up in complete disbelief. 'Are you sure *you're* not the one who is intimidated, considering you're always blushing around Lorcan?'

He scoffs, but I know even in the darkness, he's probably going red again. 'That's just allergies.' He waves a hand. 'Now tell me what is really going on.'

Great, he's onto me.

I huff and turn to him. He does the same, and now we're both looking at each other, pursing our lips in stubbornness. I glance at the Venator symbol on his armor and pull a face, knowing I have the same. We all do. 'Why did you decide to join the Venators?'

That throws him off, and he blinks, looking away. 'Well,' he starts, clearing his throat. 'I never met my parents. I was raised by a woman instead who died a year ago. I didn't have anywhere to go, so what better place to join than where free meals and shelter are given.'

I tilt my head, wondering how hard that must have been, never knowing who your parents were, and then the one person who did look after you like a parent . . . died. 'And you're okay with killing dragons?' I ask softly.

'If I'm honest, I'd rather not kill anything. But you must not care, considering you were a trapper, and well—' Brown eyes skim over me from top to bottom '—seem deadly.'

I'm somewhat tempted to roll my eyes as I walk off again. 'I'm not as deadly as you think I am.'

He catches up to me. 'That's what all the guilty people say.'

Solaris, how many guilty people has he come across that have said that?

'Would you look at that,' he cheers. 'She smiles!'

To my distaste, I start laughing and hit the side of his arm. Behind us, two trainees murmur to one another. I recognize them as Alex and Jaron – both never keep quiet.

'Yeah, right.' One of them scoffs. 'I doubt the shifters will stand a chance now that they've found the Neoma tree's blood weakens—'

Shifters . . . Blood?

Planting my feet on the ground, I turn and grab Alex by the neck of his armor. Frowning, I demand, 'What did you say?'

Alex's face turns ghostly even in the dark. Bringing his hands up in surrender, he widens his eyes.

'Nara!' Jaron says, but I don't look at him. All I can think about is the word blood. 'We're just mentioning what we overheard the General talking about with some of the leaders.'

Rydan curses, coming beside me as his hand touches my arm. 'Ambrose, I know I said you seem deadly, but I don't think I need a demonstration right now.'

I admit I could have dealt with my impulsiveness towards Alex in a far less . . . threatening way. Still, I can't seem to let go as I urge, 'Tell me what you overheard.'

Alex glances at Jaron, then Rydan, and sighs when his gaze is on mine. 'It—it was something about the Neoma tree and how it can weaken dragons.'

I look away, gathering my thoughts, hoping to remember that name, but nothing comes to mind. 'What is the Neoma tree?'

'It's the one at the center of the city,' Rydan answers, and I whip my head at him – the three of us do. 'Marigold leaves?' He sighs when I frown further. 'The story behind it is that it bleeds real blood. Some say it's Solaris and Crello's blood from the creation of this world. Others think it's cursed and are waiting for the reincarnations of the sun and moon to bless it and make it sacred again.'

The Marigold tree I've grown so fond of since the moment I stepped foot into the city. It's what captivated me the most, but I was never taught the history behind it. Idris made sure to educate me after he couldn't afford to send me to the local village schools, but I'm not sure he even knew of the tree at the time.

'What I don't understand is how you two nitwits heard this before me!' Rydan hisses. 'And how did they figure out it was the blood of that specific tree? No one is allowed to touch it.'

'Then,' Jaron adds, running a hand through his long golden strands. 'A Venator must have realized it, because apparently a shifter down in the dungeons was heavily injured with it.'

A grim taste fills the back of my throat, as I remember the shifter, the vial, the blood.

The faerie blood that isn't even faerie blood at all.

Is this why Lorcan had asked where I got it from? Wondered why I had it?

As for Ivarron, it doesn't come as a surprise to me. For as long as I've known him, he's handled things illegally for years, conned people from every village and town in Emberwell. Stealing blood from a supposed magical tree and passing it off as faerie blood is one of the many things he might have done in the past.

But . . . considering I am the one who ended up with the vial, why didn't Lorcan tell me?

'Can you let go of me now?' Alex's gaze darts to my fisted hand. I nod in a daze and release him, watching him trip and scatter off with Jaron deeper into the woods.

'I won't lie, I truly thought you were going to kill—'

I spin, facing Rydan dead on. 'What else do you know about that tree?'

He takes a quick step back and raises his palms. 'Ambrose,' he says slowly, 'you have that murderous look again.'

Tipping my head to the side, I glare at him.

'But I will say that I don't know much, apart from what I said just now.' He takes a big breath. 'Maybe one of these days, you'll see a preacher standing in front of it, asking if you are the one to bless it again. I once got asked, and obviously, I said yes—'

I stop listening to Rydan and tune into the sounds of snapping trees, the air thickening like a blast of heat. I turn in the direction of where all the Venators have ventured, and after a splintering second of sudden silence, shouts emerge followed by screams and a cry that definitely couldn't have come from a human.

My stomach plummets.

Rydan's wide gaze meets mine as I look over at him and then . . . I launch myself into a sprint. I careen through bushes, slapping away at leaves until I reach a clearing and set my eyes upon a few Venators bludgeoned on the floor. The grass is stained almost black under the night sky.

I shift my gaze around, wary of the dragon nearby, not wanting to imagine how it did this so quickly.

Rydan's footsteps quieten beside me, and he swears. 'How many do you think are still alive?'

I stammer just as someone on the ground chokes and gasps out a plea. One of the leaders – Zadkiel, reaches out his bloodied hand to Rydan and me. I rush over and kneel down to assess his injuries.

'It's going to come back,' he rasps, and horror fills me as I see that his knee is bent the other way. I stare back at the blueness of his eyes, dimming as he repeats his words over and over.

I'm trying to cover his chest which has been clawed at and is spilling blood just as Rydan pulls at me.

'He's still alive,' he says, grabbing someone from under the arm and dragging them up to their feet.

It's Alex.

I search among others for Jaron but I don't see him. Looking at Rydan, I say, 'Take him back and inform the others of what's happened.'

'What about you?'

'I'll be there shortly.'

He doesn't look convinced. Neither am I, but if there is a chance the dragon does come back, I want to help it.

'Go!' I exclaim hurriedly, and he grimaces, shaking his head as he turns with Alex, staggering out of sight.

'You should have left.' Zadkiel coughs after a while. No matter what I do, he won't stop bleeding.

'I didn't want to,' I whisper when he grabs my arm. His eyes cold and red.

'It wasn't—' he swallows '—it wasn't a dragon that attacked us.'

Dread swirls in my veins like a vortex before Zadkiel's hand goes limp from my arm, leaving a trail of blood as I breathe, 'What—'

The wind gushes past me, warm and harsh until I know it's not the wind, but a vibrating snarl pulsing behind me.

My breath trembles from my lips. Slowly I rise and turn on my heels to face inky eyes, skin like a snake but the head, body, and wings of a dragon.

Its mouth peels back, revealing sharp teeth and a clear, viscous liquid seeping from the canines.

Venom, like a rümen.

It looked like a dragon were Adriel's words once. I believe him.

The creature lowers its head, the nostrils flaring to catch my scent. I stand frozen, remembering Adriel had also said they cannot see, but just then, it stops, and jet-black eyes lock on mine.

Can it . . . see me?

It tilts its head. Then recognition clouds my mind. The memory of me at my cottage, the day my father died, plays out again. The same eyes were on me, staring like it could sense me. I felt compelled to touch it back then, but my brother shot that arrow through its chest, and since then I have lived with the scar, hating the existence of all dragon forms . . .

My chest now burns, and for the first time since that day, the same intense fear ripples through me.

It was never a dragon.

It's always been the new breed.

The creature's gaze never strays, and my fear is replaced with an overpowering need to reach out to it like before. I stretch out my arm to the center of its snout, but right when I'm about to touch it, I catch a figure stumbling to a stand from the corner of my eye.

Jaron.

His face scratched and unrecognizable as he draws back an arrow against his bow, aiming it toward the creature.

No, no, no, that will make it worse.

'Wait, don't!' I shout, but it's too late as he releases the arrowhead, and it rips through the air.

The creature shrieks, wings spreading, and with desperation, I unsheathe my dagger, raising it when its wing collides with my body and the weight sends me crashing back against a tree.

I collapse onto the ground, and my ears buzz; my surroundings shake and it takes me a while to register a stinging pain spread through my abdomen. I lift my head enough to see the creature now demolishing Jaron and forgetting I am here.

Screams and crunches of bones splitting and breaking fill the air. It won't be long before it's charging at me, and I can't die here. I can't let the same creature that killed my father kill me.

Scanning the forest, I look for a sign, for a getaway, when I remember something.

They can't see.

I spur into action, rolling onto my back and swallowing a scream as I drag my gaze down to discover a thick branch protruding from my lower abdomen.

Dear Solaris, help me.

Mustering my courage, I tear the branch free from my stomach, covering my mouth as I let out a guttural cry into my hand. Agony, pure agony shoots through my wound as I clutch it, and blood spools onto my fingers. Blowing a few quick breaths, I squeeze my eyes shut and lean on my side, but the pain almost makes me blackout.

Using my other hand, I dig into the dirt until I get to sludge. I plaster the muck onto my arms, my face, and hair, then whimper as I cover it over my wound.

There's a low growl. I freeze as the creature's tail slithers among the leaves. It's searching and sniffing for me.

As it moves closer, and I start to pray as its head peers over my body.

Seconds go by, one.

Two.

Three.

I think it's all over for me until a roar rumbles throughout the clearing. I feel it in every inch of my body, powerful and vicious, but it's not from the creature.

It's a dragon.

The creature's head shoots up, as does mine. The dragon stands at the opposite end on all fours. Large with silver scales adorning the sides of its body while the rest glistens in onyx.

It charges for the creature, and they clash, claws out. Shrills from the creature unleash within its throat as they go at it.

I attempt to get up.

Nothing.

My legs are giving out, my head spins, and I drop onto my back, staring up at piece of the sky. Light gleams above me. Orange, and shades of the sun flare in the air like fire. I manage a smile, saying to myself, 'Ardenti.'

Then the smile fades, and I let my hand fall to the side as my breathing turns to gasps.

Maybe I'm dying. Maybe this is what it is like . . . Numbness taking over you.

I don't want to die here, not like this.

I start to think of my brothers – Idris, how he'd never forgive himself if something happened to me. Illias and how lost he'd be when I've always protected him, then Iker, who came to me with any issue he had because he could trust me.

I would do anything to be with them again, to protect them, even travel through the Ocean of Storms if I had to.

A tear slides down the side of my face and into my ear. I no longer hear any fighting between the dragon and the creature. I'm fading in and out of consciousness. An excruciating groan just about slips past my lips, then I feel hands come underneath my back and legs, scooping me up against someone's chest.

My arm latches around a neck while the other hangs lifelessly. 'It wasn't a dragon,' is the first thing I murmur, unable to see because everything looks out of focus – like a dream.

'I know.' It's the voice of a man, deep and distant. I recognize it, yet I try to shake my head because that is not what I meant.

It wasn't a dragon that killed my father. It was those creatures, I say in my head again, like a chant, and I want to voice it, but my eyes begging to close. They shutter at last, and darkness swallows me before I can make out whose arms I am in.

Chapter Thirty-Five

My eyes flutter open as a path of sun gleams through the windows, warming me up. Head aching, I lift my hand to shield the light and frown at the unfamiliar wood-paneled ceiling. I tilt my head to the side then widen my eyes when I come across two large obsidian ones blinking at me. 'Hello, again, Miss Nara!'

Tibith.

I'm facing Tibith, which means—

'Darry t-told me your name wasn't Miss Misty.' His ears flap in disappointment, and his fur glows at every hit of sunray. 'I quite liked that name. It sounded magical—'

'Why am I here?' I demand, but my voice comes across hoarse as I sit up amid a pile of blankets. I wince at the dull pain in my lower abdomen, and as I glance at it, my fingers feather over the newly wrapped bandages.

'Because I saved your life,' comes Darius's answer, sharp and deadly. I whip my head up and gaze at the far end of what looks to be a cottage where Darius rests one leg on the wooden table, sinking back against the chair. His golden-skinned chest peeks through his black linen shirt. The first thing I do is search for a weapon.

'If you're looking for something to stab me with—' He doesn't look my way as he flips a coin. '—I'd advise against it. I'm not up for winning another fight with you.'

It was him: the dragon who'd fought the creature. He took me back to his house. 'Why did you save me?' A whisper of some sort.

'I was feeling heroic.' He grins. 'If I wanted you dead, I would have done it myself a long time ago.'

I narrow my eyes, shifting between him and my sheath lying in the middle of the table. 'You first told me you preferred the idea of hunting me down, and here months later, you've saved me. Even bargained with me though you lied straight to my face about it, and then . . . then you gifted my brother the crystal I helped you steal from Tarron in order to pay off my debt.'

He chuckles, looking away. 'I see that my powers were too weak to work on your brother then.'

In the corner, Tibith scarfs down bread on his small made bed, entirely in a world of his own. I take a forceful deep breath, staring at Darius. 'I'd have found out eventually.'

He shrugs it off. '*Eventually.*'

Annoyed, I say, 'not to mention how you used your Merati powers on me after the ball when I dreamt—' I stop when his frown meets my glare.

'Merati powers?' He says, stifling a laugh. Embarrassment creeps up my cheeks when he adds, 'Goldie, I may have used my glamor on you once, but I've not used it since.'

So, I had dreamed of us in the throne room on my own accord . . .

For Solaris's sake.

'Well.' My voice cracks, adding to my humiliation. "You should know that I find you incredibly annoying, like a persistent cough that won't go away.' 'And you're always so rude, Goldie. Never a "*thank you, Darius, for all the times you've saved me from certain death.*" '

'Twice.' I have the need to remind him, not wasting my time to scold him on his high-pitch imitation. 'You've only saved me twice.'

'Good to know you can count.' He catches the coin in his hand, causing it to make a clinking noise. 'I was beginning to think your brain could only comprehend the simplest of things.'

Funny, very funny.

I pinch my face into a forceful smile. He's a thief, an impertinent one, and maybe he's killed – done everything to survive for twenty-five years. It's like wants others to think he is more dangerous than he really is, enough for people to keep away. At least from what I've witnessed so far.

'How did you know where I was?' I ask with a sigh, changing the subject.

His boot slides off the table, and this time I notice the black walnut wood, expensive but beautiful to carve on. 'I was nearby and caught your scent until you covered yourself in mud,' he says. 'Though it appears this creature can cover *their* scents just like us shifters.'

I nod slowly, looking at the dried-up mud still all over me. Remnants of a moment where I felt twelve years old again. 'Is the—is the creature—'

'Dead?' He finishes off then shakes his head. 'No . . . It retreated to wherever it came from.' A tick in his jaw makes me believe he's disappointed that he didn't get to kill it.

We don't speak for a few heartbeats until I notice a cut on his wrist, fresh but healing fast. I look at the bandages on my stomach and ask, 'Did you do this?'

'You were feverish, and your wound wasn't going to heal on its own, so . . . I gave you some of my blood.'

My brows shoot up as I mutter, 'Ironic.' His lips twitch at that before I'm stretching my legs. I steady myself onto my feet and press my lips together, hiding a wince though a small grunt escapes.

Darius is off the chair by the time I'm fully standing, making his way towards me. My head tilts up to meet his heavy gaze, and a sudden flicker in my stomach as his palm skims my back.

I distance myself in a matter of seconds, wrapping my arms across my wound. 'I um—I can stand on my own.'

He rubs the nape of his neck, and I'm surprised he's not giving me any hint of playfulness or mockery. He glances back at the table as he says, 'you should wash that mud off.' Averting his eyes, he gestures his head behind me. 'There are spare clothes over there if you want to change into something else.'

I look over my shoulder at the bundle of gold coins, crystals, and books splayed along the floor. To the right is a teal kirtle with laces at the front, draping over a cabinet. 'Do I want to know where you got that from or stole?' I ask dryly, shifting my gaze to see his golden eyes burning in irrepressible mischief – his usual self.

'Not really, no.'

I scoff and snatch the dress from the furniture. Darius grins at my testy attitude and points to the left. 'Down the hall, only other room in the entire cottage.'

He eyes me as I storm away with little to no pain anymore from my wound. I pass the hall, and I wonder where, if there is only one room being the bath chambers and the rest of the cottage mainly holding stolen goods, does Darius sleep? Tibith has his own space, and if he brings anyone here regularly—

I shake my head at the stupidity of those thoughts and enter the bath chambers, shutting the door behind. A tub lies in the center, already filled with water, like he'd done it prior to me waking up. Buckets are to the side of it, and a rosewood scent rises from the soaps inside.

Dropping the kirtle, I begin stripping, the leather sticks to uncomfortable parts of my body so that I find relief once I'm completely naked. My hands grab the ends of the bandages, peeling them off, and as I look at where the branch had impacted me, I take a breath of surprise. Nothing but a scar line that is already starting to disappear.

My brows narrow as I glance at the door, then at my hand where the other scar lies. Mud covers most of it, but for half a second, I'd thought Darius's blood could have healed that too.

How delusional and selfish of me to want that.

I sigh, walking up to the tub. I dip my fingers into the water, thinking it'd be ice cold, but instead it's hot. Boiling almost. He must have used his Ardenti powers to keep it heated.

I climb in, lowering myself. Candles flicker along the sides, and I pick one of the soap bars, scrubbing to get rid of the dirt on my body. It's then, when I close my eyes to go underwater, it all comes to me like thunder striking those memories back to life.

Everything sounds louder, the movement of water rippling, the steam hissing, as I think of that creature. For nine years, I believed a dragon killed my father, for nine years I loathed them, nine years hoping to eventually kill one myself.

And I did.

But not on my own accord.

And I loathed every second of it.

My throat burns with the desire to turn back time and save the dragon before she was captured. I don't know where to go from here; I never imagined I'd end up in a shifter's cottage after almost dying.

Knowing I've been under too long, I resurface, gasping for air. I drag my hands over my hair, and spots blur my vision until I notice something orange in the corner of my eye.

'Tibith!' I screech when I see him standing so still. I cover my breasts with my arms and cross my legs together. 'You're not supposed to be in here.' I shift my gaze to the door, annoyed I hadn't locked it.

A crinkle above Tibith's eyes forms as he plops onto the floor. For a creature that lacks certain features and is covered in bright fur, it's outstanding how expressive he can be. 'But-but Darry assigned me as your second protector last night.'

'Did he now?' My eyes slit mirthfully, wishing I'd heard that conversation. 'And is watching me while I bathe protecting me?'

Tibith's eyes glisten like a child as he inclines his head and whispers, 'you could drown, Miss Nara.'

A few minutes ago, I might have. I don't say that, but I do smile, whispering back, 'I think I'll be safe inside this tub for now.'

He angles his head, staying quiet for a moment. 'Can I tell you a secret, Miss Nara?'

I look at where my hands are and flick my eyes up at him. 'Now?'

He nods, standing and shuffling towards me. Opening his mouth, his fangs poke out, and he quickly closes it looking back at the door then at me again. 'I don't think you're a creature murderer anymore.'

His innocence makes me chuckle. It's a breath of fresh air from what I do think of myself. 'Is that what Darius still thinks?' The question slips out, and my brows pull together. It shouldn't matter if he does or not.

'Darry could never think that, Miss Nara,' Tibith says, turning to walk away, which only causes my brows to crease further and my mind to tie in knots.

'Tibith?' I call out at the last second, and he spins around. 'There's no need to call me Miss. Just Nara is fine.' My smile is sincere, and his ears twitch.

'Okay, Miss Nara!' He smiles, and I release a small laugh as he shuts the door.

I'm not sure how much longer I spend in the bath but as soon as I get out, I dry myself. I bend down to grab the kirtle, pausing midway when I see a dark brown shirt and breeches hanging off the hook.

I let go of the dress immediately, reaching for the other set of clothes. Bunching them up in my hands, the corner of my lip lifts into an impish smile. Well, I doubt the kirtle will fit me anyway.

I step into the living area, rolling the cuffs of the ample shirt and clear my throat. Darius looks up from the kitchen, stirring a pan, before he stops. His eyes rake over my attire.

'What?' I ask calmly, waltzing towards the table as Tibith blinks at me from the side. 'Upset I'm wearing your clothes instead?'

'Oh, I'm not upset.' Darius folds his arms over his broad chest. His bottom lip puckers as his gaze lingers on the clothes and then he gives me a roguish smile. 'I never got around to washing those.'

I pull a face, disgusted, as I sit. 'Of course, I should have known. It's *you*, after all,' I grumble, grabbing my sheath and checking to see if my carving is still inside one of the pockets. Thankfully it is.

He ladles soup into a bowl and sets it before me as well as a chunk of bread for Tibith. He takes a seat opposite me and narrows his eyes with mirth while Tibith's child-like gasp becomes muffled as he gobbles up all the bread. Darius then smirks at me as I glance at the bowl of soup with a scowl on my face.

'Relax, it's not poisoned or anything,' he says. But that wasn't my initial thought. I was more startled.

I lift a brow at him. 'And I'm supposed to believe that?'

He shoots me a withering look. 'Why would I save you and go through the effort of tending to your wounds, just to then finish you off with some poisoned broth?'

I bite the inside of my cheek to keep from laughing at how offended he sounds.

'Look, if you don't want it, what else would you like—' He leans forward, clasping his hands together on the table. A sardonic smile graces his lips. '—*Your Majesty?*'

My frown fades at the sound of that title. 'My favorite . . . strawberry pie.'

He tilts his head slightly, so that the sun bounces off his hair and raven strands shine. What I had said seems to delight him. 'Sadly, we don't have that here, Goldie.'

I shrug my shoulders, taking the spoon and dipping it into the soup. 'I thought not.'

He chuckles, leaning back just as I freeze, swallowing the rich taste of herbs and spices. A shiver skitters across my arms and neck but not the kind I've felt before when I'd faced the Queen down in the dungeons or the creature last night; no, it's a great one – a shiver of jovial memories.

I stare at the broth and sigh because it tastes exactly how my mother used to make it.

'Thinking of ways to say how disgusting it is?' He teases, and I glare at him, taking another spoonful and trying not to show how badly I want to down it all.

'I suppose it's not the worst I've tasted.'

He hums like he knows I'm lying, and I continue eating, savoring each mouthful before dropping the spoon and looking at him.

'The Queen knows I helped you,' I say, but he doesn't look surprised; he just keeps his eyes on me.

'Figured.' He takes out another coin and spins it at the tip of his finger. 'Stealing has never been easier than it was with the pendant. At least she didn't hang you after all.'

No, she did worse.

The reminder of what happened the next day after Noctura must be obvious because Darius's brow arches in suspicion.

I turn my head away. I fear if I stared too long, he'd get it out of me: cheater and whatnot. 'You should be careful,' I say. 'She seems to know what she's doing—'

'So, you did end up deciding the Queen wasn't one to trust.'

My gaze cuts to him, and I nod. 'I know more of her story. There are just a few more missing pieces I need to uncover.'

He releases a sigh, borderline tired as he focuses on the table. 'If you think I have all the answers, I don't. Sarilyn is known for her conniving ways among us shifters. We've heard what others have said . . . some of us witnessed it ourselves. But no one will know the true extent of it other than the Queen and the Rivernorths, *if* they had lived.'

'Or the Elven King,' I add with no hesitation. His head lifts, and he frowns. He must not have known that part. Glancing around the cottage, my eyes connect with the hearth, a wooden chest beside it, displaying the crystal I'd once used to lure him. And next to that is the Rivernorth pendant.

'I'm assuming she took it from a Rivernorth when she killed them rather than had it gifted to her,' I say more to myself as I stare at the gold luster of it, remembering what she'd said after the meal.

Darius's silence urges me to look at him, but his gaze is on the pendant, an expression so bleak that I wonder what thoughts must be crossing his mind.

'Darry.' Tibith tugs at his shirt, gaining his full attention and shaking off whatever look he'd had. 'The den.'

'Den?' I inquire with curiosity, placing my elbows on the table and folding my hands under my chin. 'Is that another place where you keep more of your stolen treasures?'

Darius chuckles quietly, staring at me like he's deciding whether to say what he's thinking. 'Well . . . would you like to see the supposed stolen treasures?'

'Is that a trick question?'

Rolling his eyes, he tips his head back. 'You know, I think it's time you stop wondering if I'm going to attack you halfway through a conversation—'

'Like we have ever had a normal conversation—'

The chair scrapes on the floor as he stands. 'I don't have all day, Goldie, and most likely, your little anti-shifter army is out looking for you. So will you be joining me, or would you like to go back and keep pretending you're just like them?'

I inch back, sliding my arms off the table while blinking at his words. I think about Freya, Link, Rydan. If he'd gotten back to the barracks and warned them all. Then . . . my mind goes to Lorcan. He must be terribly worried while I'm here with the one they all deem their enemy.

Yet that small curious side of me itches to go with Darius.

Inhaling deeply, I swipe my sheath off the table and rise, pointing my finger at him. 'This still doesn't make us friends.'

He grins and says, 'I would hate nothing more than the idea of being your friend, Goldie.'

Chapter Thirty-Six

Birds are chirping and whistling from high above the trees. I'm standing in the middle of the forest, a few miles from Darius's cottage with verdant pines and a cool breeze that we never tend to get in Emberwell during the day. 'This is—' I say, staring straight ahead as twigs crunch beneath my boots. 'What am I supposed to be looking at?'

Nothing, I am looking at nothing, that's what.

Turning to the side, I watch as Darius cocks his head while Tibith rests on his shoulder. They smile without a word. Irritated, I say, 'Is this where you plan to dump my body? Your ultimate plan to end my life? Saving me so I would believe you don't mean harm to then trick me—'

I pause when Tibith and Darius both share a knowing look. Tibith slides down his arm as Darius steps towards me. Aware of my skepticism, he just smirks and leans into my ear with a tender whisper, 'Close your eyes.'

My eyelids instantly droop heavy, affected by his voice, and then the strangest rush of sparks prickle my skin, a surge of power and a sensation I don't hate. It's . . . liberating.

A silhouette then appears, followed by soft purrs, causing me to gaze up at the sky. Shock pounds me, as a dragon flies overhead, and I turn with it to see a herd of them. Lavender aster coats the greenery where dragons rest and play with one another. Large rocks encase the area, and as my eyes shift to every corner, I see an inn far ahead.

Its earthen hues match the forest, with vines sprawling its sides, enchanting and a haven. That's what I imagine this is, a safe haven for dragons.

'Many Merati's joined their powers to glamor this entire side of the forest,' Darius says, as Tibith runs past, jumping in the air to catch a butterfly. 'It wasn't until I first came here two years ago that I decided to hide endangered dragons and creatures.'

This is what the Venators have been in search of. 'Why two years ago?'

'The one who leads most of the shifters approached me. He wanted me to join them.'

'But you said no.' I turn to him, thinking back to the attack in the city.

He lifts a shoulder, stroking a dragon near him by the snout. 'I prefer working on my own, but it doesn't mean I haven't helped a little here and there with building their resistance to steel and bringing back fledglings. It's the only place a shifter can feel . . . normal.'

I feel a sudden shame at how we mortals have had it so much easier than shifters for the past 300 years.

'I—' My need to apologize cuts off as a soft rumbling echoes from the side. I turn to see a dragon whelp crawling across a rock. He lets out a small squeak as if yawning, and I angle my head, closing in on it. The scales glisten almost silver with hints of blue in them. Its wings are barely developed. I bring my hand out as the dragon sniffs and its golden slit eyes gaze at me.

'He likes you,' Darius comments, and I look over my shoulder as a soft smile takes over his lips.

'Yeah . . . I guess he does,' I say, focusing on the whelp again. It nestles its head into my palms. Before I can stop myself, I'm smiling freely. Both a smile and a soft laugh that hurts my cheeks and evokes such love.

I wish this feeling could last a lifetime, but too soon am I forced to think of the fledgling I killed. It's as if I want to remind myself of it, to not let it go, because all the guilt trapped in my heart won't let me forget.

My hand hovers over the scales, and it trembles, and so does my entire body. I suck in the air, then out, and I'm back in the dungeons; the chains crash against my ears while the dagger falls perfectly into my palm.

I drop my hand and shake my head before I blink, swallowing the harshness in my throat. Staggering, I look to my left, where Darius holds my forearm, so I don't fall. His other arm slides around my waist, steadying me.

The vision of the dungeons disappear, and I'm back in the forest while my heart twists and aches in my chest.

'Are you going to tell me what's going on with you, Goldie?'

I can't. 'Nothing is going on.' I almost stumble as I push myself off him. 'I'm just still weak from the attack.'

He stares at me in absolute silence. His eyes drift from my face down to my chest, and in an instant, I know he is trying to listen to my heart. I start to walk back the way we came, before he can sense my lie, and I mumble in panic, 'Shall we head out – I should –'

'You haven't even gone in yet.' He stops me, and grabs my shoulders, turning me towards the inn.

Oh, Solaris, no.

'Darius, no! They will notice I'm not one of them, not to mention I killed a few during the attack. I'm not ready to be torn apart. It'd be too unfair, especially when I'm still weak and have no weapons,' I hiss as I spin to face him. Still, my words only seem to amuse Darius even more as he folds his lips but ultimately can't help letting out a laugh.

My face burns and I'm positive steam is billowing out of my nostrils. 'Why are you laughing!'

'Just trust me, Goldie. No one will do anything if they see you are with me. Plus, I'd hate to have to—' He pauses for a moment, his gaze sliding from my eyes to every other part of me before settling back on them. '*Tear* apart my own kind.'

'I'm flattered,' I say dryly.

He clicks his tongue. 'Can't have the only person Tibith likes, dying.'

'He is right, Miss Nara!' Tibith says from the ground and then skips to the doors of the inn.

I groan as Darius leads me to the entrance. Anyone would think I'm idiotic for agreeing to any of this, but as we enter through the doors, chatter and jeers greet me.

It's a dimly lit tavern busy with shifters sitting and drinking on round tables. A polished oak countertop serves warm food that mix with the heady scent of ale. Pale yellow walls darken with the shadows of everyone, then lighten as some shifters unfurl flames from their palms, laughing as they flick it to others.

I jump back as Tibith rolls past with a giggle and disappears into the crowded inn. I clutch Darius's arm as people seem to stop what they are doing. Mugs slam onto the tables, and the music stops. They all turn their heads to us – specifically *me.*

Grave faces look toward me, and nostrils flare as they catch my scent. I glance up at Darius and frown as he looks at my fist tightening on his shirt. My hands unlatch from him in record speed before he turns to the shifters.

'As you were.' A graceful bow, borderline mocking, as the corner of his lip lifts into a stunning smile.

As if nothing has happened, they resume talking and drinking. My gaze widens as a goblin passes us, smiling up at Darius while waving his drink in a matter of greeting.

I recognize the same bat-like ears and remember the goblin that Archer – Darius took back from the Draggards.

Darius notices my gaping expression and says, 'Told you he was safe.'

He really is . . .

I shake my head in disbelief, but then a man yells Darius's name. His voice is gravelly and hoarse, reminding me of a rustic violin. Darius and I turn our heads to the man slapping the backs of other shifters; he halts before shaking Darius's hand in a friendly manner. Though shifters do not age past thirty, you can notice when one is mature just by the structure of their face: firm, sharp lines across the forehead, like the shifter back at the dungeons.

Flecks of brown and green sparkle in his eyes as he gives me a once-over. Obsidian hair rests on his shoulders, matching the thick beard and bronzed golden skin. Leaning towards Darius as if trying not to be conspicuous, he asks, 'What is a mortal doing here?'

'She's no threat, Gus,' Darius says in the same whispering tone. *Do they not realize I am right here?*

Gus's brows rise and lips thin. 'I hope you're right—'

'You must be the leader,' I interrupt them as Gus's eyes shift to meet mine.

He takes a step towards me, looking at my face with the sternest expression, much like Idris's stare at others when he wants to intimidate them. "The one and only." replies Gus.

Crossing my arms over my chest, I glance around the tavern. Some shifters chant at someone who strips down nude at their demand and stands atop a table scattered with dice. Wanting to clear that image from my mind, I look at Gus. 'Is it normal for you to let your people walk around naked? Or is that too much for you to control as a leader?'

His eyes narrow a fraction, studying me. I raise my brows as a response before he bursts into a bright laugh alongside Darius.

My forehead scrunches at what is going on in front of me. Gus pats his hand on Darius's shoulder and glances at me, this time with a warm smile. 'What's your name, mortal?'

'Naralía,' I answer firmly. I did not expect that reaction. 'Ambrose.'

He smiles, waving his hand for us to follow him. 'Well, Naralía, *that* over there is called the Liar's Dice with our own spin on it.'

Darius places a hand on the small of my back, nudging me forward. Shifters stop to glance at us again, but my gaze locks onto the brown woolen shawl covering Gus's tunic.

'Anytime someone challenges a bid and wins, the other has to strip naked as a bet,' Gus continues as we stop by a table of four male shifters. 'Darius always makes a spectacle of stealing their clothes, though.'

Of course he steals them, though I make a face, unimpressed by the outcome of this bet. My guess is that it was Darius's idea in the first place. I turn to him, drawling my words, 'And here I thought you had their garments for different reasons.'

He chuckles under his breath and inclines his head as he closes any space between us. His bottom lip traces the curve of my ear as he whispers, 'Just because I take their clothes doesn't mean I don't sleep with them before hand, Goldie.'

A sudden tightness engulfs my throat, and I fight to swallow. I scowl as he straightens with a half-satisfied smile, and I stare at the dark liner around his eyes. It creates such contrast to the brown and golden colors that remind me of the dawn.

I clear my throat, letting my gaze wander away from him. 'Well, have you ever lost?'

'He never has,' one of the shifters grumbles, getting up from his stool.

'Even if he did lose,' Gus adds. 'I know for certain he'd have no shame in walking around bare.'

'Always exposing me, Gus,' Darius comments with a light-hearted laugh.

'Someone has to, kid.'

'I can agree to that,' I say and clap my hands together, releasing a breath at the sudden confidence in me. 'So, how do you play this game?'

'Why?' Darius drawls wryly as I look up at him. 'Eager to lose against me, Goldie?'

'Not at all,' I practically whisper, drawing nearer to him this time as I stare into his eyes. 'I'm always up for a challenge.'

Everyone breaks out into amused murmurs as I step away. 'Where'd you find this girl, Darius?' Someone calls out, but Darius's gaze never leaves mine as I make my way to sit down.

'More like she found me,' he murmurs with a smile that can only mean he's thinking of how we met and how he'd won.

That prompts me to think of something.

'I'd like to place a different bet,' I announce, ignoring the confusion flooding Darius's eyes. 'Whoever wins gets to ask five questions the other can't refuse.'

Questions he can't back out of like he usually does, even if I'm aware I could be the one to lose.

He grins, lowering himself onto the barrel stool. 'Quite tame of you, Goldie.'

I hum in agreement, extending my hand out to him. 'I guess I'm just not as eccentric as you.'

Another laugh, melodious and deep, as he shakes my hand. It's a deal.

Gus stands at the side, citing the rules as Darius grabs a cup with five dice inside. I survey him as I pick up my own cup of dice. It's a game of lies and deception, with a bit of luck on the side. Once we roll a hand and flip the cup down on the table, you hide the dice from your opponent. We then begin bidding what we believe is the value under both cups until either of us challenges the other, calling them liars and showing what we have underneath.

If the amount the person bids is correct, the other loses.

'You're not going to try and listen to my heart, are you?' I slant my head, pouting my lips in sarcasm as I shake the cup. 'Because now that would be cheating.'

He chuckles. 'If we all did that during the game, then there'd be no point in playing it, would there?' We both slam the cup face down as he gestures a hand to me mockingly. 'You first.'

Shifters surround us, watching avidly. And since Darius expects me to disagree, I choose to tilt the cup enough to see all the dice. Three sixes, one four, and one three show under the rim shadows.

I gaze up at Darius, my voice neutral. 'Two fours.'

His lip tugs at the corner, and then he lifts his cup. 'Three fours.'

'Confident, are we?'

'Always, Goldie.'

'If I win you won't be anymore.'

'Well, if I lose, I take it with pride, unlike you.'

I glower at him then huff a breath. 'Four fours.'

'You know I've noticed something about you.' He cocks his head, pursing his lips. 'Whenever you're flustered, more of your freckles come out.'

I want to touch my skin, race to a mirror to check, but I don't want to give him that satisfaction. My fingers grip the cup tightly as I say with force, 'I'm not flustered.'

A shake of his head, smiling down at his hand. 'You're only proving me right, Goldie. Five fours.'

Solaris, it's like he tries to do this on purpose.

Gus chuckles at that, and others murmur, clinking their mugs.

Exhaling sharply, I count my dices. He's said five fours, while I have one, if I'm to call him out as a liar, he could have four fours, and my one will count as five, making him win. Deciding to play on luck and a bit of fakeness, I let my eyes dart across the room as if on high nerves. 'Six sixes,' I say quietly, taking a gamble.

Shifters now laugh at me for bidding so high, and Darius's smirk darkens with a sensuality to them. He leans forward. 'Liar,' a velvety whisper that heats the back of my neck.

Keeping my eyes level with him, we both lift the cups revealing our dice. His show three sixes and two fours. Equaling the bid to six sixes with mine.

I've won.

For once, I've won.

Shifters cheer incredulously, and the excitement that flurries through my veins is endless, as Darius's brows rise at the total of the dices. When he lifts his eyes at me, I'm smirking just like he was.

'What a foul mortal you are,' he croons.

I grin wickedly. 'Only the best against a dragon pig.'

'I'd like a go with the mortal,' a young golden-haired male says, squeezing between others. He shoots me a wink, making me scrunch my nose. 'Minus the question bet you made, I'd rather the nudity.'

Brave of him to go after I'd beaten Darius, and how unfortunate for him to believe I'd undress over this game. With greedy eyes, his hand goes to the cup that Darius's palm still lies over but—

'I'd advise against touching the cup,' Darius says with fierce lethality as he slowly glances up at him. 'Cutler.'

Cutler gulps, nodding uncontrollably. 'Right, sorry, Darius,' he mumbles. I stare wide-eyed as he retreats. Gus drags him away by his neck, muttering something about being idiotic.

I roll my eyes and force a smile at Darius. 'You owe me five answers now.'

'Once you have the questions, you'll get them, don't worry, Goldie.'

His playful tone makes me believe otherwise. Then music swarms through the air, and I lean to the side as shifters join the center of the tavern. Some play on flutes, creating an upbeat tempo along with gitterns and drums.

'What are they all doing?' I ask.

'What does it look like, Goldie?'

I carry on staring as female shifters shake their gowns and stomp their feet on the ground.

Dancing, they're dancing.

Darius gets up and extends his hand, and I blanch.

'I don't know this dance either,' I say warily. I do not need a repeat of the Noctura dance.

Darius smiles wide, grabbing my hand. 'You don't have to.'

'Wait, Darius—' I protest, but he pulls me from the chair, dragging my stubborn body to the center. I try to dig the heels of my boots into the wooden floorboards. He lets go as people start twirling one another, raising their hands in the air to clap in rhythm. Darius disappears from my view as a girl with ebony locks links her arm around mine, facing the opposite way, and smiles. She spins me with small jumps in her step and then switches arms until she passes me onto someone else.

My eyes go round, trying to adjust to a new person. I search for Darius, tipping my head in every direction except when my partner is whirling me around. I'm with another: I squeal with delight as a man with russet locks picks me up by the waist and pivots me before I'm dropped onto the floor, joining arms with him.

The drums beat to the same movement of our feet and clapping of hands. I forget where I am for a moment. These are all shifters I never thought I'd even approach other than to detain or . . . kill.

And the reality is they are not so different from a human – from me.

Somehow the scent of mead pervades our movements, reminding me of home, back when I would join my brothers on the night of Noctura, dancing to the gold stardust falling around us.

I loosen myself, closing my eyes as a grin sneaks its way onto my lips. Tipping my head back, I continue smiling. Another shifter now holds my hand upward, spinning me consecutively until it all becomes a blur, and I collide with the next person.

A laugh bubbles in my throat as I press my palms against the man's chest for support, but as I drag my gaze up, the blur becomes a clear image of Darius's eyes twinkling at me.

'Dreadful dancer, Goldie,' he murmurs brazenly.

'Really?' I drawl. 'Because I'd say I took inspiration from you.'

His eyes brighten in mischief. 'Ah, so what I'm hearing is that I inspire you,' he states, and before I can retort, he's grabbing my hand and twisting me outwards.

I shake my head, unable to contain the amusement as he reels me back in and dips me far enough for my eyes to line with the tables and stools upside down.

And just then, the music comes to a stop. I convulse with laughter, making my shoulders shake, and my head whips along with my body as he pulls me upright. Everyone else cheers and whistles to the ending of the dance while Darius keeps a grip on my hand. He inquires, 'Have you thought of your first question yet?'

I slow my breathing. Any trace of smile flees from my lips. I have too many questions that five will not suffice. 'Not yet,' I say.

His laugh is soft and sultry like a harp as his other hand tightens around my waist. 'Make sure each one is worth it, Goldie.'

They will be, at least, I hope.

A different sound of music plays, a bright tone from the fiddle. Darius and I don't move as others start to dance again. He looks as if he's tracing my entire face with a stare I don't recognize. I want to question him, but a woman appears, tapping his arm. He glances over his shoulder as she asks him for a dance. When he looks back at me, I shift away from his hold in a daze. I nod for the girl to do as she pleases with Darius, and I make my way up to the bar counter where Gus stands behind, overlooking the entire tavern.

'He's a wild one, huh?' He gestures his chin towards Darius.

'Worse than that, I'd say,' I mumble, sliding my bottom up onto the stool. My feet dangle off the barrel as I stare at Darius, now lifting the girl off the floor and spinning her around. I can just about hear her laugh over the instruments.

Gus chuckles. 'It's rare you get these moments.'

That draws my attention away from Darius and onto Gus as I frown. 'What do you mean?'

He rests his forearms against the counter. 'Well, despite him salvaging creatures and playing a game or two, the nights always end with him drinking far too much.'

'So, it's rare to see him sober?' I analyze, tipping my head forward.

'It's rare to see him *himself*,' he clarifies, and his gaze returns to Darius with a sigh. 'That boy has dealt with too much since a young age. Trust doesn't exist for him. It took him one drunken night to tell me a snippet of his life.' His words catch me off guard. My frown only deepens as he looks at me pensively. 'But with you, it seems like you are the first he trusts.'

I don't know what to say or how to respond to this assumption. Trust is the last thing I'd have imagined between us. Before, I'd wanted to kill him, capture him, and still to this day, he aggravates me in more ways than one. Why would he trust me?

I look at Darius one more time. Tibith now joins him, rolling up his shoulder, and I even wonder why I'm trusting him myself.

Chapter Thirty-Seven

I graze my thumb over the crescent carving as Darius and I walk through the forest. It'd become nightfall by the time we left the den. Tibith had ventured back to the cottage while Darius knew my silence and my wandering mind meant it was time for me to head to the city.

He offered to walk with me until we reached the area where I'd seen the creature and mentioned he'd stand watch in case it reappeared, but . . . Gus's words concerning Darius kept echoing the entire time. And the longer I'd spent with the shifters, the stranger I felt.

There were kids, families, and they welcomed me despite who I am.

Gazing at Darius beside me, I put the carving away and study him. The shadow covering his jaw, a breeze in his hair, the short strands curling at the neck. Trust clouds my mind; he trusts me. He'd taken me to the den. I'm a human who is supposed to become a Venator.

'Staring for so long can make someone very uncomfortable,

Goldie.' The corner of his lip lifts into a smile as he glances sideways at me.

I scoff, staring at the clearing ahead. The same clearing where that creature had attacked us. 'I'm sure it boosts your ego more like,' I mutter, and he chuckles without a word.

Slowing down my steps, I gaze at the darkened grass, no blood, no bodies like there were that night. Darius stops a few meters away from me and turns as I look at the broken branch on the other side. My hand traces my abdomen, already healed. No one would guess I suffered an injury or a significant loss of blood.

'I think I have my first question,' I say, but I don't, not really. I have too many, some that make no sense, others that I'm not sure how to phrase.

'Ask away, Goldie.'

I look at him, and at the faint smile on his lips as glowing fireflies drift among us. Blues, greens, all colors combine that if it weren't for the sudden question dawning on me as I watch them, I'd love to catch some. 'Why is it that you can't fly?'

A beat of silence, and then Darius sighs, nodding at the ground. 'Do you want the long version or the short?'

'Surprise me.' I raise my hand in the air and wait for a firefly to land on my index finger. Its wings buzz vibrantly, and I can hear Darius release a short chuckle.

'When I was five years old,' he says, and when I glance at him, he's pensive. 'My powers were uncontrollable. Barely even knew I held one power, let alone three.' He chuckles. 'I had nowhere to go, so I went around the streets looking for food – for shelter when Venators saw me accidentally wield fire.'

My hand falls to the side and go numb, already imagining the worst at the mention of Venators.

'I remember them chasing me. Mortals blocking pathways so I wouldn't get through.' He's avoiding my gaze, reliving every detail. 'I'd never once shifted before then, but at that moment, I did, only for one Venator to catch my wing and sever the top part. I still managed to escape but . . . haven't been able to fly since.'

I swallow. He was five, and they were ruthless enough to sever part of his wing. If he hadn't escaped, they'd likely have slaughtered him in front of everyone. And people would cheer because his kind is what we've grown to loathe.

'What about your parents?' My voice is a mere whisper; I'm surprised he hears me as he lifts his eyes and narrows them. A speck of humor glistens in them though I know it's a front. I can tell because Iker had reacted the same way whenever mentioned Mother or Father to him.

'That counts as your second question, Goldie.' He saunters over, tilting his head as he looks at my shoulder and extends his hand before retracting it with a firefly on his finger.

I chuckle. 'It's a good thing I have three left.'

The firefly flies off his hand, and he glances up at the sky, heaving a sigh. 'You just had to pick the hard ones.'

'You don't have to answer it, I just thought—'

'I never met my father,' he says, and my mouth is left half-open. He rubs at his forehead. 'My mother only told me he left when I was born and failed to ever utter his name. Whether she despised him or still loved him, I couldn't tell, and I never found out because she died protecting me.'

Something cold settles in my stomach at his admission.

'And after my wing was torn, I was taken in by someone else who happened to be a mortal obsessed with dragons, so there was that.' He waves his hand like it's nothing, but I think of what Gus told me.

Darius's drunken nights, his distrust of everyone else, how he's dealt with too much.

I do the unexpected.

I wrap my arms around his neck.

He stays deadly still, and the side of my face rests against his well-built chest. Rosewood and something familiar fill my lungs as I breathe it in. His hand then spans across the back fabric of my shirt, hesitant at first before his other arm comes around me, as if he is shielding me from any danger in the world.

'Your mother died a hero,' I whisper and slowly pull away. His eyes stay glued to mine for minutes like he's not sure what to make of our embrace or what I said. Noting I must have made things awkward, I clear my throat and add a little pointedly, 'I know I didn't say it earlier, but I am grateful that you saved me. And I'm not one to embrace someone so easily, especially a dragon, so consider this a one-off.'

His head rears back in mock surprise. 'Is that—' He points at me, almost smiling. 'Is that you being nice to me, Goldie?' He places a hand on his chest. 'I'm touched.'

My brows lift in complete disapproval. 'And now I'm reminded why it is that you anger me so much.'

He's back to laughing brightly, the mischievous glint in everything he says or does. I huff and glance at all the fireflies that disappear from the clearing. 'I can't believe I've been out for this long and with a shifter too.'

'Is that such a crime?' He snickers, and my brow flickers upward because it is exactly that – a crime. 'Kidding, Goldie.'

With a sharp smile, I say, 'Goodbye, Darius.' And head past him, remembering the route back to the city when his hand grips mine.

'Wait,' he says, and fingertips graze my skin as I turn to him. He's not smiling. In fact, any trace of amusement is long gone. 'Are you really going back to them?'

Did he want me to stay with him? 'I—' A sigh. 'I have friends there who most likely think I've perished.' I glance at the ground and shake my head. 'I have my brothers thinking I'm going to follow in my father's footsteps and become a Venator. There's just too much going on.' Closing my eyes, I reach for the crescent again and stare at it.

'You seem awfully fond of that carving,' Darius says, his voice a soft caress in the wind.

I drag a breath in, the carving warming under my palm. 'It's been my source of luck for years now. It belongs to—'

'Lorcan.'

My eyes shoot up to Darius. He's staring at my hand while I frown at how he'd guessed that. After I'd almost said Lorcan's name, he must have assumed. And he's not wrong as he gestures a finger to it. 'One of their greatest wishes was to unite and dance among the stars.' His focus goes back on me. 'Solaris and Crello, it's what my mother used to say.'

A smile tickles my lips, but I don't show it as I let my eyes roam the crescent, the polished oak that even after years looks like it'd been carved yesterday.

'For no love greater shared than the moon and the sun,' I echo my own mother's words and shove the carving in my sheath.

My shoulders lift as I inhale, and the next few seconds go by so silently until he asks, 'Is a Venator what you truly want to be?'

Years ago, anyone could have asked me that, and my answer would always be yes. I'd begged Idris to the point he got headaches from hearing me speak of it.

And now it's the hardest answer I can give.

'I don't want to discuss this right now. I've been gone long enough.'

'When then?' Frustration suddenly taints his voice. 'Every second points to you not trusting Sarilyn, not even your own people, and I know that the person I first met at the jeweller's wouldn't give up so easily. She would fight to win.'

I flinch at his words, not because I'm offended but because he is right. 'I don't give up.' My head snaps to him. My defensive walls barricade me once again. Before he can say anything, I'm already raising my arms in the air and slamming them down at my sides. 'Did you expect me to ask you to take me back to your house? Play pretend dead for a little longer? I mean, why does it matter if I become one or not? You were more than happy to tell me I was just an asset to you. You're supposed to hate me just how I am supposed to hate your kind for killing my father, yet it turns out they never did!'

Stop, stop, stop.

I don't.

'I've spent so long believing that your kind killed him. All my life, the only thing I wanted to be was someone who could fight off dragons, protect the city and help my brothers. I dreamed of becoming a warrior for years, yet it only took a few months for everything I'd ever thought to change.'

Darius just looks at me, processing my rant, my outburst at the aggravation I'm feeling over all this, over everything. I find myself pinching my lips together and my brows furrowing the more he stays quiet. He always has something to joke about, to tease, to flirt, to annoy.

Joke, tease, flirt, annoy me for Solaris's sake.

I run my hands over my face. 'I don't know what I'm doing here. I shouldn't even be with you right now. Every day is leading up to those trials, and I just—'

'Then complete them,' at last, he speaks up, and I freeze. His words shoot into me like an arrow, splintering right through my heart.

'What?' I breathe.

'Complete the trials and become a Venator,' he says, tight enough I'm convinced his jaw will break. 'You keep hesitating to make a decision, so make it easier for yourself, choose the one thing you've always wanted to be.'

I shake my head. 'It's not so simple—'

'After all, you're right. I do think of you only as an asset to me. Maybe I thought for one moment you had it in you to help us. A way for shifters to be free without risking myself.'

I bite back my vexation. 'Liar,' I whisper, just like he'd done to me back at the den, except I can't contain myself. I grit my teeth at him. '*Liar.* You can't even look at me.'

His eyes flicker up and bore into me. Even against the dark skies, the moon manages to illuminate the gold in them. He reaches for my hand and lays it flat on his chest. 'You're just an asset to me,' he repeats carefully, and I watch his expression never change as the beats of his heart are slow and steady under my palm. 'Am I lying now, Goldie?'

I yank my hand away from his grip. The phrase hurts more than I can admit, but I was the first to mention it, to remember that day in Chrysos when he'd first said it. 'I will never understand your desperate need to be hated by so many.'

He smirks without a glimmer of amusement in his gaze. 'Don't act like you ever stopped.'

My groan is frustration and anger built into one. 'You know for one moment, I thought you were a decent person. Helping me pay off my debt, protecting those creatures. Instead, you're confusing, arrogant, deceitful—'

'Selfish?' He whispers, and it takes one single step for him to be looking down at me, his breath to fan across my forehead and his eyes to pierce through mine.

I wonder if he can hear the raging thump of my heart forcing its way out of my chest or the tightening of my fists at the need to add more to that list. But I can't, I can't seem to speak, I can't seem to think, I can't seem to *breathe.*

'Go, on, say it,' his voice low and enticing, as his gaze wanders to my mouth momentarily.

Say it, say it, say it.

We stare into each other's eyes. Unspoken rage sparks between us and then . . . our lips clash, weapons out, and a battle ensues.

His hands rake through my hair and the force of him on me has us stumbling back against a tree. There's nothing gentle in the way we kiss. Our tongues collide like we are both fighting to prove a point. His lips are soft, almost silken when they move with mine.

'You're infuriating,' his voice is rugged, as he shakes his head, nipping my bottom lip. My legs threaten to collapse on the spot, and I let out a whimper, which unleashes something dangerous in him, a wild lust as he kisses me furiously again. Fire, shadow, and mind, just like his powers, I'm caught in every single one of them.

'I hate you so much,' I say against his mouth, as one of his hands slides from my hair to underneath my thigh and lifts it up against his. My hands fist through his hair as he tilts my head back and his lips come down on my neck. Warm shivers spread out in a wave from between my thighs, making me wish I could hate it, hate it as much as I hate him—

'Completely feel the same for you—'

'Shut up,' I breathe, pulling him back to me.

A groan releases from his lips, dominating, which irritates me because it only makes me want more.

My breath comes out in short pants as his mouth moves down my jaw, then he twists me around, my back against his chest before his hand slides up my neck reminding me of my dream. I close my eyes, tipping my head back with my body setting aflame. My lips find his over my shoulder as his other hand roves the plane of my stomach in sweet, seductive motions.

This doesn't mean anything, this doesn't mean anything, this—

He stops.

A sudden emptiness fills me as he lets go and I turn around. I'm breathing too hard to hear anything but the buzzing in my veins.

His back is turned to me. I walk up beside him, thinking he stopped because of what's happened but I realize by the frown on his face he's focusing on his hearing, his *scent.*

'What—' It goes too fast for me to comprehend as Darius pushes me out of the way. My side thumps onto the grass, and I squeeze my eyes shut, holding my breath for a few seconds before I lift myself onto my elbows and look over my shoulder.

My heart pounds as Darius stumbles back, clutching an arrow in the middle of his chest. He tears it out as fluorescent red pours from the arrowhead and stares at it just as his legs buckle and he slumps to his knees.

'Darius!' His name falls from my lips in a gasp. Fluorescent red . . . the blood from the Neoma tree.

No, no, no, this can't be happening.

I sit up, trying to rush to Darius, but I hear the hollow hooves of horses as Venators approach, reaching Darius before I can. Two men dismount and grab him by each arm, lifting him up as he winces.

'Wait!' I rasp, staggering to my feet. More Venators surround the clearing, and I spin to face each one until Lorcan barges through.

He's here. They're all here. How—how did they know?

He slides off his horse, running towards me. His hands grab the sides of my arms, but my vision is warped in a haze. 'Were you hit?'

I shake my head, swallowing as I look at Darius, still conscious yet unable to fend off the Venators.

'I told you to wait for my signal before we shoot at him,' Lorcan says roughly to someone behind him.

It's my fault. I should have left long before, and I should have warned Darius; instead, I pushed it all to the back of my mind, dancing, drinking, freeing myself with shifters. 'How did—'

'Glad to see that even after all these years you still kept your promise of one day capturing me,' Darius cuts me off, directing his words to Lorcan with a weak, breathless laugh.

My brows knit together as I glance at Lorcan. He keeps quiet, but his rage is palpable. I shift my gaze to Darius, and my veins turn to ice as he adds, 'Brother.'

Chapter Thirty-Eight

The word brother clings onto every part of me. My lips part, but nothing comes. Just deep breaths as I look between them.

They're brothers.

How is this possible?

'Are you not going to come and greet your brother?' Darius lilts casually, but Lorcan doesn't answer. 'Last time you'd tackled me to the ground, now you can hardly look at me.'

I still can't form a sentence or the courage to question it, not now, not like this.

Darius laughs again, weak but not without his teasing edge. 'Pity really, remember when we were kids, and you'd beg me to tell you stories—'

'Enough,' Lorcan's voice sharpens, unlike ever before, as he turns and storms up to Darius. Shivers run through me to the point of pain as I watch Lorcan point his index finger at Darius. 'You and I will *never* be brothers.'

If any of the Venators knew this, they hid it well; their faces now fixed in a warrior stare. Darius's golden skin pales as he looks to his left, and the General, along with the Queen, emerge from the woods, both with smug looks on their faces.

Sarilyn spots me straight away, and all my strength evaporates before her as my eyes roam her red ruby gown, similar to what she wore on Noctura night. It slides among the grass like a river of blood and shimmers as if she'd sourced it from the tree of Neoma.

'Naralía, darling, so glad to see you aren't hurt.' Her hand skims over my shoulder as she walks around me, and I shiver at the fiendish smile shaping her lips. 'If it weren't for you, we would have never found out what a simple tree can do to weaken and drain a shifter of its powers.'

My gaze flickers over Sarilyn's shoulders to Darius. Hurt flashes in his eyes, and I shake my head, starting towards him. 'I didn't—'

'Who knew the youngest child of Nathaniel's would prove useful to us.' The General's spiteful voice stops me. Even as I look at him, the disgust on his face matches his tone.

Sarilyn chuckles. Whatever kindness I'd seen in her at first has long gone since the dungeons. 'Now, Erion, Naralía has always proven she has what it takes to become a Venator. Her brothers will be so proud,' a cruel whisper as she smiles. She knows how to get to me: threaten to hurt my brothers as she did in the dungeons, and she will carry on doing it as much as she pleases.

My fingernails curl into my palm and tremble. My entire body does. Is it fear? Worry? I can no longer seem to hide it.

She lets out a breath of satisfaction, glancing over at Darius. 'Shackle him.'

'No, don't!' I protest without thinking, spreading my arms out as if that will stop every Venator.

'Nara.' Lorcan proceeds forward, his tone a warning before Sarilyn raises her palm in the air and he halts.

'No need.' Her eyes stick to me. 'Do you object to this, Naralía? I thought we already established whose side you were on.'

You threatened me.

You made me kill a fledgling.

You used me.

'They're not any different from us,' I whisper through clenched teeth, and her gaze tears through mine. It's like she's digging and twisting a blade to extract another answer.

'Well,' she breathes, as the whistle of the breeze breaks her out of her scrutiny. 'If you believe that, perhaps you should join him.' Her eyes shift behind me, and a Venator grabs me by the elbows, forcing them behind my back. I struggle and notice Darius light up with such fury, as the Venator's grip digs into my skin.

It's like he is trying to reach for me, even in that state, weakening by the second.

'She doesn't,' Lorcan says, and my head swivels in his direction as he cuts a pointed gaze at me, hoping I'll agree. 'Right, Miss Ambrose?'

The air feels electric. My gaze jumps from Lorcan to Darius, and our eyes meet for a split moment before he bows his head. I've broken his trust, no matter how I truly feel about his kind.

Even if I agree, Sarilyn knows my true feelings. I can tell by her eyes and how she speaks to me. And she uses this as another means to mess with me. Cruel and how I imagine Aurum must have acted like with mortals.

As Lorcan waits for my answer, a twig snaps in the trees. Sarilyn shoots her head to the sound, and then a blur of fire and fur rolls past, shouting, 'Murderers, murderers, murderers!'

Tibith.

My grin is that of relief, knowing he must have followed us out. Venators stare at him racing around and swinging past legs. Some unsheathe their swords, and the Venator's hold on me loosens enough for me to take advantage. I throw my head back, and he cries out as a crunch resonates in my ears. I tear free from him, twisting halfway to see him stumbling backward.

I turn to run for Darius but stop short once the Queen slams her hand down onto the ground, catching Tibith by the neck. He uncurls, thrashing and kicking as she raises him to eye level. 'What a curious little thing,' she muses, and a wave of protection charges through my veins as I urge myself forward. However, the Venator I hit grabs my arm once again. 'Who would have thought a thief had a Tibithian care for him.'

'Let him go,' Darius rasps. He sounds so defeated. He'd collapse if it weren't for the Venators holding his arms.

My lungs tighten like someone's pressing an anvil on me, restricting movement. I'm culpable for this. I'm the reason for them figuring out that blood weakened shifters. I'm what caused Darius to get caught.

The Queen makes a sound of fake sympathy, pouting her lips. 'But such a creature would do wonders in the Draggards.'

'Darry was right about you!' Tibith swats his arms at her, but she just looks amused. 'A ma-maniacal monster!'

I can't hide my proud smile at that. Sarilyn doesn't notice as she rolls her eyes at Tibith and hands him to the General. 'Throw him in a cage, will you. I grow tired of him already.'

Glowering, I pull at my arm as an instinct for Tibith, but Sarilyn blocks my view when she saunters over. 'So,' she says, twirling a strand of my hair between her fingers. 'What will it be, Naralía?'

For several minutes I stare at the twilight in her eyes and the narrowing of her brows. Something in the way she looks at me makes me think of the Liars Dice. A game of deception, lies, luck . . .

'I'm waiting,' she says in total mockery.

Make her think you are vulnerable, play on your luck, lie to her no matter if she knows the truth.

I dip my chin. 'No. I don't believe it.' I lift my gaze at her. 'Your Majesty.' It takes all my effort to say that without a bite to it.

She perks up with a smile, yet the Venator still doesn't release me. Turning her back to me, she walks towards Darius. Lorcan has his gaze on me. I feel a stab of guilt.

'I'm going to enjoy getting answers out of you.' Sarilyn drags her nail down the center of Darius's wound, and he hisses at the contact.

My teeth threaten to shatter at how hard I bite down, hating her cruel intentions.

Darius cocks his head to the side, huffing a laugh though he's barely conscious. 'What makes you so sure you'll get any?'

Sarilyn's shoulders go rigid. I can tell that he's angered her. She clears her throat, flicking her golden nail off Darius's skin, and says to the two Venators, 'Take him away and inform the city of the great news that we finally—' she drags the word with a smile '—have the Golden Thief.'

With a curt nod of their heads, the Venators start dragging him away. The other Venator finally lets go of me, and Sarilyn gives me one last smug glance before following the others out of the forest. The stone-cold glare I want to provide her with dissolves completely when Darius looks over his shoulder at me. A swell forms in my chest at the tightening of his jaw. He's not mad; he's disappointed.

Trust me; *I* want to say, *just please trust me, I can still fix this.*

His eyes leave me. Everyone mounts their horses. I hear the creaks of the doors of a carriage opening and shutting, and then I'm standing with Lorcan, the only ones left.

We stare at each other, and the dull ache from when I hit the Venator now surfaces. I don't let it show. I'm more speechless than anything.

Lorcan's chest heaves with a deep breath as he presses against the horse's saddle and lifts his legs off the ground to climb onto it. Stopping in front of me, he reaches his palm out, but I don't grab onto it. I can't.

He sighs in frustration, and dismounts again. In a strained voice, he says, 'Nara, please.'

I ignore that *please.*

'Brother,' I can hardly say it, shaking my head before emphasizing, 'He's your brother.'

He swallows, anger flooding his eyes again. 'Not by blood.'

I huff a hysterical laugh and shake my head at what I'd just learned. Darius is *his brother*, meaning the man obsessed with dragons Darius had spoken of must be Lorcan's father. 'Blood or not, he is still your family.'

He focuses everywhere except me, and at this point, I'm not sure whether I want to scream, cry, or have the pleasure of making the Queen feel the same way I have since that day after Noctura.

'Does the Queen . . .' I trail off, and Lorcan's nod proves me correct.

'And the General,' he says.

How could I have been this stupid? When Lorcan told them I knew Darius's name at the dining table, Sarilyn and the General didn't seem fazed. My head spins. 'All this time, we've spoken of him, and you never once told me—'

'Because he killed my father when we were still children, Nara, he bit him, and I had to watch my father die a painful death,' he says, that last line uttered like I'm supposed to be horrified by his ordeal.

'But you've also killed hundreds of his kind,' I argue, my face burning enough for the volcanoes up north to erupt. '*Some* were still hatchlings. Those are newborns, Lorcan!'

'I don't expect you to understand—'

'Because you don't tell me anything!'

'Neither do you!' It's the first I've heard him raise his voice in this manner. An unleashing that sounds almost beastly. 'Did you think I wouldn't question why you're trying to defend him? The fact I was standing there watching him kiss you? Or . . . your moment with him at the Noctura ball?'

I almost stumble backward. Of course, he had seen, he had seen *all* of it, but him having witnessed it isn't what has me so shocked and confused. When I kissed Darius, it was different, it *felt* different. A forbidden danger and hatred beneath the thick desire of each kiss.

My voice is a shameful whisper. 'Did the Queen tell you of the ball?'

A tight-lipped smile as he says with lethality, 'You just did.'

My lower body becomes so numb that I fear I won't have anything to hold onto if I fall.

'I suspected it from the moment he came in as Archer,' he goes on, leaning his head forward with disdain in his words. I don't move as he lowers his voice. 'Your *nerves* at the idea of dancing with him.'

Now I realize why he'd pulled me aside in the Draggards and told me if anything was ever wrong, I could tell him. He'd looked at me like he knew I was hiding something. He wanted to see if I would mention Darius, but I didn't.

'It may have taken a while to finally see him sent to the dungeons, but I know Darius, I know what he's like, and he himself knew he'd eventually get caught.'

'Hate can drive you to extremes, Miss Ambrose,' he'd uttered that to me the first day of training. Had he meant Darius? The reason he's now a Venator.

He touches my arm, soft and attentive. My gaze shifts to it as he says, 'Look, Nara, I need you to tell me if he took you to any hideout, any place where other shifters might be.'

The den, Gus, all the dragons Darius had taken into his care. I've lied to Lorcan too often, too much, but I can't in good conscious tell him that I know where other shifters reside.

'Just an abandoned cottage,' I partially lie, and his silence either means he doesn't believe me or he's choosing otherwise.

'Did he try and harm you in any way?'

My eyes jump to his, at the worry in his tone. *No, he took care of me.*

Without being able to voice it, the words lodge in my throat, and I shake my head. As much as I have more questions, I can't seem to ask them. My chest cracks as each minute passes, knowing Darius is on his way to a cell and Tibith to the Draggards.

Lorcan releases a breath, one of stress, tiredness, and everything I imagine myself feeling. 'Let's go.' He gets back on the horse, and that same palm is out, waiting for me to accept it.

I can't.

I still can't.

'It's late, Nara,' he says, a hollowness to his tone. 'Please don't make this any harder.'

Any harder?

My molars grind, and my vision is a teary blur as a tempest whirls within me. I decide not to retake his hand. Instead, I climb onto the saddle myself. His hand is left untouched as I wrap my arms around his middle.

'The first person I met at the jeweller's wouldn't give up so easily.'

Lorcan stares at his palm for a few seconds more before he tugs at the reins, and the horse gallops past the trees.

She would fight to win.

Darius's words whisper in my head, and the speed of the horse's hooves clapping on the ground causes my hair to flow behind me in the brisk air.

I shut my eyes then open them to the glistening moon and silver starlight.

I choose to fight.

And I will make sure I win at all costs.

Chapter Thirty-Nine

The streets fill up with people parading and spilling their ale on the ground while Freya and I push through. After the Queen made the public announcement this morning about Darius, everyone assumed that it meant all the shifters would soon be captured too.

The irritation of hearing them cheer and shout '*hang him!*' welled up in my chest. I wanted to explode then and there, but Freya had to squeeze my hand to stop me doing anything drastic. I'd already tried hard to ignore Lorcan since I arrived back at the barracks – even if part of me struggled to – and with the lack of sleep, one might assume I'm on the verge of collapsing.

'Nara, wait a moment.' Freya tugs at my forearm from behind and I stop to face her. She pants and drops her voice to whisper, 'Do you not think informing the shifters of the Golden Thief—I mean Darius's capture might do more harm than good?'

When I told Freya last night everything that happened, she'd not expected Lorcan to have grown up with him, neither had I, and I'm not sure I can get used to it yet. She also found it hard to grasp why I was so resolute on getting Darius out. I understood her confusion. Darius's relationship with me went from one extreme to the other. There was no in-between.

In the past I'd have preyed upon this moment. Now, I have to tamp down my anger at the memory of that arrow in his chest.

You're infuriating, another memory I can't seem to shake off about him. I draw a sharp breath. 'It won't be long before the news travels back to them.'

'And then what?' She asks, biting her lower lip, worry coating her deep brown eyes. 'We wait until the whole city burns down?' My non-response makes her raise her brows. 'Don't tell me you're thinking about that.'

I frown. 'I'm not.' Well, partly yes it might have been a thought during the early hours of dawn until it became clear I was thinking deliriously. My frown smooths as I sigh. 'But I do know who can help us . . . Leira.'

Freya's forehead pinches, a few civilians knock into her, and I grab her hand before she can trip. Guiding her towards the entrance of the Draggards I start to explain, 'She's a witch, and for as long as Zerathion has existed, they are known to share a bond – a tether of some sort with shifters. She could perhaps talk to them.'

Freya makes a whimpering sound. 'But do we have to go back there? I had this strange sensation last time I was in that room, not to mention commoners all staring at us like they were ready to tie us to a wooden pole and burn us to death!'

Specific, dramatic and the only words that could make me laugh at this moment in time. I cast her an amused look. 'And you are someone who I've seen shoot arrows at targets with your eyes closed. *We* wouldn't be the ones burning to death.'

She sucks in a breath, her obsidian curls plummeting over her shoulders as she kicks at the ground. And as I start dragging her through the cobbled roads, someone yells our names from behind.

It's not hard to tell who it is when you hear the names, 'Frey-Frey' and 'Ambrose.' Freya and I twist halfway as Rydan taps his foot on the ground, crossing his arms. Link bites his nails beside him, looking half confused and anxious.

'Well then.' Rydan arches a brow. 'I have to say you've offended us deeply.'

I mimic his facial expression but more the incredulous – what way did I offend you – type.

Rydan coughs, nudging his shoulder against Link's. Link then stumbles forward and mutters, 'I was dragged into this, I'm not entirely sure—'

'Link and I heard that you are the reason the Golden Thief got caught,' Rydan interjects, and a sudden drop occurs in my stomach making the food I'd consumed this morning a gurgling mess. I'd not had time to speak to Rydan or Link, they only knew I'd turned up safe, though I felt far from that. 'Do you have any idea how frightening it was to inform everyone of dead bodies in the forests and that after the first search you were missing? Then I come to find out you were with the thief, and right now I'm both madly jealous, and—'

'Can we perhaps withhold this conversation for another time?' Freya urges and I can't agree more.

Rydan slowly raises his chin, and his brows draw inwards. 'What are you two up to and why are *we*—' He gestures a hand between him and Link '—not involved?'

Freya and I side glance each other, aware that while I've mentioned every little detail to her since the day after Noctura, Link and Rydan know nothing. Even with Freya it took me a while to confess, and only because I hated how worried she was for me.

I realize though that Link and Rydan's thoughts on becoming a Venator aren't far off from my own views – the recent ones that is.

Restless at the idea time is running out and the trials are approaching in less than two weeks, I look over my shoulder at Link and Rydan. 'Do you trust us?'

Link nods vehemently, as Rydan dramatically raises his palm. 'Ambrose, one day we will be wed, and you will become Nara Alderis. Of course I trust you despite your murderous tendencies—'

I stare impassively at him then turn away and ignore the last of his words as I stalk through the Draggards, I'd tell them everything after I achieved what I came here to do. Freya follows me which leads Link and Rydan to do the same.

Women and men fix their glowering gazes on us, some mutter things such as 'Venator bastards,' or 'don't they get enough with extorting us for taxes?' I drown them out, darting my eyes to every stall, and peeking my head above market tents until I spot a familiar stand near Leira's tavern.

I pause. Air leaves my lips in a sign of relief at the orange fur coming into view. The brief sensation is overpowered with my blood boiling when I see Tibith in a small cage hanging off a hook above the roof tent.

Freya yells after me when I take off. Tibith's eyes perk up with delight as he clutches the iron bars. 'Miss Nara!' He squeaks.

'A Tibithian?' Rydan asks behind me, confusion lacing his voice, but I ignore it as I focus on Tibith. No vendor is around, and four other cages hang from the tent. Three goblins, and a pixie the size of my hand.

'I'm going to get you out of here, okay?' My eyes hook on his in a promise.

He blinks nervously, nodding. 'And—and Darry?'

I don't answer for a few seconds. My lips tug down before I try smiling. 'Him too,' I whisper even as the disappointment on his face still gnaws at me.

'You again?' A gruff voice says, and I turn my head to see Tig's glare on me. His crinkled eyes run over my attire, and then a thick laugh cracks out of him. 'Well, this is a surprise, turns out you're one of them.'

I back away from Tibith's cage. Every step towards Tig is civil even as his larger frame towers over me. 'I want to take this Tibithian with me.' My eyes shift to the set of keys jangling from his belt. '*Please.*'

He scoffs, lines crease on his hairless head as he raises his brows. Crossing his arms, he gestures his head towards the end of the street. 'He's not for sale.'

None of these creatures should be. Guilt tries to wiggle its way back into my mind, knowing this is where Ivarron sent all the creatures I'd trapped for him. 'He doesn't deserve to be here.'

'Neither do you, so go on.' Tig flicks his hand for us to head out but none of us budge. Tibith growls from inside the cage.

'Not without him,' I say firmly. My patience hangs on a thin line.

'Or what?' He narrows his eyes like the thought of me standing my ground is humorous to him. 'You and your little warriors will detain me?'

My gaze burns with unyielding fury, and my fingers twitch at my side, holding back from grabbing my dagger or strangling him.

Freya clears her throat softly and stands next to me, but I don't take my eyes off Tig, not for one second as she says, 'We just want the Tibithian, so name your price, sir.'

I detect the tremble in her voice, but Tig only laughs, shaking his head. 'Venators like you are all the same, treat us people from the Draggards as if we are filth and think you can get away with everything else.'

'You shouldn't speak to her like that!' Tibith says and Tig looks at him, pushing the cage, causing Tibith to tumble backwards. All my patience deteriorates and my temper sparks.

'Get out of here, Venators—' Tig goes to shove me, but I seize his hand. I snap his pinky in the opposite direction.

He lets out a silent yelp as I say, 'I am *not* a Venator.' I grab his thumb, bending it backward until bones snap and I can hear Rydan and Link's wince along with others looking our way. 'And I plan to take every creature that you've trapped in these cages with me.' My eyes jerk to a wide-eyed Freya, and I tip my head at the set of keys around Tig's belt. She nods, scrambling to get them as Tig looks at me mortified. I bend another finger of his and grit, 'So I suggest you shut down this business of yours indefinitely.'

Once Freya unlocks all the cages the creatures step out, coming behind me. I thrust Tig's hand away and he staggers, clutching his hands as he stares at the awkward position his fingers are now in.

'Have a wonderful evening.' A threat lurks beneath my deceptive calmness, and I don't waste my time listening to his insults as I spin to face a smiling Tibith, a pale-faced Link and Rydan, and the other creatures looking up at me. The pixie flies over to my shoulder, her blue skin glistens like droplets of water as she whispers a thank you in my ear.

I smile but can't help but let it slip into a solemn expression before

I heave a breath and say, 'Let's go.' I walk between Rydan and Link with Freya catching up to me. I lift my eyes at the sign of the Crescent Eye and pick up my pace. When I reach the door, I notice the silence from within. 'Both of you stay here.' I glance over at Link and Rydan and immediately they frown.

'I don't—'

'I need lookouts,' I say, cutting Rydan off. Already showing up with creatures to Leira's might make things questionable. I had too much to explain to her, to Rydan, to Link. I have the feeling that I'm running out of time and in some ways I am.

Before Rydan opens his mouth to protest, I enter the tavern with Freya and the creatures, slowing to a stop when I see what is in front of me: tables knocked over, shards of glass scatter the wooden flooring and not a single soul in sight.

'What in Solaris and Crello's world . . .' Freya whispers.

Tibith climbs up my leg and sits on my shoulder. 'Everything is broken, Miss Nara!'

Dread pounds against my head. I slide the dagger Idris gave me from my thigh. The twin blades unsheathe as I press my fingers under the trigger point. Freya lurches back, as the creatures gasp.

I creep across the tavern, cautious of the crunching glass under my boots while Tibith slides down and curls into a ball.

Moving the ripped drape aside, I enter Leira's room, and I'm greeted with the same mess: jars smashed on the ground, and the table I sat at with Leira overturned.

My throat closes and I think of the worst until my name is softly spoken from the side.

Leira crouches on the floor, dusting off dirt from books. Aelle is helping behind her.

'Leira,' I breathe, sheathing my blade and rushing to her. I grab her arms, helping her up as Freya does the same with Aelle. 'What happened?'

Her face flushes in fear in the dimness. 'Venators raided the place a few hours ago. We didn't get here until after.'

Venators . . . hearing that alone makes my body stiffen.

'Why did they raid the place?' Freya asks as she steps over a piece of wood and picks up a few jars, trying to clear the place. 'Did they have a reason for it?'

Darius is what first comes to mind, but how? He'd never mentioned Leira, unless somehow—

Bile fills at the back of my throat wondering if the Queen had managed to get answers out of him, but Leira banishes that thought when she shakes her head and says, 'The barmaid said they came in search of all the witches living in the Draggards. They wanted to know if we'd worked for the Golden Thief. Apparently, he's used glamor to wander around the city.'

As Archer.

I'm exasperated, not knowing where to go from here. Leira's eyes flicker over my shoulder and her brows pucker. 'Who are these—'

Glancing behind I answer, 'Creatures I salvaged.'

The goblins nervously blink their glossy eyes, and then Tibith's feet patter towards my side, smiling. 'Hello there, Miss!'

Leira's frown turns into peculiar amusement, and I let go of her arms, taking a step back. Freya and Aelle continue to salvage what was not damaged, but I focus on what needs to be done. This place is no longer safe for Leira or Aelle, and it's likely their cottage isn't either.

My sigh alerts Leira to shift her gaze to me. 'Look, I need your help,' I say.

From my sleepless night I imagine I already look rough, but Leira senses my worry and clasps both her hands around mine, bringing it to her chest. 'Anything.'

I'd not had much affection except from my brothers, since my parents' death. But then I came here and found Freya, Leira . . .

My breath quivers as I inhale, and I tell her everything I can remember. The attack, the creature, how Darius took me to the shifters' den, and I hated it because I enjoyed every minute, every *second* of it until Darius pushed me, letting that arrow hit him.

I'm panting by the end, describing the shock of Lorcan and Darius's history before finishing with what I have chosen to do.

It's so quiet even with Freya and Aelle cleaning in the background. Leira finally sighs, lowering her gaze. 'Nara, this is you risking—'

'Please, Leira.' I probably reek of desperation, but I don't care. 'I can do this and—' I glance at Tibith for a second '—Tibith can take you to the den.'

Tibith peers up at me, a nod followed by a smile, and I return it just as I look at Leira again. 'You just need to hold the shifters off for a little while until I sort a way to get Darius out.'

Tibith, Leira, Aelle and the other creatures would be protected, at least for now.

'What about your brothers?' Wariness floods her eyes as my heart caves in. It might as well grind into dust.

They were the first thing I thought about as soon as I returned. Idris had mentioned they would be back to watch the trials, but that was another issue added to the many I had going on right now. 'I'll handle it when they come.' A further promise: I am *not* going to let anything happen to them.

Leira bites her lip, glancing at Aelle behind her who simply gives her an encouraging nod. 'Alright, I'll—'

'What's this?'

We turn our heads to Freya holding a large, leather-bound book. Amethysts adorn the center of the cover as she narrows her eyes at it.

'My sister's grimoire,' Leira answers. 'I haven't taken it out in so long. It was in one of our cupboards. She'd given it to me to look after before she—' A deep pause. I understood this was already a hard topic for her '—left.'

Freya doesn't take her eyes off the grimoire, and a certain suspicion within me makes my head tip to the side.

She goes to flip the cover, but Leira says, 'Do not bother, child, only witches are able to open a grimoire and read the magic from it, it's—'

The words trail from Leira's lips and shock slams into me. My eyes widen as Freya opens it with ease and I look at Leira, her lips part and even Tibith murmurs something.

Only witches are able to open a grimoire. And Freya has opened it.

'Brigid,' Freya whispers to herself, running her fingers along cursive writing.

It's only a second, but a second in which it takes me to realize what this means. I slowly make my way toward her, extending my hand out to make sure she's okay. 'Freya?'

Her eyes start skimming wildly across the grimoire and then she looks up at Leira, the warmth of her bronze skin dulling. 'Where is your sister now?'

Leira hesitates to answer, before whispering, 'She died . . . seventeen years ago.'

Freya was three when her mother died . . .

I gulp. Freya trips on her feet, her breaths ragged as she looks between us all before dropping the grimoire. The thud echoes the walls as she storms out in a frenzy with me yelling her name. I turn to Tibith, telling him to make sure they all make it to the den safely. Aelle holds on to a stunned Leira as I run out of the room in pursuit of Freya.

CHAPTER FORTY

Barging through the doors of the barracks, Rydan, Link and I trail after Freya. She'd fled Leira's as if it was a mission to get back here, and I already knew she was going to confront General Erion.

She pushes the wooden doors wide open, and we enter the room. Velvet curtains brush back as everyone sitting at the long table looks up. Lorcan, a few Venators and the General himself.

I linger behind as Freya slams her hands down on the table, not caring about the others. 'Were you ever going to mention my mother was a witch?'

My eyes land on two vials shaking from Freya's movements, atop the map, each containing grey ash. I lift my head towards Lorcan and a deep line forms between my brows. My mind recalls the raided tavern at Leira's: Venators demanded whether witches had helped shifters.

If Lorcan—

'Niamh, Roman,' the General's clear voice jerks me out of my thoughts as he addresses the two other Venators. 'You may leave.'

Everyone else stays put as Niamh and Roman head out and close the double doors behind them. We all lapse into silence and I try to remain still, despite the heat of Lorcan's gaze on me.

'Freya.' A soft expression drenches Erion's face, one I've never seen on him. It's almost too hard to believe. He rises from his chair, wood groaning, then his boots drag across the marble floor. 'What did I tell you about interrupting meetings—'

'Answer my question,' Freya demands, her hands fisting.

Erion freezes in front of her, and his fatherly gaze dissipates into a humorous frown. 'Where did you hear that?'

'Mother's name was Brigid and I happened to open a grimoire.' Freya tilts her head. 'How does that occur, Father, when only witches can access a grimoire?'

My eyes slide to Link and Rydan, both seeming to read my mind as their eyes widen and I shoot them a subtle nod of my head.

Erion barks out a gruff laugh. An underlying tone of bitterness coats it. 'I didn't expect my daughter to go snooping around.'

'I didn't expect my father to keep the fact that I'm a half witch from me,' Freya retorts. Her anger crackles inside the room like bolts of lightning waiting to strike.

It makes sense if she were a half witch. Her admiration for amethysts, how she can't bear to attend any dragon fight at the arena, let alone kill one.

After silent seconds, Erion scrubs at his face. 'I did it for your own good.'

'How?' Freya's voice rises with a crack. I move nearer, as does Rydan. His protective side appears as his eyes narrow on the General; I'm as surprised as Link by his sudden change. 'How could you possibly think it was for my own good? That my mother was a witch, that I—'

'Witches aren't particularly liked,' Erion says. 'For a while, I didn't know your mother was one herself.' He places his hands on her shoulders, and she flinches, only a second but it's enough for me to notice. 'She never loved us, Freya,' he says softly. I believe it for a moment, and would have kept on believing if not for the cruelty dripping from his next words, 'She only wanted a way to deceive me and take the Venators down. All because she'd fallen for a *shifter*.'

I know because my sister fell in love with a shifter over twenty years ago.

Where is your sister now?

She perished.

Everything Leira had said the first day I met her pointed to Brigid, and she hadn't even known – known that she had a niece living behind these castle walls.

'You'd told me she died from a dragon attack,' Freya's voice is barely audible. The General's face drains of color. His hands slip from Freya as he stares at her.

No answer. His chest puffs and then a faint grin sneaks onto his lips.

Something inside me ricochets off the walls of my chest, disgust and rage wanting to unleash at the General. He doesn't have to say it. He doesn't need to show a sign for me to understand the truth.

'You killed her,' Freya whispers, realizing it herself as she steps back.

I wince at the words. Lorcan shifts in his spot as if he wants to come toward me. But all I want is to reach for Freya.

'I did what I had to do.' Erion's smile vanishes. Gone is the concerned father. In place is the General I've come to know. A man who'd kill the mother of his own child; a man who treats his daughter like she is nothing to him; a man who loathes any form of happiness.

Freya slowly shakes her head before turning and pushing past us toward the doors. Rydan and Link run out of the room, but I stay. I stay and stare at the General. He doesn't even show a twitch of emotion, no remorse, no pain.

I walk over, as I bite out the words, 'You're disgusting.'

He lifts his chin; a condescending smile deepens at the side of his lips. 'Interesting . . .' He flicks invisible dust off his cape. 'The thief said the same earlier. Though at least he managed a smile before I cracked a whip against his back—'

His head turns as my palm strikes him across the face, harsh and cold, echoing off the walls of the grand room. I do not regret it. General or not, he deserves it.

For Brigid.

For Freya.

For Darius.

He doesn't look at me, nor does he lift his hand to his cheek. He inhales a sharp breath through his nose and then carefully glides his eyes to meet mine. Their brownness reminding me of the rich dark soil of the forest, trapping you in whatever harsh reality there is underground.

I wait for him to snap back, to order my dismissal or worse because his eyes say it all – iron-willed hatred. Yet he straightens up and says, 'You're just like your father . . . a disgrace.' He walks off, and without hesitation I turn to go after him, my fingers already curling into my palms, causing indents on my skin.

But Lorcan says, 'I need to talk to you.'

I move in a slow circle until I'm looking at him straight on. A slit of light slashes across his eyes yet no glimmer shines in them.

Struggle grips at my heart and I let my defenses down. If he can see it, he decides not to mention it as I clear my throat, diverting my gaze to the other side of the paneled walls. 'I can't right now.'

Cedar and spices mix with the heaviness of the boardroom as he stands inches away and says quietly, 'I didn't know Freya's mother was a witch.'

Is that supposed to make me feel differently?

My eyes flash up at him, remembering Leira's tavern. 'If you did, would you have disowned Freya just like you all do to other witches?'

His jaw flexes as he swallows. 'Nara, I know that you're mad—'

'I'm not mad, I'm—' *Frustrated, confused?* I sigh and my lashes flutter as I glance down. 'You never told me about the Neoma blood, you were . . . *distant* with me even after you showed me my carving, you—'

'What difference would it have made if I told you?'

None at all. I would have reacted the same way.

I knew about the tree's blood by the time Darius took me into his cottage. I wanted to tell him, I almost did but I ended up putting it off once we made it to the den. I could have prevented many things if I'd been honest with myself.

Wiping my nose with the back of my hand, I look at Lorcan. His brows narrow as I say, 'I guess none.'

I whirl to leave but his hand closes around my upper arm, the span of his fingers gripping my skin tightly as he twists me. 'Nara,' he whispers in turmoil. 'I know it may not seem it, but I'm trying to protect you from—'

'Protect me from what? Your brother?' My brows flick up. His nostrils flare and I tilt my head, lowering my voice by an octave, 'Or from you?'

'Why do you defend him so much?'

'Because he is *not* the enemy.' We – the Venators, the Queen – are.

Lorcan shakes his head. 'What happened, Nara?' The disbelief in his tone matches his expression. 'What happened to you hating his kind, what happened to you helping us capture that dragon in your village?'

A knot forms in my stomach. It doesn't loosen a bit as I think back to that dragon. My hands are clammy and something hard compresses my chest, weighing me down.

I'm sorry, forgive me.

Glistening eyes, fire and gold, youthful and peaceful.

Thick liquid pools onto my hands—

'What happened to the times *we* spent together?' Lorcan's words crash back into me, his forehead falls on mine and his hand traces my arm until it's by my waist.

I can't shake the unease of the memories over what I'd done. My breaths rush out from my throat, ragged and tense. Lorcan pushes me backward and I hit the edge of the table. I almost stumble onto it, but Lorcan's hands are already there holding me as I press my palms on the scaled armor of his chest.

'Lorcan—' I sigh, closing my eyes as I try to move my head away from his, 'I can't do this, I can't—'

His lips catch mine regardless. And at first, I fight to part from him, but his grip doesn't yield. His tongue darts inside and I say his name between breaths, pleading to let go.

My thoughts go to Darius, his lasting impression from when we kissed. *This isn't the same.*

One hand lowers from my back to my thigh before he whispers, 'What about our carvings?'

Reality quickly lances through me, and Darius's voice, deep, annoying, tantalizing seeps into my mind.

One of their greatest wishes was to unite and dance among the stars.

My eyes shoot open, and I twist my head as Lorcan's bottom lip grazes the side of my neck.

'For no love greater shared than the moon and the sun,' I say to myself. I press with my hands and shake my head. 'Lorcan, stop.'

His arm tugs me closer and I say it again and again until I push with enough force and shout, 'Stop!'

He staggers back, panting as shock shadows his face. 'Nara, I—'

'You can't expect to kiss me and think everything is okay,' I say, feeling suddenly small. Nothing is right at the moment: the trials, Darius in the dungeons, Freya a half witch. Rubbing at my arm, I huff a breath. 'I need to go check on Freya.'

He tries to say something, but I cut him off, 'We'll *talk* later.' I don't wait for his response as I rush past him and out the doors in search of Freya, Link and Rydan.

Later indeed came, but I was focused on Freya. She did not want to speak, instead she went out to train. She expected Rydan, Link and I to leave but we didn't. I went and grabbed a fletcher while Rydan fetched swords, and the four of us trained in silence, supporting her in any way we could.

'I think I get it now,' Rydan says quietly as I lead him and Link to the door of my room. Freya had fallen asleep early on, but we stayed with her until now.

I cross my arms over my chest, and he continues, 'Why you freed the creatures . . . stayed with the Golden Thief.'

My shoulders loosen but my arms remain where they are, unsure of what to say to that. I don't know myself most of the time and I have yet to explain everything to Rydan and Link. But between everything going on it's been hard.

'I thought becoming a Venator is what I needed to be to protect

Emberwell but—' He pauses, glancing down at Link, and he nods at him. 'It turns out they don't protect; they ruin this kingdom.'

My throat tightens at his words, at both their comforting expressions. They understand, they're on *my* side. I throw my arms around both of them and smile.

'Link don't move. She might break our hands next,' Rydan whispers, and I draw back, swatting his arm. 'So vicious, Ambrose,' he teases, and I half laugh, shaking my head.

'So,' Link draws out the word, looking over my shoulder. 'Freya is a half witch.'

I glance behind me as Freya's curls cover half her face, and her lashes flicker each time she breathes. 'I guess she is.' I'm not entirely sure what she thought of it herself, but I know that when she is ready to talk about it, I'm here.

Link mentions how I need rest, and both he and Rydan agree to vacate our chambers. As I bid my goodnight to them, I close the door and take a deep breath, leaning the back of my head against it.

The only source of light is the moon gleaming through the open window of our room, splashing across the beds and chest of drawers.

You'll figure this out, you'll figure it all out.

Sitting at the edge of my bed, I focus on the crescent in my hand. A new day has surfaced after another sleepless night. At least Freya awoke in good spirits, focusing on new hobbies she wants to try as she plaits a few thin strands of my hair at the front while the rest lies loose.

Meanwhile, I've not stopped thinking about Lorcan. Had I been too harsh yesterday? I'd not gone to speak to him when I said I would, partly because I didn't know what I would have gotten out of it.

Freya comes out of the bath chambers clad in her Venator armor before the door bursts against the walls.

Link, practically gasping for air, stretches his hand across the door as he looks at me, then Freya.

Alarmed, I stand. 'Link, what is it?'

Wide blue eyes blink at me. 'You need to come with me *now*.'

'Why?' Freya asks.

Link sighs heavily, his gaze turning worrisome. 'Because,' he says, 'they've put the Golden Thief up to fight in the Arena.'

Chapter Forty-One

I force myself through the boisterous crowd. My elbows hit the backs of others, feet trample upon feet and many swear at me while Freya and Link apologize from behind. In normal circumstances, I'd yell back at them, but this is no normal circumstance.

'Where's Rydan?' I shout, shoving a drunken man to the side. I search around the arena, stepping down the stone stairs. If I can get any closer, perhaps I can find something, anything. I don't know how or what, I didn't have much time other than to race out of the barracks.

'He tried to flirt with Lorcan first. That failed so then he tried to convince the General to put someone else up for the fight.'

Let me guess, that failed too. 'Where is Rydan now?' I stop and turn to them once we near the front.

Link holds up one finger, taking deep breaths as his golden-brown hair sticks to his forehead. 'The General put him on patrolling duty, that's why I rushed to you.' He frowns. 'Although I must say I am still confused. I know you're on the shifters' side, but I thought you hated the Golden Thief either way?'

The question stumps me. 'I do,' I say, and Freya looks at me skeptically. 'Well, most of the time I do, I—it's complicated.' I dislike Darius for a lot of reasons. His arrogance, his inability to care about the consequences of what he does or says, and he always manages to aggravate me just by breathing. But our time at the den . . . the argument . . . the *kiss*.

'Nara,' Link exhales, shaking me from my vivid memories. 'You should know he's fighting—'

The cheers increase as a creak of the gates rumbles the entire arena. I whirl back around, and my stomach turns as Darius steps out from the darkened passageways. No shirt, no boots, nothing but ripped breeches. I've always been used to seeing him in all black that I take a sharp breath as my gaze wanders the tanned muscled torso and the narrow lines indenting his abdomen. Sleek, tight and irritatingly enough for him to rightfully have that huge ego I was met with at the jeweller's.

A chain around his ankle drags against the sanded pit as he walks to the center of it. Lashes across his back look to be healing and I shake off the vision of how the General spoke of having flogged him. My face screws in distress for Darius. If he is in any pain, he doesn't show it. His eyes narrow at the people jeering, and a sense of amusement radiates from him in waves.

Then the crowd goes silent, and I raise my head toward the balcony on the opposite side of the arena. Sarilyn, with all her cruel and manipulating smiles, drops her palm to her side. The General, just like the first fight I attended, sits beside her, drumming his fingers against his knee in boredom.

'This might possibly be the greatest outcome we've had since the arena fights began,' Sarilyn says, and indeed she is right. I'd go as far as to think the entire population of Emberwell is here.

I ground my feet to the floor to stop myself from doing something utterly stupid – such as jumping into the pit.

'You're quite popular, *Darius*.' She says his name like a tease, letting the last letter linger on her tongue.

Darius's answer isn't verbal, but from the shift in the Queen's expression, I assume he must have shot her one of his mocking smiles.

Sarilyn's eyes slit and she purses her lips before a fake smirk appears. 'Well,' she drawls. 'Shall we see how you fare after today?' Jerking her chin toward the left of her, another set of gates crack and screech.

I hiss through my teeth at the horrid sound as another male saunters into the pit. Dark long strands, pale complexion and Merati tattoos on his hands.

With alarming recognition, I slowly shake my head. It's the shifter I went to for answers. *He's* fighting Darius.

It's hard to blink into focus. The heat of the sun scorches at the crown of my head, but I will myself to concentrate; to not faint in the middle of this. Solaris forbid that were to happen.

Seeing the shifter again brings back unpleasant memories. Because of me, he is the cause of everyone finding out about the Neoma blood; the same one who screamed in pain. I even felt sorry for him, but now watching as he paces to each side, eyeing Darius up and down with a smile, I don't anymore.

'He'll be fine,' Freya tries to reassure me, though her voice tells me otherwise. 'He carries the three powers of a shifter, if anything—'

'He's also been weakened by Neoma tree blood.' I sigh in frustration. 'I doubt they did that to the other shifter.' Considering he looks healthier than when I first saw him. 'It's not a fair fight,' I say to Link and Freya, knowing it never has been before, for any creature.

Link gives me a sympathetic look, then someone from above us yells for the fight to start. I glare at him despite the fact that he isn't looking at me, and that's when I turn around only to be taken aback by the flash of bright light coming from the shifter.

I place my hand up to my forehead, squinting before a roar quietens the crowd, and the shifter's claws slam onto the ground, fully transformed. Darius doesn't so much as flinch, unlike the people around me; he tilts his head as he raises his hand to the side and flecks of fire spark off his fingertips.

'Is he – is he not going to shift?' Link asks, his tone cautious, but I keep my gaze locked on Darius as the shifter springs toward him. Luckily, Darius rolls out of the way before the shifter can get to him. Stealth and precision ripple off him like he knows what tactic to use. The shifter on the other hand shakes his head from the fall and puffs air out of his snout, ready to charge at him again.

'He's going to try and wear the Merati shifter out,' I say quietly, my heart racing with unfounded certainty.

The shifter snarls, creeping forward, one claw taps the ground, slow and ominous, but Darius keeps his eye on his every move. And when the shifter pounces, Darius blinds him by flaring a flame up in the air.

I bite my lower lip out of nerves, watching the shifter go at him, each time failing. The audience groan, growing tired, as if they hoped one would be dead by now. The irony is not lost on me, watching the humans act more animalistic than the dragons themselves.

Huffing, my eyes stay glued each moment Darius dodges an attack. *Fight and win,* I say in my head, then realize with disbelief that for the first time, I want him to win. I don't know why I pray he can hear me; it's the single thought I have since the last fight where the Ardenti heard me, *connected* with me. For whatever unknown reason, I was able to give her confidence. But Darius . . . he doesn't look my way once; he doesn't *know* I'm here.

Fight and win, fight and win, fight—

A line of dust rises in the air and seconds go by where I can't see anything until it clears and everyone around me screams in excitement. I lunge forward by impulse before Freya pulls me back just as the shifter lands on top of Darius, snapping his jaws down at him. Darius crosses his arms, keeping the shifter mere centimeters away from his face.

People in front of us block our view and I twist my head to Freya. She already has that look in her eyes, the kind where she's telling me to stay put, but I shake my head and slip from her grip, moving in between two men. I meander through others, peering over shoulders to get a better look.

Sweat and dirt seep into my nose as arms flail in the air, and then a thud from the pit prompts the crowd to clamor in delight. I make it right to the other side, up against the railings and in perfect view of Darius and the shifter.

Except the shifter is no longer on him, he's at the opposite end while Darius staggers to his feet, pressing his hand to his upper arm. Blood trickles past his fingers and he gives it a quick glance before his eyes are on the shifter.

The shifter is nowhere near worn out. It's like he has twice as much energy. Irked, I gaze over at the Queen toying with her gold rings. She's smiling as if finally the fun has begun for her.

I turn my head just in time to see the shifter spreading his wings and taking flight, as far as the chains will let him.

No, no, no, Darius shift— 'Shift!' I shout, but the noises from the crowd drown me out. The shifter dives downward, his wings tuck in and I let out a small gasp right as he approaches Darius.

Yet *one, two, three* . . . seconds is all Darius needs as he crosses one arm over the other in front of him and bows his head before dark shadows encase him, making the shifter divert himself onto the ground. Swirls of silver glisten from within Darius and then he emerges, no longer in human form, but a dragon.

Murmurs of suprise run through the entire arena. I've only seen Darius like this once, but I had been too weak, too delirious, and I could barely make out it was a dragon saving me in that forest. Now I'm witnessing the full extent of him, the strength he possesses as both human and a dragon. My gaze caresses each part of him in fascination, from his silver scales shimmering among the obsidian leather skin, to the two horns curving at the head as if it were a crown.

Despite the same large build as the other shifter, Darius possesses something else, something I imagine goes beyond his powers.

I release a trembling breath, my chest heaving as I look to Darius's wings spreading. The right stretches out to a perfect point but the left . . . just like he'd told me, is severed completely at the top. Light streams between the thick skin, emphasizing scar lines running down the curve where his wing had been sliced.

I can't imagine what it must feel like for a shifter, not being able to do the one thing you were born to do. Then again, the Queen and Venators don't give them the privilege of doing that unless they want to be caught.

Wishing for this to end already, all I can do is watch as Darius and the shifter stumble and claw at each other. Sharp teeth clash on leather skin. Screeches come from them both before Darius sends the shifter flying back.

The stands rumble under my feet from the shifter smashing against the sides of the arena walls. A low snarl leaves Darius as he approaches him. The anticipation is so intense that I want to close my eyes – and that is something I'm not used to thinking.

Darius stops inches away and it's as if my heart does too. The shifter still hasn't gotten up, but Darius drops his head, sounds of pain emerge from him as he collapses to the floor and shifts back into a human. He clutches the sides of his head, and I realize that the shifter is using his Merati powers. Whatever it is, he's inflicting pain, hallucinations, *anything*.

Shit—

I grab onto the railings and tremble as the shifter hurtles from the walls to Darius. Again, I let myself feel what I normally avoid: fear.

And for the first few seconds, I can't see Darius, the shifter's whole weight covers him. People question whether it's over, but the shifter soon enough raises its head and shrieks, crumpling to the ground beside a still-alive Darius. Tendrils of fire spark from his fingertips, he's panting as the shifter reverts to his human form – chest red and raw from burns.

It's not long before they both regain some strength and the shifter fights with him, human to human with fists in the air, one on top of the other. The shifter lands the first few punches until Darius clenches the shifter's other hand within his grip. The audience wince out loud as Darius smacks his head against the shifter, startling him.

My head pounds wildly almost as if I'd received the hit. Darius reacts quick as he glances to his side and takes the long chain by his foot, wrapping it around the shifter's neck. A struggle ensues as Darius doesn't ease on his hold, and the shifter turns every color in the world.

He sputters until his hands fall limp to the side, and he falls unconscious. I think I stop breathing as the chain drops, and Darius steps back to examine. It goes eerily quiet for seconds, minutes, the moment lasts a lifetime and then . . . the cheers break through.

Copper coins rain in the air, and glancing over at Sarilyn, I see her grip the arms of her throne despite her calm composure as he stares up at her. He then turns toward the crowd, bowing at the waist with a mocking smile. He goes around as everyone whistles before he stops to bow again to someone in the crowd. My eyes travel along with his until I notice Lorcan above.

His lips are pulled into a tight line and from where I'm standing, I can see him convulsing in anger, as if that one smile from Darius was the last straw. Every part of me grows heavy with emotion. Had the death of Lorcan's father made that hatred so strong? Blood related or not, I could never hate my brothers.

Lorcan shakes his head, his brows narrowing before he shoulders past someone and walks out of the stands, never turning back.

Prying my eyes away as he disappears, I whirl my head to Darius. He's still bowing when he freezes halfway, straightening up as his gaze connects with mine from the stands. It's the first he's seen me since that night, and it's the first time since the fight ended that his winning smile disappears.

I suspect my own expression as being solemn, because I can feel it in the way my brows pucker, my throat closes and how hard my heart squeezes.

Someone says my name, but I clutch my cloak as Darius and I stare at each other. He slowly rises to his full height, powerful even after a fight, his eyes never drifting away from mine as Venators yank him back to the dungeons. Even as he looks over his shoulder at me and the gates close, he doesn't stop. It's as if he is memorizing my features.

'Nara!' Freya shakes my arm and I realize it was her calling for me. I glance at Sarilyn, her eyes on me in the same way she'd looked at me on the night of the Noctura Ball, knowing I was with Darius.

Freya shakes me again and this time I face her and Link, my mind elsewhere and my chest tight. 'I—need to get him out—'

People start descending the steps as Link and Freya share a troubled look before he says, 'Nara, it's not so simple, you know that.'

I do.

'Now more than ever the Queen will likely think you'll try and get him out,' Freya adds. 'Meaning more patrols and less chance of you succeeding.'

She keeps her hand wrapped around my arm and I lower my head, knowing she is right, but I still want to at least try.

'If I don't get him out, they'll kill him—'

'*If* they wanted to kill him,' Freya lowers her voice. 'They would have done it by now. They wanted answers from him, didn't they?'

I nod but how much torture can he withstand before telling them everything they want to know?

Freya sighs, looking at Link as if she's thinking of what to do next. 'Three days, Nara,' she says. 'Give it three days and I will find out where exactly they're keeping him and gather enough resources to help you.'

Three days . . . at this moment feels like a lifetime. I slide my hand down to hers and squeeze it. 'But what about you? Your father—'

'Is a *horrible* example of a human being,' she cuts me off. 'And if I think about it, I'm letting him win.' She looks skyward, biting her lip, and I watch her throat ripple as she swallows before focusing on me. 'My mother died . . . he killed her. He treated me like I was dirt, and when I came back after two years, he already had everything set up for me because he believed I wouldn't succeed in anything else. He may be my father and I hate that—' A single tear slides down her cheek. She wipes it away within a second '—I hate that I still love him, but I also can't let him think he's winning again, because I'm tired of feeling weak by his side, and I'm tired of always trying to make him love me when that should come naturally to a father.'

No matter the circumstances, Freya has stood beside me through everything. She has just learned she's a witch, and that her father killed her mother, but she still finds courage to help me when she shouldn't have to at all. 'You might share his blood but you're nothing like him,' my words are soft enough to nurture her. 'Remember that.'

She puts on a brave smile, her eyes squinting like she wants to cry as she nods and drops her head on Link's shoulder beside her.

'Three days.' I calm myself with a deep exhale.

'Three days,' she repeats with a whisper, and I look back to the pit, the marks on the ground and then the empty thrones where the Queen and the General once sat.

After the three days, I will only have four more until the trials. I pray those *do* take a lifetime.

Chapter Forty-Two

My hair peeks through the hood of my cloak as I keep my head low and make it past the cells. It'd turned nightfall by the time I left my chambers. Freya had made sure that for the three days I waited to come down here, she'd figure out where Darius was being kept. We realized it was where the Queen had held the Ardenti dragon. Be it some twisted joke on her part or not, it didn't deter me, and according to Rydan, fewer Venators would be patrolling the dungeons tonight.

I avoid the pleas of the prisoners, each insult they throw out across their cells, and I take a long breath. When I slow down and look to my left, I see the looming hallway I saw last time, leading down somewhere, deeper than where I already am.

Shaking away the itch of curiosity, I continue, each minute bringing me closer to where Darius is. Clatters and distant echoes sound from one of the passages, making me freeze, but the noise fades and I figure they've gone another way.

Blowing a breath, I dart my gaze around. A deathly cough

resonates through the cells before I make my way to the steel gates and place both palms flat on them. I graze my fingers along them, cold crust rasps against my skin as I count to three hoping this works. I've had the confidence for anything prior to coming to Emberwell; I don't want to lose it now.

I look to the side where the lever is and check again for any Venators. Not a single soul – for now. Once I pull on the lever, the gates rise and I stumble into the cave-like cell. It doesn't take me long to find Darius in the center. I hold back a gasp at what I see. Chains hang from above, clasped on each of his wrists. His body sags and his head tilts to the side like he's been in this position, unconscious for hours, *days*.

I peel my hood back and rush in front of him. 'Darius.' Resting my hands on his face, I plead for him to awaken. He grunts and I close my eyes for a few seconds, letting out a small sound of relief before opening them.

He lifts his head, his voice hoarse as he realizes it's me. 'What are you doing here?'

'What does it look like I'm doing?' My whisper is a loud hiss as I glance behind me. 'I'm getting you out that's what I'm doing.'

He shakes his head, and his eyes slit as he tries to stay conscious. 'You need to leave; they'll know it's you—'

'I'm not leaving.' I glance at the chains and walls, hoping there's something to pull them down but there is nothing.

'Listen to me—'

I will not. 'First of all, you should know by now I hate listening to you.' I huff. 'And second, be quiet while I take these chains off.'

'So heroic.' He chuckles but it's not the same, not the kind he always gives me where it's followed by a teasing remark. It's feeble, raspy, not a Darius laugh.

The word *sorry* wants to come out but that doesn't feel like it is enough, not for what he's endured during his capture.

I turn my focus to the shackle around his right wrist, and I can feel him looking at me the whole time. It makes my nerves spike, so I send him a small glare and his lip tilts up, but it falls too quick, I almost miss it. The reminder of our last encounter right before his capture hangs thick in the air, but he does not say a word. Inhaling deeply, I study both chains this time, the dents and the blood dripping to his elbows.

Just like the shifter I'd seen wearing these before, it is clearly some sort of steel spike or knives piercing their wrists. Attempting to yank these off won't work, it might do more harm than good. I sigh. I need a set of keys to unlock the sides; no blade I have will fit to pick the lock.

I decide to walk around him to see if there is anything else I can do. Up close I see fresh lashes across his back. Blood clots over wounds, others are such deep cuts, it makes me ache. I know they will heal completely, but with the Neoma blood weakening him, they just might not.

My hand trembles a little as I reach for one in the center of his back. He tenses. I suck in a small breath. As I trace my index finger over the wound . . . it begins to heal within seconds. I take my hand off like I've been burned, but Darius doesn't seem to notice.

I stare down at my fingers, wriggling them.

It healed?

Thinking I've gone mad, I attempt to touch another wound, one by his shoulder. It closes upon contact and my brows crinkle until he suddenly starts whispering, '*Naralía Ambrose.*' It's more like he's talking to himself as he repeats my name a few times like a sacred prayer from his lips, and a speck of liveliness seems to return to him. 'Do you have a middle name?'

My fingers still, forgetting for a moment how he's healing. I've not been asked that in a while, and I should know Darius of all people would be one to end that streak. 'It's um—it's Brielle,' I say quiet enough that I doubt he can hear me. 'It means strength. My mother gave the four of us middle names reflecting qualities she believed we'd have within ourselves.'

He pauses, like he's soaking up my answer. 'And your brothers?'

I smile and another of his wounds heals as I brush my hand against it. 'Idris Callan, protector.' And he is true to that middle name. Idris always makes sure to protect us even when I give him a hard time. Walking back around to face Darius, I glide my hands along his torso and then say, 'Illias Cedric . . . kindness, and finally Iker Alexander, nobility.' I stare up at Darius. He stares down at me, my blue eyes reflecting in the dark gold gleam of his. He doesn't respond. I don't even think there is a way to respond to this, but he does smile. It's affectionate, maybe even a sense of appreciation that makes me feel breathless. I quickly move my hand to touch what I can reach of his wrists, and he grimaces. 'Sorry.' My fingers recoil and I too grimace. 'I won't be able to take these shackles off without hurting you.'

His eyes train on me, on everything I say. 'It's fine,' he whispers before letting out a breathless chuckle. 'I'm sure you're secretly enjoying this.'

I glower. Months ago, I could have easily said yes but . . . 'Well, if it was the other way around, I'm sure you would too.'

His expression hardens. He didn't like my comment. The knuckles of his hands turn white as he clutches the chains, and tilts his head away.

He doesn't want to say something back and I don't know if I want to hear it.

'Darius?' I clear my throat, but it does nothing to the croakiness in my voice.

His gaze jumps to me in a heartbeat, and the anger in his eyes cools to a warmth of gold.

'About your capture,' I say, avoiding his stare. My heart stammers. 'I know you think I had something to do with it but—'

'I never did.' You can hear the sincerity in his voice, and when I look at him, it's the first time he seems upset – at least from what I've seen of him so far. Still, I carefully nod as a response, but regardless of it all, I don't think I can forgive myself anytime soon for what happened that night.

I stare at my feet and bite the side of my bottom lip. He looked so disappointed in me at that moment he was dragged away. Maybe he's lying, or maybe he's right and I jumped to the wrong conclusion, because if he was disappointed in me, it would have shown that he cared.

Something else pops into my mind, a question I want to know even if it's not the right time. All I'd learned from Lorcan is that Darius had bitten his father, but why did he? Was it intentional?

Insults from the other cells intensify, plucking me from that thought. *Venators*. I pop my head up and glance over my shoulder. Making a quick decision I look back at Darius and say, 'I'll return in a minute.' And without a second thought I take the crescent from my sheath and lay it flat in his palm.

He parts his lips with a frown and clutches it before I tell him, 'To take the pain away. I always believed it was quite magical so . . .' I trail off. I'm not one to just give the carving out to anyone, especially someone like . . . well someone like *Darius*. And I don't know if it is because it belongs to Lorcan that I'm giving it or because every time I look at it, it's now a reminder of him. And that despite the other night, these three days Lorcan has reverted to his cold self; the person everyone thinks he is.

Pressure clamps down on my chest at that thought. I turn to walk out before it gets worse.

'Goldie,' Darius calls out, and I stop, realizing it's the first time he's called me that today. I look over at him. His brows are furrowed in a pensive stare, and I wonder for a second what he might be thinking so hard about. 'Tibith,' he says. 'Is he—'

'He's safe,' I answer before he finishes because it's all I can tell him. Tibith believes in me enough to save Darius, and it's what I plan to do.

I walk out, pulling the lever and resting my back against the gates. My breaths come heavy, like I've done strenuous work.

'Once you get him out, go with him, Nara,' Freya had recited a thousand times before I left the barracks. *'Go with him and don't worry about your brothers. Rydan, Link and I will make sure they're safe, I promise.'*

Squeezing my eyes shut, I let out an involuntary sob, no tears, no sting, nothing, just frustration rising in my chest because I don't want to leave them, but I can't leave Darius here, as much I should *want* to leave him.

I rest my hand on my chest and inhale slowly before pushing myself off the gates. I walk stealthily through the pathways with determination settling in my gut to find a set of keys and if I must fight a Venator to get them, so be it.

Fire torches flicker as I pass them until a cry for help causes me to halt. It's distant, and sounds painful, and it happens again. I turn my head to the source and notice it's coming from the dark passageway beyond the stone stairs.

Twisting my body towards it, I clutch my hands into fists. The hallway looms darker the more I look down it. I know I should continue with what I came here to do but when I turn to go, I hear the voice again. My legs move before I can think straight.

I'm cursing myself with each careful step down the stairs. I expel a shuddering breath as a gush of cold washes over me. No torches are ignited in this part of the dungeons, but a small crack of light seeps from above, enough for me to make out more cells that lead into depths of gloom. I walk closer, my eyes scrunching as I try to take a better look.

'Help—please,' the voice comes again, and I whirl to the side to a man lying on the floor of his cell. Fingers like those of a skeleton twitch, and as I drag my gaze to the auburn hair covering half his face, horror jumps down my throat.

'Adriel.' I breathe his name out in a chilling gasp and run toward him.

Clutching the cell bars, I frown yet he doesn't look at me. Instead, he falls unconscious. I shift my gaze to someone next to Adriel, resting his head against the back wall of the cell and recognize him too.

It's the man who'd pleaded with one of the Venator leaders to spare him from paying taxes the day I was with my brothers. So many down here are breathing, most unconscious, malnourished but breathing.

It's suddenly hard to draw in any form of breath without panting. Why are they here? Adriel is supposed to be dead. I saw his bite marks. He was pronounced dead along with Oran. I watched him on his deathbed as he spoke to me, told me of the creature—

The creature.

My hands slacken from the bars and fall to my sides as I shake my head, taking a step back from the cell. I almost trip over my feet as I whisper a 'no' and everything spins.

They say it's worse than dragon shifters or a rümen.

You should know the rümen that attacked us wasn't normal.

It was never a dragon . . . it's always been the new breed—

'I knew soon enough you would come down here.'

I turn to stone, immobilized with the pieces fitting all together before I find the power in my legs to slowly turn around.

The General's face appears through the shield of shadows covering his upper half as he takes a step down the stairs, then another step and another, like an animal unleashed from its cage. His eyes skim past me to everyone inside the cell and he lets out a breath as if this is an inconvenience to him. 'They all look so . . .' He flicks a hand. 'Lifeless, don't they?'

Chapter Forty-Three

'You're the one creating the new breed,' I state as calmly as I can, but I am far from that. My gaze shifts to the stairs, wondering if I can pass him and run, but that's not what I really want to do.

Erion stares at me, observing any little twitch, any form of emotion on my face. 'I wouldn't say *new*.' He puts his hand behind his back. 'I've been this way for years.' When he starts slowly pacing to the sides, my feet stumble backwards. 'Though I can no longer shift.' He stops and twists to face me with a narrowing gaze. 'I suppose there's still downsides to a newly made breed.'

I should have known. If the General is capable of killing even the mother of his child, then he's capable of so much more. 'How—'

'It's simple, Nara. I got bitten by a rümen and I didn't want to die. So my solution?' He lifts a brow, sounding smug before a smile cracks the corners of his lips. 'Test out if I would survive a shifter's bite even if it meant I would become one of them.'

'And you did.' I'm unable to keep the control in my voice. Bouts of fury curl against my fingers. And I had thought Darius, other leaders such as the Elven King could be behind this, yet it turns out to be the very people we thought were protecting us.

'It came out with some interesting results. Two different bites, one outcome.' He looks bored now, and I know this can't lead to anything in my favor. I carefully move around, bringing my hand to the blade strapped around my thigh just as he casts a casual glance at the other cells. 'We aren't immortal. We do have an acute sense of smell, hearing . . . heal quicker than usual but we still scar, die and share all the horrid traits of a rümen.' His brown eyes cut across to me, so sharp and animalistic that I freeze. Unease creeps through my veins at the soullessness reflected in his gaze.

'What do you gain out of this?' I ask, wondering if it's mere satisfaction, if he's that cruel and delusional to want to do this? 'Out of turning humans against their will? The Queen—'

"Is *desperate* for a bigger army than just humans.' His words stun me into brief silence, and I can tell by the spiteful smile on his face that my horrified expression must be one he'd love to see every day. 'So,' he proceeds, 'around the time I was bit . . . Seers told her of a great battle in the near future, one that will bring the world close to the brink of destruction."

The knots in my stomach tighten. There'd already been battles within Emberwell in the past. Another greater one now could jeopardize Zerathion as a whole.

'And for someone without power,' Erion points out, shooting me a stern glance. 'She is prepared to go to any lengths.'

Even if it goes against her beliefs . . .

Erion continues speaking, walking up to Adriel's cell and tapping the bars. The metal clinks and rings for what seems like an eternity as he explains that some Venator leaders know about the prophecy; the ones who are trusted enough not to defy him. I think of the Queen and how her fury for Aurum led her to what is happening now. Despite him she still detests shifters, dragons. It's no longer hypocrisy, it's fear, even if she will never admit to it.

Thoughts pile up inside my head, one after the other. And when I come to a conclusion I've dreaded and have avoided thinking about since that night in the woods, I look up through narrowed brows. I grit my teeth, cutting the General off, 'You *killed* my father.'

He puffs his chest as he sighs. There's not a single bit of emotion in him. 'Perhaps,' he says, not even denying it for one second. 'But I wasn't the one who ended up with his blood on my hands.'

My brows knit and I grip my blade harder as he clicks his tongue and shakes his head. 'Nathaniel was always favored by everyone. He was good at capturing creatures, but his views . . .' He winces in mockery. 'He didn't believe it was moral to kill dragons and send others to slavery even though that's what humans once were to Zerathion. You can imagine we never saw eye to eye.'

'So, you sent someone else to kill him, another one of *you*,' I spit out. The words cause a stir of revulsion in my stomach and if it weren't for Freya, I'd delight in torturing him the same way he tortured Darius.

Erion hums almost too gleefully. It's sickening. 'When he found out about my plans to use humans as weapons, I had no other choice. I'm trying to protect Emberwell, Nara.'

I want to laugh at how paradoxical that is, but I shake my head, fixing my glare on him. 'Just like you were trying to protect Freya by killing Brigid?'

His eyes flash in rage. 'Do *not* think Brigid's death was something I wanted. She signed onto that wish the moment she fell for a pitiful shifter.'

It doesn't excuse anything. He's a murderer, out of his mind and a poor excuse of a man. 'You're sick and so is the Queen.'

He's unaffected by my words. Instead, he chuckles, cocking his head to the side. 'And what do you think of, say . . . the deputy?'

My muscles tense up. 'Leave him out of this.'

The General can't contain his smile of vile amusement. He inclines his head forward and says, 'Oh, but why should I when he is at the center of it all?'

As soon as those words flow out of his mouth, I don't want to hear anything more. And yet my trembling voice asks, 'What do you mean?'

He rolls his eyes, drawing closer. 'Come on, Nara, *think*.'

I don't want to. I don't want to at all.

Every step he takes toward me has me inching closer to the walls. 'I told him bringing you here would be a mistake.' He sighs. 'But he couldn't help it even after everything. You just seem to *fascinate* all creatures.'

Creatures, creatures, creatures.

All creatures.

My heart drums like thunder in my ears and I beg my thoughts to be wrong.

'Lorcan . . .' Erion's smile turns into a sneer. 'Was the first to get bitten by me, the one to stay strong, shift, unlike me and everyone else down here, weakening by the day.'

No, it can't be true, no—

'He was my first successful weapon, and he does everything I say.'

Nausea clutches my throat and I fight to hold it down. 'Stop.'

'*I* ordered him to kill your father, *I* made him attack you that night in the forests because it was our chance to see if the thief would appear, if he'd sense you were in danger, and we were right—'

I stumble against the brick walls, blocking Erion out as memories ring in my head. The creature's gaze on me the day my father died was the same as that night Darius took me back to his house. The scar on my hand . . . It can't be Lorcan, it—

'I did warn him you would be nothing but trouble for us. Such a waste of my time.' Erion's forceful chuckle brings me back. His tone lowers with a cruel twist as his gaze wanders from my head to my feet, repulsed. 'Although—' A thoughtful look '. you might just be what I need.'

I don't need seconds to realize what he means by that as he bares his teeth and runs his tongue along a growing fang. My eyes widen and it all happens too fast as he lunges for me.

I barely dodge him, pressing the button of my blade as I raise it to defend myself. Erion cracks his neck to the side as I pant, waiting for him to turn and face me. 'If you have any humanity, you wouldn't do this to Freya,' I spit my words at him. As much as I want to thrust this blade into him, end him for everything he has ever done, he is also Freya's father and the only parent she has left.

A slant of light slashes across Erion's eyes as he twists. Anger cascades down his face, and I know that anything I say will do nothing to stop him. I look to the stairs and charge towards it when Erion grips the back of my cloak, making me almost scream as I'm thrown against the bars of a cell.

My vision quakes as the blade drops, and the side of my head stings. Regaining composure, I rush for the blade, grabbing it in the nick of time before the General's arms come around me, trapping mine to the sides. The grip is so tight, my lungs feel as if they are slowly crushing together. I can't breathe. I try to move my hand as much as I can.

'Let's see what your brothers will think of their new sister,' he says. As soon as he mentions my brothers, rage seeps into my veins and I clutch the blade harder.

His fangs skim across my neck and just as he lowers them onto my skin, I jam the dagger through the side of his thigh.

The pressure of his arms loosens as he lets out a low grunt, and I slam my head back against his. I hear him shuffle backwards until there's a deafening smack against the wall followed by a thud onto the floor.

I choke on my gasp, hunching over as the blade quivers in my hand. Blood drips from it as I allow myself to recover and then slowly, I turn and drag my gaze to the General on the ground. His chest rises and falls. He's still alive but I don't know how long it will take him to regain consciousness.

Sheathing my blade, I spot a set of keys attached to his belt. I've been down here too long and now is my only chance. With caution I reach down and grab them as I look at the cells one last time: at the men, women, Adriel, all of them part rümen. 'I'm so sorry,' I whisper because I know I can't save everyone.

I take off, gripping my free hand against the walls to steady myself as I make it out into the main passageways.

He was my first successful weapon, and he does everything I say.

The General's words hound me, and I'm overcome with every emotion searing my insides into nothing but dust. I don't even know how I got from one point of the dungeons to the next.

I ordered him to kill your father.

I shake my head and slam into the gates.

I made him attack you that night in the forests.

My hand curls around the cool steel, and I force myself to pull down the lever. When I do, Darius is there with a weak smile of relief. I stalk up to him, breathing harsher than ever as I fumble the keys between my fingers.

He says, 'Goldie,' but I can't answer him right now as I fit one of the keys in to the lock, twisting and turning it but to no avail – it doesn't work. Frantic, I look for another one. A strangled noise leaves me when it also doesn't fit.

Nothing is going right.

'*Nara*,' Darius says, this time his voice commanding me to look at him but instead I try another set of keys. 'What's wrong.' He's not asking it like a question, he's saying it because he knows something *is* wrong.

I shake my head. 'We don't have much time—' I stop as the shackle unlocks, blades pull back and his arm drops.

As much as I want to relax at that, I can't. The blood pools down onto his hands and the crescent before I run to unlatch the other wrist, and his knees slam onto the ground. He almost takes me with him as I place my arm under his and struggle to raise him up. 'Darius,' I whisper, like his pain radiates onto me. 'Please . . .'

He stares up at me and I know he can see the urgency on my face. Nodding, he lifts himself off the floor, and I clutch his hand as I drag it over my shoulder. We stagger out of the gates, and I don't bother to close them as prisoners start jeering at us.

'You're healing my wrist?' Darius says, half confused. As I shift my gaze to where my hand is holding him, I realize it is just how I'd done with his back: no more blood, no sign of blades having lodged inside his skin.

'I—' I look at him and his eyes draw me in. 'I don't know how—'

Venator voices suddenly float through the dungeons from near the entrance. Shadows of them appear on the brick walls, and I look to my right for a place we can hide, when Darius lets go of me and tugs me back against his body without warning into one of the hidden corners. One of his arms wraps around my stomach and the other across my chest, securing me. I hold onto his upper arm as the back of my head rests on his chest, and I don't utter a word as I take several deep breaths along with him while we wait for the Venators to pass. When we hear feet skid to a stop, I clutch harder onto Darius's arm.

'Do you think the General has already killed that thief?' One of them says. My heart races. The General is still unconscious or . . . might not be anymore.

'Won't be long,' the other says. 'You saw how he left him the other day.'

I bite my tongue at their obnoxious laughter. Darius can sense my need to go at them, so he presses me harder against him. I feel his heart drum in a slow rhythm on my back. As the noise dies down, I say quietly, 'I think they're gone. You can let go of me now.' Neither of us makes a move. I'm positive my fingernails have dented into his skin.

'It doesn't seem like you want me to, Goldie,' Darius whispers against the arch of my ear. I can already feel his lips curve into a smile.

I let out a breath, sounding thick and ragged before I remember where we are and push his arms away as I turn to him with a glare. 'I see that it didn't take you long to return to your aggravating self.'

His eyes illuminate in delighted mischief before I roll mine and grasp his hand, leading him out of here. Shouts can be heard as soon as we make it past the entrance, and I imagine they've discovered that Darius is no longer in his cell.

Darius's strength picks up and we dart through the spiraling steps that lead us to the outside. The grass wisps in every direction with the wind. I look ahead to the woods.

I shake my head, realizing that he thinks I am going with him. That was the plan, but now . . . 'Wait, wait, wait!' I say, planting my feet in the ground as Darius turns to me with a frown. 'I can't go with you,' I add, catching my breath.

When he looks as if he's about to disagree I continue, 'I still need to do one thing. And don't try and say I'm putting myself at risk because I know I am. I have been since I came here, so *please* leave. Tibith is at the den, as are two witches, Leira and Aelle. They will explain what they know so far—'

'What happened when you left me back there?' His voice hardens. My breath heaves out of me in deep pants.

Your brother killed my father.

The General is behind it all.

I can't go with you because I can't leave without hearing it from Lorcan myself.

'Nothing happened,' I whisper, because if I tell Darius now, he's capable of abandoning the thought of going to the den, and he's capable of much worse.

He takes a purposeful step toward me, and his eyes show such conviction I want to do nothing more than to look away, but I can't. 'You have to learn to stop lying to me.' His hands lace through my hair, and I unintentionally wince when he touches the side of my head that was slammed. As he draws his hand back, he notices blood on the tips of his fingers.

Panic edges its way through me as his gaze lifts to meet mine, so wild with rage yet concealed for my sake. He stays silent as he starts stalking back to the dungeons, and I turn, shouting his name.

He doesn't listen, and I brace myself in front of him. 'You have to go.'

He's not focusing on me. He's zoned out from everything around him, the air, the woods, life.

'Darius, stop!' I yell, and my voice finally gets through to him. Exhausted breaths come out of me as our eyes are on each other. 'Stop pretending you give a shit,' I whisper, and the words taste bitter in my mouth. His eyes widen with incredulity, but I don't give him a chance to respond. 'I told you nothing happened. I need you to go, and I promise I will come but not now, okay?'

His jaw moves and there's something so raw in his gaze that it peels back my own vulnerability and my need for sudden comfort.

Whatever he wants to say, he keeps it to himself. It's like he knows he can't win this time, not with this argument and not with me.

He brings out a fisted hand, uncurling his palm to show me the crescent. A sharp sting pierces my chest.

I always wondered why it was so special . . . now I know.

My lips quivers. I stare at it for a minute too long before dragging my gaze up at Darius and saying with enough coldness to my voice, 'Keep it, I don't want it anymore.'

He looks at me like he knows there's more to it, like he wants to ask what's wrong. But I can't bring myself to tell him that the person who was once his only family, broke mine.

'Please go,' I say, about to lose all the resolve I have. He hesitates. Then nods. He turns his back to me and I watch him walk away. I feel a rush of disappointment, yet I know he has to for his own sake but . . . he only makes it halfway before he stops, looks off to the side, and shakes his head with a grimace as he twists around and comes back towards me.

I don't have the chance to ask him what he's doing as he drops his forehead onto mine, and I close my eyes in an instant, letting us stay like this. I don't try and fight, yell or argue like I usually would. I'm too defeated and for once, I'm scared that if I move or push him away, I won't have this feeling of peace ever again.

'I hate that you're so stubborn,' he says with a sigh.

I keep my eyes shut. 'Is that the only thing you hate about me? Because I have a long list when it comes to you.'

His low chuckle feathers across my lips, and I don't know what is happening, but I do know that I don't want it to end just yet. 'There's so many things I hate about you, Goldie, that no list will ever suffice.'

I bite back a smile. Our foreheads still press together and my eyes never open as he takes my hand in his. Somehow his are both soft and rough. The touch is gentle, but his skin is of a person who's trained, fought, and *survived.*

He pries my palm open, hands me the crescent, and curls my fingers around it. 'This isn't for me to keep,' he whispers, and I can't bring myself to protest because he's right. And with that, I no longer feel him here. A breeze whizzes over me. After a minute I blink, seeing him far ahead before disappearing between the trees.

The loss of peace is immediate. I'm alone. I have the truth of what happened and it's the worst truth I've ever had to face.

I cradle the crescent in my hands, staring down at it until it hits me all at once.

Don't cry, don't cry, don't cry.

Biting my lower lip, I clench my eyes shut.

Don't cry, don't cry, don't cry.

I don't.

CHAPTER FORTY-FOUR

I walk back to the barracks. feeling like I'm in a dream or a nightmare that I can never wake up from. It's similar to when my father died. My mother and brothers crying, all except for Idris and me. We looked at each other whilst I held my arm, the blood, so much blood I couldn't even see my skin.

Stopping outside Lorcan's chambers, I stare at the door. I don't care if it's late or if he's asleep, I *need* to know.

I barge in without so much as a knock. Sconces on the walls lighten half his room and for the first few seconds, I feel . . . nothing. Lorcan idly walks out from the bath chambers, his chest drips with water droplets and his copper hair looks almost brown when damp.

He pauses when he sees me and furrows his brows, glancing between the door and me. It's then my heart splits. I slowly drag my eyes down to the scar on his chest as he says my name, but I concentrate on that scar.

He'd mentioned it was Darius who caused it. A spear that pierced through him. But I remember that Idris shot an arrow, hitting the creature in the exact spot where Lorcan has his scar.

'How did you get that scar?' I can't ask it any quieter than this as I glance up at him, and his frown deepens.

'How did you get that scar, *Lorcan*?' I repeat, my voice firm this time. It's not even a question anymore, it's an accusation.

He looks at it for so long that the room grows too quiet but every word the General told me sounds loud and clear in my head. When his eyes are on my face again, his expression is torn yet his silence tells me everything.

I erupt.

A yell rasps from my lips as I charge at him with my fist in the air, but he clutches my wrist and twists me, so that my back is to his front. 'Nara,' he says in a guttural warning. '*Don't.*'

'You lied to me,' I say. A slice of anguish tears at me as I yank myself free and whirl back round to him. 'You *murdered* my father and yet here you stand having known all along what you did.'

He lowers his gaze. I think back to our conversation the other day. To every *other* moment I had spent saying how despicable it was of me to lie to him when he'd done worse. So much worse.

'Why?' My voice betrays me in a broken whisper. 'Why did you take an interest in me when you knew who I was? When you knew what you'd done to my family.'

His stare doesn't leave the ground. He's afraid to look at me. 'I didn't want to.'

My hands clutch the crescent so tight; I don't care if it cuts through skin and bone.

'But when I saw you that day in your village,' he inhales, shutting his eyes. 'There was an aura about you that made me feel content. You intrigued me too much to just leave you behind.'

Intrigued.

That word, that *damn* word turns to poison as soon as he utters it.

And as if he's built the courage, he draws his gaze to me. His eyes are dim and bleak and full of pain. 'I just wanted to be near you so I could always feel that way but every time I looked at your arm, I couldn't stand it because I was reminded how easily you would hate me if you found out what I'd done.'

I shake my head and don't stop as I speak, 'No. There's a difference there. You hoped I would never find out, you only wanted me in your worst moments and that you secretly plotted to get Darius in an act of petty revenge. He might have killed your father, but you also killed *mine*.' My heart twists in every direction, and what I want is to forget. Turn back to the times I knew none of this and had only my brothers. 'You're a *coward* and a hypocrite, Lorcan.'

Those two words land like a blow to him. His throat tightens as he swallows and says, 'I didn't have a *choice* with your father. Sometimes my urges are impulsive, and I turn. The only one who has kept me sane enough is the General. I *owe* him.'

'So, when he ordered you to kill my father, you agreed?'

'I was just seventeen. I didn't know what I was doing—'

'And Adriel? Did you know what you were doing then? Did you know what you were doing turning all those people into the same thing as you? Did you know you were the one who attacked me that night in the forests?'

'You weren't supposed to be harmed,' he says, quiet and desolate as if it will help me think differently.

My eyes begin to water, and I bite my cheek, holding back my tears. Lorcan reaches for me, but I shake my head, retreating backward. His hand fists. He lowers it before sighing.

'Nara, please,' he says. 'I love you too much for this to ruin everything.'

Love, a funny word that holds no value when someone is saying it to save themselves.

I laugh at him.

I curse at him.

I almost *shatter* before him.

'You don't love me.' I shake my head because maybe, just maybe, right at the start I might have thought that it was love. But now? Honed daggers stab at my naïve heart. 'You used me,' I say in realization, the words an echo from my lips. 'Just how everyone else seems to.'

'That's not true.' Determination rings in his tone. 'All this time I've been trying to protect you, but finding out you were helping a shifter hurt me—'

'Hurt you?' I repeat with such disbelief. 'You found out I knew more about Darius than most people did. You waited to see if he would appear and then you planned it all out, you, the Queen, the General. I was always going to be the bait for him, *always*.'

'And do you wonder why that is?' He snaps but I don't answer him, and his gaze hardens. 'He's always tried to one-up me. He saw us together and wanted to anger me, to mess with me—'

I let out a pathetic laugh at how wrong he is, but he ignores me and continues, drawing closer.

'If anyone used you it's him. He's the one who isn't a good person. He doesn't care for you, he doesn't care for humans. He steals because that's his fun, his mockery to all of us, he kills, he seduces anyone that comes his way and tosses them aside once he's bored. You're *nothing* to him, Nara, none of us are.'

Breathing down on me, by the time he finishes, he's not the Lorcan

I once met. He's the one who took my father away from us. He's the one who gave me a scar I cannot even look at without remembering that day. He's the first one that I—I shake my head. 'You're right, he's not your brother,' I say, without a single emotion in my voice. 'I would never treat mine like you do.' I take a step now toward him, confident enough not to show any weakness. 'And maybe I'm nothing to him.' Whether I'm lying, telling the truth or just wanting to get it out of my system I couldn't care less. 'But you, the Venators, the Queen give him a reason to feel that way about us all. If only I had that mentality when it came to you.'

His jaw tenses and those green eyes go a shade darker than any forest. He opens his mouth and I prepare myself for more lies, but he stops when his gaze travels down to my hand. 'What about the carving?'

Realizing that I'm still clutching it, I open my palm and stare at Darius's dried blood seeping through the wood. It's never brought me good luck. It's harbored the opposite.

I muster all the control I have within me before I slam it against his chest, and he stumbles back as his hands grab onto it. 'Take it,' I say. 'It was yours to begin with.' I storm out of his room, slamming the door shut and pressing the heels of my hands to my eyes.

A beat goes by. I flinch as I hear something smash against the wall from inside his chambers.

The carving.

I squeeze my eyes shut, hearing him break more things, and I choose to walk away this time, heading towards my room.

I make it to my door, slowly turning the knob to find Freya leaning against the window, playing with her obsidian curls. She turns her head as soon as I enter and widens her eyes, springing toward me with question after question, saying that she was so worried about me, she couldn't go to sleep.

I look at her, taking the keys I grabbed off Erion from my sheath pocket and holding them out in front of her. She stares at them, frowning, and grabs both my hands in hers. I still keep looking at her, at the distress grasping onto her features as she slowly takes them from me and sets them on the bed. After that she gently touches my shoulders, sitting me down. She then settles opposite me and says my name over and over in a distant echo.

I don't know where to start, I don't know how to say it to her.

The floor blurs and I blink to focus my eyes as I lift my gaze to Freya's. With any strength I have left in me, I try and explain what I can without falling apart.

She's silent for so long, without any sort of expression, but I know she's feeling too much, all at once.

She rises, taking in a deep breath as she starts nodding with intense resolve. 'I can help him.'

It hurts seeing her like this. 'Freya—'

'Before my mother's death, he—he used to smile at me. I remember he'd bring me back lilac pearls that I wanted, he—'

'Freya,' I whisper. She looks straight at me. Her shoulders begin to shake, and she cries.

She wraps her arms around me. 'I'm sorry,' she says, but I don't know why she's the one saying sorry when it's not her fault. 'I said I wouldn't cry for him but I am.' Her breaths heave out of her in short bursts. 'Why do I still care for him?'

I don't think she's saying it to me. I think she's saying it to herself. I pull back and shake my head. 'Because you are *not* him.'

Her nose reddens, and she tucks her bottom lip between her teeth, nodding. I hug her once more before she whispers into my hair, 'You should have left with Darius. It's not safe here.'

'I know,' I say and look at her. 'Which is why I need you to listen to what I'm going to ask of you next.'

She nods adamantly. I exhale, looking at the keys. 'But first I want to ask you something else.' When I look back at her, she wipes her tears and nods again. 'I know . . . being a witch means able to bond with shifters.' I recall the moment I was with Darius and how his wounds had healed. 'Is it the same for other creatures?'

Freya mulls my question over. I'm not a witch, that I know, but healing Darius, and the way animals are drawn to me like I'm there to protect them. It just makes no sense at all.

'I don't really get anything when it comes to creatures,' Freya says. 'They barely register me. The only thing I've noticed is that I've always hated any fight or capture involving dragons, but I've only ever gotten a strange feeling like—like I could help someone a few times, like when I met your brothers in Chrysos, or the ball, even the arena fight the other day with Darius.' Her eyes drift to the beds pensively before looking at me. 'Why do you ask?'

I shrug, seeing I'm left with more questions than answers. 'I was just wondering,' I say, and Freya doesn't look convinced, but I change subjects and tell her what needs to be done before I leave.

Neither Freya nor I sleep the entire night. We talk for hours about our plans and don't even realize when the sunrise casts rosy hues into our room.

She helps me pack whatever necessities I need into my satchel and rushes me toward the window when rapid knocks sound on the door. We freeze until hearing, 'Ambrose?' and let out a breath, knowing it's just Rydan.

He knocks again and Freya shouts. 'She's not here, remember?'

'Well, how do you plan on informing her that her brothers have arrived already and are downstairs!'

My whole body stiffens.

The satchel in my hand falls and everything I have in it scurries across the floor: carving tools, bread, clothes.

Freya turns to me just as I go to the door and fling it open. 'What?' I say. Rydan's brows narrow, pointing one finger at me then the other at Freya.

'Frey-Frey, was I just lied to—'

I barge past him, rushing through the corridors, not even noting that Freya is right behind me. I make it down the stairs to see my three brothers standing there, glancing around as if careful not to touch anything.

Illias is the first to notice me and he smiles, then Idris and Iker spin to face me.

No, they shouldn't be here, not yet. They are supposed to come on the day of the trials. I was going to come back to make sure that I take them with me. My panicked expression makes Idris frown with concern.

'What are you doing here?' I ask, gazing between the three of them, nerves practically oozing out of me.

Iker snorts. 'We wanted to surprise you. Your friend Lorcan sent out a carriage for us a few days ago, but Idris was too stubborn to come until he finally gave in.'

'You don't seem happy to see us?' Illias makes a face as he leans into Iker, whispering, 'This feels like the time we tried surprising her when she turned fifteen.'

Iker's brows rise at that, rubbing the back of his head with a wince. 'I'm still recovering from that.'

'What's wrong?' Idris gets straight to the point, his eyes narrowing as he looks at my fingers still covered in dried blood. He scans me whole before glancing over my shoulder at Freya. Then a familiar voice grips me to the spot.

I look to my left as the General clasps his hands in front of him. He's acting as if nothing happened last night. He looks the same except for a strained smile. 'Miss Ambrose, there you are.'

Defensive, I move nearer to my brothers for protection as Erion's gaze shifts to them. He hardly greets them before saying to me, 'The Queen has requested your presence . . . *now*.'

Chapter Forty-Five

'Father—' Freya attempts her pleas, hoping in some way she can get me out of this.

'Freya, I suggest you get yourself ready for training.' His tone is impatient, and Idris starts forward when Freya walks up to my side, puffing her chest with stern confidence.

'No,' she says, and this time the General takes his eyes off me to look at her with a mixture of surprise and anger. I do not deserve Freya's friendship.

And I don't want to get her in trouble for something that is all me.

Two Venators, leaders, join the General, their faces devoid of any emotion. I turn and grip Freya's arm to draw her attention. 'It's okay,' I whisper and level my eyes with hers. 'Remember what I told you?'

She nods rapidly, biting her lower lip. 'But, Nara—'

'Just tell them if you must,' I whisper again and let go, looking at my brothers. My chest squeezes, watching confusion on both Iker and Illias's faces while Idris's eyes cling to me almost knowingly. Something is wrong and he can see it; he's always been able to see it.

I clear the tightness from my throat and give a wan smile, promising to see them later.

Freya stares at me as I follow Erion out of the barracks. The two Venators walk in front of me before the General latches a hand around my upper arm, his hold tight and rough. We continue our way to the castle as he says through gritted teeth, 'The keys . . . *where* do you have them?'

'I didn't think to take them with me once I got out,' I lie, keeping my eyes on the flagstone pathway. 'Why? Upset that you couldn't turn me? Or upset that Darius is no longer someone you can mess with?'

His sneering laugh unnerves me, and his hold only tightens to the point of pain. 'I'm far more curious as to why you are willing to risk yourself for a thief like him instead.'

I dart a glare at him, not realizing what I'm saying as I blurt out, 'I'd do it all over again if it meant he'd be safe from you.'

My words startle me. Erion hums with triumph, dragging me when I start slowing down.

I let the warm air glide around me along with my memories of what there is beyond the castle walls: the woods, the den, Darius . . . the peace I'd had in my mind last night before he left.

I want that again.

Though the tension ramps up when we walk through the castle gates, I barely even register the bronze crest of a dragon outside or how the brief moment with my brothers back at the barracks might be the last I ever have with them.

At a time like this, Ivarron's words remain my source of strength: *ignore it and prevail.*

I always knew how dangerous this would be. And perhaps I should have thought of his words last night, but I wanted to speak to

Lorcan. I wanted to see him because if there had been one shred of hope the General had lied, I needed to see it myself.

For *that* . . . I felt stupid to have believed Lorcan all this time.

I didn't realize that we had made it to the throne room until the General releases me, and my hazy mind tries to clear away my thoughts. I lift my head toward the Queen. Poised and seated on her throne, she swirls her goblet slowly. My eyes skip to the right of the grand hall where the General stands beside Lorcan.

He's looking at me with regret, and that only makes my gut twist at what I know. Ignore *him* and prevail.

'Naralía,' the Queen says, and I shift my gaze to her as she stands, narrowing her eyes with a derisive smile. 'For all these years I've seen trainees come and go, but you by far have been my greatest piece of entertainment.' Her gown slides down the steps of the dais like a golden river, alluring but still a menace to trap you. She hands her goblet to the lady-in-waiting and tilts her head, eyeing me closely. 'Such a shame you keep lying to me though. What would your father think?'

Her words are a spear straight through my chest, my heart, *everything.* What would he say? Would I still be in this position? Swallowing hard, I settle on what I'd hope for. 'He'd be proud of me.'

Her eyes widen at my answer, and she scoffs. 'Well, that's surely different to what I once heard you say.'

That was before I knew everything.

"To honor my father's legacy," she recalls. A crack forms inside my heart at how that was what I'd wanted for so long. 'Although in a way I suppose you are honoring his legacy.' Sarilyn's crown gleams under the golden mirrored ceiling as she tilts her head to the side and takes on a pitiful look. 'He just sadly never made it out alive.'

Anger flames my cheeks. I dare not look at the General or Lorcan.

'So, is that your plan now? To kill me? Threaten me with my brothers again? Torture me?'

She tips her head back and her laugh rings against the walls at that last part. 'I already did that with the thief, before you released him. Although I must say it became quite tedious unable to get any answers out of him. Not even when I mentioned *you* did he fess up.' She purses her lips in thoughtful mockery. 'I suppose I was wrong to think he cared for you.'

I don't let her words affect me. I don't need to hear it from her or from anyone. I'm tired of it.

She waves a hand with such daintiness. 'Shifters are all the same.'

There's an underlying tone of hatred in her voice. I think of Aurum, every one of the Rivernorths she'd slaughtered; taking that crown, this castle, this kingdom. None of it belongs to her.

'Erion,' she says. 'Inform the city and trainees that the trial has been moved up to tomorrow.'

I suck in air.

Tomorrow.

No.

Lorcan steps forward, shaking his head. 'That is too short—'

'I've made up my mind.' Sarilyn's tone manages to stay graceful yet authoritative as she doesn't even glance back once.

My eyes flick to Lorcan's as he drops his head and retreats into a guarding position. Disappointment rakes through me, more at myself for believing he might have tried to do something. His cowardice has always been there since the start. I was too blind to see it.

'And *you*, Naralía,' Sarilyn says. I blink out of my misery to look at her. 'Will participate just as you had intended to unless of course . . . you'd rather risk the ones you love.'

I raise my chin, indignant at her manipulation. She can do

whatever she wants to me, *anything*, even if it wrecks me, picks apart any strength I still have, so long as my brothers are safe.

'In the meantime—' She smiles like a predator smelling fresh blood and clicks her fingers in the air. The Venators who had accompanied me and the General here come at her command, grabbing me by each arm '—to make sure you don't attempt anything, you will spend the night in the dungeons. I'm sure you are familiar with it by now.'

I'm hollow, not fighting back when I know it's no use. I can only hope Freya did as I'd asked.

The Queen dismisses us, like I'm just dirt she wants to get rid of. It unravels something in me. I clench my fists as she saunters back up the dais.

'You know, Sarilyn?' I call out to her. She turns. 'I feel sorry for you, I truly do.'

She raises her brows with a complacent smile, like anything I say will be a simple joke to her. 'And why is that?'

I narrow my eyes, saying it so everyone hears, 'Because you are so full of hatred that you've lost yourself throughout all these years and ended up becoming just like the person you despised yet . . . loved the most.'

Her smile drops and I delight in it as she clutches the side of her gown so tight, she might rip it. She storms down the dais and grips my chin with force. I try not to wince. 'Say that again,' she grits.

'I don't have to,' I say as neutrally as I can, glad I've wiped that self-congratulatory look from her face. 'You already know what I mean.'

Her pupils seem to quake the longer she stares at me. Her face tight with such an unfamiliar expression that for one small moment, she looks vulnerable.

'Your Majesty,' a small female voice interrupts from the doors behind me. 'The Phoenix warriors have arrived.'

Sarilyn doesn't answer, doesn't move. She keeps her eyes on me, and I do the same, not backing down from anything I've said. Another second goes by and then she releases me. 'Tell them to come through.' Her voice doesn't sound like hers. It's as if she's fighting for control of it again.

I'm being taken away by force after the Queen signals for us to leave. I look over my shoulder. She's dazed as she makes her way back to the throne, then I drag my gaze to the General, his face dripping in smug superiority, before it lands on Lorcan who's unable to even glance at me.

Memories of Lorcan float around me: when he walked away from me after Adriel and Oran's attack; when he'd ignored me among other Venators and the General; when we'd kissed for the first time, and then he listened to the General as if I no longer existed.

I can almost hear the crack in my chest, leading toward my heart, and I snap my gaze away as we make it out of the throne room.

'He's not worth it.' I say it so quietly not even the Venators beside me hear, and I close my eyes, thinking of my life before the city.

Chapter Forty-Six

I slam my palm against the stone wall, looking for a loose piece. It's a useless thought that there might be one, but the Venators hadn't even bothered to throw me into a normal prison cell, they'd taken me to the section where I'd found Adriel's cell.

Knowing this is where they sent me should fill me with dread. Instead, I'm restless, taking my cloak off as if that is viable enough to work as a weapon. Rotting flesh clogs the entire area, and I suppress the urge to gag.

I have no sheath, no blade, nothing to help me either way. My palm is red-raw as I hit the wall again and drop my forehead against it. The coldness of it eases my burning mind and body.

Huffing, I tip my head back and start whispering a lullaby my father would sing to me to fall asleep. '*Oh sun, oh sun, I wait for thee, basking in the twilight until your dawn. Oh sun, oh sun, how I wish to be blinded by you and mourn when you no longer shine—*' I trace the sun and moon on the ground beside me '*—oh moon, oh moon, I wait* *for thee, shining down on those who shame us. Oh moon, oh moon, how I wish to share the skies with you, and emerge in love and bliss—'*

'You were the last person I expected to see down here.'

My fingers pause among the dust and I lift my head at the weak beaten down voice.

Adriel.

A wall separates us and I can't see him, but the last time I was here, he was unconscious. I turn my head to the side so he can hear me better. 'You're awake.'

His laugh crackles like a fire. 'Since the moment you thought breaking down the walls would do something.'

I pout my lips and puff out some air, staring at what I'm surrounded by. It's futile for me to think I can escape. Luck rained on me when it came to getting Darius out, and I already had the opportunity to leave with him and I didn't.

Now I have to deal with it.

Adriel takes in my silence. Then a scraping sound, followed by grunts like he's lifting himself up against the wall, echo out into the void. 'It looks like you're still her favorite if your only punishment is the dungeons.'

I'm not sure what would be worse anymore.

'Maybe she's just *intrigued* by me,' I mutter under my breath, raising my brows in sarcasm. When he chuckles again, I inhale sharply. If only I could have prevented all of this.

Adriel's laugh fades into a wheezing cough before his next words come out hesitantly. 'Did you . . . did you figure out it was Lorcan who bit me?'

Something sharp cuts through my heart. 'I didn't want to believe it was him,' I whisper, looking toward the floor. *I wish it was all a lie.*

'Neither did I,' Adriel says. 'Then it became clear why he'd done it.'

I perk up with sudden attention. Despite Adriel being unable to see me, I frown, twisting my head over my shoulder and facing the brick wall. 'Had the General not told him to do it?'

It's what I assumed. He'd killed my father at the General's command, which was a disturbing way for him to owe Erion.

'Why do you think the day after Oran and I grabbed you outside in the gardens, we were attacked? Your scent must have been on us.'

The same night I first met Darius. While I'd fought him, Lorcan had attacked Adriel and Oran. He'd slowed down before we all left for the city and tensed as soon as he'd passed them. I shake my head. 'But Oran—'

'Didn't make it,' Adriel whispers, and the memory of Venators dragging them both back gnaws at me with every ounce of guilt. 'I suppose it serves me right. We were horrible to you and for what?' He sucks air through his teeth, and I imagine he's wincing. 'Jealousy?'

'I forgave you,' I say.

'You shouldn't have,' he says, when I no longer think he'll respond to me.

Words tangle in my throat. I want to tell him that though Oran didn't get a chance to live, everyone down here still does. Adriel does. I'd given the keys to Freya, but more Venators than usual were patrolling this time; it wouldn't be easy. None of it ever is.

I shift to the side and exhale in despair when footsteps echo from the stairs. Someone hangs a fire torch on the wall and when the flames filter through to the person's face, I see Lorcan. He looks at Adriel's cell then mine before he heads my way.

Scrambling off the floor, I rub the side of my arm and stare at him as he takes the remaining steps. If it wasn't for the bars, I'd lunge at him.

With a cautious glint in his eyes, he lifts a slice of brown bread and passes it through the slit. 'I brought you food,' he says. 'I thought you might be starving.'

Normally yes, but the events of the past few days have made me forget food altogether.

My face stays impassive as I grab it off him. He watches as I take a bite, not bothering to swallow and spit it back out at him. It hits the side of his cheek, and his jaw locks as he brushes the crumbs off. Childishly, I then throw the other piece at him. This time it knocks from his chest to the floor and he sighs, his lips pulling into a grimace.

'Nara, this is the last thing I wanted.'

I let out an incredulous breath, shaking my head. 'You should have thought about that when you lied to me about what kind of person you really are . . . the General has you in this tight hold that I just don't—'

He doesn't meet my eyes as he says solemnly, 'He's the only one who's been there for me since I was fourteen.'

He still trusts in him. 'Been there for you?' I repeat, feeling whatever I say will be in vain. 'He uses you as his weapon, Lorcan.'

He falls into silence. Maybe he does know. Maybe he doesn't want to admit to it himself.

I sigh deeply, my eyes roaming every part of him until it stops at his hand. Heavily scarred, rough even upon my skin whenever he'd touch me. 'Is that how he turned you?' I ask. Despite my feelings over what he's done, my question is gentle.

He looks at me and I motion my chin to his hand. He lifts it, giving it a thorough stare before he nods. 'Back when he could shift, he couldn't control it. I walked in here when he was trying to chain himself . . .' He lowers his arm and it's like he can't finish the rest.

'And you were there at the wrong time,' I conclude.

He nods again, tearing his gaze away.

It doesn't change anything. When I look at him all I can think about is how he's the one who attacked us, attacked *me*.

'Tell me about your time with Darius when you were kids,' I say quietly, wanting to know where it all went so wrong. His eyes shoot up at me, a dark flicker of rage pulses through them but I don't falter. 'Please?'

It's enough of a beg for his gaze to soften. He takes a long deep breath. For a brief moment, I begin to think he won't say anything until . . . 'We didn't have much growing up. My father was turning blind, and so I was always the one providing. Darius was never allowed to go out but some days I would sneak him out, and he'd be so fascinated by things he'd end up stealing them.'

An unwanted smile escapes me. *A thief from the start.*

'My father never liked that though. He'd punish Darius far too often, but despite it all, Darius continued to rebel, seek anything that was fun to him, always telling me every single wish he'd have on Noctura night.'

A twitch of a smile tugs on his lips before he masks it. How so much hatred stemmed from one thing I won't understand. So, I bite my lip and ask the question I haven't been able to decipher since I'd found out. 'Why did he kill your father?'

He exhales roughly from his nose as if he knew I'd ask that. 'I—I don't know,' he says, his gaze bleak and far away. 'I was out the whole day but when I came back, I found my father violently coughing blood and in agonizing pain. He was holding onto his arm and saying, '*the dragon did it*.' I hadn't even realized Darius was peeking out from behind the wall at the far corner of the room until I'd looked up. And when I confronted him, he would only shake his head. I was so terrified, angry and—' His lips pinch together as he thinks of the word. '—*Confused* that I told him to leave, but then his powers started getting out of control, burning everything, the walls, the tables . . . and while I managed to get my father out, it didn't take long for him to die in my arms from the bite.'

I'm not sure what to say, what to think. They were so young back then. Brothers, a family that ended in tragedy. 'And Darius?'

His gaze jumps back to me, empty. 'He ran away.'

Our eyes stay on one another, and I can tell there's more to it that he won't explain.

'Have you considered that perhaps it wasn't all his fault?' I know it's something I shouldn't say when I wasn't there to witness it; when previously I believed Darius could do such a thing for no reason at all other than being a shifter. When Lorcan stares at me like he can't believe what I'm saying, I blurt out, 'You had good memories together, he even seems—'

'Seems what, Nara?' His voice takes on a cruel edge before he shakes his head at my silence, and a muscle flickers under his jaw. 'The General was right, of course you would defend him.'

I can only widen my eyes in disbelief. 'Are you listening to yourself?' I throw him a look of frustration. 'The General this, the General that . . . whatever lies and nonsense he's fed you, you accept it so easily.'

His brows furrow, vexation sparks off him like he chooses not to think any differently.

'Your General tried to turn me into what *you* are.' I approach the bars and clutch my hands around the cool steel. 'And who is to say he won't come down here and try it again?'

'He wouldn't—' He releases a tense breath and amends his words. 'I wouldn't let that happen to you.' His hand reaches to touch mine around the bar. My first response is to jerk my hand back, the rough touch of his fingers on mine lingers on my skin; an unwanted presence.

His gaze turns pleading just like last night, how he'd mentioned he loved me. I step back even further, curling my fingers on my chest.

'If this is what your idea of love is supposed to be.' My throat tightens the more we stare at each other, and I whisper, 'Then I do not want it, nor will I ever accept it.'

I spot the change in his eyes, the hurt flaring in them as his hand lowers from the bar. He nods once like he understands but he doesn't. I don't think he ever will unless he realizes what kind of person the General really is.

Just leave, my gaze says, and he complies, pausing by the fire torch. He looks off to the side and clenches his fist before becoming nothing but a silhouette as he walks out.

'Word of advice, Ambrose?' Adriel says after a minute or so of me standing here, staring at the ember flames of the torch. I don't say anything back. 'Unless it's Crello itself, don't fall in love.'

His tone is a weak tease, maybe to make himself – make *me* feel better.

I close my eyes and hug my abdomen for comfort. My words a soft timbre on my tongue. 'I won't.'

Chapter Forty-Seven

There's a herd of trainees by the time I arrive through the cave passageways of the arena. A few are fastening weapons on their backs, to their sheaths and across their chests. I didn't have enough time to grab anything; the Venators had arrived within hours since Lorcan left and tossed me the trainee attire.

Inhaling the stale and damp air, I jerk my arms away from the Venators and glare at them as they walk off.

Freya squeezes past two trainees, a quiver of arrows hangs across her back as her wide eyes take me in. She wraps an arm around my neck, pulling me in as she breathes out my name in such worry that it drills deep into my chest. 'Thank Solaris, you're okay,' she says and steps back to look at my face. Lines pinch at her forehead. 'I didn't know what to do once I'd heard where they took you. My father made sure I couldn't go down there and then the trials were pushed to today—'

I shake my head to cut her off and clutch her hand. 'My brothers? Are they . . .?' It's too hard to even say it.

'They're safe,' she replies, understanding what I meant and what I *needed* to hear. 'I did what you asked me to.'

I nod, releasing a short breath when she scrunches her eyes in mild amusement. 'Idris however – was furious.'

I imagined so, even the thought causes my lips to twitch. 'I knew he would be. I'm surprised he hasn't tried anything.' The last thing I expect is Idris to be calm.

'He wanted to until I managed to calm him down,' Freya says thoughtfully, her gaze lingering at a spot over my shoulder.

My eyes narrow, surprised more than anything that Idris managed to listen to someone that isn't his cranky self.

'Oh!' She snaps out of it, clicking her fingers as she reaches for something in her quiver. 'Um—' In both her hands, she holds the blade Idris got me and extends it toward me. 'I kept this safe for you.'

I take a deep breath, forgetting the sting prickling the back of my eyes and carefully take it from her. Before anything else, I lock my arms around her and whisper my gratitude as I blink a few times, letting thoughts of my brothers flutter away like a flock of birds.

When I let go, she opens her mouth, looking like she has something else to say, but Rydan appears from behind Freya's shoulder and grins. 'You're still alive!'

I fix him a stern look as Freya turns to him and smacks the side of his upper arm. 'Rydan!'

'What?' He frowns looking from Freya over to me. 'I was worried.'

A breath escapes me before I roll my eyes and stand on my toes to hug him.

'It's beginning to get rather odd that you keep embracing me, Ambrose,' he says, and I shake my head in mirth at his ability to annoy me into smiling.

'How do you know I'm not—'

'Miss Ambrose . . .'

My shoulders tense at Lorcan's voice coming from my right. Hesitantly, I pull back from Rydan. I don't look, I don't turn to face him, I just don't want to.

He awkwardly clears his throat as I don't respond. 'I hope you are all ready for the trials.'

This time I can't help snapping my head toward him. My gaze cuts through his exterior as I clench my fist around my blade. 'It's not like I have a *choice*.'

His expression fills me with remorse and tightness engulfs my chest – a mixture of anger and remembrance of the times I thought he was genuine.

'I am ready, Lorcy,' Rydan announces, and one can guess he is trying to help. 'Far more ready than the rest of these trainees.'

Lorcan's gaze pulls away from mine unwillingly as he looks at Rydan with a raised brow. 'I'd believe that if you hadn't fooled around during training.'

Rydan runs a hand over his chin, and the side of his lip creases into a flashy smile. 'So, what I am hearing is that you were always watching me?'

Lorcan doesn't say anything. He stares at Rydan with a stone face before shaking his head and strolling off to speak to other trainees. My eyes linger on the back of his armor, and something unsettling flutters deep in my gut. Dread almost.

'Are you sure he betrayed her because—'

'Rydan?' Freya hisses. 'Not helping! Besides how are you so calm right now?'

'Frey-Frey, in all honesty, I'm shitting myself but if I show that I'm shitting myself then that would mean others would take that to their advantage, therefore I'm acting as if I'm not shitting myself to gain the upper hand, do you understand?'

'No.'

'Then you clearly don't have the mental capacity—'

Rydan and Freya begin quarrelling in harsh whispers like siblings as I rest the palm of my hand just above my stomach. I drag my gaze away from Lorcan at my side and find Link looking down at an item in his hand, brows furrowed and ignoring everyone around him.

'What have you got there?' I ask as I walk up to him.

Link lifts his eyes at me and sees that I'm looking at his hand. He opens his palm and a grey talisman – like a stone carved with a star in the center rests in it.

I instantly recognize it, and an airy smile graces my lips.

'Illias gave it to me on the night of the ball,' he murmurs, staring at it. 'He said it's his talisman, that it's meant to promise—'

'That you'll both see each other again.'

Link glances up at me again, dark caves or not, his eyes still glimmer like sapphires at my response. I remember the meaning because our mother gave it to Illias before her death. She told him to give it to the person he would one day grow to love.

Not even Kye ever got it.

'You'll see him again, Link,' I assure him as I nod at the talisman. 'We both will.' *That much I trust.* 'No trial can stop that.'

Though his smile is weak, shy and hesitant, I know it is what he wanted to hear.

Murmurs then come from the front and dozens starts shuffling towards the gates.

Terror tightens Link's face as he looks at me. Freya and Rydan make their way to us, and I try so hard to keep the anxiety over these trials at bay.

I look over my shoulder, as if running might still be an option, but I lock eyes straight away with a Venator's glare.

The iron gates crank and judder, causing Freya to flinch as the light seeps through the cave. I close my eyes and a flash of my younger self appears.

My father getting ready to set course to the city, golden hair feathering his shoulder as I stand by the door.

'Father? One day I'd like to be a Venator . . . like you.'

He chuckles, it's sad, it's hollow, it's not my father's usual guffaw. 'You wouldn't want to be one, Nara.'

I frown and he sighs, lowering himself on one knee. His thumb rubs my cheek. 'Chase your own adventure, don't follow someone else's.'

Freya's voice wrenches me back into the present, and I open my eyes to see her concerned and waiting for me to walk with her into the arena. I do, numb and lost. I look around feeling infinitely small compared to when I'd been up with the crowd, watching fights ensue.

I squint as the ravenous sun burns into the middle of the pit. Wooden defense walls taller than a human coat the arena like a maze, making it hard to see where to go.

The flock of people cheer above us, but I drown it out as I raise my head enough to see the Queen seated atop her throne with the General at her side along with rulers of other lands.

Bitterness dances in Sarilyn's eyes as she scans the trainees, then darkness and almost sorrow once they find mine.

Confidence flares inside me as I straighten, defying everything she hopes I'd be right now. A Phoenix warrior clad in red and gold armor is the only one to notice Sarilyn's tense shift and follows her gaze to where I am.

The phoenix narrows her eyes at me. Hira, the woman to whom Lorcan had introduced me at the Noctura Ball. I analyze her from afar but there's no malice behind her stare; it's that same curiosity she'd shown back then.

'Nara,' Freya whispers by my side as we all stop, and the crowd grows silent. 'I should tell you. About the plans, we'd made, I may—'

The second my stare breaks from Sarilyn, she addresses us all, cutting Freya's words in the process. 'Months of training, proving you are fit to become a Venator has now come to this—' She rises from her throne, lifting her chin with authority and smiles '—*the trials*.' Whistling and claps echo through the arena, but Sarilyn's words have never sounded fouler. 'They will take place over three days. You will be tested on your agility, how you work as a team . . . *courage*.' She cuts a gaze in my direction, and her smile strains before she clears her throat. 'Today is the test of survival.'

My eyes shift to Freya as she releases a nervous breath. Link blanches, almost dropping his sword.

The uncertainty of what can happen burrows into my bones, and I gaze back at the Queen as she waves a hand and says, 'Good luck . . . and let the first trial begin.'

Chanting starts up from the stands, intensifying each second as rocks skitter and reverberate beneath my boots. I look at Rydan on the other side of me just as someone blows a horn and horrid shrills, ones I should recognize like the sound of my own voice by now, rise from the other side of the arena.

Rümens.

CHAPTER FORTY-EIGHT

My back slams against the wooden walls as I slouch down with panting breaths. I hold my blade to my chest, listening to the painful cries from other trainees possibly injured . . . and on the verge of dying after charging into the pit once the trials began.

'Of course, it had to be rümens,' Freya mutters beside me, clutching her bowstring like it's the only thing tethering her to life. We look at each other as she says with an assertive nod, 'it was likely my father's idea.'

Likely, no, for certain, yes.

Rydan and Link converge on the opposite wall to us. While Rydan looks relatively calm, Link presses his hand against his heart, counting to himself. His worries have doubled and so have mine.

'Were all the trials like this?' Link asks, then flinches when a shriek booms again.

Freya nods. 'Death was certain, that I know.'

And the General is hoping for my demise I suppose.

'Death or not at least I got to stand on the same grounds the Golden Thief was on,' Rydan suddenly says with a faraway smile. My brows draw together. I should be used to this by now, but before I can add to that he continues, 'That shifter got to live out my dream of being choked by him.'

I don't even blink.

'Seriously?' Freya hisses, but it's cut too soon when a rümen lunges from the corner of a wall, catching us off guard as it heads toward Link, throwing him down onto the ground.

Panic encircles me as I shout his name. He uses his sword to barricade himself from the rümen's ferocious bites. I rise to my feet, swinging my blade in the rümen's direction but I don't land the blow. Rydan does.

The rümen's severed serpent head rolls onto the floor and blood spills from Rydan's sword. I stare with wide eyes between the three as Link frantically shoves off the headless rümen's body and stands up, patting at the bloodied stains on his armor. 'I think I'm going to be sick.' He swallows as Freya tries to comfort him and Rydan places a palm out below Link's mouth as a precaution.

My gaze can't help wandering to the deceased rümen. I haven't seen one since that day near the Screaming Forests. I'd killed it, but not before it'd looked at me like every other creature does in the world. To know that part of *this* is what killed my father, only wounds my heart further.

I look behind me, and start walking to the edge of the wall, peeking from the side to where every scream, every cry and every painful crushing bone is heard.

My eyes then dart upward and spot the Queen's brows pinch with frustration as she watches the pit. The General, however, smiles with malice at the chaos unfolding.

A sick twisted man.

If anyone survives with but a simple a scratch, he'll just use them as part of his supposed army.

Even after everything you just seem to fascinate all creatures.

I think of what he'd said that night in the dungeons.

Whether I liked it or not, he's right.

I do fascinate them.

Glancing at my left hand, I trace the scar with my eyes, and for half a heartbeat I almost search for Lorcan in the crowd but stop myself. I take a shallow breath, seeing that because of him I wanted this, the title of a Venator. That shortly after my parents died, I became a trapper to learn . . . to one day kill. But truthfully, never was it for Ivarron or for my need to feed the anger I felt towards dragons, but because it's the only time I'd be . . . closer to creatures, and I hated that truth. I hated it so much because I didn't want to care for them.

And then that Ardenti dragon came, and I did care.

Too much.

I clench my hand into a fist and stare at the blade in my other palm. An idea—a mad one blooms.

'Nara?' Freya's voice echoes and I whirl my head to her. 'Are you okay?' Her mouth moves but the sounds don't come out with it. I just stare. My breathing loud in my ears and my heart in my throat as I look back to the pit.

It's a moment of instinct. My legs move before I can even think of it, walking between the maze-like walls toward the center of the arena and turning corners until I am there. The crowd's uproars are just a reflection in my existence as I take the blade in my hand, letting the sun beam off the metallic edge.

I know Sarilyn's eyes are on me. She has a direct view of where I am, to her, to everyone.

Ignoring it, I press the blade against my palm and inhale as I slice across it. I hold back a wince as people from the crowd start asking each other what I am doing.

My blood *drips.*

Drips.

Drips.

On to the ground and I close my eyes, raising my hand in the air. I hold my breath and wait.

A screech rasps against the walls of the arena, then another and another until it's a chorus of them approaching me.

My blood thrums with apprehension as wings flap my hair back and then . . . there's silence.

With each heartbeat, I will myself to open my eyes and when I do, the sight before me is unlike anything I've ever seen.

Dozens of rümens rest at my feet. A short laugh of surprise comes from me as each of them tilt their heads up. Some hiss in curiosity, others look as if they are trying to see me through the slits of their eyes. It's the first time they seem normal – a simple creature in need of guidance.

'She tamed them?' Someone says from the stands and so does another, inciting curious chatter before I raise my head to Sarilyn.

Her chin lifts as she looks at me without a glimmer of shock. A faint smile tugs at her lips while the General's fades. He shifts on his stone-crafted throne, and if I'd never seen him angry before, I sure have now.

He beckons a Venator behind him and whispers something into his ear. Whatever he said, I know it can't be good as the Venators rush to inform others. I keep my fist in the air, needing to think of a plan, *anything*, when a splitting creak of gates cracks against the grounds and a thick, monstrous cry makes my head snap to the right.

The rümens turn to it. As dust flies into the air, out comes a larger one, the size of two humans – the leader.

Every rümen has a leader to go back to . . .

My fist slowly drops as its nostrils flare, sniffing out my blood and communicating a low rumble to the other rümens. I creep backward, breathing heavy because no matter how I managed to tame them, I don't think I can with the leader.

All the oily skinned heads snap in my direction. Their mouths widening to show those teeth, sharp enough to tear you apart.

In the span of a second the leader charges at me, curving its wings as it slams against walls. I leap into action, running as fast as I can. People shriek, not for me but for themselves, and I only have a minute to look high above and see dragons filtering through the crowds and Venators rushing into the pit.

Shifters.

Nearing a dead end, my boots slide as I turn the corner and lose the rümen, though I know it's only seconds before it sniffs out my blood again.

I pant and my heart hammers at full speed as thuds, roars and clashes erupt in the distance.

Freya. Get back to Freya.

I bend down, cutting away at the leather of my Venator armor around my ankle. Biting down on the middle base of my blade, I wrap the piece of clothing over my palm, tightening it into a knot to stop the bleeding and sprint the other way until I land straight into someone's arms.

With the person's hand clutching my elbow, I stagger on the spot as my gaze draws up from the leather jerkin to the playful amber brown eyes gleaming at me through a mask. 'Darius?' I frown as he begins perusing the blade in my hand. 'What—'

'I should be used to your reactions by now, Goldie,' he murmurs, deep and mocking. The tip of my blade just about touches his neck. 'But I have to say this one offended me.'

Right . . . it's clear he is anything *but* affronted by that.

I yank my arms away and step back enough to see Freya, Link and Rydan over Darius's shoulder. Yells sound from within the center of the pit before Tibith squeaks out a 'Hello, Miss Nara!' from the ground.

My eyes dip to him and I breathe out a smile even as realization prickles my skin. When I glance at Darius, I can't form a coherent sentence or understand how he came back here after I'd made him leave me. 'I . . .' A shake of the head. 'I thought you weren't fond of attacks?'

'Well, that was until your friend—' He looks over his shoulder at a sheepish Freya '—told me you landed in the dungeons, and as the gentleman that I am, I had to come and return the favor of getting you out.' His attention shifts to me as his lips arch into one of his alluring smiles – still annoying, conceited, idiotic.

However, knowing that Freya had told him of what happened means this was what she'd been trying to tell me. She already knew the shifters would come.

Relief fills my chest before I lift a brow judgingly towards Darius. 'With your mask?'

His smile only brightens like he was waiting for that comment. He shrugs saying, 'It brings out my eyes.'

A retort won't suffice, not under these circumstances and not when, aggravatingly enough, Rydan interrupts with a wistful sigh. 'It really does.'

Darius looks back at him and by the "oh my," swooning reply from Rydan, I imagine Darius flashed him a smile. 'I need you all to head back to the den,' he says turning to me after Freya jabs Rydan in the stomach. 'Your brothers are waiting for you there.'

'Shall I go with them, Darry?'

Darius smiles down at Tibith. 'You're here to protect them, aren't you?'

Tibith nods, then another roar ripples above the arena, and with time limited for us, I quickly say, 'Wait.'

I look between Darius and the rest, knowing that I'd previously had a plan and that I want to make sure still happens. Walking past him, I reach Freya and she blinks up at me. 'Do you still have the keys?' I whisper and she nods.

'I made sure to keep them safe.'

'Then get them out, first,' I say without any other explanation. Freya's eyes become a mask of determination, and our talk the other night about wanting to free Adriel comes back to mind. 'I'll see you three soon, I promise.' My eyes jump to Rydan and Link, both staring at me like they're not sure whether to believe me or not.

But I will, for the sake of Solaris, my brothers, *them*, I will.

Freya envelopes me into the tightest hug imaginable before she regards me with a saddened gaze and retreats backward with Tibith running at their sides.

I watch as they disappear into different sectors of the arena, and then turn halfway around to Darius. His eyes are on me but there's a strange gleam in them. It crackles with heat between us as I tell him, 'You didn't think I'd leave you here to claim all your glory in saving me, did you?'

His laugh comes off arrogant, but a smile full of soft amusement stays on his lips. 'Of course not, Goldie. I expected you'd take charge instead.'

I grin at him before lurching toward the screams and roars.

Chapter Forty-Nine

I grind my feet to a stop, skidding across the floor as a rümen blocks my path. Taking a slow step backward I bump against someone and sneak a glance over my shoulder, seeing Darius's back facing the other way to me.

Another rümen is at the other end of his side. Walls entrap us and everywhere I look, more people scream and push past others, trying to escape the arena. Dust and smoke ascend through the air, blocking the sun. It's hard enough to breathe, let alone concentrate.

Still, I try and focus on the rümen in front of me, snarling as its wings flutter outward.

'Now would be a good time to tame them again,' Darius lilts quietly.

I don't have time to ask him how long he'd been here, if he'd watched everything from the stands. If he'd used his glamor. If he'd believed in me enough to get me out of this.

'They don't seem to be on my side anymore,' I say, and the rümen cocks his head with a growl at me.

'Right then,' Darius mutters, and a hiss of power sounds from behind me before there's a screech and the rümen in front of me pounces forward. I lift my dagger just as teeth near me and the reek of carrion filters through my nostrils. I swing my blade across its neck, and I exhale sharply at the crumple of its body hitting the ground.

I've always thought myself to be confident but just then, even the death of an awful creature makes my stomach turn unlike before.

I wipe the blade clean at the side of my thigh and glance above the maze walls. Squinting up at the balcony, Sarilyn is no longer there, nor is the General and phoenix warriors.

Flames fly into the sky, causing my gaze to jump there. 'Is Gus here?'

He's normally been the one to plan the attacks in the first place.

Darius chuckles. 'Spent one day with him and already prefer him to me?'

'Yes.' I spin around but he's already facing me. A burnt rümen lies where he'd used his powers to kill it. My brows narrow as I look up at the mock amusement behind his eyes. 'Does that hurt your ego?'

'Not at all.' He drawls his words into a whisper and leans his head closer to mine. 'But to answer your question, he stayed to look after your brothers and those lovely witch friends of yours.'

I exhale a long breath out of my nose at the mention of my brothers again. Darius must notice the sudden drop in my expression because he says soft and quietly, 'The three of them are fine, Goldie.'

My head snaps up at him, and I hardly nod. I know they are safe, but I'd also kept so much from them.

'Your older brother though—' Darius huffs a laugh and looks off to the side for a moment. 'Was adamant that if you get hurt, he'll shove a sword through my skull.'

That makes the corner of my lip pull into a smile. 'And what did you say?' I ask, as his eyes cut over my shoulder, and then a wave of shock floods me as he places the palm of his hand against my lower back, pulling me to his chest.

I furrow my brows, letting out a startled noise as I gaze up at his half-smile before he blasts a whorl of fire with his other hand behind me. A shriek rattles my eardrums and then Darius stares down at me, his gaze swallowing me whole as he says, 'That for as long as I live, immortality or not, I will make sure nothing ever happens to you.'

His words leave me breathing slower, and I urge myself to think of something worth aggravating him for, but the truth is I'm speechless. My eyes drift to his lips, the reminder of that night – our kiss, it's such a wild memory.

Darius's fingers brush my hair away from my face. 'Have I told you that—' His head dips to the side of mine as he whispers, 'You look like an absolute mess today, Goldie?'

That breaks me out of the unwanted trance, and I hum a short laugh as he leans back to look at me. His eyes speckled with humor.

'And has anyone told you how that mask doesn't favor you at all?' I lift my brows and smirk at him.

His lips curve into a grin, looking as if he is about to respond, but the ground rumbles beneath us and I glance up as the leader of rümens barrels toward us.

I get out of the way as its claws slam down on the floor, and Darius and I are separated.

'You have to be kidding me,' I say under my breath as it roars its shrill cries and heads toward me.

I run.

My shoulders slam against walls as I swerve corners and I don't look back, but I know the rümen is on my tail. Three pathway walls come into view, leading to the center where shifters and Venators fight among one another.

Feeling relief, my steps pick up and the rümen starts to sound distant, but as I'm about to reach the middle pathway, a force knocks me to the ground. The blade slides from my hands and a buzz fills my ears, as I blink away the haze of dust clouding the air.

For what feels like eternity I can't process what just happened until I'm rolled onto my back and hands grasp my neck.

My eyes widen, coming face to face with the General hovering over me, and all the air starts waning from me as I take ragged breaths.

'You just never stop.' Fury ripples from Erion's voice as my head spins and I claw at him. 'I should have made Lorcan kill your whole family that day.'

Anger builds up in my chest but I can't release it as his fingers tighten around my throat.

'You corrupted Freya's mind.'

I thrash underneath him.

'You ruined *everything* by siding with the shifters.'

My lungs start to ache.

'Lorcan became too *weak* because of you.' His eyes now burn with emptiness. 'And now? You will be the one at fault for destroying our world.'

Clawing my fingers at his hands, I strangle out the word, 'No,' and gain some strength as I say, 'you and the Queen already did that.'

He glares at me, hazel eyes wrathful as his grip slips the slightest. I take the chance to drive my leg into his abdomen. He lets go in an instant and I gasp for air as he falls to the side, releasing a low grunt from his lips.

With the hideous burn of his fingers imprinted on my neck, I rise to a seated position and try to recover as I spot my blade at the end.

Stumbling on my hands and knees, I reach out for it when Erion yanks me back by the hair, grabbing the blade before me as I cry out with a wince.

No, I need to—

'Erion!' Darius shouts, stalking through the dust as I lift my eyes to him, but Erion jerks both me and himself up, pressing the edge of the blade against my neck.

Darius halts, glancing between the dagger, me, and then Erion.

My breath stops short and I look for a loophole as Erion chokes out a laugh, and I grimace with displeasure at the sound of it.

'Darius *Halen,*' he announces, with a taunt to his voice. 'The despicable adopted son. And the one shifter Lorcan missed, even after I brought him here, he'd always say how much he missed him.' He croons with a malignant edge. 'His *brother* Darius.'

Darius's hands curl into a tight fist, and that only makes Erion nudge the blade further into my skin.

'You turned him against *me*.'

'I turned him against all of you.' The pride in Erion's words is sickening. 'And like the naïve boy he was, he believed *everything* because I'm the one who was the father he craved, the one who turned him into the creature he is now . . . half dragon, half rümen.'

Darius hadn't known, yet he does not react. 'A man like you does not deserve the title of father.'

'Then, kill me, thief,' Erion seethes. The pressure of the blade eases from my neck as he shoves me toward Darius. 'Kill me like you did Lorcan's father.'

I cling onto Darius by the arm, turning to look at Erion as he spreads his arms out by his sides.

He's smirking, daring Darius to do it.

I attempt to step forward, anger raging through me when Darius's arm comes across me. His gaze sweeps across my neck, and as if I feel it, I run my fingers along, drawing back blood onto the tips of them. When I look up, Darius eyes aren't on me anymore.

'He'll only hate you more,' Erion taunts, and that smug grin of his remains even as Darius considers his words. It's the first time his face is impassive until his lips lift into a cold smirk that's brutal for anyone who ever dares cross him.

'Well,' he says, 'it's a good thing I *adore* being hated.' He approaches Erion, shadows crackling within his hand at his side as he studies the sudden cowardice washing over Erion, despite my blade in his hands. 'Send my regards to Aurelia.'

Aurelia?

Erion's brows furrow, like he recognizes the name as he whispers, 'Aurelia,' to himself.

'My *mother*,' Darius grits out. A heavy weight pushes down on my chest.

Erion must have been the one to kill his mother all those years ago.

Recognition dawns on his face as Darius raises his hand. Shadows form into blades, except a rush of ice sweeps down my spine as I look to my right.

Lorcan stands there at the edge of the wall, aiming an arrow toward Darius.

Shrieks become muffled as Lorcan glances at me and though his expression is solid, unmoving, his eyes share a charge of regret.

Wait—

'No!' The word sounds too weak from my lips because the second I say it, the arrow springs out of the bow and instantly I squeeze my eyes shut as I am seized with terror.

The sound of someone choking on blood freezes me.

No, no, no.

I open my eyes to blood spluttered on the ground, shocked when I realize that it doesn't come from Darius.

Shifting my gaze to the General, his mouth gapes wide open as he clutches both hands to his neck. An arrow pierces through his throat as he collapses to his knees and blood pours through the gaps of his fingers.

He looks at Lorcan. Betrayal fires up in his wide eyes, then he slumps, no longer moving.

Lorcan killed him.

He heard everything.

I glance toward Lorcan, not knowing what to feel as he lowers his bow and stares at me and Darius.

He nods once, signifying truce, and I smile.

It hardly lasts a second as the leader of the rümens breaks through one of the walls.

I shout a warning but it's too late. Time slows and my voice echoes into a gasp as Lorcan spins toward the rümen. Its sharp taloned wing scatters out, puncturing Lorcan through the chest.

My feet take off towards him, as the strength of the wing sends Lorcan smacking against another wall. Picking my blade up, Darius charges toward the rümen with whorls of fire just as I reach Lorcan and collapse with him onto the floor. His bow tumbles out of his grip and with a panicked gaze, I press my hands against the blood surging from his chest.

It's fine, he is part dragon, he will heal, he will heal, he will—

'I'm sorry,' he rasps, the rose-tinted lips now seeping blood from his mouth.

I shake my head. 'You can say that to me later. Let's just get you out of here.' I search around, looking for Darius but he's on the other side, fighting off the rümen.

'I lied—' Lorcan's whisper draws my attention back to him. Pale, he's too pale. 'I lied—'

My head shakes again but before I can speak, he grabs my wrist, prying it away from him as he places something in my hand.

I stare at him, my lips parting as I look down at my palm.

The sun.

My carving.

Orange hues from the flames behind, lighten the wood now tinged red with Lorcan's blood.

'Tell Darius to go after his wish.'

I look at him, and my throat hurts.

He's saying goodbye. He thinks he won't survive.

No . . . I refuse that idea, no.

'You can tell him yourself.' My stubborn voice fails me as he smiles for a little while before his eyes become dim. Within seconds they close.

'Lorcan?' I say, gripping his other hand and shaking it. 'Lorcan, wake up—wake up—' My breaths come out fast and short. No tears form but everything surrounding me, all the carnage in the arena, become a blur. 'Please?'

No movement occurs.

So I shout his name. An arm comes around my waist from behind, attempting to pull me up. I instantly know it's Darius, but I struggle against him, breaking free for just one second as I scramble back to Lorcan.

I shake his chest.

Wake up, wake up, wake up.

An arrow from a Venator lands straight by my side but I do not care.

'Nara,' Darius says, his arms now crossed around me. Even with such command in his voice, it's also breaking.

'No,' I say and grab onto his arms to try and yank him off, but his grip is unyielding. He starts dragging me, but I press my heels into the ground and say the same word over and over, '*no*.'

Lorcan's body lies so still ahead of me and each time I look, it's further from view.

I blink and then it's my father, my cottage, Idris hauling our crying mother away.

It's all the same.

My head falls back onto Darius's chest, tired from thrashing in his arms. And though my chest burns, I still don't cry. I can't.

As smoke and rubble cover the arena, I can no longer see him.

CHAPTER FIFTY

Golden hues of the early dawn gloss over the skies as dragons fly outside my window.

It's the one thing that's given me comfort since the trials last week – a way to ease my mind from that day. I haven't cried, not once, but I've stayed here in one of the rooms of the den, wishing I could.

It's as if crying will make what happened real.

And I don't want to believe it was.

I gaze at my hand and the sun carving it holds and the leather fingerless glove Leira had found for me. Then there's a knock at the door.

I look over my shoulder, putting the carving into my pocket and say, 'Come in.'

The door opens, and my three brothers slip inside. My smile is weak as I walk up to Iker. He holds a plate of strawberry pie in his hands, and I take it from him with a light chuckle. 'So, *you've* been the one bringing the pies to my door this past week.'

His brows pinch together in puzzled amusement face. 'Well, I—'

'You haven't left the room since you arrived.' Idris's curt words draw my gaze to him by the wall. I hadn't managed to speak to my brothers much, nor tell them of my time at the barracks. Still, they know enough by now.

'Or eaten, for that matter,' Illias adds, grimacing at my plate. 'You love your food.'

Well . . . at least I've eaten the pies set by my door each night. 'I've not been hungry,' I murmur truthfully.

'Why didn't you tell us, Nara?' Idris seems to lose his patience, sighing as he shakes his head at me.

I thought I could fix it on my own.

Now I know it's foolish to think I could have.

'Idris, we said we weren't going to—'

'No, it's fine.' I draw in a breath, holding my hand up to interrupt Illias. I shift my gaze to Idris and say, 'I should have been truthful since the beginning. After all, you were right about becoming a Venator. It was never a good idea.'

'I don't care about what I once said.' A vein pulses at the side of his neck. 'I care that my sister has been struggling while I was back at our village, thinking you were out here living your dream.'

My head lowers in shame at how far I'd let it all go. 'Scold me all you want, Idris—'

Something odd happens.

My words are cut off, breathlessly, as Idris takes a step toward me, wrapping his arms around my neck.

I blink, holding the plate of pie out at the side, as he doesn't let go. It's an embrace that no matter how long it lasts, it seems as if it's not enough, because the thought of losing me is harder than anything else for him.

'I promised mother I'd look after you.' His voice cracks on the last word, a sound I've never heard come from him. All my life Idris and I clashed because we were too similar. Not once had I seen him cry, not even when his lover perished. He keeps it all in a tight grip against his heart. A protective spell to keep the emotions at bay.

'I know,' I whisper, using my other hand to reach around him. 'I'm sorry.'

We pull apart. His blue eyes illuminated by the morning light fix on me in hope. 'You don't need to apologize.'

'Without you,' Illias says, and Idris looks over his shoulder at him. 'You'd never have found out that shifters aren't all that bad.' He chuckles, and the softest brown curls shake along his forehead. 'Who would have thought that would be the case.'

For the first time this week, a natural smile tugs at my lips as Iker joins in with a mumble, 'They've treated us better than our village did, but I still won't forgive Idris for leaving Dimpy with Miss Kiligra.'

That breaks the solemn atmosphere as we chuckle, and then the door creaks open with Freya popping her head through. 'Oh,' she says. 'Sorry, I thought you were alone—'

'We were just leaving,' Idris goes back to his stern self, and Freya opens the door wider. Her curls skim past the purple tunic she has on as she pulls her bottom lip between her teeth, and nods.

I don't miss the strange averting of her eyes as Idris walks past her, along with Illias and Iker.

She takes a breath and smiles at me once they all exit the room. Freya was the first one I saw as soon as I came here with Darius. She grinned with excitement at how they'd freed Adriel and the others.

It broke me to see that smile vanish as I told her of Erion. But her way of grieving differed from mine. She involved herself with others, came by my room each day while I tried to isolate myself from the rest.

Sighing, I ask, 'How are you?' *It's always the worst question to ask.*

'Better,' she says, taking the plate from my hands and placing it on the bed as she sits down. 'Leira told me more stories of my mother when they were young, though it's rather odd isn't it?'

I quirk my head to the side, sitting beside her. She takes in my questioning silence and glances around the thick wooden walls, at the basin in the corner, and a chest of drawers by the door.

'That we've ended up here,' she continues.

It's truly ironic, but . . . 'We can't stay here forever.'

Her eyes find the bruises on my neck, and she looks away with a painful wince. 'I know that,' she breathes, running her hands along her thighs. 'I actually came here to tell you that Gus informed me he'll be speaking to all of us at noon. He's counting on you to be there.'

I nod slowly, but my thoughts go to Darius, wondering if he'll be there. According to Freya, he hadn't left his room either. Only Tibith came to check on me, as he was still intent on being my second sworn protector.

We hadn't discussed Lorcan. We hadn't discussed what happened that night before his capture . . . nothing. Perhaps it should stay that way. Perhaps he regrets it and I should too.

It was a moment of weakness, that is all.

Breathing out a thoughtful sigh, I place my hand over Freya's, and her gaze snaps at me. 'I'll be there,' I say, and she smiles.

'Why can't we just attack the castle?' One of the shifters shouts across the tavern. 'We've built enough resistance against steel, the arena is destroyed, and the Queen's army have weakened in numbers. We can easily end her.'

A few agree, raising their tankards in unison. My eyes shift to Illias and Link sitting beside each other on some of the barrels. Link rests his shoulder on Illias's, while Rydan sits next to them, drawing circles with his finger on the bar top rather solemnly.

I frown, understanding that this is all so new to him. Lorcan's death had taken a toll on him more than we'd all expected.

And Darius? He never came down from his room.

My expression smooths out, however, as Gus paces across the middle of the tavern, answering the shifter. 'And what is that going to do for the rest of the mortals? It will only make them despise us more.'

That quietens most of us down, and I cross my arms over my chest, thinking it through.

'Sarilyn has rebuilt this kingdom to have everyone at her disposal,' Gus continues. 'With or without magic, she is still the most powerful person.'

She also fled the arena as soon as the shifters attacked.

'Then she has to be afraid of something,' Leira gathers from one of the tables. She's not wrong. I saw how the Queen's cold façade cracked beneath my words the day I was sent to the dungeons. There is more to her that not even the shifter I'd spoken to knew.

'Or *someone*,' I say, thinking I was whispering it to myself until everyone's gaze lands on me, and I glower.

Clearing my throat, Gus smiles at me in a way that reminds me of my father, encouraging and attentive.

I speak up, 'A shifter in the dungeons told me not long ago of how Sarilyn managed to gain entrance to the Isle of Elements. She obtained the Northern Blade and whatever happened with the elves led to the King creating that forest.'

A few exchange wary looks, and others mutter something about me being the mortal Darius brought over.

I ignore it and close my eyes for a decisive minute. 'I was told—' I puff a breath '—that seers predicted a battle between many that could destroy Zerathion.' *A future I want to change.* 'What if . . . what if we can get help, fix it, or prevent it?'

Gus's brows draw together. 'What are you implying, Nara?'

Before I can answer with the only idea I have, someone says it for me: 'That we go to the Isle of Elements ourselves.'

We all look to the right as Darius makes his way past everyone's stares. Confidence brews within him and tumbles over each of us as he stands before me with his shirt unlaced, and says, 'And to do that, we need to go to the Elven King.'

I narrow my brows at the smile taking over his lips. Though, I notice the darkness beneath his eyes, like he hasn't slept at all. Tibith climbs up his arm and sits on his shoulder.

'Not a chance I'm going through those forests,' the same shifter from before says.

'Then don't.' Darius's eyes stay hooked on mine. 'I'll go.'

Why am I not surprised?

'Darius,' Gus warns. 'Your powers won't work in the forest—'

'No,' I blurt out. Heads tilt my way, but I don't break Darius's eye contact. 'He needs a trapper.'

Darius lifts his brow, teasingly.

'I know most creatures and animals like I know the back of my hand. I'll go.'

'Nara—' Idris says, but Darius's chuckle has a sardonic bite to it.

'Goldie,' he says. 'Not even Solaris knows what creatures lie in those forests. I doubt *you* will.'

Oh, how I want to prove him wrong already. Calming my irritation, I state with sarcastic amusement, 'Even if that's the case, why should you be the one to go? Are you going to charm your way through the forest? Enamor creatures and then do the same to the Elven King?'

He shrugs with such nonchalance before smiling at me. 'If it comes to it.'

I huff, knowing I should have seen that coming and whirl around to Gus. 'I'll do it.'

'No, you can't just go on your own.' Idris comes to my side, and I stare up at him as he grabs onto my upper arm. 'I almost lost you to the Venators. I'm not going to lose you to the Screaming Forests because you want to play the hero again.'

'I don't want to play the hero,' I say quietly, snatching my arm away. 'I just want it to end.'

The silence between us overlaps the other shifters' murmurs. I can see, as always, he's struggling to agree with me. After all, he's only just gotten me back.

But he also knows when it's something I *want* to do.

'Seeing as we can't come to an accord.' Darius claps his hands, and I twist to him. 'And you know certain things about the Queen, I – charming as always – suggest you and I then go,' he says and smiles, '*together.*'

Oh, for the love of Solaris.

'Can I come too, Darry?'

I soften at Tibith's sweet innocence, and Darius looks to his shoulder with a playful grin. 'I was already planning to take you, Tibith.'

Tibith's ears flap, and I sigh in defeat. 'How long will it take us to pass the forest?' I ask Gus.

His forehead crinkles, marking the lines of his maturing face. 'It depends.' His pensive stare at the floor has me on edge. 'No one has exactly lived to tell.'

My back tenses at that as I inhale, and Idris curses under his breath.

'Wait.' Leira rises from her stool as her eyes travel from everyone to me. 'There is a map. I remember my sister spoke of it. It's supposed to guide you through the forest with a high chance of survival, but no one has ever managed to obtain it.'

Surviving the Screaming Forests . . . I'll take any thing that gives me a chance at it.

My mind flies to one possibility. A place I've been to multiple times, where I've seen trinkets, jars and maps of all kinds, ones that didn't even look like they were from this world. 'I think I might know where to find one,' I say.

'Then it's settled.' Darius comes over. His words aim at me specifically as he towers over me. 'We will leave here at dawn.'

After saying my goodbyes the following morning, I sheath my blade across my thigh and lower my grey tunic over my leggings. It rests above the knees with slits at the sides to give me free movement. I then lace up my leather arm braces just as Darius walks down the steps of the tavern with Tibith trotting after him. I straighten my back, staring at how his long-sleeved black tunic and breeches show the strength of his arms, legs . . . and annoyingly, everything else.

'If you keep staring, you might drool.'

My eyes snap to meet his irritatingly golden ones. A smirk molds his lips as I scoff. 'I don't ever drool, which is more than I can say for someone like you who rolls around in jewels half the time.'

He feigns a shocked expression. 'How did you know I do that, Goldie? Did Tibith tell you?'

I roll my eyes as Tibith shakes his head, wobbling on his feet, and then a whisper of my name comes from behind. Turning, I notice Gus gesturing his head for me to walk over to him near the bar counter.

Looking back at Darius, I see he's now busy, sheathing blades of his own, and I oblige, heading over.

Gus rubs at his jaw as he takes a few seconds to speak. 'I want to wish you luck on this journey.'

Genuine words, but I can't help thinking he wants to say something else.

I smile at him, but I no longer have belief in myself.

And he can see that as he says gently, 'You are quite the brave lady, Nara.'

I chuckle, though it's painfully feeble. 'I'm not brave,' I whisper. 'But I like to think I can be.'

A kind of pain rises in my chest. I can feel it again in my throat and my eyes just by remembering Lorcan. I shake it away.

Gus then hums as if that's hard to believe before his gaze flickers past me. 'You know he sees something in you.'

I glance behind at Darius, kneeling in front of Tibith with some bread. My brows lift as I look back at Gus. 'Disgust, you mean?'

He laughs. 'You see something too.'

My body heats up and I part my lips to protest at his assumption, but he speaks before I can. 'If you didn't, you wouldn't have risked yourself to free him from the dungeons.'

Now, I have nothing I can say to disagree with that. I did risk myself, and I would do it again to guarantee his freedom.

'Just . . . take care of each other.' Gus places a hand on my shoulder, shooting me an anxious smile before he walks past.

As I turn to go after him to ask what he means by it all, Leira stands in my view and stops me. She sighs with a doleful gaze. 'Is there any chance that you will change your mind and stay here?'

My expression is apologetic as I lower myself and wrap a single arm around her neck. 'Idris already asked me that,' I say into the coils of her hair.

Her chuckle sounds like she's on the verge of crying as we break apart, and she holds my arms in her hands. 'And of course, you said no.'

I smile and nod. 'It will be good for me to get away from this land, even if it's a dangerous path we're going towards.'

Anyone else could easily go with Darius, someone stronger, a person of his own kind, but I'm not one to sit around. I don't wait, I act upon any situation. Perhaps it's a way of escaping or a need to take control myself. Especially after everything.

'Miss Nara!' Tibith snaps me from my reverie, curling into his usual ball and rolling up to us. 'We need to go!'

Chuckling down at him, I bite the corner of my lip as Leira tugs at my arms, causing me to glance at her.

'Nara,' she says, inhaling a deep breath. 'I just want to say thank you for bringing my niece to me.'

A burst of delight wells in my stomach. The first since before the trials even occurred. Before I knew of what Venators truly meant for Emberwell.

Leira removes her hands from my arms, and I feel a sensation much like loss as I straighten, hoping I can pull through this.

Following Tibith to the center of the tavern, Darius whirls to me, eyeing me with a certain heated scrutiny that makes me shift on the spot. His eyes finally fall on my face as the side of his lips tease a soft smile. 'Ready, Goldie?'

I hesitate, looking over at the other end where my brothers, my friends . . . shifters watch us.

Freya stands beside Idris, smiling at me with glossy eyes.

I had already said goodbye once, thinking I was heading towards a new future. A new future for me and my brothers. Now I'm doing it all over again but for everyone in Emberwell and for the sake of Zerathion.

A blinding emotion builds behind my eyes as I return my gaze to Darius. I raise my chin and breathe out, 'Always.'

His smile lights the entire tavern. 'Then let's go meet the Elven King.'

ACKNOWLEDGEMENTS

Mum, thank you for always believing in me when I never did. Growing up, your passion was to write stories, and now that same love and devotion you had, inspired me to write this book. You've listened to my ideas, fangirled with me over my characters, and supported me through everything. I love you.

Dad, you're the one person I've always hoped to make proud someday. It's not been an easy time having to deal with me (lol), especially in the past few years or so, but you're the best dad anyone could ask for. From your crazy stories to your jokes every time we enter Waterstones and you ask the sales assistant if they have my books, to embarrass me. Let's hope one day they will say they do.

My siblings (Eddy and Noelia) thank you for being the best sports over my book, even though I had to explain the plot to both of you about one hundred times.

George, six years ago, we met in the most book-worthy way, and here we are now with your endless support and belief that I can do anything I set my mind to. You've been with me through this entire journey, helped me when I had writer's block, and loved me unconditionally whenever I doubted myself. Without you, I don't think I would have had the courage to pursue publishing this story, and for that, I'm eternally grateful I have you.

Stacey, my other half and my best hype woman, you've been with me since the start of my writing journey. You were the inspiration behind Freya because of your strength and kindness. We all need a little bit of you in us.

Para mi familia en España, os quiero tanto y ojalá algún día podais ver mi libro en las tiendas.